Darling
Energy

Cover design by Kristen Solecki

Dedicated to my students: past, present, and future. They are the best teachers.

The truth is an anagram of an anagram.

— Umberto Eco

ONE

Dylan Geringer's anagram names were *Daringly Green* and *Darling Energy*. She hadn't done the unscrambling herself. Her friend Steven had, combing through different letter combinations in Dylan's first and last names—using each letter once—until he found what he thought would make appropriate alter ego names for his seventeen-year old friend. There was a website online that would work out every possible solution and do all of this tedious work for him, but Steven, new to the task, liked the challenge. His school notebooks since September were filled with people's names mixed up into jumbled letters and words. Their tiny, sweet friend Michelle Samson became *Ms. Melancholies* in Steven's notebook.

Their English teacher, Trevor Drake rearranged into *Dr. Overtaker*. That was one of their favorites, a perfect villain name if they'd ever seen one. Fortunately, Mr. Drake was no villain. He was a sweet man in his fifties, mustachioed and sweater-vested. He wore glasses too, but they hung from a string around his neck, worn only when he read from the text or from the yellow pad of paper clipped to his clipboard. Dylan and Steven could never tell what was on that pad of paper, but they had fun imagining.

"It's a list of gifts he'd give his wife if he had the money," Dylan said.
Steven disagreed. "No, it's a self-portrait he adds to a little each day."
"It's his will."
"A novel."
"It's his name in giant bubble letters."
"It's a penis."
"Mr. Drake would not draw a penis."
"Why would he be any different than the rest of the boys in this room?"
"No."
"I didn't say it was *his* penis."
"Is that supposed to be better??"

Dylan and Steven agreed they never wanted to find out what was actually written on the yellow pad of paper. Steven was tempted one day when Mr. Drake left the pad unattended as he answered the classroom phone, but Dylan shot him a look. She was right. It would ruin everything.

While it was a frequent point of interest—the lives of their teachers beyond the school walls—their conjectures were more fun than the scary possibility that they'd actually run into one of them in the grocery store, wheeling a sad cart through the produce aisle.

"Can you imagine seeing Mrs. Dwyer sitting at a bar? Or Mr. Steele at the gym?" They couldn't. They didn't want to. Maybe in theory, they did— but only because the prospect made them laugh uncontrollably.

They liked to play a game where they would pretend that Mr. Drake became Dr. Overtaker when he went home to his wife, that his teaching gig was a cover for something dastardly. He was an art thief, a deep web hacker, an al Qaeda operative, an SAT question-writer for the College Board. He had the mustache, so curling it between his thumb and forefinger was a real possibility.

They were both sitting in Drake's classroom when Steven texted Dylan the results of his anagram efforts for her name.

Dylan: I love them!!
Steven: They're good, right?

Neither Dylan nor Steven wrote in shorthand, abbreviated text form. Steven said it was uncouth.

Dylan: Darling Energy is like a superhero.
Steven: Look out! It's DARLING ENERGY!
Dylan: Daringly Green is sweet, too.
Steven: But also spicy. Not just any green. A daring shade.
Dylan: Daisy's green light. . .
Steven: Ha!

Mr. Drake was just then talking about chapter one of *The Great Gatsby*, where Nick first spots Gatsby staring out at Daisy's single green dock light across the sound. Dylan had already read the novel back in the seventh grade. It was her sister Daphne's favorite book in high school,

TWO

The Geringers lived in a modest suburban home that backed up to the hospital. The window in Dylan's room looked out onto the helipad. At least once a week, she'd wake to the distant whirring, and eventual thumping, of a helicopter hovering over her house and settling down outside her room. She rarely saw the helicopter during the day. She wondered if people only got into serious accidents at night—ones serious enough for the chopper.

Dylan treated each arrival the same way. Before she got up out of bed, she'd reach for her phone on her bedside table and turn it screen-side down. This wasn't a superstition or obsessive compulsion; she imagined it to be a small sign of respect to the grave nature of what was happening outside her window. She didn't want her phone to go off when she looked out onto the dramatic landing and careful unloading of the injured. It had happened one night when she was staring out the window, and it felt all wrong, that her phone would interrupt this sacred and sad delivery. (Steven, who never slept, sent her texts throughout the night.) Since then, it became automatic, the way some people immediately turn off the radio good metaphor, she would not dress as a sponge for Halloween. She smiled thinking of *Darling Energy*, but what would that costume even look like??

The helicopter blades slowed to a halt and her phone buzzed again. Someone had left a message.

THREE

"It's a post office."

"I thought you already had a post office."

"But this one fits the theme. See the tiny hitching post?"

Steven looked at the tiny hitching post.

"See. A Pony Express post office."

Steven did not want to have this conversation, but he knew it would be worse if he said what he really thought. This tiny Christmas village—now Western-themed—occupied his mother, and he didn't want to go back to the unoccupied mother of two years ago.

"It's cool," he managed.

"It's cute, isn't it?" she said.

That was all she needed. She balanced the tiny building in the palm of her hand and disappeared into the living room.

"It fits perfectly!" As Steven climbed the steps to his bedroom, he thought she sounded like a little girl, like one of the Smith girls that lived across the street.

Steven longed to be a Smith. He used to tell Dylan that. The sweet anonymity of sameness, he thought. A Smith was just some guy everybody knew. They were easy to ignore but not invisible, and that had been Steven's goal ever since he could remember. He simply wanted to be a bit player, an extra, content to fake talk to the rest of the cast in the background. If he had any other ambitions he hadn't spoken them out loud yet.

His own last name, Lilly, had not been too kind to him. His middle name, Andrew, created the unfortunate combination, Steven A. Lilly. This unintentional appositive—*Steven, a lilly*—was shouted across playgrounds for what seemed like years. His tormentors, sensing his otherness, his "sensitivity"—he hated that word, but could find no appropriate substitute—watched as he made quick friends with many of the girls in his class, as he eschewed kickball for coloring. Once he tried to stick up for himself and made the mistake of telling some jerk that he liked his last name, that he thought it was *pretty*. He'd heard his mom say as much. The reaction of the Royces of the world let him know he shouldn't have used that word, but it was too late. For weeks, they'd ask Steven's opinion on anything in the vicinity: "Hey, Steven a lilly. Do you think this desk is *pretty*?"

He tried his best to ignore them after that. He didn't think the desk was pretty, but had he answered them, he would have admitted that *yes*, the jungle gym actually was kind of pretty when the sunlight cast a web of shadows underneath it; that the green and gold of Green Tree Elementary's tree logo was sweet in its own way; that, sure, you could find some prettiness in the library—the spectrum of book spines, the symmetry of the shelves; that, Mrs. Dunwoody, one of their cafeteria ladies, with her apron filled with straws was certainly pretty despite her crooked smile and matching teeth. There was plenty *pretty* to go around if you

24/7 with no commercial breaks, no scouring eBay for more cigarette cases. He might return to an obsession, but not until he'd exhausted himself on his current one.

This was the monastic, monogamous way Steven lived his life. The only exception to the rule was Dylan. Despite everyone else's unwanted opinions and insinuations, Steven didn't think he was gay. The only person he'd ever been attracted to was Dylan. And Dylan was a girl, so he assumed he was straight.

It would be more accurate to say he never really thought about it—his sexuality. He wasn't sure what he was supposed to think anyway. If he was supposed to be overcome with hormonal urges and thoughts, maybe he had something wrong with a gland. Movies and TV taught him that boys only ever thought about one thing, but there were too many interesting things in the world for Steven to be so easily distracted by sex. He thought of himself as *Silent Valley*, his Steven A. Lilly anagram name. That's how he felt most of the time.

Dylan was kind to him. Steven couldn't really remember when their friendship had started. It was eighth grade, but he couldn't recall the day or the context. They just found themselves in each other's company. He could, however, recall the first time she visited his house.

He'd become obsessed with the concept of having a friend that would visit him by climbing in his window. It was an impractical TV cliché, but that didn't stop his planning. There was a tree outside his window, but its branches were about three feet short of reaching his room. There was no ivy-covered lattice on the side of house, not even a gutter to shimmy up.

There was, however, a ladder in the garage. Before his dad had moved out, it was used to clean the gutters and once to retrieve one of Steven's kites out of a tree. That afternoon, Steven unhooked the ladder from the hooks in the garage and brought it over to the side of the house. He leaned it there carefully, its top rung square outside his window. Dylan could climb it easily, he thought. He'd text her and tell her about it.

"What are you doing??" Steven's mom had just returned from the grocery store and was getting out of her Toyota Camry. "What are you doing with that ladder??"

"One second." Steven tested it to make sure it was sturdy. Mrs. Lilly put down the shopping bags she was carrying and walked over to the side of the house.

"Are you running away?" The question made little sense. It was the middle of the afternoon, Steven was already standing outside, he was expecting company, he wasn't carrying any bags—but his mother asked it seriously, and it came across as more of a statement than a question.

"No. What? No, I'm just setting this up for Dylan."

"For what?"

"For Dylan. She's coming over tomorrow."

"And. . ."

"I just wanted—"

"She can use the front door." Mrs. Lilly was used to Steven's theatrics.

"I know. I just—" Steven couldn't think of a way to describe what he was doing.

"You're going to hurt yourself. Put it back where you found it."

Steven looked up at his window and sighed.

Mrs. Lilly made her way back to the car but stopped halfway and turned. "Unless you want to clean the gutters. Lord knows they need it." She was happy that Steven had invited someone to come over. She couldn't remember the last time that had happened. And ever since Foster had left, the yard, the landscaping—really the entire house, minus her Christmas village—had been a disaster.

"I'll clean the gutters." He said it too eagerly. His mother gave him a funny look.

"Can you help with the groceries, please?"

Dylan arrived in her mother's minivan promptly at 1 o'clock, as promised. Unlike the Lillys, the Geringers were always on time. Mrs. Geringer and Mrs. Lilly, once classmates themselves, met and talked briefly, though Dylan's mom stayed in the car. If this bothered his mother, Steven couldn't tell. Less than a minute had passed—Dylan and Steven had barely said hello—before Mrs. Geringer's minivan pulled out into the road, letting out a squeal, and Mrs. Lilly let the front screen door bang closed behind her. Dylan and Steven looked at each other and laughed as they stood alone in the driveway.

"That was quick," Steven said.

"She was very glad to get me out of the house," Dylan said.

"Why?"

"I don't know. Sometimes she's just like that."

"I know what you mean. You wanna come in?"

"Sure."

Steven looked over at the ladder.

"What?"

"Want to do something fun?"

She hesitated. Dylan was still looking at the ladder.

"Wanna climb up to my room?"

No, she didn't want to climb up to his room. But this is how it was with Steven; she knew she would be climbing into his window in the next few minutes.

"Why would I want to do that?"

"That's how it happens in the movies. The girl next door—"

"I'm not the girl next door." This epithet she would not allow.

"Well, yeah. Of course. Far from it. You're the girl two neighborhoods away. It's just that close friends like us should have easy access to each other's rooms."

The *close friends* line worried a bit, but she played along.

"I could just climb the steps. That's pretty easy."

"But it's not fun. Come on. Let's try it. It's not even that high."

Dylan surveyed the climb. She said nothing. But then tried on a smile.

"Good. But give me a second. I've got to get upstairs and open the window."

From his room, Steven looked out the window at Dylan, standing at the base of the ladder. She rolled her eyes and sighed, as she stepped on the first rung. Steven was leaning out the window with a big grin on his face.

"Don't look down my shirt."

"I'm not." He wasn't until she made the suggestion.

"Go sit on your bed. I'll be right there."

Steven did as he was told. He was giddy. This image he'd cooked up was coming to life. In a moment or two, a friend of his, his only close friend, Dylan, would climb into his bedroom as he sat expectantly on his bed. At the last moment, he decided he'd sit at his desk and pretend to work on homework. That's how the trope usually went.

Dylan's face peered over the sill. Steven turned and was about to speak.

"Shhh," she said as she climbed in. "Turn back to your desk." Dylan directed the scene. Her voice, lowered a half step and affected some nonchalance: "Hey, Steven. I was bored and thought I'd stop by." She knew the lines!

Steven swiveled his chair to face her. "Hey, Dyl. I was just thinking about you." He never called her Dyl.

They laughed. It was exactly as Steven had imagined.

For the next three years, every day after school—give or take a few—this scene played out exactly the same way. Steven kept promising he'd put the ladder away, but after a while, Mrs. Lilly stopped noticing and asking.

Three years later, sitting in his bedroom at the computer, Steven imagined a montage of these visits—only the seasonal backgrounds, outfits, and hairstyles changing. Steven couldn't sleep again. He'd been on his computer for hours now, and when he looked at the white background of the Google homepage, he thought he could see individual pixels spinning around in all the colors of the spectrum. He looked out the window instead, but the image burned in inverse against his eyelids.

The moonlight caught itself on the silver rungs of the ladder. Just once he wished Dylan would visit in the middle of the night. He texted her often when he couldn't sleep, trying to convince her to walk the two miles between their neighborhoods, and climb the ladder into his room.

"That's not part of the script," she'd say.

***

He heard a buzzing somewhere that sounded like his phone. But where was it? Steven checked by the desk and around his bed. It wasn't in his book bag, either. It must have slipped out somewhere. He spotted the light from under a discarded sock, but it had stopped vibrating by the time he got to it.

Unknown number. That's all it said. Telemarketers, likely. One final buzz signaled a message. He opened his messages and hit play. It wasn't a telemarketer.

By the time, he finished replaying it for the hundredth time, he still couldn't understand. What did this mean?? It was almost time to go to school. He wondered if everyone else had gotten the same message. There was only one way to find out.

FOUR

Trevor Drake felt sick. Unfortunately, he had little luck acquiring a diagnosis. That's all he wanted, just a doctor who could point at something, preferably literally, and say, "There's your problem."

This was his fault. If his sickness had a narrative, he could not tell it. He had no setting to describe—his pain, or the *general dullness*, as he'd taken to calling it, had no epicenter. The characters involved—creaky joints, headaches, an occasional sharp pain in his sides, the exhaustion—weren't very flushed out ones. It was a *malaise*, a word he'd just taught in class, ironically. In offering a sample sentence, he wrote on the board, "His *malaise* had kept him in bed for days." Sometimes, to amuse himself, he would work his own life onto the whiteboard.

"The old man had lost his youthful *ebullience*."

"Lying on the couch, he grew more *listless*."

"Life can get so *convoluted*."

Trevor often found himself frozen in place when he was at home, whole minutes going by before he'd realize he hadn't moved. He remembered reading *Watership Down* to Benjamin and the word *tharn*, a word au-thor Richard Adams used to describe the "staring, glazed paralysis" that comes over terrified rabbits, as they watch oncoming cars or weasels bear down on them. He was more exhausted than terrified, but he felt like he was waiting on an approach, some impending, sudden thud. Trevor had gone tharn.

When he couldn't sleep, he'd flip open an anthology of Shakespeare's plays. Tonight it fell open to *The Winter's Tale*. He knew the play, had probably read it in college, and maybe even wrote a paper about it, but its details were lost to him now. There's a line that stopped him the other night, something Camillo says about how a person can carry an illness even though they are free of disease.

> *There is a sickness*
> *Which puts some of us in distemper, but*
> *I cannot name the disease; and it is caught*
> *Of you that yet are well.*

Shakespearean scholars are intrigued by the amount of knowledge he seems to possess about sickness and disease. It may have been, as Trevor had read recently, that it was a sign of the times, that the London of the 1590s was such a breeding ground of disease because of its unsanitary conditions, that the merely observant man would seem an expert in maladies compared to our WebMD-outsourced knowledge today. Shakespeare witnessed the plague, for god's sake. Trevor was reasonably sure he didn't have the plague, but he was getting more worried every day. He was only fifty-one.

Mrs. Drake, Elizabeth, was not a great comfort to Trevor. Not lately, at least. He didn't blame her. It was hard to be sympathetic to an unnamed and unpredictable sickness like his. He was careful not to complain about it too often. Elizabeth would often tell Trevor that he was overreacting, that he was just getting old and this is what happens. She hadn't yet called him a hypochondriac, but Trevor saw the word form on her lips a few times. Elizabeth worked at the hospital in the claims department. She was the vice president there and spent her days on the phone with insurance companies and with patients and families who complained loudly enough to make it up the chain to her. Her job had trained her to look at concrete details to resolve a conflict. She dealt in diagnosis codes, fees, PPOs, Medicare. Her wing of the building was safe from the sick and the dying, from the plagues of the patients. Trevor's undiagnosed condition flummoxed his doctors, but for Elizabeth, it hardly registered. She was not unkind, though. Whenever Trevor got frustrated with her, he would tell himself that: *she's not unkind.*

The English teacher's life is filled with papers. Trevor had been carrying the same set of essays with him every day for the past two and a half weeks. They came out of his bag when he got to school. He put the pile on his desk, evening them into a clean stack. If he could find time during a planning period, he'd sit and give them a go. That was the plan anyway. Most of the time they went untouched and would get placed in the bag for the trip home where they would stay. He couldn't bear taking them out at home. There was no comfortable place to sit and grade. It would make sense to just leave them at school, but teachers who left empty-handed received odd looks. *Look busy* was good advice for a new teacher.

He prided himself on providing meaningful comments to his student writers. Whatever blank space was left at the bottom of the last page, Trevor would fill it with thoughtful ideas and suggestions, and encouraging praise. His strength, he thought, was finding the good lines. No matter the level and ability of the student, Trevor could find the one true line, or a particularly poetic combination of words that stood out from the rest. He had this trick— not an official pedagogical strategy—where he'd hold the essay at arm's length and scan it, looking for words that popped off the page, like some divination. He'd been reading papers for so long that one look was a pretty accurate assessment of its success. He told the kids that their writing was a conversation with the reader. Trevor thought of his comments as the same. But ever since this dullness had attached to him, he was finding it more difficult to do his part.

He and Elizabeth occupied very different worlds at work. As much as ham-handed politicians wanted to turn schools into businesses, the corporate model never worked. Once they treated students like products, it had all gone to shit. Standardized tests, teacher performance valuations, graduation rates, AP test scores, student-teacher ratios, reading proficiency rates, college readiness indices—everything was a number, and the numbers, along with everything else, got crunched. The number of acronyms was staggering: AYP, CCS, ELL, GPA, IEP, LRE, PBL, STEM. Outside the classroom, the only one that mattered to Trevor was CYA— and he'd been covering his ass for years. In the classroom, *the room*, as he called it, only the ABCs concerned him. Even as bureaucracy imposed itself on the school, there was always the sanctity of the room. Save for a few observations each year, Trevor was alone to create a safe and comfortable environment for his kids. Behind his closed door, all he needed was a book, some paper and pens, and thirty young minds and hearts.

Since Benjamin died, Trevor depended more and more on the room. Elizabeth found the logic and math of her job comforting. Each claim her department processed was another problem solved. It had been ten years already since the accident, and Trevor knew they were grieving in different ways—that was clear after the first week. It was painful the first year back at work, staring at all those young kids, older versions of the son they'd lost, but when summer rolled around, he longed for the classroom again. One of the unintended consequences of losing Benjamin was that Trevor threw himself into teaching more. He attended NCTE conferences, volunteered for district committees, started an after school writing workshop three days a week. He poured all of his energies into the profession. But something was different now. He wasn't sure what had changed. It may have been that it was just catching up to him. Maybe a man can only put off his grief for a decade.

Benjamin had a sweet voice. His mother and father encouraged his love of music. Every week Benjamin sang in the Men and Boys choir at the Church of the Good Samaritan. He was one of the younger boys, joining the group when he was only eight years old. He enjoyed the pomp and circumstance of the Episcopal church. He got to wear a robe and cassock and process down the aisle into the choir stalls every Sunday with his dad. He loved singing the descants the best, high counter melodies belted out over the hymn verses. His voice sounded like a bell. It was hollow and round and always on pitch. Some of the older boys resented his near perfect ear.

The boys practiced twice a week and we're given a ten-minute break in the middle of rehearsals. There was a blizzard the winter Benjamin turned ten, forcing the church custodial crew to plow high mounds of snow off to the side of the parking lot. The tallest one formed a wall around the cemetery. The boys played King of the Mountain and staged snowball fights on either side of the snow wall. Two of the older boys, Greg and Tom, found Benjamin to be an especially easy target. Benjamin was quick for a ten-year-old, but he was no match for the two of them. There wasn't a safe side of the mound; Greg or Tom could always flush him out into the open.

Trying to outwit the boys, Benjamin climbed to the top of the mound, one day, and laid low between two jutting banks, while they circled around calling his name. Mr. Beaumont, their choir director, came outside and rang the bell signaling the end of break time. Benjamin peered up and over the bank, planning a safe path back to the church. Greg and Tom saw little Benjamin's head and tossed the snowballs they'd been carrying at him. Benjamin scrambled to his feet and took a few steps down the snow wall and lost his footing. His arms windmilled, trying to regain his balance, but his forward motion carried him right off the snow bank. He tripped over one of his boots, and he landed head first against a headstone. It happened in a fraction of a second. No one on the scene even heard the sound of head against stone—just heard the soft flop of Benjamin's blue winter coat into a foot of snow. His arms and legs splayed out, his neck twisted at a right angle, the impression underneath him like a cruel snow angel.

The emergency responders came quickly and rushed him off to the hospital, but he was dead before they got there.

The grief was unspeakable, but for a while, the first year or so, Trevor and Elizabeth relied on one another. They spoke sweetly and softly in conversation. They were always checking in with the other one, to see if they could do anything, get anything. They held hands a lot—as they sat at breakfast, went food shopping, sat at church, walked around the neighborhood. The church, too, was a comfort for a while. The congregation and ministers prayed and visited and offered counseling and advice. They named the choir stall after Benjamin. The plaque read *Benjamin Drake "Sing to the world a new song," Psalm 96*. There was a tiny bell in the right top corner.

After the first year, though, things changed. Elizabeth didn't offer her hand to Trevor much anymore. Besides kissing right before bed, they hardly even touched. Even when walking by each other in the house, as one walked into the kitchen and the other back to the living room, their bodies didn't even brush against one another, as if there was some kind of magnet keeping them apart. They both noticed but neither spoke of it. They were afraid to hear what they might say. Even the day that Elizabeth boxed up Benjamin's toys, books, and clothes for the basement, even then, when Trevor noticed them missing, nothing was said. When he found the boxes under the basement steps, they were unlabeled. He found a marker and labeled them: *Benjamin's Belongings*.

Ever since then, Trevor carried the label maker around the house, looking for the uncatalogued.

This was the scene tonight as Trevor found himself asleep on the couch again, the label maker on the coffee table. He heard his phone buzz.

The clock read 2:30 a.m. He reached for his school bag, but knocked it on the ground. Fifty student essays slid out onto the floor—and his phone. He reached it by the fourth ring and listened to an automated message he didn't understand. He hung up and couldn't move. He looked as if he'd seen a ghost. Trevor had gone tharn again.

FIVE

The following is a message from the Great Valley School District:

March 15th. March 15th. March 15th. March 15th. March 15th. March 15th. March 15th. March 15th. . .

A computerized voice intoned the date over and over in a loop.

In the main office, Deedee handled about a hundred calls on the morning of the first message. By eight o'clock they brought in Kim to help answer the phones. Neither had an answer—no one had an answer. They told confused parents that an explanation would be posted on the school's website and the district was sorry for the inconvenience.

The principal, Dr. King, met with her administrative team to come up with a properly worded response. The tech director was already working with IT and the service they used for their all-calls to figure out why over 2,500 phone calls went out at 2:17 a.m. last night. The service was rarely used, except to inform the community about the three or four snow day closings a year. Other questions lined up, too: *Was this a computer glitch? Who was responsible? How do we assure this doesn't happen again? Why "March 15th"?*

While administration dealt with the technical concerns, the rest of the building—students and staff—were more interested in that last question. What did the message mean? What was special about March 15th? Some teachers and kids sloughed it off as a weird computer glitch and didn't see what all the fuss was about. These people had no joy in their lives, Dylan and Steven thought. Something had happened in a place where nothing ever happened.

More exciting for Dylan was the fact that March 15th was her birthday. In the middle of the night, having just watched the helicopter take off, listening to a computer voice say her birthdate over and over, Dylan didn't know if she should be amused, concerned, or freaked out. She settled on all three. She couldn't go back to sleep. Steven called Dylan right after he'd heard it.

"Did you get that message?"
"Yes!"
"Well, happy birthday, I guess."
"What was that all about??"
"This seems sort of a desperate plan on your part."
"It just kept saying it over and over."

After trying to hash out what was going on, confirming that they'd gotten the same message, they spent the next hour texting "March 15th" back and forth to each other, trying out different emojis, making each other laugh. By the morning, Dylan was more intrigued than freaked out. At school, they'd taken to whispering it in the hallway. A later variation had them touch the side of their nose knowingly, and then point at a friend, or a startled-looking freshman, when they passed between classes. They doodled the date in their notebooks. It became mantra. They tried working it into conversations.

Michelle asked, "When do we need our permission slip in?"

"March, 15th. March 15th. March 15th. . ."

Marta asked, "When is our Spanish test?" They tried a Spanish robot voice.

"El quince de Marzo. El quince de Marzo. El quince de Marzo. . ."

By second period, Steven had fashioned a few lame memes.

Dylan spent most of her free third period googling *March 15th*, looking for some significance. Obviously, it was the ides of March too, the day Julius Caesar was assassinated. Neither Steven nor Dylan had ever read the play, but the line *Beware the ides of March* was familiar enough. The possibility that the message was a threat was not lost on Dylan and Steven—and certainly not on Dr. King and her staff, something about the tone, the repetition. As much as they were enjoying the mystery of the day, they noticed a weird energy around the front office and wondered if the administration was thinking the same thing.

"That's too obvious," Steven said.

"Maybe it's not a warning. Maybe it's the beginning of a story."

"It's a pretty bad story. Unless it's about you."

"That I'm going to be assassinated?!"

"No. Something else. Anything."

"It's other people's birthday, too."

Dylan googled more. Also born on that day: Andrew Jackson, Fabio, Ruth Bader Ginsberg, will.i.am. It seemed unlikely it was a message from any of them. A check over other non-assassinating historical events yielded no other interesting results. This year, March 15th, Dylan's birthday, would be on a Tuesday, and Tuesday as Dylan always contended was the least compelling day of the week. A quick check into its anagram—for this occasion Steven used the internet—offered no clues. (The fact that March Fifteenth could be *Hatchet Men Riff* didn't seem convincing of anything.)

They filtered the month, date, and year through some half-assed numerology. 3 + 15 + 15 = 33. Three's the magic number. Thirty-three, the age when Christ died. The atomic number of arsenic. The human spine has thirty-three bones. Islamic prayer beads are arranged in sets of thirty-three. The number printed on Rolling Rock bottles. Records spin at 33 and 1/3.

Nothing.

Like a lot of their obsessions, Steven and Dylan wouldn't be satisfied until they'd exhausted it, rendered it meaningless. It was a gift, their single-mindedness, one that multiplied exponentially when they were together. They could entertain a thought for hours—take it for a walk, out to dinner, back to its place. They could interrogate it under a hanging light bulb and play good-cop/bad-cop. This mysterious phone message was almost wrung dry by sixth period that day, ready for its post-mortem, until Mr. Drake's class stirred it up again.

A kid who sat behind Steven asked Mr. Drake what he thought of the message. "What do you make of it?" Colin asked Mr. Drake. "It's clearly some sort of—" Colin, whose idea of a personality was telling people his theories on things, was cut off abruptly by the unfamiliar sound of Mr. Drake's raised voice.

"WE'RE NOT GOING TO TALK ABOUT IT!!"

It stopped the class dead. Dylan and Steven both considered turning to one another, but didn't. None of them had heard this all caps voice from Mr. Drake before. He never lost his cool, never had ruffled feathers. Never had feathers to ruffle, presumably.

He seemed poised to yell something else. He put his hand up to his mouth and put a finger across his mustache like he was about to sneeze, forming a second mustache. It should have been funny, but it wasn't. They became oddly aware of the whir of the air vent overhead.

"I DON'T HAVE TIME FOR THIS! WE—WE DON'T HAVE TIME FOR THIS!" He caught himself. He exhaled slowly. If he inhaled, no one noticed.

"We have things we need to get through. Could you please take out your books?"

And that was it. As quickly as this other person emerged, it disappeared again. *What the hell was that?* Dylan thought. Seconds later a buzzing in her back pocket from Steven that she would read later: "WTF??" She wanted to grab for it, but didn't dare now.

Was that *Dr. Overtaker*, incarnate, just then?

Whatever was going on, Dylan was surprised Mr. Drake continued with his lesson plan—a discussion of chapter 3 of Gatsby. Lots of teachers lost their cool, and their anger resulted in the assigning of some quiet desk work: a sad worksheet, note taking, silent reading. Teachers could be as moody as their students, often more so.

Instead, Mr. Drake soldiered on. Dylan and Steven knew how to play their student roles well; they often rescued a flailing teacher with a raised hand or thoughtful comment or question. Dylan's listening skills were especially good in these uncomfortable situations. She made eye contact with Mr. Drake/Dr. Overtaker—part from fear, part sympathy—and nodded her head, willing his lesson into the room.

"The opening to the chapter is filled with *things*, isn't it? Motor boats, aquaplanes, a Rolls Royce, station wagons, mops, scrubbing brushes, hammers, shears, oranges, lemons—and that's just the first page. The rest is populated with all these *things*—" Mr. Drake kept emphasizing *things*, like it was a dirty word. "And what about that butler, juicing all those fruits?"

They weren't sure if this was a rhetorical question. He paused a little too long, the rage still pulsing dimly in his eyes. Dylan quickly looked down at the text, searching for something she could add, wanting this awkwardness to stop.

She didn't raise her hand, just spoke up, reading: *"Pulpless halves."*

"Exactly!" Mr. Drake zeroed in on Dylan. "What about that??"

She wasn't sure what to say next. The odd pair of words just leapt off the page. Steven and the rest of the class turned to Dylan. What was she talking about? Marta Wainwright put her hand up but was ignored.

"It just sounds. . .gross," Dylan began. "He's got all these people working for him, setting up for these parties. And the oranges and lemons, sitting outside the back door are 'pulpless halves.' I mean, the party sounds amazing," she wasn't sure what she wanted to say. "It's just—it's also sounds—" She was disappointed that the right word wasn't coming to her. "Gross." Her face flushed; everyone was still looking her way.

Steven came to the rescue. "Well, I mean he describes the partygoers as *moths*. And it's not the butler who's pressing that juicing button two hundred times, it's the *butler's thumb*. Like he's just a thumb for juicing. And he keeps writing about how things are *permeating, swelling, weaving*—" Steven's copy of the novel was marked up. Dylan wanted to be that kind of reader, but she wasn't yet.

Now that Steven had started, there was no stopping him. "And no one's invited, they just show up. And they never meet him. And they're all gossiping. Like on page 44, he calls it *casual innuendo*, but Jordan's friend is 'given to *violent* innuendo.' I circled all the negative words, like: *graceless, tortuously, notorious*—"

Dylan joined in. *"Vacuous, corpulent, discordant. . ."* Marta, whose hand was still up, huffed. Dylan and Steven were on a roll.

Mr. Drake was loving it. He was the nodder now. "Yes," he kept saying, each time with greater emphasis. This happened every once in a while, a moment where a teacher and a few students zoned in and left the rest of the class in their wake. Some turned to their laps and played with their phones.

Mr. Drake took over. "But then it changes. Look at the bottom of fifty-one. After the champagne, Nick says the scene transforms, becomes 'something significant, elemental, profound.'" He sat back down behind his desk with the book and flattened the book open on top of his yellow pad of paper, like he'd had the "two finger bowls of champagne," too.

***

The rest of the period slowed, their flurry over. Marta Wainwright wanted to talk about Jordan's line to Nick about the kinds of parties she likes: *And I like large parties. They're so intimate. At small parties there isn't any privacy.*

"What does that even mean?" But the bell left that question hanging there, like everything else Marta ever said.

It was Dylan's favorite line, but she didn't want to talk about it. Certainly not with Marta. She didn't want anyone to know she knew exactly what Jordan was talking about. Merging into the crowded hallway, she and Steven became two moths weaving gracelessly into the crowd.

SIX

It was a bad idea and Dylan spent most of that night angry with herself (and at Steven) for agreeing to his plan. She was angry because she had lied to her parents about where she was going, because she agreed to something that was likely illegal, because she had schoolwork she'd been neglecting all week, but most of all because Steven had shamed her into coming along and she had no logical comebacks to shut him down. This didn't seem like one of his *divertissements*, as Steven had taken to calling them. He'd called her a bore, and she wouldn't allow that. She was angry about being called a bore, angry that she feared he was right, and angrier that she would care at all.

By the time they'd made it to Mr. Drake's house—*Trevor's house*, as Steven referred to it—fear and excitement replaced the anger. Steven had a copy of a faculty directory he'd found last year in a recycling bin at school. Like his copy of *Gatsby*, it was annotated and full of marginalia. Dylan was surprised when she first saw all the markings.

"Someone's going to find that and think you're a stalker. Or worse.

Why is it all marked up?"

"Everybody's a stalker."

This was a common construction of Steven's: take a personal slight and twist it so it applied to everyone. Dylan knew he liked the Zen quality of those absolute statements, regardless of whether they were true or had any real meaning. He'd fail a test and tell Dylan, "We're all failures, really." Steven's mother would comment on the mess in his room and he'd say, "Everybody's a mess." (To this point, Steven's mother—agreed, and let it go.) He and Dylan watched some asshole at school leave his trash on the cafeteria table: "Everybody's an asshole." Dylan knew better than to argue these points. *I'm not an asshole. You're not an asshole*, she thought. But a second thought, a second later, and she wasn't sure anymore. *I guess I am an asshole, sometimes.*

"Orchard Drive seems an appropriate street name for Trevor," Steven said.

"You'd say that no matter what it was."

"Probably. I don't see any orchards."

"I can't see anything. Why aren't there any streetlights?"

"People that live out here, don't need streetlights. The worst thing that happens out here is someone doesn't clean up after their dog."

"You're sure this is the one?"

"503."

"What are we looking for exactly?"

"We don't know yet. I'm just *worried*."

As cynical as Steven could be, he was also completely earnest—and weirdly compassionate. Dylan was worried, too. After his blowup, Mr. Drake had been off the rest of the week. He was short with students. He'd read whole passages of the text aloud and forget why he'd chosen them and what he wanted to point out. On Wednesday, he snapped at Marta: "Marta! Could you please wait till I finish?! Instead of waving your hand in the air like you're drowning!" Any other week, Dylan and Steven—the entire class—would have viewed this as a small victory. Someone had finally said something to that girl. Mr. Drake could get away with these lines occasionally. He was good at disarming with a bit sarcasm. But in the wake of Mr. Drake's bad week, it sounded mean. On Friday, he'd come to class ten minutes late. No one left. They all just sat and waited. When he walked in, he mumbled an apology, but the rest of the class period felt like the first ten minutes. Mr. Drake was completely and helplessly absent—a shell of the teacher they had grown to admire that year.

503 Orchard Drive was a beautiful house made less beautiful by its similarity to all the other houses in the development. It was bigger than they had imagined a teacher's house to be. "He must have married well," Steven said.

A lamppost lit the driveway. Two sconces cast sharp pyramids outside the front door. An upstairs window blinked blue and green lights, presumably from a TV. Downstairs, from a front window on the garage side of the house, came a soft yellow light.

"There."

"But what are we supposed to do?"

Steven shushed her. He whispered, "I just want to look in. I just want to make sure he's okay."

Steven grabbed Dylan's hand and slinked around the side of the house to get a better look into the window. They had never held hands before, but it wasn't unpleasant, Dylan thought.

Mr. Drake sat at long wooden dining room table. On it sat manila folders, a label maker, some sort of blue robe, a cardboard box, a plastic crate, a three-ring binder, and his yellow pad of paper. He wasn't grading papers; he was in the midst of a big organizing project.

Dylan tapped Steven on the shoulder. She pointed to a second box sitting on one of the dining room chairs. It read, "Benjamin's Belongings." Dylan and Steven had heard, in bits and pieces—mostly pieces—about Mr. Drake's son. He died some years ago. They didn't know his name, but in an instant, it occurred to them it must be *Benjamin*, that these must be his things Mr. Drake was going through.

Dylan was immediately uncomfortable. They shouldn't be here. What were they thinking? This was someone's house. Someone's moment. Someone they didn't know. Not really. Why had she let Steven talk her into coming out here? They needed to walk away, now. Dylan grabbed hold of Steven's elbow. He turned, and she implored with her eyes. But Steven froze there—he couldn't look away. She didn't like what she saw in his eyes, like he'd seen a ghost. Maybe they had.

She whispered, "I'm going." Unable to move, Steven let her hand slide off his arm without comment. "Come on," she said as she crouched a few paces away.

But then, a cat. From out of nowhere, a black and white cat jumped on the window sill, its eyes hollow and translucent. Dylan let out a scream.

It was quick and sharp, but it was loud. Not knowing what to do next, she made for the driveway. She would not get caught looking into Mr. Drake's window. This was not her stupid idea. She was getting out of there.

These thoughts flew through her head, but just as quickly flew away when her feet found the garden hose. She tripped and fell in a tangled pile, her face in the mulch.

Steven hadn't turned to look at Dylan yet. Mr. Drake put down a folder and walked toward the window. The cat, oblivious, rubbed up against the curtain. Steven thought if he didn't move, maybe Mr. Drake wouldn't see him. He was wrong.

"Steven??"

Steven remained still. Dylan struggled with the hose.

"What are you doing??" Now seeing Dylan: "Is that Dylan with you?"

Steven stood up. "Yes, sir." Steven had never called anyone *sir.* "Yes, it's me. And Dylan."

"Stay right there."

Steven came to help Dylan untangle, but she pushed him away.

"Just get off of me! I can do it myself." She threw the hose down in a pile. Black mulch smeared the left side of her face.

"You've got some—"

"I know!" Dylan scrubbed it off as best she could.

The front door opened and Mr. Drake emerged, still holding his yellow pad of paper.

"Come in here." That's all he said. He didn't appear angry or surprised, more like he'd been expecting them. They followed him inside because they had no other choice.

As they followed Mr. Drake into his dining room, it felt like they were on stage at the theater.

The inside of the house was immaculate, everything in its proper place. Recessed lighting cast soft spotlights on abstract modern art hanging on the wall. The soft hum of classical music wafted in from somewhere. There was a candelabra on the piano. The only sign that this wasn't a staged, real estate model was the mess on the dining room table.

Mr. Drake walked into the room and surveyed his progress at the table. Dylan and Steven looked at each other, unsure what to do. Trevor sighed.

Dylan started right in: "Mr. Drake. I'm terribly sorry. We were just walking through the neighborhood, and—"

"No, we weren't. We came here on purpose," Steven said.

"No. No. That's not—no—"

"We're sorry, Mr. Drake." Steven would not let Dylan explain this away. "I hope you can forgive us. The thing of it is—"

"Can I get you some water?" Mr. Drake pointed to the kitchen.

"Some what? Some *water*? Uh, sure."

"No, I'm good. Look—" Dylan bulged her eyes at Steven.

"I'll get you both some water." Trevor left them alone in the dining room.

"What are you doing?" Dylan asked.

"I'm saying I want some water."

"We're bothering him."

"We're not bothering him. He just invited us inside. Now we're going to drink some water."

"Is this what you wanted?"

"I didn't want anything. I just wanted to see if he was okay.

"Unbelievable," Dylan said, but she didn't believe her own assessment. "Everything's unbelievable."

Mr. Drake returned, carrying two small tumblers of water. "Here."

"Thanks," Steven said.

"Thank you," Dylan said. She drank, but her mouth was still dry.

They stood there sipping quietly for a long beat. Trevor was the first to move when he returned to his seat at the dining room table. Dylan couldn't help but do a quick inventory of the table: crayon-drawn pictures, certificates, legal documents, a few articles of clothing, a blue robe, some books. Trevor motioned for Dylan and Steven to sit as he resumed the shuffling and dividing of papers. He grabbed his yellow pad of paper and sighed again.

"March 15th."

"The phone message?" Steven asked.

"March 15th will make ten years since we lost Benjamin."

Steven didn't miss a beat. "I'm sorry, Mr. Drake. He was your son, right?"

Dylan envied Steven. He seemed completely comfortable in this conversation. He always had an easy time talking to adults. She couldn't decide if it was his sophistication, ignorance, or vanity, or some combination.

She merely listened, reprising her good student role. Steven was good at conversing, but Dylan was the listener. Together they made a whole person, she thought.

"Yes, he was. Benjamin was our son." Trevor straightened a pile. "It's not just the 15th. It's every day, really. But a decade? A decade of every days is a long time. It feels like yesterday. But like a yesterday that happened ten years ago, if that makes any sense." Trevor directed most of this to Dylan.

"It does make sense," Steven said. How could Steven possibly know, Dylan thought.

"Obviously, it's worse around the *anniversary*. I don't like that word. But I don't know how else to put it. But then that message—whatever that was. Brought it all up again. I don't know if you can imagine what it's like to hear that. . .*intoned* the way it was. In the middle of the night. Out of context. Like it was a ghost. Even by computer. Maybe, especially by computer. The date of Benjamin's—the date we lost Benjamin."

"It's also Dylan's birthday," Steven offered. Dylan turned to Steven. What is he thinking, saying that?

"I'm sorry, Mr. Drake." Dylan wasn't sure what she was apologizing for.

"Is it? Well, that's nothing to be sorry about. Your birthday?" He shook his head. "Huh. Benjamin would have been around your age now. A senior, I guess."

"Is that what's made you out of sorts, lately?" Steven asked.

"I guess so, yes." Trevor turned to Steven. "Has it been that bad?"

"It's been fine," Dylan assured him.

"It's been a little weird. In class. We wanted to make sure you were okay."

Someone moved upstairs. "Who are you talking to?" came a voice from the top of the stairs.

"I'll be right up," Mr. Drake called back. Somehow this was a good enough answer to the woman upstairs.

Steven plowed on. "That's why we were here. We just wanted to see if you were okay."

Trevor put down his yellow pad of paper. Without wanting to see what was on it, he'd put it right in front of Dylan and Steven. There was nothing written on it. It looked brand new—unwritten upon. One mystery solved?

"We're sorry to interrupt your evening. I'm mortified. Really," Dylan said.

"Isn't that one of our vocab words?" Mr. Drake managed something like a smile.

Dylan hadn't realized that. It was hard to have a conversation with someone who was teaching you what to say, how to say it. Every word sounded different coming out of her mouth, next to Mr. Drake.

"Yes. I guess it is."

"So are you? Are you going to be all right?" Steven asked.

Mr. Drake sat back in his chair and looked at all of Benjamin's belongings. He grabbed a nearby label maker. "I'll be fine."

Trevor typed something into the label maker, and when he hit the print button, a thin white tape ejected from the back panel. He pressed another button to cut the tape, handed the label to Steven, but looked at Dylan. He repeated the words printed there:

I'll be fine.

Mr. Drake showed them to the door, and Steven and Dylan walked home without talking.

SEVEN

"Y"ou'll be a seasonal employee," Ken said. Ken looked no older than she did, despite his attempt at a beard.

Dylan liked the sound of *seasonal employee*. She'd never been any kind of employee before. A seasonal one sounded like a good way to begin. Maybe she could concoct a life of seasonal employment: ski instructor in the winter, lifeguard in the early summer, a picker of fruits and vegetables at the end of summer, and then find herself here at Halloween Adventure every fall, helping kids find the right fake teeth.

"When it gets closer to Halloween, when the customers start rolling in, you'll need to be in some sort of costume all day. If you read through the packet, you'll see some of the suggestions and restrictions. You can get 25 percent off any item, but there's usually enough broken or factory reject wigs and props that you can manage to put something together for free. It can't be anything too scary. A witch is okay, but no fake noses. A zombie is crossing the line. Anything that strongly evokes death is a no-no. A lot of the girls dress as fairies or princesses. . ."

This was the line Dylan would not cross. She would not be in a dress, tutu, or in wings.

"Liz was a mermaid last year. The little girls that come in—those are the ones they like. The costumes they like. There's some good upselling opportunities there, too."

"Some what?"

"Upselling. If a girl comes in and says she wants to be a mermaid, you try to upsell her mom. Get her to buy the makeup, the glitter, the press-on Rhinestones. The hand-fins."

"Hand-fins??"

"We've got gloves that look like fish fins. Fish hands. They double for the Creature of the Black Lagoon costumes."

"Mermaids have human arms. Human hands, though."

"Yeah, see, there. You're not thinking like a salesman there. Why couldn't a mermaid have fish fins??"

"Because they're. . .human on top?"

"Look. It's Halloween. If a kid wants fish hands, we sell them fish hands. Got it?"

"Okay." Dylan got it, but she didn't want it. Or she sort of did—this job, at least. She'd been bugging her parents to let her get a job ever since she turned fifteen. "Other kids' parents force their kids to get a job," she'd argued.

"You'll be working the rest of your life. What's the rush?" her dad said.

When she was younger, her favorite characters in books were the young kids who had to go to work to help *pay their way* or *help out around the house*. There was Darry in *The Outsiders*. He had two jobs to support

Ponyboy and Sodapop. Meg and Jo in *Little Women* had to pitch in, too. She wouldn't mind being a governess, she thought. Even Oliver's life on the street as a street urchin, pick-pocketing strangers, was weirdly appealing.

Her feminist heroes now were more complicated, older certainly. She'd blazed through all the Jane Austen books the summer before Daphne left for college, and most of the Brontës. She'd been the only one in her class last year who liked *The Scarlet Letter*—who'd actually read the book. Hester Prynne, living out in the forest with her sins—above the reproach of the town. Later, her mother gave her an old dog-eared copy of *Gone with the Wind*. Scarlett O'Hara was strong and selfish, a survivor, a businesswoman. She liked how she did things for herself, how detached she could be. These two Scarletts. Occasionally, Dylan would try to affect this attitude at school: a Hester, holding her books to her chest, looking out past the lockers on the way to class. Or as Scarlett, ordering Steven around in a bad Southern accent. She was unsuccessful on both counts. The only evidence of these two women in her life was the scarlet lipstick she wore to school every day.

Dylan wasn't ready for the role of Hester, Scarlett, or Steven's suggested Darling Energy, and she doubted she would ever be. As much as she wanted to be one of these independent women, as long as she lived where she did, how she did, it would be an impossible assignment. Everything in Dylan's life had already been provided for her. Her parents weren't as loaded as a lot of the families at the other end of her street, but by any other measure she wanted for nothing.

It embarrassed her sometimes: how she had the newest, nicest phone, her pick of fashionable sweaters and expensive jeans, a Martin acoustic guitar she still hadn't learned to play—the base level one, sure, but still. Sometimes she would feel guilty, and then she would feel embarrassed about her guilt, and guilty about her embarrassment. At night before she fell asleep, she'd remind herself that all she should feel was lucky—but luck was not an emotion, and emotions were all she really knew.

The only thing she didn't have access to was her own car. However, unlike the rest of her friends who had just turned sixteen, Dylan had no interest in driving. The thought scared her, actually, and she'd hadn't even brought up the possibility of driving, either getting a car or even just taking the driver's test. Steven gave her grief about it, despite not having a car or license of his own.

"You'll be surrounded by little kids all day," he reminded her. "Touching everything. Screaming."

"I like kids."

"No, you don't."

"I do like kids. How would you know?"

"I just know. Who could like kids?"

"There's a lot of things I like you don't know about."

"Name one."

She gave it a second or two but nothing came up. Ever since that night at Mr. Drake's house, Steven's insistence and opinions grated on her. The job would be a nice break from him, too.

"So every day after school??" He sounded insulted.

"No. Two days tops. Maybe a weekend day here and there." She didn't like the look on his face. He was in a snit. She promised him it wouldn't be a big deal, climbed out his window, and walked home.

For a few weeks, it confused her that her parents weren't all in with her employment plans. She assumed they were being overly protective or worried about how it would interfere with her schoolwork. But the week before she overheard them discussing the idea in the kitchen. It surprised her to learn they were more concerned about how it might affect their *own* schedules.

"How is she going to get there?"

"Right."

"What about public transportation?"

"Why not?"

"I don't want her on that bus."

"She's on a bus every day."

"A school bus."

"What's the difference?"

"Well, I can't drive her."

"Well, you *could*."

"We've talked about this. Has she even mentioned the driver's test yet?"

She didn't stay to listen to the whole conversation, but it stuck with her for the rest of the day—thinking of herself as a parcel needing to be delivered was upsetting. She hadn't considered that before. They'd spent most of their lives dropping her off and picking her up, like some sort of persistent dry cleaning.

She didn't want to drive—not yet, anyway—but she used this information to strike a deal: she would get the job so she could save money for gas.

"I don't want to put you two out."

She had never used that phrase before, but it sounded remarkably mature coming from her lips. She almost meant it. They agreed to help her get to work, but maybe she could befriend someone at work who could drop her off at the end of her shift?

When she found out who else was working at Halloween Adventure, her befriending idea had become the best plan she'd come up with in a while. His name was Norman. She was very aware how much Norman looked like Steven—the same sad eyes, the same cowlick, even Steven's abrupt guffaw. He had all of these things, but he was a half-foot taller and his chest puffed out under his oxford shirts like he was Clark Kent. He had the athlete's build, but played no sports. His six-foot-three frame stood at the back of the school choir, singing baritone. It stood behind podiums at debate. He managed both conspicuousness and modesty.

For the first few days at Halloween Adventure, Dylan unpacked boxes, scanned bar codes, and hung plastic bags filled with wigs. It was mindless, tedious work, but she appreciated all the organization it entailed. She was put in charge of stocking the girls' section. She hung up Alice in Wonderland, the Pink Power Ranger, a Prom Queen corpse, a ballerina-zombie mashup imaginatively called Zomberina, vampires, werewolves, four different leopard print costumes, a cop in a miniskirt, Batgirl, Catwoman, Wonder Woman, witches of every variety, and princesses—Elsa, Mulan, Belle, Ariel—Miss Sock Hop and her Poodle skirt, and a *Hunger Games* rip-off called Hooded Huntress. The accessories were more tedious: gloves, leggings, leotards, shoes, tutus, wings, and an entire corner dedicated to tiaras. So many tiaras.

The women's section featured most of the same costumes save for the word *adult* or *sexy* in the title. Dylan knew she was supposed to hate all these costumes—the easy, thoughtless objectification of women—but she couldn't help staring at all the cleavage, at the *bosoms* as her grandmother called them, and feel some envy. The models wearing the Adult Tavern Maiden, the Adult Maiden Native American, and the Adult Hot SWAT costume with handcuffs were busting out of their skin suits. Adult Day of the Dead Señorita didn't seem so bad. Not that she would ever wear something like that, or the Adult Fancy Yellow Plaid School Girl or the Adult Sultry Scarecrow.

"Adult Sultry *Scarecrow*?!?" she said out loud.

A Frankenstein overheard her and galumphed down the aisle.

"Dylan. Where's your costume??" It was Norman. It took her a while to recognize him. His face was painted green. He had two plugs coming out of his neck. He still looks good, Dylan thought. She might have been nervous to talk to him under normal circumstances, but it was easier talking to him as a monster.

"I can't decide. Adult Hot SWAT or Tavern Maiden." Norman looked at the pictures on the bag. His eyes widened. He stuttered out a low sound. It was not un-Frankenstein-like.

"I'm kidding." She let him off the hook.

"Oh, yeah. I *know*." He landed hard on the word, like it was obvious she wouldn't wear that. But she didn't know if he meant because she was *above* that or because she couldn't pull it off. Her face must have looked confused because Norman broke the silence again.

"I mean, not that you—I mean, if you wanted to—" He put his arm out to lean on one of the hooks, but it immediately slipped out of the peg board. A pile of fishnet thigh-highs and nude smoothing control-top boyshorts fell to the ground. Norman picked them up quickly and handed them to Dylan. She thought he would make a joke—Steven would have—but instead Norman hurried away with a muted apology. She couldn't see through the green face paint, but she was sure Norman was blushing.

Dylan might have found his response adorably awkward had it been what she expected of him. But he was easily embarrassed, prudish even. He was too tall to be like that.

She replaced the stockings and shorts on the hooks when she spotted a Red Riding Hood costume and was struck with an idea for her Halloween costume this year. With a few alterations, a stitched letter *A* on the *bosom*, and she might just have something.

When Dylan turned around, she was face-to-face with a young girl half her height.

"Where do you keep the severed fingers?"

"I think they're on aisle nine. Near the front." Dylan was a fast learner.

EIGHT

The second message arrived the next month, on October 30th, during dinner time.

The following is a message from the Great Valley School District:

Three Thirty-Three. Three Thirty-Three. Three Thirty-Three. Three Thirty-Three. Three Thirty-Three. Three Thirty-Three. Three Thirty-Three. Three Thirty-Three. Three Thirty-Three. Three Thirty-Three. Three Thirty-Three. Three Thirty-Three.

Steven hated Halloween. The only day worse was Mischief Night, as his house was a frequent target. Halloween fell on a Saturday, and so it was today, Friday the 30th, that brought the holiday to the school hallways. There were a few rules the school put in place, but no one paid attention to them. There couldn't be masks, and there couldn't be weapons. But sure enough, the first person Steven saw that morning, struggling to open his locker, was Royce Caulder wearing a Jason Voorhees hockey mask and carrying a plastic dagger. Apparently Royce was back from rehab. Had it not been such a terrible idea, Steven contemplated telling Royce, *Jason carried a machete, you dipshit.*

Halloween gives everyone permission to act like a dick, Steven told Dylan the night before.

"Everyone just dresses up like their inner monster."

"Yeah?"

"All those slutty costumes girls wear. All the future date rapists dressing like superheroes or in camouflage. Or worse, the boys that dress up like women because they think being a woman is funny. Angry loner kids who get sent home because they're wearing *real* scissor hands. It all just seems so dark."

"It's supposed to be dark. It's Halloween. You're no fun."

"What are you going to be then?"

"You're the expert. What's my *inner monster?*"

Steven didn't like where this was going. That's the sort of question he might ask. He didn't like the sound of it from Dylan.

"I don't know," he said.

"Maybe I should come dressed up as you."

"There could be worse ideas."

"Maybe I will. That might be fun." And then added, "And easy."

"Shut up."

"How hard would it be?" she said. That stung him a bit. He wanted to know what she thought dressing as him meant, but was afraid to ask. He didn't consider himself an easy study.

"You should come as *Darling Energy.*"

"You know, I thought of that. But I'm not sure what the costume looks like yet."

Steven changed the topic back to mysterious message number two.

"So I guess we've got ourselves a time of day now," he said. "3:33, right?"

"That's what I thought, too. But AM or PM?"

"That's a good question. I've already put it in my calendar."

"Me too."

"Dylan?"

"Steven??" Sometimes in the middle of the conversation, Steven would just say Dylan's name. He liked how it sounded.

"Dylan, let's make a promise right now."

"Go ahead."

"Let's promise that no matter what, we will get together on March 15th at 3:33."

"What do you mean, *no matter what*?"

"I don't know. I just mean, let's clear our schedules. If nothing happens, we'll just do something fun."

"Okay."

"You promise?"

"I said *okay*." Steven was silent. Dylan knew he needed to hear it, so she gave him what he wanted. That was easier. "I *promise*."

It was the first long conversation they'd had on the phone or in person in a few weeks—since their visit with Mr. Drake. He had to call her after this second all-call school message. His excitement—*their* excitement about the first one—had diminished with time. He'd resigned himself to the possibility that it was just a computer glitch after all. But this new message—Steven had called it a *clue*—meant there was a still a mystery for Dylan and him to solve, together.

He was glad she promised, but there was something different in Dylan's voice over the phone. He kept saying that during the conversation. She told him not to be stupid. Part of the change was Dylan's new job—they were seeing less of each other, and when she came over to hang out at Steven's house, it was for a shorter stay than before.

Steven knew it was something worse than the job. She'd taken up with Norman Lewis, anagram name *Normal Swine*. (Steven rejected other possible combinations that included more complimentary words like *manlier, lineman, and seminal*.) Norman was aggravatingly nice. Steven had always been suspicious of anyone who was overly enthusiastic. People referred to this Norman as a *solid guy*. They meant that he was sincere and dependable, but Steven was convinced they were taken in by his size—lazy thinking that viewed the big and tall as sweet and kind if they just smiled occasionally. Before Dylan took up with him, Steven joked to Dylan that he was a lot like Lenny from *Of Mice and Men*. Steven thought he remembered Dylan laughing at the comment, but maybe she didn't.

Dylan had had other boyfriends since she and Steven became friends. He'd felt jealousy before, but it was always short-lived. She never seemed to genuinely care for these other boys. She betrayed them to Steven, confiding in him about the stupid things they'd say, their awkward attempts at romance, or some gross habit. This Norman *relationship* went without commentary, just that she thought he was a nice guy. This worried Steven.

***

Dylan, on the other hand, loved Halloween. Working at Halloween Adventure, although tedious, had given her some time to come up with her outfit. It took little effort to turn Little Red Riding Hood into Hester Prynne. She'd learned to use her mother's sewing machine last summer and, while no work of art worthy of the *ignominious* seamstress (one of her vocab words!), her scarlet letter "A" didn't look half-bad. In fact, it was half-good, she thought.

She got the reaction she was hoping for from Mr. Drake when she walked into English.

"Well, if it isn't Hester Prynne!" Mr. Drake had improved a little since their visit to his house.

She knew Steven would have something to say when he saw her, so she avoided making eye contact. She didn't want to see his eyes roll. That didn't stop Ted Lavender's crack from the back of the room.

"Who's the lucky guy?"

Dylan wasn't sure he was talking to her or not. "What are you talking about?"

"Who'd you commit adultery with??"

The class gave Ted a big laugh on that one. She hadn't considered that someone might make that joke. She was always overestimating her peers.

"Norman Lewis?" Ted suggested.

That got an even bigger laugh. She turned red. Why was everyone laughing? Did people already know she liked Norman? She wasn't even sure she liked him. Why was she blushing? Fuck Ted Lavender.

"Okay," Mr. Drake said, trying to deescalate, turning to the board.

And then, out of the blue:

"Why don't you *shut* the *fuck* up??" Steven turned to Ted. One of his eyes went a little crazy.

"Hey!" Mr. Drake turned around, surprised. Shocked. He felt a sudden flush of heat on his forehead. Every head in the classroom craned back onto their spines. Eyeballs bulged. "Hey," Mr. Drake said again, with the exact same intonation, like someone had pressed a button. "You can't talk like that in here," he said.

Steven was staring hard at Ted Lavender and then shrugged. "I'm sorry, Mr. Drake. But he's an asshole. He should shut up."

"Just stop. What are you doing?" Dylan asked.

"Steven," Mr. Drake said.

Dylan had never heard Steven like this. He'd been confrontational before—to her, alone in his room, yes—but not like this. Ted Lavender was just as surprised. He might have even been scared.

"Take it easy. Jesus," Ted said.

"*Take it easy?* That's good advice, Ted, why don't—"

"Steven! Stop it," Dylan tried again.

"Look. You're can't yell out like that." Mr. Drake walked up to Steven's desk.

Steven stood up. "Mr. Drake, I apologize."

"You should probably head down to—"

"Got it. I'm on my way there." Steven grabbed his book bag and made for the door—but then stopped. "But: before I go, let me just say: *Fuck* yourself, Ted Lavender." He gave a quick look to Dylan, opened the door, slung his backpack over his shoulder and walked out of the room.

Everyone turned to look at Dylan. She folded her arms over her stitching.

Dylan was furious. But she couldn't make up her mind about what. What was that even about?? She didn't need him to protect her honor. Her honor was not at stake. It didn't help. It was just more evidence that boys were only capable of joking or yelling, that they could only belittle or attack. She took a deep breath, straightened her dress, and tried to channel her inner Hester.

***

Trevor had no opinion on Halloween. He had few opinions these days. That wasn't always the case. In fact, as a younger man, he was somewhat of a contrarian. When he was an undergrad, he'd lost a few friendships arguing over the merits of popular foreign films or a new Broadway success. He was wary of popular culture and popular opinion and tried to live as unpopularly as possible—looking for fellow radicals he could kvetch with. Actually, back then he and his progressive college friends had a memorable Halloween, dressed as Patty Hearst and the Symbionese Liberation Army. Trevor's Patty was pretty enough, but the fake guns and genuine berets of his friends—and the authentic drugs they were holding—saw them locked up overnight at the police station. They managed a great photo behind bars that Trevor had planned to show Benjamin when he was older.

Seeing his students in Halloween costumes struck him as redundant. Students were always wearing *costumes*. Especially the boys. A good number of them wore heavy hooded sweatshirts, loose-fitting, many-pocketed cargo pants, and oversized Timberland boots with the laces untied. Despite coming from upper-middle-class families, they wore the uniform of the day laborer, ready to tackle roofing and construction jobs, instead of study hall and trigonometry. The pockets on the cargo pants were comical, each one unused and bunched up from the washing machine, the hammer loops never knowing a hammer. The boots made them shuffle through the hallways, pretending to be men. It was just—silly, really. He didn't blame them. Boys were always pretending to be men. So were men. Besides, it wasn't their fault that individuality wasn't rewarded in high school. It was safer to look like everyone else, to be like everyone else. High school is the great middling, he'd always thought.

There were exceptions. Dylan and Steven were two of those this year—an observation cemented by their unannounced visit to his home last week. The worlds of home and work infrequently collided like that. He knew how surprised students would be to see him in public. Trevor used to joke that the closet in the back of his room was a Murphy bed and he slept there overnight. He kept making that joke despite their not knowing what a Murphy bed was. By all rights, he should be angrier about Dylan and Steven's intrusion into his home, but they both seemed genuinely concerned, which both comforted and saddened him.

Dylan was an *old soul*. She seemed wise beyond her years—not that she'd been able to show it much in class. There wasn't a lot of concrete evidence for this hunch. Her essays were good but not great. She'd stumble on an occasional good line, a graceful turn of phrase, but it was often lost in a pile of unformed thoughts and unsupported assertions. You could see the paper's intention like it was a watermark under the text. But it was her classroom demeanor—her attentive face and encouraging smile, and the way she'd jump into a discussion just to help him out. Trevor relied on those students. She was on the perfect trajectory. With any luck, it would all come together in college; she'd peak in skills and curiosity and friends at exactly the right time. Too many students tried to rush this process, mistaking knowledge for learning, filling their heads with blind ambition and thoughtless worry. Dylan will be great, he thought. He didn't worry about her.

One of the benefits of teaching for so many years was the déjà vu of meeting students who reminded you of former students. Dylan, and the other old souls, stitched a single thread of optimism for Trevor, like they were reincarnations or genetic mutations of one another, budding off through the decades. Were there, what, seven types of students overall? Trevor wondered.

Teaching made you philosophical like that. There aren't many jobs where you can witness the same people over and over again doing the same things over and over again, year after year. He tried to make that point to a friend of his recently—a salesman—but failed.

"It sounds like that guy with the rock. Syphilis, right?"

"*Sisyphus.*"

"Right," his friend sad. "I don't know how you do it."

That was a short view, though. If you thought about the day-to-day every day of the week, you'd want to pull your hair out. Trevor preferred the broad view—the authorial view. He kept a limited omniscient third-person perspective, and it had made all the difference. This perspective was harder when he thought about Benjamin, but he reminded himself to try anyway.

Besides, there was something beautiful about this sameness, this thread of recurring characters—like he was watching twenty-seven seasons of the same TV show. And while some of the story lines were the same, the plots were new to the students. It was always a cold read for them.

"It's sweet," Kathy Barham, Trevor's former colleague said to him one day. "Everything is *new* to them." This was invaluable and true advice, but unfortunately, some of his colleagues forgot that point from time to time. They would get easily frustrated. But Trevor was never surprised when they didn't know how to pronounce a word or know its meaning, or understand the complexities of race or gender or history, or how to gracefully request help and guidance. They were sixteen or seventeen—what does anyone know at that age? He worried about the ones that already knew too much of the world.

It didn't surprise him that Dylan had Steven. Dylans always seem to have a Steven by their side. Not that Steven was a sidekick by any means. But like Dylan, Trevor recognized that kid right away. He'd taught kids like Steven A. Lilly before, and as much as he enjoyed having one in his classroom, he'd always felt he had failed those students. Besides Steven's obvious creativity and his capacity for literary empathy—he could stick up for any character in a book, no matter how unlikable or small—there was such a heavy sadness to Steven, like a green patina on a penny. Whatever spark Steven managed for the text inside the classroom, outside the classroom he was surly and defensive. He was angry. Whatever gifts he had to make connections with fictional characters were lost to the rest of his peers—besides Dylan. Mr. Drake never quite knew what to say to a Steven. Trevor wondered if Benjamin had lived to be a high schooler, maybe he'd be better equipped to help. Benjamin's short and sweet-natured life had hardly given Trevor the opportunity to even try out tough love or to dispense disappointment as motivation.

But yelling *fuck* out loud in the classroom was not something Trevor expected. It wasn't a shock either. Part of him was envious when he thought about it later. Being in high school every day of his career allowed Trevor a few daydreams about what he would say to his own tormentors in school, knowing what he knows now. He'd have to write Steven up. Not because he felt personally obligated to—he would have been happy just to talk to him after class—but because his outburst came at the expense of another student, in front of a room of witnesses, and if he didn't say anything, someone else might, and that sort of undocumented anger could come back and slap Trevor. Steven needed help anyway, he thought. It was an obvious, trite thought, but true nonetheless. He would take him aside the next time he saw him. He'd think of something to say.

NINE

Norman Lewis's house backed up to the train station on Theronside Lane. His father joked that they lived on "The-Ron-Side-of-the-tracks," and this dad-pun was also entirely accurate. The Lewis house was the only residential home on their side of the tracks, sandwiched between the tailor and the cobbler—the last holdout of a razed housing development built in the late 40s. The other neighbors' families had all moved across the street in the early 60s, but the Lewises (well, at least Norman's grandfather Ronald) preferred the southerly view and refused to move. The construction of a new train platform built in the '90s now blocked the view. Norman's dad, Evan, cursed that bad decision every chance he got, and had Steven ever told Mr. Lewis his anagram name, *Lane's View*, Evan Lewis would have found no pleasure in the irony.

After Steven's classroom cursing, Dylan fretted the rest of the day. What she had always feared was playing out—and playing out like a bad teen movie. A jilted just-friend boy gets envious of a tall, good-looking new kid and makes a public spectacle of himself. She texted him after lunch and to her surprise, he called her right back.

He offered no defense. In fact, he shrugged it off, pretended it was no big deal, and didn't even address the subtext Dylan assumed would keep them at bay for a month or more. He sounded relaxed on the phone, nonchalant. When Dylan offered to "explain" Norman, he shrugged—or at least that's how it sounded from over the phone, his shoulder joint bringing his shirt up against his cheek, a rustling. And that was it.

That was it?

"I'm sure he's great," he said the following day. And he sounded like he almost meant it. "Love to meet him."

"You *have* met him."

"Right."

"Well, I'm going over to his house after work. We're helping his dad hand out candy." She and Norman had a three-hour shift before Halloween that afternoon for last-minute shoppers. In a week her seasonal job would be over.

"Do you. . .wanna come??"

Why did she say that? She was just filling the silence.

"Over to Norman's house?" She was about to take it back. Before she could change the subject, Steven agreed. "Sure."

She hadn't even been to his house yet. It wasn't her place to even offer an invitation. What was it going to look like bringing Steven with her? Could she un-invite him?

"Is your mom dropping you off?" Dylan still didn't have her license.

"Yes."

"I'll meet you at your house and we'll go over together." Steven hung up.

Dylan put her phone down, walked over to the window, and stared at the helipad.

"Shit."

***

All of this—whatever this was—felt very liberating. Steven had never let his words spill out like that. Before he yelled at Ted Lavender, he'd never confronted anyone in public like that, not in such a direct way. He was more of a natural resenter—an angry one, for sure—but never a confronter. He'd mutter snide asides, but if caught, he'd feign innocence and hurt. Victim: that was a role Steven was good at.

It was instant. "Go fuck yourself" felt like freedom. After he left Mr. Drake's classroom, he unleashed it again—this time to an unexpecting freshman boy who was barely five feet tall. He walked home that day, and four cars driving past heard Steven's new motto. He knew immediately what it meant. *Go fuck yourself* meant *I love you, Dylan Geringer. I love you, Darling Energy*. Steven was positive Dylan would realize that. No one else was yelling on her behalf. This Norman Lewis guy, this brute-sized boy, had nothing on him. It suddenly seemed obvious. So yeah, I'll go meet this kid, Steven told Dylan.

When he and Dylan arrived at 27 Theronside Lane, he was surprised at the sight. He had talked the entire ride to Mrs. Geringer; they had an easy rapport. It wasn't unlike his conversations with her daughter. It was just more polite, a little more generous. Dylan stared out the window and wondered how long she'd have to endure this awkward meet-up—dropped off by her mother in a minivan, accompanied by a doting childhood friend, at the house of a guy she was interested in—before she and Norman could make plans to hang out properly, unobstructed. For the first time in her life, she understood what it would mean to have her own driver's license.

She'd lost the Hester Prynne costume for a makeshift Hermione one, compiled with Daphne's never-returned graduation gown, a Harry Potter scarf she already owned, and a stick for a wand she'd liberated from a Japanese maple. Steven was instructed that—hating Halloween or not—he had to bring some sort of costume. He brought Groucho Marx glasses, complete with the attached mustache and oversized nose.

There was no driveway, so Mrs. Geringer pulled up to the curb and put on her hazards. The three of them stared at the tiny house for a beat. A second later they watched as two men, the tailor and cobbler they assumed, walked toward the respective windows of their storefronts. It happened in unison, both of them stopping to rest their hands on their hips, staring out at Mrs. Geringer's minivan. They were either expecting them or anxious for a customer. It felt like the opening village scene of some summer stock musical. Dylan turned to Steven; Steven turned to Dylan; they both turned to Mrs. Geringer who was already staring at them.

She broke the silence. "Well, all right then. If you can get a ride home that would be great." She hit the button to activate the side door. It opened slowly and Dylan and Steven slipped out onto the sidewalk and shuffled to the Lewis front door. The tradesmen took one look at Groucho and Hermione, turned, and walked back into their respective backrooms.

They had about a half an hour before the trick-or-treaters arrived so, after an awkward exchange of hellos—for Steven's part all in a bad

Groucho Marx impression ("I've had a perfectly wonderful evening. But this wasn't it," he quipped), for Dylan's part, a failed explanation for Steven's presence—they headed upstairs to Norman's room.

It was an austere bedroom, and the only color belonged to a set of red storage crates. His bed sat off the floor on top of cinder blocks and a piece of plywood. A weight bench sat on one side. The attached weight looked cartoonish to Steven, as if Norman had doubled the plates before they came over to impress them. A three-piece suit was slung over the bench. He removed it when they came in and apologized for the mess. But there was no mess. This was the neatest, most organized room they had ever seen—everything had a place. To make more room, Norman grabbed the entire weight bench (with the weights and bar still attached), and lifted it into the corner. It was as graceful as it was impressive. This boy was no joke. As they sat and talked, Norman, this Clark Kent-looking boy—without a whiff of self-awareness nor any visible sense for how perfect a picture it was making—removed from his closet a Superman sweatshirt and a red cape. He got into costume like he was getting ready for work.

Steven looked through Norman's bookcase: a few volumes of debate textbooks, a modern-looking translation of the *Odyssey*, several biographies—Benjamin Franklin, Winston Churchill, PT Barnum, Steve Jobs, some Model UN booklets, a whole food diet book, a Civil Air Patrol manual, and several self-help books. It was the bookcase of a middle-aged man, Steven thought.

"So you're supposed to be Groucho, I take it?" Norman asked Steven.

"Do you know him?"

"Yeah. My dad likes a lot of old movies. We've watched all those Marx Brothers movies before. And Laurel and Hardy. Stuff like that."

"You live with your dad?"

Dylan had told him that before they came over. She didn't know why he always asked questions he already knew the answers to.

"Is he older? Like an older dad?"

"Steven." It was like he was a police officer. Dylan wondered what she had gotten herself into.

"Older than most, I guess. What made you—"

"The photographs downstairs. There's three of you?"

"Yeah. Me and my brother and my dad."

"Your brother's older?"

"Two years, yeah."

"What's his name?"

Norman paused for a second. "Why? Are you going to give him an anagram name?"

Steven laughed. "Did Dylan tell you that?"

"She told me what hers were. What was it? *Daring Energy*?

"No. *Darling* Energy."

"It sounds like a sports drink."

"No, it doesn't," Dylan corrected.

"His name's Lester. My brother."

"Lester?!?" Dylan and Steven said it at the same time.

"Yeah. I know. Lester the Molester. People call him Les. It hasn't been good to him."

"Did he go to Great Valley?"

"For a while." Norman walked over to the window—and good lord, his cape even billowed. The view looked out on a small slice of backyard, surrounded by a chain-link fence. There was a small vegetable garden along the side with a few peppers still growing.

"My dad's home." Dylan and Steven joined Norman by the window. They watched as a man closed the driver's side door of his Ford sedan and open the backseat door to retrieve a wide, brown leather briefcase and two plastic CVS bags. His khaki raincoat got caught in the door jamb when he slammed it shut. The three of them watched without comment while he negotiated its release. They had a good second-story view of his balding head.

"He looks like a private eye," Steven said. Dylan laughed. He did. Then she felt bad for laughing.

"He is. He's a private detective." Steven couldn't tell if Norman was kidding, but before he could ask, Norman was leading them back downstairs.

Mr. Lewis banged the kitchen door open and was already mid-sentence.

"Norman! Oh, hi, kids. Look Norman, you've got to bring those cans in. It's a miracle they didn't get kicked over last night, and I don't want trick-or-treaters tripping over them and suing me. One of the lids is against Mr. Rutigliano's dumpster and I'm worried he'll throw it out if it stays there any longer. Can you grab these please?"

Mr. Lewis handed Dylan one of the plastic bags. It was full of drug-store candy. "Just put those down over there, hon. Who are you supposed to be? I recognize Groucho over there. How you doin', Groucho?"

"Good, thanks." Steven was glad someone knew who he was supposed to be.

"Don't tell me." He sized up Dylan's costume. "What—are you in a choir or something? Or is that a graduation robe? Oh, I didn't see the stick. Are you a choir director?'

"She's a character from a book, Dad."

"Well, that's not going to help me then."

"It's a character from *Harry Potter*. Her name's Hermione," Dylan said.

"Herman-y?? That's almost as bad as Lester. Norman, will you take these up to your brother, please?" Mr. Lewis tried to give the other plastic bag to Norman.

"I thought you wanted me to get the trash cans."

"Get the trash cans. And that lid. And then take these up to your brother. Excuse me, kids." Norman left out the back door.

"Nice to meet you, Mr. Lewis," Dylan said as Mr. Lewis threw the plastic bag onto the kitchen counter before rushing into the bathroom under the stairs. Dylan and Steven were—alone. The throw had been off and the contents of the bag spilled on the floor—three prescription bottles tumbled at Steven's feet. He looked at Dylan, who shrugged at him.

Steven wasn't going to just leave them there. "You would just leave them there, wouldn't you?" he said to Dylan. Sighing, he picked them up. He read one of them. "Whoa."

"Well, don't read them!" The toilet flushed. The back door opened. Norman stopped in the door frame and stared at them.

"They just fell out onto the floor," Dylan explained.

"Your dad missed the counter."

"Don't worry about it," Norman said as he grabbed them from Steven and placed them back in the plastic bag. "He's on a lot of drugs. My brother." Dylan and Steven accepted this fact quietly. Mr. Lewis walked back into the kitchen.

"See if Les wants to help out tonight," Mr. Lewis said.

"I don't think we'll need *four* people, Dad." Norman didn't look at Steven, but Steven felt uninvited for the first time. He hadn't once thought about what a night handing out candy from some other kid's house would be like, a kid who liked Dylan as he liked Dylan. He was just along for the ride. He struggled to imagine the three of them—and Mr. Lewis?—all sitting in the tiny front living room handing out candy to snotty kids.

The curiosity that kept his interest was Lester Lewis, Norman's brother, who apparently was upstairs this whole time. Lester Lewis, who was dealing with some serious shit, if that pharmacy bag was any indication: a combination of antidepressant and antipsychotic drugs. Steven recognized the Zoloft—he was on that briefly in ninth grade—right after his dad left. It was an unkind drug to Steven, and he made his mom promise not to force him to take any more drugs like that. The other drug was Clozapine. That one was serious—especially taken along with the Zoloft. Lester must be bipolar or psychotic. Though he knew sympathy was in order, all he felt was intense curiosity. Steven wanted to meet Lester.

This evening was more than he had bargained for. He was flush with what was likely a false and fleeting sense of bravado. Instead of attending the wake for the Dylan-Norman relationship, Steven felt like he was backstage at some play, one he was only understudy for. He'd been holding his Groucho Marx glasses in his hands for a while, but decided to put them back on.

Steven grew silent and removed himself from the scene for a minute. He found himself on a well-worn wingback chair by the living room bay window. He watched as Hermione talked to a private detective; he watched as Superman emptied Halloween candy into a plastic bowl; he looked outside and watched two skeleton boys and a witch run by. (Had *he* taken the Clozapine?) But mostly he watched the staircase, listened to a door open and close, saw a shadow move against the landing wall, and wondered who Lester Lewis was and what was wrong with him—and when he would make his entrance.

"Norman says you're a private detective," Dylan said.

"Well, I do some detecting work, yes."

"That sounds exciting."

"It's not. Not like TV. It's a lot of fraud stuff. Business fraud, insurance fraud. Or serving warrants. Mostly warrants."

"Oh."

Norman-Superman was bounding down the stairs, having just delivered the plastic bag of drugs to his brother.

"Like search warrants?"

"No. A criminal summons. I let bad guys know they've got a court date."

Steven got an idea. "Hey." Steven got up from his chair. "I think I left my coat in your room."

Norman shrugged. "Yeah, sure. Help yourself." Steven made his way for the stairs as the doorbell rang for the first of many times that night. Wrong side or not, the Lewis house saw a steady stream of candy beggars.

He thought about snooping around Norman's room—but with a real-life private detective downstairs, it seemed a little risky. Steven wondered what that must be like. A detective as a father? Could Norman hide anything from him? Norman didn't seem like a hider-of-things, anyway. He seemed conspicuous, an open book—a boring, open book, maybe an encyclopedia. What prompted this ruse was his interest in the other Lewis son. He made his way down the hallway and stopped in front of Lester Lewis's half-open door and looked in.

Lester Lewis's room was the opposite of his brother's. Steven saw a little of his own in it. The floor was covered with books stacked in piles that somehow looked both chaotic and organized. A corner desk bowed a little under the weight of a massive computer and at least three monitors and other assorted peripherals. There were maps on the wall. A large abacus leaned against the only window. Its last calculation let in some of the streetlights from outside. A beaded, crenellated pattern of shadows marked the floor. The whole room looked like a missile command center.

"Yes?" A voice behind him.

"Oh, hi. Sorry."

Lester slid by him and into his room.

"Sorry, I came up for my coat. I'm a friend of Norman's." He wasn't a friend of Norman's. It just seemed the right thing to say. Lester sat down in front of the largest computer screen. Steven thought about just heading back downstairs, but he couldn't help himself. "You've got a lot of books," he tried. Nothing. He tried again: "You have an Nvidia graphics card?!" Steven spotted an empty box on the ground. Of all his obsessions, computers had lasted the longest. The hours he'd spent playing games on his computer—especially throughout middle school—embarrassed him a little. He'd promised himself he'd do something more constructive with his time. But if he'd had an Nvidia graphics card, like Lester Lewis's here, it might have been a different story.

This got Lester's attention. He moved his head to the side: "You have one?"

This was enough of an invitation, so Steven walked in, avoiding a tower of books. "God, no. Can't afford that. I hear they're amazing." Lester mumbled something in agreement. "Must be great for games." Nothing again. "What games do you play?"

"I don't play many games anymore. Sometimes, if I'm really bored, I'll wander back into *WoW*." *World of Warcraft*—Steven had played that one for a while. "I'm mostly into coding now." Norman knew nothing about coding. He'd tried one week last summer, but had no patience for it.

"Cool." Lester grumbled again and went back to his screens and keyboard. "What are you working on?" A stiff breeze hurtled in the open window and the abacus fell with a crash to the ground, its beads carried it for a foot before it stopped moving. One of them had gotten loose.

"Shit." Lester moved over to the window and struggled to put it back together.

"Steven?" Dylan was calling from downstairs.

On the side of Lester's desk were a pile of papers. He would have ignored them, turned around and headed back to Dylan downstairs, but something caught his eye. He could only see the top of the paper, the beginning of a list:

1) *March 15th*

2) *3:33*

There was a three, but Steven couldn't make out the last item.

Lester returned to the desk and covered the paper up with some loose pieces from the abacus. "I've been trying to figure out those phone messages, too. Do you think—"

Steven thought he'd found a fellow puzzler. "I'm in the middle of something." Lester slid past Steven, sat back down, and turned his attention back to the screen.

"What are you doing?" Dylan was standing in the doorway.

"I was just talking to Lester."

"Les," he corrected.

"I was talking to Les."

"Did you find your coat?"

"I don't think I brought one." Dylan huffed and turned for the stairs. Steven followed. "Nice to meet you, Les." Lester mumbled again.

It seemed the world could only sigh, huff, and mumble. *Where were his fellow Go fuck yourself-ers?*

They spent the rest of the night taking turns at the door. Dylan and Norman had worked out a bit of theater for the kids:

SUPERMAN: Hi, kids. Are you here to fight for truth, justice, and the American way? Or are you here for candy??

KIDS: Candy!!

[Hermione casts a spell over the bowl of candy and Superman hands them out.]

HERMIONE: [as the kids walk away] You are the most insensitive warts I have ever had the misfortune to meet.

It wasn't particularly funny, but Dylan and Norman couldn't stop laughing. Steven didn't fare too well. Not one kid who came to the door knew who he was supposed to be.

Are you Johnny Depp? Are you Anchorman? Borat? Mario? Ned Flanders? The Pringles guy? By the end of the night, he wordlessly answered the door and dropped the candy into pillowcases.

Norman received a text. "You guys want to go to a party? Down the street. Do you know Chris Strawbridge?" They didn't. "He's a good guy. Just a few folks hanging out. Let's go for an hour. I'll drive you home after." Norman was their ride, so they weren't going to argue. Dylan wasn't sure about another event with Steven as a chaperone, so she left it up to Steven. Steven was ready to go home. He had something he wanted to look up, but he shrugged his shoulders. Despite how he felt about Norman, it felt wrong to reject an invitation to adventure from a man dressed as Superman.

"Sure."

Norman nodded his big head. "Good." He called upstairs to Mr. Lewis, who had already retired for the night. "Dad, we're headed out for a little bit. Just down the street. The Strawbridges."

"Turn out the porch light, please."

Dylan and Norman made for the door, but Steven took one last look up at the thin bar of blue light from underneath Lester's door.

"It's a short walk," Norman said—and they were off.

TEN

They used to leave a bucket of candy on the doorstep, but their neighbors reported it was emptied the last couple of years by Royce Caulder, a former student of Trevor's who lived in the neighborhood. Trevor saw him earlier that day at school, back from his *alternative placement*. Now that was a euphemism Trevor could appreciate. He would take an alternative placement if anyone was offering one. Royce dressed as Jason from *Friday the 13th*. Mr. Drake told him to take off the hockey mask. He slid it off his face and onto the top of his head. By the time Royce had reached the other end of the hallway, he'd already slid it back down. It wasn't worth the fight.

He'd bought bags of candy again this year, thinking it safe from a hospitalized Royce, but he thought better of putting out the bucket now. Even though he was eighteen, he knew Royce would wander around tonight, dressed as a murderer, ringing people's doorbells. He worried that in five years Royce wouldn't have to play the part. Before they lost Benjamin, he and his wife made fun of the Halloween-bucket households. After Benjamin, it seemed the only solution. They couldn't weather all those young children coming to their door, just to walk away. The bucket made them feel like they hadn't given up completely. Tonight they would just turn off the lights and lock the door behind them. They would go out to dinner.

Trevor had taught a lot of kids like Royce. He could empathize with them. He told himself if he ever lost that, he'd just quit. As a younger teacher he was frustrated to learn that empathy and concern weren't enough. The bubble around school made all things look possible back then. When a student was flailing in their courses, distant from their peers, there were counselors and intervention programs; there were meetings and discipline referrals; there were heart-to-hearts held after class; there were the distractions of clubs and sports and music and theater. Of course, there were parent phone calls and conferences, too, but Trevor learned quickly that these last two interventions were harder to predict. He assumed that most parents would take the school's side, would form a united front to get their kid back on track. Unfortunately, that wasn't always the case.

Suspicion could creep into some of these conferences, a sort of defensiveness. If there was a problem with their child, there must be a problem with *them*, some reasoned. Other parents were willfully uninterested—or put out by the intrusion into their day. More persistent were the parents who sought answers legally. If their child was failing in school, the school was failing and accommodations were drawn up. These IEPs were a necessary and important part of designing learning strategies for the students who needed them, but some were written so vaguely, or were so impossibly specific—and often for kids that didn't really need them—that Trevor and his colleagues couldn't help but roll their eyes from time to time.

It made sense that a student with *school anxiety* might need an extended time for long-range projects, but what student didn't have school
anxiety? It made sense that a student with ADHD might need a moment
to get up and walk around the room, but when giving him a task or direction, how exactly could you manage to observe whether he began the task
within one minute and remained on task for a minimum of ten minutes
independently with no more than two prompts on eight out of ten independent tasks? Trevor lacked the math skills for that word problem. If
he accommodates a student's need for movement breaks and the use of
self-regulation strategies, how exactly can he observe the student demon-
strating the ability to attend to a task 75 percent of the time? Is *attending*
to a task the same as *completing* a task, or is it just not avoiding a task?
With the use of Cognitive Behavioral Intervention, Trevor was told, student X would reduce instances of negative comments and gestures to an
average of one instance per hour, across all classroom settings, as mea-
sured over six trial days. He needed to read that one over a few times. If
he understood it correctly, it meant that Student X could curse and flip the
bird once per class for the next week.

Trevor needed this intervention for himself. He could probably control any sudden gestures, but negative comments—ever since his blow-
up last month—had been spilling out into the faculty room and into his
vocabulary sentence examples on the whiteboard. "'What a *capricious*
world,' he said as he shook his fist at the sky," he wrote yesterday. Did
they know he was trying to communicate with these sentences? Steven
Lilly's explosion the other day seemed like a much more direct and effective approach.

Trevor knew better than to minimize the struggles of his students. It was tempting to point thirty miles down the road to the Philly schools that struggled to attract and keep good teachers, that squeezed every dollar of a diminishing budget to pay for supplies, that had to contend with crime and poverty, that suffered a fractious city and state government that had no clear plan for their success. While his students needed this lesson in humility, it didn't shame away the depression, anxiety, and suicidal tendencies of his at-risk students. After all, they were all *at-risk*, all the time.

True, Great Valley's average household income was well above the national average. Most of its neighborhoods filled out giant developments, outfitted with two-car garages, in-ground pools, and finished rec-room basements. Their population lived comfortably among the trees and cul-de-sacs. Trevor was one of them. But despite this idyllic backdrop, something nagged at Trevor as he walked his dog around the neighborhood. He sensed a quiet inhaling sound, like the wind in reverse—some sort of vacuum. It felt like years since he'd seen kids on bikes or heading back to the creek behind his house. Except for a few other dog walkers, the only foot traffic he noticed in his neighborhood came from the joggers—his adult neighbors, out in the dark before dawn or late at night after dinner.

Most of the drivers sat behind massive Yukons and Tahoes and Suburbans. He'd wave at them as they passed, but the tint and glare on the windshields made it hard to tell if anyone waved back. Was anyone inside at all? Was he getting a preview of a world with only self-driving cars? The only sound that reverberated throughout the neighborhood those days were car doors closing. It was hard to tell where the dull thuds were coming from, but a few echoed around at intervals just long enough to make you forget the last one.

Trevor's own childhood seemed so much louder. The Royces in his neighborhood would have been outside working on their cars, souping up an engine, firing off BB guns, blowing up amps in the garage. Shouldn't the kids today be blasting their stereos, so the neighbors could hear their musical rage, and not sticking plastic white shells in their ears and pretending they were in their own private movie?

It's not that Royce Caulder scared Trevor. The silence that followed him around did. If Benjamin had lived, Trevor would have some insight into these houses, fellow dads to barbecue with. He would have been able to find and follow all these missing sounds, find the source of the vacuum. But he didn't, and now everything was so quiet—and it was just getting quieter.

The quiet followed kids into the classroom, too. It occurred to him the other day—right after Steven's eruption—that he hadn't had any major discipline problems in years. He hadn't witnessed one food fight, nor one after-school parking lot fight. Not even many outbursts of anger, really. Where did all that kinetic anger go? It struck him how much childhood depression had changed over the last decade, how private and quiet it had all become. There was plenty of time for quiet desperation when you became an adult. Trevor could have told them that.

The kids had it all wrong. Adults were the ones who were supposed to harbor their frustration and anger inside their hearts. Kids should be bursting and leaking all over the place. He tried not to be the old guy who blamed the cell phone and its social media for all these problems, but it must have coded a lot of their fear and anger into an algorithm pressed into a microchip. Theirs was a virtual and passive-aggressive hurt, often dampened by medication.

Many of the girls he taught described their mothers as their best friends. This seemed like more evidence of the growing insulation of the kids he taught. What did this BFF status say about them, or their other friends, about their inability to form the same bond with someone their own age? He'd overhear them talking in the hallway—despite trying his best not to—about how they had a party at their house and how their parents were there, but it was still cool. He knew enough of his neighbors to know this was going on. The logic was: *if my kids are going to drink, at least they're going to be safe and under my roof.* No one's going to get in a car and drive drunk. It was strange logic, he thought.

Using this same logic—allowing potentially dangerous or illegal activity only under supervised parental control—would parents let their kids cook their own meth? *Look: I know you're into meth, but if you're going to cook it, you'll do it under my roof, in my kitchen—with your mom's skillet.* Were these the conversations for sex, too? *Look, if you're going to have sex, you're going to have it here, under my roof, in your parents' bedroom. And you will make the bed after, mister!*

What used to compel privacy and personal discovery was in the public domain now, and what used to be public record had receded back into the shadows. The world was topsy-turvy, Trevor thought.

These were the charming thoughts Trevor had ricocheting in his head as he sat across from Elizabeth at dinner.

Trevor had always had the best view in any restaurant. Elizabeth was a stunner—a "striking woman," as his mother had called her after they met for the first time—and even years of silent grief hadn't dimmed her beauty. Had Trevor been more observant he may have even noticed that she was more beautiful now than she was then. She had become one of those late-night joggers who ghosted through their neighborhood. She'd always been fit and a mindful eater, but the last decade brought on a dedication to health and fitness that Trevor couldn't keep up with. He knew she needed something to throw herself into, and it was silly to begrudge her this healthy and stealthy new hobby.

But he'd grown to begrudge it anyway. At first he tried to join her out on the road, but her pace kept her a first-down farther than his did. He didn't think she was running away from him, but the image was hard to shake. It was a good escape for her, he told himself when he was feeling less selfish. But then the meals at home changed, too. There were juice cleanses and protein drinks and hard-boiled eggs. Dinners were lightly grilled fish and steamed broccoli, a pleasant enough meal, but their frequency was depressing. Trevor volunteered to cook, thinking he could spice up their life with his chicken parm or one of his crockpot stews, but Elizabeth declined. It wasn't part of her meal plan now, her "regimen," as she called it. Ten years ago, Elizabeth and Trevor would have laughed at the idea of a "regimen," but here they were. They didn't exercise together; they didn't eat together. They went to bed at different times. They still made love once every few weeks, but Trevor had recently noticed that it was *always* a Sunday night. Was this, too, part of her *regimen*?

"What are you going to have?" He knew but asked anyway.

"The Caesar with the salmon." She knew what he'd say next.

"But you eat that at home."

"I like it."

Trevor pretended to see something interesting out the window, so she wouldn't see he was annoyed. Elizabeth didn't turn to see the thing that wasn't there and took a drink of her club soda.

That was the other thing: club soda. Trevor and Elizabeth used to go through a bottle of wine at dinner, easy. She allowed herself an occasional glass, but more often than not, it was club soda. There were many towns painted red in their dining history, but Trevor drank alone most nights now.

He knew Elizabeth didn't enjoy being out in public anymore, but he was happy that they still found a few nights each month to get out. He had the sense it was another necessary part of her routine, but he hoped it was also a gesture of love, too. Even after ten years, they knew people watched them when they were out in public. Looking for what? Some mark of what happened? There were all sorts of looks: pity with its raised eyebrows; guilt with its stares at the ground; fear masquerading as enthusiasm; suspicion at their continued existence; jealousy, even, as people tried to rebrand the Drakes' childless fate into opportunity for travel. Others avoided them completely, like the death of a child—or simply bad luck—was a disease they might catch.

Trevor ordered the gnocchi with a gorgonzola sauce. It was a decadent favorite of his, and it was the only thing that felt good right now. His fear that his body would become like his father's—with pants latched up over his prodigious belly by suspenders—had kept Trevor from letting it get too far away from him, but his body had been consistently softening as Elizabeth's tightened. In this way, their combined mass had stayed the same.

"How was it?" she asked.

"It was tremendous." He got the last of the sauce with the leftover bread.

"I'm leaving."

Trevor looked up at Elizabeth. *Leaving?* Is that how it was going to happen? She was just going to declare it, right here in public, as he stuffed his face. His face froze. Sauce fell from his bottom lip. For the first few years after Benjamin, he kept waiting for this to happen. He knew the statistics about marriages that suffered the loss of a child. But even with all the distance between them, after this long, he had stopped imagining the possibility.

Elizabeth screwed up her face. "What's wrong?"

"What. . ." was all he managed.

"I said I'm leaving. Next week. To New York. That first week of November. That Wednesday, I think. It's just one overnight."

"Oh." He tried hard to hide the misunderstanding that had just passed through his head and onto his face. He didn't want her to see it there. If she saw it, she might recognize it, might want to suss it out. He couldn't let that happen. If the thought ever formed between them, it would never go away. He reached for his wallet instead—to pay the bill.

"What's that?"

Trevor saw it at the same time. Stuck to his black leather wallet was another sticker from his label maker. This one dumbly read: *wallet.* Yes, he had labeled his wallet, *wallet.* Trevor laughed, and then they both laughed.

"I was just playing around with the—I guess I forgot I put it there."

"You've been busy," Elizabeth said and attempted a smile.

"I have." He gave the waiter his credit card.

It was an opening, so he took it. "I *have* been busy. I just think that that stuff should be labeled. There's a lot of stuff still. And, look, I don't mind you putting it into boxes, but the boxes were just sitting there next to all the other boxes. Next to our old tax stuff. Next to pairs of ice skates and yoga mats. I mean. Just with everything else. I mean." He kept saying "I mean," hoping it would take him somewhere. Elizabeth didn't try to interrupt. "I mean space is not a problem. We have all the space in the world. I understand it's painful, all these things, and like I said, I don't mind you putting it in boxes, but the boxes should at least be labeled. I'd prefer if they were in a crate, really, so I've been thinking I'll get some crates instead and label them, and then we can feel good that his things are safe. And sound. There's mold down there."

Elizabeth reached over and calmed Trevor's right hand. She grasped his fingers together. Looking at Trevor, she nodded her head.

The waiter put the bill alongside their hands.

"Have a great night. Thanks for coming in!"

Like a mirror, Trevor matched Elizabeth's nods, and they silently agreed to agree.

ELEVEN

The walk from the Lewis house to the party at Chris Strawbridge's house reminded Dylan of Francis Ford Coppola's film *The Outsiders*. She and Steven watched that film every day in the summer after eighth grade. The brisk fall evening was filled with blues and blacks, with streetlights forming ellipticals on the ground, table lamp–lit house windows softly illuminating little one-act family plays. By 8:45 p.m. when they made their walk, all the young trick-or-treaters were already home, counting and separating their candy. But the streets weren't empty. Wild spotlights of flashlights streaked against trees and puddled on the pavement, only to be clicked off suddenly, swallowed up with the sound of laughter and door slamming. Every few blocks they'd see the backs of some kid-pack turning a corner, or watch the last wobble of a punched stop sign.

Dylan lingered a few steps behind Norman and Steven. From behind, in the dark like this, now that they were out of their costumes, Dylan laughed to herself about how much these two boys reminded her of some evolutionary chart of early man—Steven's small Neanderthal to Norman's more upright Cro-Magnon, together with their respective shadows. Even with the size difference, neither seemed remarkably evolved to Dylan. She was not following Modern Man, certainly.

She'd been reminded by her mother that boys developed more slowly than girls. Her mother offered this as a consolation when Dylan grew three inches the summer after seventh grade. In size, this was true, but she'd yet to meet a boy—even mild-mannered Norman, or precocious Steven— that seemed all that mature. Three years ago her complaints were about how spazzy they were, how their uncontrollable bodies bounded around corners and jumped up from their seats. They'd raise one hand to answer a question and use the other to rub their exposed armpit. They touched everything. If they got up to get a tissue during class, they'd touch all the desktops on the way there. They'd yank four tissues from the box, blow their nose, play with the Purell bottle, push a magnet along the white-board, and spin the pencil sharpener for no reason.

She wasn't sure when it happened, but three years later, as the rage of puberty was coming to a close, they were strangely different. Now it was their sullen nature that disappointed her most. They traded their mania for indifference. They perfected nonchalance and stoicism—and *ennui*, another Mr. Drake vocab word. They stayed in their seats now, but spent their time there stretching, always stretching. They were less interested in blowing their noses and more interested in yawning. They slouched and slid on their plastic seats until their legs stuck out at odd angles in the path of a pacing teacher. They'd sit back up when they could slouch no farther, but it was temporary. Slide, reset. Slide, reset. Like overgrown boys on an undersized playground slide. Most days they were just a bunch of mopes.

She may have been moody, but she was no mope. Moody people were unpredictable. As much daily confidence as she lacked, she could always depend on her moodiness to reset the scales. At this point in her life, it was Darling Energy's only superpower, and she wielded it proudly. At school, she often pretended to be depressed because she knew it would get the attention of her friends.

"What's wrong?" they'd ask.

"Nothing," she'd respond, as she emphasized the point unconvincingly with her eyebrows.

"Are you sure?"

"Yes."

"Cause you seem a little down."

She'd pause and deliver an exhaled, "I don't know." She could always think of something to complain or worry about. It felt manipulative, but it never felt like lying. She was seventeen, and there was always something to be offended by.

When they weren't eliciting sympathy from one another, they were building each other up with wild emoji-filled hyperbole. It had died down a little this year, but their affected poses in their Instagram posts (in their "real" accounts and their fake *finstagram* accounts) elicited rabid praise— "YOU ARE SO PRETTY!" or "OMG YOU ARE A GODDESS. I WANT TO KILL MYSELF!!" Most posts were selfies, thoughtfully conceived and edited images of their new dress or a haircut. While there was the occasional passive-aggressive slight here and there, it remained, mostly, a safe place for Dylan to be, if not *Darling Energy*, at least a little *Daringly Green*, a pretty young girl with few cares in the world. She thought it was odd how happy they could all be for one another in the public, virtual world of the internet, but how anxious and depressed real-life personal contact could make them.

She would never float this "mope vs. moody" theory to Steven, who would have disagreed with her assessment that he was a mope. Had she ever said this to him, she would have conceded that while he was more open to culture and capable of conversing on a wide range of high- and low-brow topics, he was, by no means, a bon vivant. True, he got her to tag along on the occasional adventure, but it was always *his* vision that pulled them along. She wasn't so much his partner in crime as much as his Girl Friday. And whenever the plan fell apart, he'd pull the plug, and sulk back home to his room.

Steven watched his shadow get over-shadowed by Norman's shadow. He played a game for the rest of the walk: he swung his arms by his side, feinting and connecting his shadow with Norman's dark silhouette, until Norman gave him a weird look. Steven grew uneasy about heading over to Chris Strawbridge's house. He hated parties, and he hated people. He liked a few *persons*, but couldn't stand people. Though it was just the three of them under the glow of the streetlights, Steven felt the push and weight of all those people he was about to encounter. He resented Dylan and Norman, the easy way they could approach a gathering of people and not want to puke. Puke, he thought. Will there be puking people there? Drunk kids consoling each other in a parents' bathroom? In the movies, he was disturbed to witness how a boy would hold a girl's hair as she emptied her stomach into the toilet. Maybe if it were a Gatsby party he'd enjoy himself? It would still be too crowded for Steven's sake, but at least people would be dressed nicely.

He slowed a little to fall in step with Dylan.

"What?" Dylan asked.

"Nothing."

The Strawbridge house was a monstrosity. It sat at the end of the cul-de-sac, at the end of a long driveway. It embarrassed Steven.

"Jesus," Steven said.

"I know," Norman said.

"It's terrible."

"It's remarkable."

"It's like Gatsby's house," Dylan said.

"It looks like a hotel," Steven said.

"There's at least eight bedrooms, I think," Norman said.

"Actually, it looks like some fancy assisted-living facility," Steven said.

Dylan laughed. Steven hadn't made her laugh in a while.

"Who has a four-car garage?"

"People with four cars?" Dylan said.

"It's a five-car garage. See?" Norman said. Dylan and Steven looked again and saw. "They've got more than five cars. There's a separate garage out back for Mr. Strawbridge's performance vehicles."

"Who has an odd number of garage spaces?"

"What's a performance vehicle?" Dylan asked.

"You know, I don't really know. I guess ones that...*perform* really well?"

"If they have eight bedrooms why do they only have a five-car garage? If they have guests not everyone will have their own space in the garage." Steven was trying too hard.

"What do his parents do for a living?" Dylan asked.

"I've asked that before. Chris couldn't describe it. Consultants, I think," Norman replied.

"I never know what that means."

"That's what all the richest people do. They just consult people on how to do their job. They just show up to some company and say, 'You're doing this all wrong,' and then they go to the next company and do the same thing."

"Is telling other people how to do some other job, a *job*?" Dylan asked.

"Sure. That's what any boss does."

Steven felt like arguing. "Yeah, but you don't really do anything yourself. It's not like he has a company of his own. He doesn't have his own business, his own product."

"That *is* the product: *advice*."

"Sounds terrible." That sounded like a line out of one of Norman's self-help books. They still hadn't reached the garage yet. Somehow this driveway seemed to get longer as they walked.

"I don't know. Lots of jobs are about giving advice. It's better than taking advice."

Dylan nodded in agreement at Norman's take. Steven felt like picking a fight, but Norman was right on that point.

The bass thump from a nearby subwoofer was the only sign of life. Steven pretended to check his phone. When he looked up again, Norman and Dylan were already walking around the side of the garage to a staircase that led to a second floor. He considered turning and walking back to Norman's house and chatting up Lester. He'd settle for Mr. Lewis. Maybe tonight was a lost cause.

It was just a few weeks ago when he was making Dylan accompany him to Mr. Drake's house. Instead, tonight, he fell in line behind Dylan on the steps, and as the door at the top of the stairs opened, he closed his eyes and took one long inhalation.

No one noticed them as they walked into the upstairs garage apartment. Dylan and Steven shot each other a quick look, somehow feeling both relief and disappointment at the sight. The walk up to the house, talk of performance vehicles and eight bedrooms, promised an extravagant display of wealth—maybe wall-to-wall televisions, arcade machines, a mirror ball spinning little orbs of light, a smoke machine. What they walked into was a sad, but huge, apartment-like-thing, filled with mismatched and oversized sectionals and awful drop-ceiling lighting. The walls were bare, save for one long mirror that faced the three of them as they walked into the center of the room.

Bodies packed the room in dense clumps. Some spilled onto the sectionals or sat on armrests of black pleather chairs. A gangly boy with an eye patch stood on top of a matching ottoman. Next to him, another boy yanked the adjustment bar of his recliner, trying to make the girl sitting on the footrest fall to the floor. Dylan recognized many of the costumes populating their way around the room. A coven of sexy witches were taking photos of one another by the driveway-side windows. There was the Adult Hot SWAT costume, riding up the butt of Rory from homeroom. And good god, standing by the keg, it was the Adult Sultry Scarecrow! Someone actually bought that. She pointed it out to her fellow employee, Norman.

"No shit. . ."

"Yeah."

"What?" Steven asked.

"The scarecrow over there."

"Wow. If she only had a brain." Steven made them both laugh. Maybe he could survive this if he could manage some occasional pith.

There were few boys in costume. There was a sad-looking Dracula standing next to what was either an evil Charlie Chaplin or a goofy Hitler.

Most of the boys were holding court by a folding table that held two turntables and a mixer. Two giant speakers sat to either side. One girl Dylan recognized from math class sat atop one and tried to yell over the noise.

"Turn it up!"

"What?" the gang pretended.

"Turn it up!"

The music was already shaking the walls. Neither Dylan nor Steven recognized the track. It was all drums and bass with some sort of flanged hi-hat.

Dylan remembered the speaker-rider's name after the second scream: Nicole. She was the only freshman who was in her Calculus class. She was clearly smart, as she must have skipped at least two years of math—but her airy and persistent cackle found every math pun Mr. Steele used in class hilarious, beyond anyone's idea of rational enjoyment. "Why was the calculus textbook unhappy? Because it had lots of *problems*." It was a student's job to only groan at teachers' puns, but Nicole found them uproarious and celebrated each—even the repeated ones—with her high-pitched plosives. The first time she let loose her giggled flurry, the class laughed along with her. Maybe she was being ironic, this little freshman kid, they thought. But after witnessing this reaction every day for the last two months, the class just stared at one another, wondering what was going on. Math class was no place for laughter. The best a math class could hope for was resigned acceptance, and Nicole ruined their commiseration. No one talked to her because, well, she was a freshman, but mostly because she was a far superior student than the rest of them. To anyone's knowledge she hadn't gotten a single question wrong on any assignment, homework, or test the entire year. Dylan couldn't figure out how someone so silly could be so smart. She also couldn't figure out what a freshman girl was doing at this party. Dylan practiced few prejudices, but she let herself be unreasonably disgusted by freshmen. It was a high school birthright. Plus, it was never good news when a freshman girl hung out with upperclassmen. Dylan entertained the idea that maybe she should be worried about this girl instead of annoyed, but then Nicole yelled again.

"Make it louder!!"

Nicole repositioned herself and pretended the speaker was a horse. She was wearing jean shorts that were 75 percent dangling pocket liners and 25 percent jean. She waved a pretend hat.

"Turn it up!" she yelled again because no one was paying attention.

Chris Strawbridge floated in from a back room.

"*This* guy? *He's* Chris??" Steven said to Dylan out of the side of his mouth.

Dylan tried to hold back a laugh. She remembered a day last year when she and Steven watched this guy, Chris apparently, talking to some of his friends in the parking lot. As they waited for Dylan's mom to drive them home, they made up his monologue from afar. It took little effort.

Chris was an easy study and made for easier improv. Dylan and Steven cracked themselves up and were crying with laughter all the way home.

Chris was an eighteen-year-old trapped in a forty-six-year-old man's body and clothes. He wore pleated khaki Dockers that were too short. He wore an untucked polo shirt with a white undershirt underneath. He wore penny loafers and a leather-roped dangling belt, and when he walked, it looked like he might fall backward. Keeping him upright was his dad-belly and the sense that nothing, at any time, could possibly go wrong. You could read that on his face. That was the only feature that belied his true age. Behind his giant, tortoise-shaped glasses and underneath his receding hairline was the babiest of baby faces, oblivious to anything but the present nature of any situation. He looked like a walking Lipitor ad, fresh from a slow and uneventful match of tennis. After seeing the Strawbridge estate on their way in, Dylan and Steven could easily understand Chris's nonchalance. He had never wanted for anything. He clapped some of his friends on the back like they had just made a long putt, and mimed a lasso in Nicole's direction. He was spinning around with his magic lasso, slapping his knee, when he spotted the triangle of Norman, Dylan, and Steven.

"Norman!" He walked over with his hand extended for a handshake, as if he might say "old sport." Thankfully, he didn't.

"Hey, Chris. I brought Dylan and Steven over, too."

"Oh, yeah. Sure. That's great. Hey, guys. It's great to have you." He shook both their hands.

Steven wondered what the hell was going on. He saw the same expression on Dylan's face. Somehow they smiled through the greeting. Did this guy just shake their hands?

"Do you live up here?"

Before the answer came, Nicole fell off the speaker and with her, her red Solo cup. Two of her friends laughed and pointed. One boy walked over and yanked her up by the arm.

"That's the second time that's happened tonight," Chris said. "I don't even think she's drunk. She's been nursing that same cup all night. I don't mind. More for the rest of us."

"She's not drunk?" Dylan asked.

"No. But she plays one well, doesn't she?"

"Why?" Steven asked.

"She's Katelyn's friend. My sister. I don't even want her up here, but she's sort of tagging along with Dylan these days." Chris motioned to Dylan Bowers. He was pretending to tie Nicole up with a loose USB cable.

"Stop it!" Nicole's plea was unconvincing.

"Help yourself to whatever," Chris said as he motioned to the built-in kitchen along the back wall. By the time Dylan said "thanks," Steven had already made his way over to the keg.

"That was quick. Is he a big drinker?" Norman asked of Steven.

"Steven? God, no. He usually . . ." Her voice trailed off. She was watching Steven gulp down an entire cup in one long pull. He filled up a second one.

It occurred to Steven, despite his usual reluctance about drinking, that maybe a beer or three would loosen him up a little, get back some of the swagger from his recent classroom outburst. And, more to the point, maybe it would steel up his nerves to finally say something to Dylan. He wasn't sure what that would be, but he was tired of watching Clark Kent sidle up to Dylan all night. He may have miscalculated Dylan's interest in Norman, but it occurred to him that if he didn't do something tonight, it might be too late. Dylan couldn't keep rejecting boys forever, and besides, they'd agreed that if they were dateless, they would go the prom together. That was still many months off, but it wouldn't take much to ruin the rest of the year.

Dylan raised an eyebrow at Steven from across the room. Steven raised his beer back at her.

"How's your brother?" Chris asked Norman.

"My brother?"

"Yeah, how's your brother?"

"He's fine."

Dylan watched as Norman tightened up a little.

"I think it's a bum deal, what they did to him." Chris could see that talk of Lester was making Norman uncomfortable. "I'm sorry, man. I just mean, I think your brother got a raw deal. And that a lot of worse kids do. . .worse things all the time, and no one says a thing. Deal drugs, whatever, you name it. I mean, Lester is the kind of guy that Fortune 500 companies hire all the time. They hire the best hackers all the time. Usually after they've broken into their network or something. He should do that. He should work for one of those big companies. Tell them what they're doing wrong." Chris was clearly a consultant's son.

Norman smiled through Chris's assessment. He didn't offer any agreement. He just nodded his head and said, "Yeah."

"Do you want a beer?"

"Thanks. I'll help myself." Norman grabbed Dylan's hand and walked over to the keg, glad to not be talking about his brother to Chris Strawbridge.

"What was all that about?" Dylan asked. Why was he holding her hand to walk over to a keg?

But Norman didn't answer. Steven was polishing off number two as they approached.

"What are you doing?" For Dylan, seeing Steven drink a beer from a red Solo cup as Taylor Swift sang in the background was not a scene she would have ever imagined. But here it was.

"What do you mean, what am I doing?"

Dylan tried a laugh. "Well, come on. You gotta admit, if I told you you'd be drinking a beer at—"

"I'm having a drink. I'd like to unwind."

"Well, you could use a little of that," Dylan said.

Norman was still holding Dylan's hand. She saw that Steven was watching their hands, so she let go. Norman tried to find something else in the kitchen to focus on.

"What time is it?" Dylan asked.

"We just got here."

"I know. But my mom's gotta come get us. Back at Norman's house."

"I can drive you home," Norman offered again.

"Yeah. Norman can drive us home. Thank you, Norman."

"You're drunk."

"I am *not* drunk. I just started. I don't think you could get drunk off this crappy beer." He finished off number three. "See?" He mimicked doing a little soft shoe to prove his coordination, but smacked his hand against the counter when he tried to windmill. "Shit!"

Dylan rolled her eyes and walked away back toward the music. She'd let the boys talk to one another. It was too awkward.

Norman pumped the tap and helped himself to a drink.

Out of nowhere, Steven asked, "What's the deal with your brother?"

"You too?"

"Me too, what?"

"Nothing."

"Here." Steven was, actually, a little slurry. "Stop me if I get this wrong—your brother's really smart. Lester, I mean. Lester's really smart, a whiz at math and computers—"

"Perceptive."

"Hold on. But he's always hated school. Probably because he was so bored because he was so much smarter than everyone else." Norman let him continue. "I guess it's safe to say, too, that he didn't have a lot of friends either. And that he spent most of his time on the computer, playing *World of Warcraft*, programming, coding, building his own machine. And I'm gonna guess you two didn't get along much growing up, he not being a very active, let's-go-have-a-catch kind of older brother, and also his being so much smarter than you—" This was coming out wrong. "Not that you aren't smart, but your brother's on a whole different level, and anyway, I'm guessing he did something at school, when he was in high school, some kind of hacking or something, that got him kicked out." Steven waited for a second to see how he was doing. Norman offered no expression. "I'm right, then?" Still nothing. "Was it a grade-changing thing? Like Ferris Bueller?"

"My brother is nothing like Ferris Bueller."

"What was it then?" Steven could see Dylan out of the corner of his eye. Now she was talking to some other guy. This party was stupid, but he wanted to figure out this Lester thing first. "What did he do?"

"It had nothing to do with grades." Norman finished his beer. Steven would not let up, and for some reason, Norman felt like talking to someone about it. He would have preferred Dylan, but here he was. "It was an email thing."

"Email? What was he doing?"

"He was writing emails to a teacher."

"Oh. Like a teacher he liked?"

"No."

"What then?"

"I don't really want to get into it," Norman said, but he stayed right there and didn't move or change the subject.

"Did he threaten someone?"

"Not really."

"Porn?"

"What??"

"Was it porn?"

"Was *what* porn?"

"The email he was sending."

Norman sighed. "It wasn't porn."

Dylan walked back over. "We should go home soon. I need to be home by 11."

"What time is it now?" Norman asked.

"Hold on. Can we just finish this story first? So it wasn't porn?"

"What wasn't porn?" Dylan had no idea what was going on.

"He found out about something he shouldn't have and then sent emails to one of the parties involved."

"Like blackmail?"

"It wasn't blackmail. That was the point. They tried to say it was blackmail. But it wasn't blackmail. Honestly, I don't think he knew what he was doing. I just think he was trying to start shit. He's always trying to start shit. Or used to, anyway."

"What are you talking about? Your brother?" she asked Norman.

"Wait—" Steven's eyes bulged. Norman and Dylan waited. "Wait, wait, wait!"

"We're waiting," Dylan said.

"It's your brother!"

"What is?"

"Your brother is sending out those phone messages!"

"What? No." But even as he said it, Norman seemed unsure.

"Of course it's him."

"It's not him."

"Are you sure?"

"I'm sure. I mean. . ." Norman didn't finish his thought. "He just. . . wouldn't."

"Why would he do that?" Dylan asked.

"Why would anyone do that?"

"He doesn't mess with phones." Norman knew that sounded stupid.

"It's not a phone thing. It's a computer thing, these systems they use."

"I don't know." Norman seemed less sure now. He sighed and looked at the ceiling. Kanye came on the stereo. "Look. . ." Steven and Dylan gave him a second. "The police have already come around about this phone thing. Last week, after the last one." They were about to get a story. Maybe they would figure this thing out after all.

"I guess he was on their watch list. Because of the other thing. They just came by to ask him some questions, but Les wasn't home—he was at the doctor's—and my dad knew one of the cops and said something that made them drive away. I came down to see what was going on, but he didn't want to talk about, but I could tell that he was upset. Or worried." Nicole was back on the speaker again. "But I really don't think he had anything to do with it. Seriously. It's just too. . .too *something*. I don't know."

Steven was going to tell them about the list he saw on Lester's desk, but it seemed bad timing now.

"I'm sure you're right," Dylan said. She changed the topic. "We should probably go. It's 10:30 and we still have to walk back to your house."

They tried to get Chris's attention on the way to the door, but he was doing shots with the sexy SWAT girl. Nicole spied Dylan on her way out. She blocked the door.

"Hey, it's you."

"Dylan."

"Yeah, Dylan. Hi. I'm in your—" She was definitely not *pretending* to be drunk.

"In your math class, yeah."

"Right. You're so pretty. I'm Nicole. Can I walk out with you?"

"Uh, sure."

"Is there any chance you could drive me home?"

"I don't have a car." She didn't want this freshman girl tagging along now. It was weird enough with Norman and Steven.

"Where do you live?" Norman was so nice, but Dylan found the trait annoying right now. There was a bad energy in the room, and she wanted to get out of here.

"I live by school."

"I can drive you home."

"Oh, you're so sweet." She attempted to hug Norman, but she was too drunk and short and Norman was too tall and not interested.

"Oh, boy," Steven said. "I think you left your cowboy hat."

She turned to Steven and saw him for the first time. "It's a cow*girl* hat." She tried to sound serious, but a hiccup ruined it. "Let's go." Uninterested in the hat, she skipped to the door, and bounded out.

Norman shrugged at an annoyed Dylan.

A sharp crack sounded outside, followed by a screech that was followed by a "FUUUCK!!"

Nicole was on the ground at the bottom of the steps. She held her ankle and screamed like a banshee, not a cowgirl. Dylan rushed down the steps to help.

"Oh my god. Oh, shit." It was bad. Really bad. She looked back up at Norman and Steven, who were just standing there. "Don't just stand there! She broke her leg!" She looked at it again. "It's bad." Norman ran back inside. Steven came down a few steps. He wasn't good with blood or pain. He didn't want to look.

Nicole would not stop yelling. The curses gave way to a weird, confused guttural emission. It only stopped when Nicole took a deep, anguished breath, only to start again. Norman came back with Chris.

"Jesus Christ. Nicole. What happened?" He reached the last step and looked. "Oh, shit. Fuck." Steven and Norman had finally come to take a look. They saw bone, stretching the skin around Nicole's ankle.

Dylan was the calmest. "Nicole, just hang on. It's like a sprain or a break, but don't look down at it. Just hold tight and we'll get an ambulance."

"We're not getting an ambulance," Chris said.

"She's got a bone sticking out of her leg!" Norman yelled. Nicole made a panicked sound.

"Norman!"

"Sorry. It's fine, Nicole. It will be fine." And then to Chris: "Man, you've got to call an ambulance."

"I'm not calling an ambulance! It's bad, yes. But can we just take her to Urgent Care?" This seventeen-year-old in a forty-year-old's body now seemed every bit his age. "I don't want my dad to find out."

"Well, maybe you shouldn't have invited forty people to your house," Steven said.

Chris shot a quizzical look at Steven. "What are you talking about? He knows about all of this." He motioned up to the party. "He's home. I just don't want him to see an ambulance pulling up."

"He's here?" asked Dylan.

"Listen, asshole," Steven started. The beers and the last few days were talking. "We need to get her to the hospital. No one gives a shit about your stupid fucking party. Or you. You dress like somebody's dad. You look like you're about to give a PowerPoint presentation to a bunch of fraternity date rapists." He was off-script now. Dylan stared up at him, her face furrowed in a confused gape. Steven imagined the line going over better than that.

"What the fuck are you talking about?" Chris lunged to push Steven, but tripped over Nicole's other foot, prompting the worst cry yet. Norman pushed Chris back like he was swatting a fly.

"Stop! She needs help now." Chris looked at him. "What?"

"Can you drive her?"

"What??"

"I can't drive. I'm drunk. I'm sorry, Norman. I'm really sorry. Help a fellow scout out." They had been scouts together as boys, because of course they had.

"Oh, god. Fine. But I don't have my car."

"Here." Chris already had his keys out of his pocket. He flashed the BMW key chain in front of Norman's face. Norman grabbed the keys, and with Steven and Dylan's help, they slid Nicole into Chris's convertible and took off to the hospital.

The drive took them down Theronside Lane, right by Norman's house. As the car did a rolling stop at the stop sign at the end of the street, they all saw Lester Lewis standing in the middle of the street with a backpack.

"What the actual fuck?" Norman said to no one in particular. Lester didn't move as they approached and Norman had to stop the car.

"Where did you get this car?"

"Les, get out of the street. We're driving to the hospital. This girl broke her leg."

"I'm coming with you."

"What? No, you're not. Get back inside before dad sees you." But Les was already opening the passenger side door, slipping past Dylan in the front seat, and climbing into the already cramped back seat next to Steven whose lap was propping up Nicole's broken foot. Steven hadn't been able to look down at it, but he couldn't stop staring at Lester now, wondering what was in his backpack and why he was in the middle of the road and what was going on and how this was probably the most exciting night he could ever remember.

Lester turned to Steven when they reached their next turn and spoke quietly. "I need your help with something."

TWELVE

S
now came early that year. The week before Thanksgiving saw an eight-inch snowfall that canceled school on a Wednesday and delayed Thursday by two hours. For Trevor, it meant more drinking and less planning of his *Streetcar Named Desire* unit

As he'd gotten older, and now that Elizabeth didn't drink, he did most of his drinking alone at home. He didn't enjoy it, but he liked the formality of making a drink, the mixing of ingredients, the shaking of a cocktail concoction, cutting up a garnish, and sometimes, when Elizabeth traveled for work, he even muddled—some mint, maybe fruit if there was anything in the fridge. It was not lost on him that his cocktail-muddling was more evidence of his general life-muddling.

He looked it up in the dictionary:

mud·dle /ˈmə-dl/ — verb
gerund or present participle: muddling

1. bring into a disordered or confusing state. "They were muddling up the cards."

2. confuse (a person or their thoughts). "I do not wish to muddle him by making him read more books."

3. busy oneself in a confused and ineffective way. "He was muddling about in the kitchen."

The last few years fit meaning #3 to the tee. His state Wednesday, Thursday, and most of Friday were closer to meaning #1. He was too old to be hungover at work. School was a disordered and confusing state all on its own.

That's why Trevor was surprised when he heard himself accept an invitation from his colleagues to happy hour. But there he was on Tuesday night at Brownie's Tavern, with the first of his gin and tonics, as he and his younger colleagues watched the weather report on a muted TV up in the corner over the bar. The snowstorm was a "sure bet" according to the closed captioning, and despite many missed snow forecasts the year before, the air was pregnant with the promise of snow when they walked into the bar that afternoon. The calm before the storm was heavy and quiet. It was inevitable—the best kind of snow.

"You gotta drink like we've got a snow day." This was Kevin McConnell's line, and he delivered it every year at the first mention of snow. Kevin was a history teacher who Trevor and his English colleagues had adopted over the last few years. It may have been because each department had their own department work rooms, but Great Valley's faculty remained mostly segregated. This wasn't necessarily a bad thing.

Trevor was happy with his department. They were a good mix of veterans and youth, of skeptical union reps and fresh-faced recent grads. They loved books, and for the most part, this was enough.

"That's the problem with the History department," Kevin said. "They think history is about facts. They don't understand it's all about stories." It was a point Trevor and his literary colleagues appreciated. It must have been a point Kevin made often to his History colleagues, often enough that they no longer invited him to their own happy hours.

Trevor avoided voicing the comparisons, but if anyone had ever asked, he could have provided good reasons why the English department was where he belonged. Besides their insistence on facts, the History department was composed of a number of angry and often stubborn teachers. It had always struck Trevor that History and Social Studies attracted professionals who liked hearing themselves talk. The uninspiring History teacher is merely a lecturer, the sage on the stage, a pontificator, whose lessons plans were as dusty and predictable as the subject they taught. He knew that was an unfair assessment, but years of watching students compose pages of tedious textbook notes convinced him he might be onto something.

Science teachers were a different lot. Trevor was never sure what was going on in those classrooms. He envied the active status of their labs—students who only an hour ago were adding missing apostrophes to an essay draft were wearing an apron and burning chemical compounds over an open flame. Though to be fair, the other four days of the week, they sat slack-jawed in the dull glow of PowerPoints. The new push for a STEM curriculum, focusing on science, technology, engineering and mathematics, spawned dozens of new, impressive-sounding science clubs and competitions. He admired the hard work of the science students, but it often felt like they were in pursuit of a job, not an education. Trevor knew he was in a growing minority—advocates for the liberal arts, for the broadening of knowledge as opposed to the narrowing of ambitions. Didn't they know great scientific discovery comes from an ability to think in metaphors?

After a disappointing day when students had failed to read the assigned text and the class discussion had become more monologue than dialogue, and when unread essays were obscuring his desk blotter, Trevor wondered how his life would have been different had he been a math teacher. He daydreamed about having all the answers in the back of a textbook, about teaching a formula, then assigning homework, then having the kids write their answers on the board, and then pointing out if they were right or not. And then doing that for thirty years. It might crush his soul, but at least he would know what to expect and he could leave it all at work. Despite the predictability of their days, it was the math teachers who had the shortest tempers. I guess they had the most difficult sell, math. It was a quiet tension they carried with them—exasperated snorts when their copies were collated incorrectly, muttering to themselves in the parking lot. They rarely left their rooms, but when they did, it was at a brisk, speed-walking pace. There was a math study room called "The Math Lab." Every time Trevor passed the sign he could have sworn it read "The *Meth* Lab." Trevor thought it best just to smile and keep his distance as far as the math teachers were concerned.

The other alternate teaching reality he imagined was life as an art teacher. He could draw a little. He admired the workshop model of the art teacher's classroom. All that attention to process. He'd been trying to bring this attitude to his writing assignments with mixed results. The art teachers seemed to have it figured out. John Matthews, who was about to retire, was a good example. From Trevor's room, across and above the small courtyard, he watched John work in his pottery studio, milling around, pounding clay, working a wheel. When the weather was nice, John worked with the kids outside and took breaks to walk over to the small vegetable garden the Horticulture club took care of. He was essentially living in the Italian Renaissance down there. If one could win at teaching, John clearly had them beat. Last year, at another teacher's retirement dinner, John held court with some of the young teachers.

"What's the secret of teaching?" they asked.

"Find your humanity elsewhere," John told them.

The Foreign Language department? Who knows? They dressed well, they sang songs, they laughed the loudest, and, he was pretty sure, they were all sleeping with one another. Or at least it seemed that way. Maybe it's because they relied so much on their body language to coach their students, but it always seemed like they were leering and winking and raising their eyebrows, like everything was a double entendre. Maybe everything *was* a double entendre, and the rest of the monolingual staff and students were out of the loop. What they weren't lacking in was enthusiasm. But despite all their enthusiasm—or maybe *because* of all their enthusiasm—when Trevor looked into the language classrooms, the students gazed out into the hallway like a bank full of hostages.

No, that wouldn't have worked for Trevor. It was a lifetime of English for him. *So be it,* as one of his favorites, Vonnegut, would write. So what was the English teacher's greatest sin? "Reading too much into everything," they'd say. "Why can't a tree just be a tree? Why does it have to be mean something else?" It wasn't a bad question, really. Sometimes a tree was only a tree. But even a passing glance would remind a reader of the humanity of its shape, its reaching branches, its sturdy trunk, its *roots*, for god's sake. Most of the students were so literal, and a suggestion that something might be more than it seems would stymie them. It took some time for them to get used to the idea that a novel was more than its plot. But Trevor wasn't there to discuss plot, except if it needed explaining. They were in the room to discuss ideas and people.

The idea that there could be a truth of reality—of action and consequence—and also an emotional truth—of hearts and minds—and that those two truths might not always match, blew some minds. Trevor reveled in this, in the ambiguous and dynamic nature of literature, and how simple black strokes on a white page could reveal so much grayness. Of course, this was the classroom and not real life. This controlled laboratory, with texts and assignments he knew so well, was a safe place for him, too. Outside of it, it was hard to spot the patterns and motifs. It was hard to find the hidden meanings. Lately, trees really were just trees.

He would not teach his students something merely practical. He would teach them words—and with words, thoughts and feelings. They'd use those words to think with, to fall in love with, to tell stories, to find their own story in someone else's. What could be more important than that? These rationalizations were as close to prayer as Trevor got.

***

Trevor went through all these thoughts as he listened to Kevin

McConnell talk about the weather. Despite the sureness of the forecast, the district would always wait until the last minute, an hour or two before school would begin, to call off school. Privately, some teachers wondered if it was to avoid exactly what was at stake right now: hungover teachers for a snow day that never arrived.

"Drink like it's a snow day," Kevin repeated as he raised his mug. The line was superstition. While students were at home wearing their pajamas inside out and placing spoons underneath their pillows, their teachers, exercising their own superstitions, were having their first tentative cocktail. An entire community came together at the prospect of a day off. It was their only true, collective school spirit.

"Another round?" The offer came from the youngest and newest member of the English department.

Trevor might not have come at all if it weren't for Benjamin Whitermore, one of the new English department hires. Besides the obvious—sharing his son's name—Ben reminded Trevor of himself at that age. It would have been difficult for Trevor to name what it was, but it had something to do with his level of interest. He was interested in conversation, in curriculum, in the kids, in the school. He often asked Trevor for advice and it felt good to be useful again, Trevor thought. Teaching was one of the few professions left where you could realistically expect to have a job for thirty years, which made young teachers like Ben even more important. Without them the building would be full of remember-whens.

He had an earnest gaze when you talked to him—not a trait Trevor had seen in many of the kids he'd taught recently. Ben, at twenty-four, was young enough to have been one of Trevor's students only six years ago. But unlike them, Ben didn't stare at the floor when he had a request or expressed an opinion. Trevor didn't worry about his students' dwindling reading habits—he figured that was his job to address and inspire—but the lack of social intelligence was more concerning. Midway through the year, students struggled through their request for a college recommendation. They'd look off to the side and stare at the whiteboard, shuffle their feet around, and begin a run-on sentence that would never end. "I was talking to my guidance counselor. . ." Yes? ". . .and with the end of the year coming up. . ." Go on. ". . .it was probably a good time. . ." Do tell. ". . .to think about college recs. . ." Yes, good idea. Trevor, despite how painful this communication was, found it entertaining to let them spin around for a while, to see how long it would take them to get to the question. Others who couldn't manage a face-to-face conversation merely emailed. Those communications were even worse. One long sentence with little punctuation.

"Trevor?" Ben tried again.

"Oh, yeah. Sure, thanks." And so arrived G & T number three. This was the last one, he knew. There was no way he was driving anywhere if he had another drink.

"So, what do you make of this last message?" The question came from Elaine. She taught the tenth graders.

"Maybe it's a clumsy attempt by the National Parks Service to get more people to go to the park," Ben said.

"The Memorial Arch isn't that exciting of a monument. It's just an arch." Trevor still hadn't bought into the excitement around these messages. They annoyed him. Not to mention this last one came at 12:03 am on a Monday morning. This last one just said *Memorial Arch* over and over again.

Memorial Arch. Memorial Arch. Memorial Arch. Memorial Arch.

They had all assumed it was referring to nearby Valley Forge Park's monument arch, situated just a few minutes from school.

Kevin sensed Trevor's uninterest. "Come on. You're not even slightly interested? It's like the beginning of a story." Kevin was about to go on about stories again. "March 15th. 3:33. Memorial Arch. We've got a setting."

"But no characters," Ben said.

"*We're* the characters," Elaine offered. Elaine was sitting next to Mary and Larry. They came as a pair, those two. People always assumed they were married. *Work spouses,* they explained. They finished each other's sentences, carpooled, lunched together. They even wore matching scarves. Sitting closely as they were, it looked like one giant scarf tying them together.

Trevor thought Elaine might have a point.

"Maybe I'll plan a field trip for that day. Take the kids there," Kevin said.

"I don't know about that. There's too many unknowns. Someone might be planning something horrible," Elaine said. She worried about everything. Trevor appreciated Elaine—they had come into the district the same year—but she was especially gifted at seeing the worst in any situation.

"What if someone's planning to blow up the arch?" Mary asked. Larry nodded in agreement.

"Why would someone want to blow up that arch?" Trevor

played along.

"People are blowing up things all the time now," Larry said. Mary nodded in agreement.

"I prefer to think of it as an invitation," Kevin said.

"Did anyone else think the voice sounded different this time?" Mary asked.

"I wondered the same thing," echoed Larry.

"It was a slightly higher pitch, right?"

Trevor had noticed that, too. There was something familiar about the voice this time, but he kept that observation to himself. Maybe it was because there were more specific words and no numbers this time. It was only five syllables—*me-mor-i-al-arch*—but you could hear a lot of someone in five syllables. As his colleagues tried out different hypotheses, Trevor stirred the ice in his drink and thought of other five-syllable phrases: *a son of a bitch, get down on the ground, get over yourself.* Like the first lines in a haiku. *Take care of yourself,* his dad used to say on the phone.

"It's snowing," Elaine said. They all turned to the window, just as the students would at school. Mary and Larry *oohed.*

"I should probably head home," Trevor said.

"I'm with you. I've got to let the dog out." Ben had a fiancée, but he talked more about the dog.

Ben and Trevor settled up their tab at the bar. As they made their way to the parking lot, the snow had begun to stick to the pavement. Giant snowflakes floated in the air. Trevor searched for his keys and a wise or witty exit line, but nothing popped into his head. Ben stopped to look up at the sky. In that frozen moment, he looked more twelve than twenty-four.

The sight struck Trevor.

"Do you mind driving me home? I'm not sure I should drive myself."

Ben lowered his head and without missing a beat said, "Sure. No problem."

On the ride to Trevor's house, they talked over the low, peaceful hum of a Terry Gross interview.

"How's the year going?" Trevor asked.

"It's good. It's been fun."

"Fun??"

"Yeah!" Ben hit the word hard, trying to convince Trevor. "I mean, not a lot of fun. Not the kind of fun I imagined. But it feels good more than it feels bad."

"Good."

"Maybe it's not *fun* fun. But the kids are pretty cool for the most part. Some are lovely, really." The word sounded too sophisticated or British for this young American kid, Trevor thought. He'd gone from *cool* to *lovely* pretty quickly.

"Lovely?"

"Yeah."

Trevor thought for a second. "You're right. There are some very lovely kids."

"And there are a few kids who are driving me crazy. But they're ninth graders. What can you expect?"

"Anyone stand out?"

"Oh, sure. A bunch of them."

"Like?" For some reason, Trevor wanted to hear what Ben would say, how he would describe a student, what he liked in one.

"Jack Richter."

"What do you like about him?"

"I don't know." Ben thought for a second. "Wait, do I turn here?"

Trevor had forgotten to motion for the turn into his development. "Yes, here. It's the last house on the left. Downaways."

Ben picked up the thought. "Jack is just a good kid. He's thoughtful. He doesn't talk a whole lot, but when he does he's willing to try out an idea in front of the class. Float out a thought that's kind of playful but also kind of serious. He's not the best writer in the class. He's not bad. He's good. He just hasn't figured out how to get it all out on the page yet. But mostly he's just a great kid."

"I think I may have taught his sister."

"What about you?"

"Keep going through the stop sign." Orchard Drive was a long drive.

"Any standouts this year?"

"There's this girl Dylan. Dylan Geringer. And her friend Steven. Steven, whose last name escapes me right now."

"Steven Lilly?"

"Yeah. Do you know him?"

"Yeah, he approached me about starting a foreign film club."

"Oh, yeah. That sounds like Steven. He's a character."

"I got that impression."

"Right here." Trevor motioned to his driveway. "You need characters in the classroom. I'm worried about boring him, honestly. He's one of those creative, smart, slacker kids. The ones who see behind the curtain, so to speak. Always looking at the big picture through the small details. Keeps me on my toes." The gin had made him very talkative. "Emotionally, though, he's all over the place. Moody. He had this out-of-nowhere blow-up the other day. Yelled "fuck" in the classroom. He was yelling at some kid who said something about Dylan. It was pretty innocuous, really, but Steven seems pretty protective of Dylan. She was dressed up like Hester Prynne for Halloween." Ben put the car in park in the driveway and waited for Trevor to finish. He had that open look on his face again. "Dylan sounds like your Jack. She's *lovely*, too. Warm, genuine—a kid who seems generally curious about things, and not too caught up in all the competition or the drama. . ." Trevor trailed off as he looked at the hose he still hadn't put away for the year, the one Dylan had tripped over last month when she and Steven had stopped by. He thought about telling Ben that story, but it had too many parts, and their driveway conversation was feeling like the end of a weird date.

"Anyway. Thanks again. I guess I'm not seeing you tomorrow."

"Let's hope not," Ben said laughing. An inch of snow already covered the street. Trevor closed the car door behind him and noticed the cat sitting in the window, watching a finch spill birdseed out of a feeder onto the ground.

THIRTEEN

Dylan and Daphne helped with the salad. Neither had many skills in the kitchen, but they could manage slicing tomatoes and spinning the lettuce in the salad spinner. Dylan liked the soft whirring sound the spinner made. It sounded like a departing spaceship.

"I think it's done, dear." Daphne had taken to calling her sister *dear* and *doll*. *Dear* when she was playing a motherly role; *doll* when she wanted a partner in crime. Either was fine with Dylan. She was happy to have her sister home for Thanksgiving.

"But it's fun," Dylan said. She gave the leaves a few final spins and dumped the lettuce into a bowl. Daphne finished with the tomatoes and mixed lemon juice and olive oil for a dressing.

Their mother, Sarah Geringer, was a good cook. (Steven had to include her middle initial to find her anagram name, *Greater Garnish*.) She'd been briefly enrolled at the Culinary Institute before she decided she hated all her classmates. It was shocking to learn how cutthroat the industry was, so she gave up that short-lived dream. Instead, she studied graphic design at Moore. She'd worked for some local firms designing logos and websites for a while when the girls were younger, but after her parents had died, the money she inherited helped pay for an addition to their house that included a small art studio. Now she spent most of her time painting portraits of pets and designing her own small line of greeting cards.

Dylan admired her mother's creativity, her nonchalant approach to new projects. It was evident in the kitchen, too. Sarah rarely used recipes or cookbooks. It was always a little of this, a little of that, and voilà. In fact, she often uttered "voilà" when she brought out the main course. Daphne had been a picky eater when they were younger, always requiring a separate meal. Dylan realized early on she could please her mother as the more adventurous one, so she always ate what her mother created. She enjoyed the meals almost as much as she enjoyed the moments when she and her mother ganged up on Daphne.

Despite all this creativity, Sarah was not the kind of mother who palled around with her kids. She encouraged their creativity, but she didn't sit with them and make scrapbooks. She never once took them aside and taught them how to draw or paint. They baked the occasional cookies together, but her skills as a cook were her own, for herself. Daphne and Dylan weren't rejected, but they weren't invited either. There was something in their mother's face when she painted or cooked, a mix of seriousness and playfulness, a Gene Wilder–as–Willy Wonka grin. Dylan saw the same expression in her sister's face and she envied it. She tried to practice that look in the mirror but was unconvincing. She was more her father's daughter, another listener. There was no voilà.

Dylan's dad, Tom Geringer—*Shaggier Mentor* in Steven's book—was an audio engineer at a studio down in Philly. He took the train there in the morning around nine and returned most nights after dinner hours. He could get out early and take vacation days off, but for the most part, nightly dinners were usually just the girls. His work was mostly commercial—advertising voice-overs, film sound mixing and design, documentary TV packages. Occasionally, he'd have artists and bands come through, but they were rarely that exciting, certainly not to Daphne and Dylan. Still, being part of the industry, he could get good tickets from time to time for major acts, ones his girls approved of. His favorite part of the job was designing sounds. Like his wife, he'd tried his hand at a more ambitious training. In his twenties he lived out in Los Angeles and worked on films—mostly independent ones. He wrote music for a few small films, but found better work as an assistant audio engineer, designing and mixing sounds. He was rarely in a bad mood. He never took a hard stand when it came to arguments in the house. He was reasonable and rational and knew how to calmly concede a point, if only to point out how his opinion was more sound. Yes, Dylan wished she were more like her mother—confident and creative—but only if it somehow pleased her dad.

"It *does* sound like a spaceship. Huh." Tom gave the spinner a few spins, holding his ear close to the opening, but the sound had changed now that the lettuce was out. "It sounds like a helicopter from about a hundred yards." Sarah smiled at her girls as they set the table. Her husband was always comparing sounds. They usually rolled their eyes at these comparisons, but since they lived a hundred yards from the hospital helicopter pad, they all nodded in agreement.

After the first round of turkey and mashed potatoes, Daphne poured wine for her parents.

"Do you want some?" Daphne asked Dylan.

"No," Dylan's mother answered for her.

"She can have a glass of wine if she likes," Dylan's dad said.

"It's Thanksgiving." Daphne seemed to think this was a good argument.

"She can have *one* glass," Sarah said.

"I don't want one." The response came out angrier than Dylan intended.

"Fine," Daphne said, but it disappointed her. "I was just offering. You had one last year. You and Steven both had one. Why couldn't he come this year?" For the past three years, Steven had Thanksgiving-ed with the Geringers. They all liked him, Daphne especially.

"I'm not sure," Dylan said.

"Didn't you ask him?"

"I think so."

"What does that mean?" Sarah asked. "I hope you let him know he could come if wanted to." Dylan took a bite of mashed potatoes. "Dylan?"

"What?"

"Did you at least invite him?" her dad asked. Steven had interned with Mr. Geringer at the studio last summer. They traveled into town on the train together—another point of jealousy with Dylan. It annoyed her, all this stupid jealousy.

She was tired of thinking about Steven, and she felt herself about to lose it. They had been having such a nice family night. Steven was not part of her family. Yes, she loved Steven. I mean, that's what you say about a longtime friend, right?

Since Halloween she and Norman had become a little more serious. They'd make out in the car a little before he dropped her off. It was nice, Dylan thought: the leaning in and his hands around her back; the warmth of his face against hers; the softness of his mouth. Only once or twice did his hands trace the ribs along her side, sliding against her breast. She liked how small she felt in his arms, like he could pick her up effortlessly, be weightless. The spell broke when she noticed once how Norman kept his eyes open the whole time.

"What's wrong?"

"Nothing."

"Your eyes are open."

"Okay."

"What do you mean *okay*?"

"I mean, okay, my eyes are open. Is that weird?"

"A little."

"Okay." She only meant to tease him, but he'd taken it as a criticism or something. She couldn't tell. Steven reacted the same way whenever she questioned him. Boys were so easily offended, she thought. They loved to criticize but hated criticism.

"I wasn't complaining." She squeezed his shoulder.

"Okay."

"Are you only going to say *okay*?"

"Okay!" He tried to say it ironically, but it felt disingenuous. The moment was lost.

Dylan kept her eyes closed after that, trying not to notice if Norman's were open. But the last few times, it was all she could think about. She felt his eyes against her face when they kissed. Something wasn't quite right. He looked the part, he felt the part. He was nice and liked her, but she wondered why he never tried anything else, why he never tried to grope her. She wouldn't have stopped him. Maybe she was doing something wrong, she thought.

It was illogical, but her frustration with Norman made her more irritated with Steven. She tried to hide it as best she could. She found that with Steven, the more you pushed back, the more it made him want to argue, and Dylan hated arguing. It was important to Steven to be right, whatever the topic. When they were younger, she enjoyed how he took charge, how he planned their days, how he introduced her to cool music and movies, how they bonded over their hatred for mean girls and stupid guys, how it was just the two of them surrounded by dolts and bores. If *Darling Energy* had another power, she would transplant some of Steven's passion into Norman's kindness. Or vice versa, she wondered. Couldn't you be kindly passionate or passionately kind? Maybe *she* needed the transplant.

She decided she would try to kill Steven with kindness instead. Maybe if she was nice to him—the way *friends* are to another—she could pretend not to notice his infatuation with her and it would just go away. She channeled this more rational approach in her response to the dinner table. How would her dad handle the situation? She mentioned Thanksgiving to Steven, but he said he was busy. She wasn't sure if he was just saying that because he didn't want to annoy her, or if he was actually busy. Either way, she found it an annoying response. She was annoyed thinking that maybe he just wanted her to ask him again and make him come over, and annoyed if he was really busy and didn't offer what his plans were. She didn't try to loosen the truth from him, afraid her interest would only encourage him. Dylan didn't know what to think anymore. And why didn't her parents ask about Norman? They'd met him and liked him.

"I asked him, and he couldn't make it. I'll let him know you were all asking about him." She tried smiling.

"Please do. How's his mother doing?" Mrs. Geringer was not a fan of Mrs. Lilly. Dylan explained that she still wasn't well.

"I'm not sure she was ever *well*." Dylan's mother was a kind woman, but Steven's mother was a topic that revealed a frustration that sometimes sounded like anger. Sarah had gone through grade school with Steven's mother. Tom sensed the anxiety at the table and changed the subject.

"Can you pass the cranberry sauce?"

***

"Can you pass the cranberry sauce?" Steven's mother asked.

Steven and his mother, Lillian—yes, Lillian Lilly—sat next to each other at the corner of a long dining room table. The cranberry sauce was within reach, but she was doing her best to make their Thanksgiving conversation seem ordinary. She did not make many attempts at being ordinary, so Steven passed the cranberry sauce.

Lillian Lilly was also back at work on a regular basis. For as long as Steven could remember, his mother had worked at the hospital gift shop. As a young boy, Steven liked visiting his mother at work. He liked spinning the Get Well and New Baby card carousels. He liked the bouquets of flowers, the balloons, the stuffed animals. He liked the formality of his mother's name tag.

"Lillian Lilly! Is that your real name?" the customers would ask.

"Why, yes it is." His mother answered back in a faux Southern

Belle accent.

This truth pleased the customers.

Some days, Lillian—with her store discount—would come home with a stuffed animal for Steven. One was a Get Well teddy bear that came with a leg cast and crutch.

"But I'm not sick," he said as he looked it over. "I didn't break my leg."

"But you might."

At ten, his mind found this response both logical and frightening.

His mother had insisted they dress up for Thanksgiving dinner. She wore a sleeveless black dress and a string of pearls, and had, for the first time in many months, styled her dark brown hair into a sleek ponytail. The look was only somewhat betrayed by her bare feet. "It will be fun," she said. Steven was unconvinced, but he didn't mind the opportunity to wear a white dinner jacket he'd ordered off eBay last week. It was very Sean Connery-era James Bond—black pants, bow tie, his hair slicked back. He knew his mother didn't mean *formal*, and indeed she sighed when he came down the stairs. He knew it would have this effect, but if she wanted to playact, he would have to find some way to enjoy himself. His descent down the stairs played like a prom date pickup in reverse.

"What?" he said but knew.

"Nothing." It wasn't worth it.

Finding a way to enjoy himself was Steven's unofficial motto. In the Lilly house, for the last two years since Steven's father left, it was more a necessity than a motto. Foster Lilly's anagram name—his first name, at least—was the first name Steven unscrambled, and its uncovering was a prescient description of his father's departure two Aprils ago. It was an accident, this discovery. Steven wrote his dad's name over and over again in a notebook a month after he left, after it had become fairly certain he wouldn't be returning home any time soon. The writing was not a sign of sadness—that would come later—but instead, it was the result of Steven practicing his father's signature. He'd needed a permission slip signed for a field trip to the art museum, and his mother had gone catatonic. She sat at the dining room table—the one they were sitting at right now—and just stared out the window. During those months, Steven cooked for himself and did his own laundry. He tried not to bother her with many requests. His mother's signature had always been such a graceful one, all those lilting *l*'s swooping on the page. It was too perfect to perfect. His dad's, on the other hand, was a sloppy *F* and an indistinguishable *L*, connected by an inky lightening bolt. He figured this new skill would come in handy.

He wrote *Foster* over and over again, until one time he'd interposed the *s* with the *f*. *Softer*, he wrote. He never noticed how similar those words were before—why would he? But it struck him, this realization. He didn't know what to make of it, but it felt good to unscramble something at a time when nothing made any sense.

He stared at the word for a while and finished it off: *Softer Lilly*. The phrase switched something on inside Steven, and for the first time since his dad left, he broke down and cried.

The tears were complicated. Foster Lilly left Lillian Lilly for a man. "His revelation," his mother called it when she found the words. Steven was sure they were his father's. Steven's mother didn't use words like *revelation*.

The first grief was not for the abandonment. At first, his father called often enough that it felt like a long work trip that had stranded him at an airport. Mr. Lilly was an engineer of some sort—Steven had never understood exactly what kind or what sort of work he did—and often trav-eled for his job. Instead, the first wave of sadness that swelled up inside him was witnessing the change in his mother. When she wasn't staring out the window, she organized and reorganized the clothes in her closets. She laid them out on her bed in small piles, sometimes by color, only to hang them back up in an hour. Steven thought it was weird the first day, but when it continued for a week, he got nervous.

She wasn't eating or sleeping either. Or talking much. That was what most unsettled Steven. Lillian was a talker. That's how she had always figured out what she thought. She was also a self-narrator, providing her own play-by-play and color commentary for her day-to-day actions. "It looks like we're out of pepper. Going to have to fill this up with some pep-percorns, aren't we? We can't have salt without pepper. Can we, Steven? That just wouldn't be right. Yep. Need some peppercorns." She would al-ways overdo it when Steven was within earshot, or wearing earbuds pre-tending not to hear, because she knew it aggravated him. After Foster left, Lillian gave up the literal descriptions and went quiet.

The second wave of sadness was all subtext. Beyond his leaving them, what did it mean that his dad liked men now? What assumptions had Steven held that were now false? About dads, men, love, marriage, life? His dad had never been one of the most masculine of men. He wasn't in-terested in sports, though he was an avid runner. He wasn't much of a drinker (that was his mother's job). He didn't care much for cars, prefer-ring to drive the same Camry for the entirety of Steven's life. He was rare-ly angry. He wasn't fat. He was handy, but in more a tinkerer sense. He would try to fix the air conditioner himself, but hired someone to mow the lawn. Steven knew these traits were based on ungraceful, small-minded notions of what men were like—embodied by Homer Simpson and the Lillys' neighbor, Mr. Smith—but his father's divergences from the American dad stereotype, had seemed more original than conspicuous. It had been a point of admiration. Now Steven wasn't sure what to think.

Like most dads, however, Foster was quiet. He was comfortable sitting without talking. Steven and he used to drive an hour out of town for his piano lessons without talking or even listening to the radio. Steven didn't think this was unpleasant; it was just how things were. The few family car trips they took were dominated by the narration of Steven's mother, anyway. Steven had always assumed his dad went into a peaceful, Zen-like silence, but after he left, he wondered if his dad's insides were arguing with themselves, if he imagined leaving Steven and his mom at every rest stop.

The third wave of sadness finally turned inward. What had he done to be rejected so? It was one thing to fall out of love with your wife—Steven could imagine that, he guessed—but aren't you biologically obligated, legally obligated even, to love and protect your own son? And if you reject that, and leave with another man, and only call your son once every few weeks, and express sadness but not remorse, if you make no promises about when or if you'll return, and if you sound *different* on the phone, a more relaxed version of yourself in spite of the turmoil you've unleashed, what does that mean? What does anything mean?

What more does it mean, if a part of you wants to understand this irrationality, if a part of you knows what it feels like to want to escape your current predicament, if you feel a kinship with your abandoner that is unnameable, if you wish for a love that would make you leave everything else behind, if you wish to care so much for something that you can care for nothing else?

"Do you?" his mother asked.

"Do I want what?" Steven floated back into the scene.

"More turkey?"

"No, I'm good." He had an idea. He wanted to leap up from the table and go up to his bedroom, but he saw his mother's serene face in the candlelight.

"I'll clear the table," he said instead.

"Thank you, dear."

As Steven stacked the plates in the dishwasher, he knew he had to tell Dylan about what Lester had given him. He had an idea for message number four.

***

After dinner, Dylan and Daphne sat on the back porch. Daphne was into her third glass of wine.

"What's he like?" Dylan asked her sister.

"Jay? Jay is—" she searched for the word. "*Himself.*"

"Well, that's not much help."

"He's just completely himself. It's hard to describe. He. . .doesn't worry about himself all the time. Most of the guys I've dated have this obsession with the future. Like, what job they're working toward, how they're building their résumé, how they're going to get to point B."

"That doesn't sound so bad."

"Well, it's not bad, but with some people it's a blinding purpose. And it's anxiety. And it's selfish, of course." Daphne took another sip of her wine. Dylan kept quiet and let her sister figure out what she wanted to say. "I'm not saying he doesn't think about those things, about the future, it's just not his sole purpose in life."

"Are you his sole purpose, then?"

"No. It's not like that either. We just have a good time together, and we're just. . ." Daphne finished off the glass. "We're just living."

Dylan was surprised. Daphne was usually more articulate than this, and not one for New Age–sounding platitudes. "So he's not like Gatsby then?"

Daphne laughed. "Well, he looks great in a suit." Daphne reached down beside her chair. Dylan hadn't seen her come out with the bottle. She refilled her glass and motioned for Dylan to take a sip. Dylan wouldn't reject her sister again and took a long sip.

"What about you?"

"What about me?"

"What's this *Norman* like?"

"He's sweet."

"That's good."

"Yes," Dylan said, but she sounded unconvincing. "He's very nice. And cute."

"That's a good start." Dylan reached for another sip of her sister's wine. "But. . ." her sister prompted.

"But nothing. It's good. He's a good guy. It's not serious."

"You haven't. . .?" Daphne raised her eyebrows.

"No. We haven't."

"Do you want to?"

"Maybe. Yes. I don't know."

"Has he been asking?"

"No," she answered a little quickly.

"What does that mean?"

"I don't want to talk about this."

"Come on!" Daphne offered another sip of her wine.

"I guess I don't know."

"You're not sure how you feel about him?"

"Well, I thought I was."

"What happened?"

"Nothing happened?"

"Why not?"

Dylan thought about it for a second. "I don't know. I don't think he wants to."

Daphne frowned. "They all want to. Maybe he's just shy."

"Maybe."

"Or he's gay."

"He's not gay."

"How do you know?"

"He's just not."

"But how do you know??"

"Why do you want him to be gay?"

"I don't. I'm just asking."

"Not everyone is gay. Why does everyone have to be gay?" This sounded ridiculous, and they both laughed. Their mother looked out the window and made an unconvincing angry face at the wine bottle. Their father led her away.

"Has Steven's dad come back?" Daphne asked.

"Nope. He calls every few weeks."

"That's just horrible. Just to leave like that. I mean, I don't think he should have stayed married, and I respect his lifestyle choice. You shouldn't live a lie, etcetera. But if you have a son, a son in high school—a great kid like Steven—and you just take off without. . ." She took another sip. "I don't know."

"I know. It's terrible. We're lucky." Dylan looked in through the window at her parents in the blue hue of the TV.

"What does Steven think of Norman?"

"I think he wants to not like him, but it's hard to not like Norman. He just dislikes him on principle."

"On what principle?"

"On the principle that I like him."

"God. I don't miss high school." Daphne offered the last of the wine to Dylan, who downed it.

"You should date Steven. I've always told you that." Dylan gave Daphne the same look she always gave her for this suggestion. "I'm serious. He's smart and funny. And cute, in his own way. He's a little short, but that's no big deal. And you two are great friends. You've been as thick as thieves for years now. You need a partner in crime. Life is short, and there are many crimes." Daphne tried to take another sip from her glass before realizing it was already empty.

"You aren't going to ask if Steven's gay?"

"Steven isn't gay. Why, because his dad's gay?"

"No."

"Because he's into art and dresses well?"

"Of course not." She didn't like how her sister was making her feel small-minded. "I don't know. You should have seen how they used to treat him at school. The things they used to say about him." Daphne turned to look at Dylan. "They were cruel. I was the only friend he had. I'm still the only friend he has." Maybe it was the wine, but Dylan's eyes filled with tears.

"What's wrong?" Daphne asked.

The question and the wine made the tears pour out. Dylan hated not knowing why she was crying.

***

Dylan blamed her sister this time, not Steven. If not for her encouragement, and her bottle of wine, Dylan would not be climbing into Steven's window at 11 p.m. on Thanksgiving night.

"You've never come at night before." Steven was still wearing his white dinner jacket and bow tie.

"What are you wearing?"

"Long story. Actually, it's not. Come over here." Steven was not sitting at his desk as the scene usually unfolded but by his desk and computer. A second computer sat on the side of his desk, attached to what looked like an external hard drive. "Look at this," Steven said as he motioned to the screen.

Dylan looked. It looked like an Excel spreadsheet filled with phone numbers, addresses, and names. Steven highlighted one. "There's your phone number." He scrolled past Geringer down to Lilly. "And here's mine." A few rows above were the Lewises.

"Lester?" she asked. It seemed obvious now. "Did he give you all this?" She motioned to the screen and the second computer.

"He did. I sent the last one."

"You sent the last message out? You sent *Memorial Arch*?"

"I thought we needed a setting. Now we've got one. March 15th, 3:33, at the Memorial Arch."

"What does it mean?"

"I don't know."

"What was Lester trying to do? Does Norman know?"

Steven explained what little he knew. Lester cornered him that night at the ER when they had dropped off Nicole. Steven said yes right away, without really thinking of any possible ramifications. There were a host of details he didn't understand. As best as he could figure out, Lester just wanted to see if he could figure out how to do it, how to send an automated phone message to the entire community, just to see what would happen. There was some anger there, but Steven couldn't figure it out, though presumably it all stemmed from Lester's expulsion a few years back.

"What do you want me to do?" Steven asked him.

"Just hold onto it for a while. I can't have it in the house. They've already stopped by. The police."

Steven was disappointed to learn that Lester had no plan. He'd picked March 15th randomly. As far as 3:33, three was Lester's favorite number. Steven had the culprit but there was no clear motive, no sense of narrative. It was a lame mystery. Up to now, Steven thought. Maybe he could change that.

"I just wanted to see if I could do it," Lester had told him.

"So it was all just random?"

"Well, there's no such thing as random, really."

Was that a riddle? "Why me?" he asked Lester.

Lester just shrugged his shoulders. "Why not? You seemed interested in my computers. I don't know you at all. And you have a look."

"What look?"

"That one." Lester pointed at Steven's face. Steven felt his face holding an expression, but he had no idea what it looked like.

It would have made perfect sense to reject this offer. He didn't know Lester, didn't know what he was really giving him, or what kind of liability he was exposing himself to, but at the end of that Halloween night, sitting in the middle of an ER waiting room featuring two injured zombies, watching Norman and Dylan together, he thought Lester's offer seemed mostly harmless, and maybe even exciting. By the time he'd gotten the hardware back to his room and powered it up, a whole world of possibilities opened up.

"So now what?" Dylan asked.

"Let's finish telling the story."

Steven threw some clothes off a nearby chair and brought it over to his desk. This could be fun, Dylan thought, as she sat next to Steven.

"How does it work?"

FOURTEEN

Trevor decided he would go for a run. Maybe that would clear the fog. Thanksgiving and a Friday of leftovers made him round and stuffed. He needed to treat his body better. Every year he entertained the idea of making his body the priority. Instead of using his free time to read or write, not that he did much of that anymore, he'd just devote himself to exercise. Maybe he'd be able to keep up with Elizabeth. The plan passed him by again this year. It was the end of November and his plan would have to wait until the calendar changed.

He preferred listening to his feet against the road rather than a motivating playlist. He convinced himself he was working harder that way. Perhaps if he'd been listening to music, he wouldn't have stopped to look over at the Caulder house. It was in the middle of Orchard Drive, set back thirty or forty yards from the street. Whenever Trevor was on a run, he'd look over at it. It was a house like any other on the street: a stone and stucco colonial house, a two-car garage, a basketball hoop in the driveway. The Caulders had moved in three years ago, when Royce was a freshman. Trevor had waved to the parents from time to time, on a run or in his car.

They each had broad smiles and seemingly cheerful dispositions. On the weekends they both worked in the garden. They were the first in the neighborhood to rake their leaves in the fall and the first to mulch in the spring.

Trevor knew better than to judge the happiness of a family by the outside of a home, but he still found it difficult to imagine Royce, angry and depressed Royce Caulder, inside this lovely house on this lovely street. He had a treasonous thought now and again when he found himself relieved his own son didn't have to feel so alone and angry. He would give anything for Benjamin to be alive, but the memory of his son was so perfect. He really was a charmed boy—sweet, kind, smart, generous. The thought he might have struggled like Royce, might have felt alone, despite not being alone, and, that he might have felt angry and been unable to express it, shook Trevor. He and Elizabeth would have found a way to help, but it was a moot point now, and Trevor felt awful for that relief.

A white Tahoe swung around Trevor. As he waved a *thank you*, a squirrel darted out in front of the car and couldn't decide if it should keep going or turn back. He tried to yell a warning—to the driver, to the squirrel, but it was too late. Trevor heard a dull thud and a small squeak. Trevor could only grab both sides of his head. He saw the driver in the side mirror react—a wordless opening of her mouth—and drive on.

The squirrel's mouth was agape, but its tail still twitched. Its middle was crushed. It looked like a magician's trick. Thankfully, it was thrown against the curb, out of the way of the next car. Trevor came to a stop to look at the body. He watched for a minute until the tail stopped twitching, and he caught his breath.

It was a squirrel. He wasn't going to let this ruin his day. Yes, it's upsetting to watch something like that, he conceded, but he can't let that send him down another spiral. That was the squirrel's *tharn*, not his, right? He watched its indecision and the inevitable impending doom. He wouldn't react that way now.

It was this state of mind that prompted Trevor to look back at the Caulder house. He looked at the upstairs windows, at the bay window into the living room, at the front door, at the pachysandra that led over to the garage. Something drew him up the driveway, like he was attached to a rope. He was sure he was seeing things, imagining smoke coming out of the garage. Halfway up the driveway his slow walk turned into a jog. It *was* smoke coming from under the garage doors.

It couldn't be what he thought it was, but at the same time, he knew it was. He yelled "Hey!" for some reason. He reached for the handle, but it was locked. He yanked it but it only opened an inch. "Hey, hey, hey!" he yelled at the house itself and then back at the door. He looked back to the street for anyone. Trevor ran over to the front door and banged on it. He rang the doorbell and banged somewhere. "Help!" he yelled out to the street.

Grabbing the garage door handle again, it budged open six inches. He grabbed the bottom of the door and tried lifting from there.

"What's going on?" A young kid from next door ran over holding a basketball. His younger brother and sister stood by his side wide-eyed.

"Help me open this door!" Trevor said. The boy came to Trevor's side and grabbed the bottom of the garage door. More smoke billowed out. "Cover your face," he told the boy. The boy lifted his T-shirt over his mouth. They yanked at the door together. "Call 911!" he yelled at the other two. The girl, who was no older than eight, ran back to her house. The younger boy couldn't move.

They yanked one more time and heard a loud crack. The garage door gave way and opened enough for Trevor to run inside. "Stay out," he yelled at the kid. The room was thick with noxious smoke. He managed to see and step over the hose attached to the exhaust pipe. The stereo inside the car was on. He felt the bass reverberate against the window. He was holding his breath, but his eyes burned and he struggled with the front-door handle before it gave way. A body slumped against the steering wheel. Trevor reached one arm behind the back and linked the other around the waist. It was Royce. Unconscious, Royce slipped off the seat and into Trevor's arms. Trevor dragged him out of the garage and deposited him on the lawn.

Trevor had been CPR-trained once, but it was a long time ago. He couldn't tell if Royce was still breathing, but before he leaned in to check, Royce gave out a violent-sounding cough and a desperate inhalation. Trevor went to steady him, but Royce jerked to his side. The vessels in his face pulsed and his eyes teared, but he was alive. He coughed again and spat up onto the grass.

"Go back inside, Drew." It was the mother from next door. "Take them both back inside," she said as she motioned to her two younger kids. "Are you okay?" she asked Trevor.

Trevor held Royce's back as he continued to cough and spit.

"Did you call 911??" Trevor's heart was beating out of his chest.

"They're coming, yes," the mother answered. "I'll get some water."

Trevor moved Royce's hair out of his face. He heard the sirens from down the street. "You're going to be okay," he told Royce. "You're going to be fine." Royce tried to roll onto his knees. "Just stay right there. You're fine. You're fine." Trevor moved to the other side to look in his face, but Royce turned it to the ground. "Someone's coming for you. They're almost here." He wasn't sure what he should say. Royce kept groaning, so Trevor just rubbed his back. One of Royce's bloodshot eyes turned to look at him. He tried to say something but nothing came out.

"You're going to be fine," he told him again.

The ambulance screeched to a stop, followed by a police car and an EMT vehicle. They had Royce on a stretcher and fitted with an oxygen mask in seconds.

"Are you his father?" a policeman asked.

"No. I'm not. I don't think they're home."

Trevor was there for another half an hour. He was checked out by the EMTs and cleared. He talked to the police and the next-door neighbor. He rejected an offer to drive him home. "I live down the street," he told them. When he knew the parents had been notified, that they were on their way to hospital, he walked back home. A landscaping truck pulled up to the Caulder house. Two men got out. One rolled the tractor off the trailer and the other gassed up a weedwacker. It was November, and the grass looked short. Trevor didn't see any weeds. Wearing red noise-canceling headphones, the men got to work on the Caulder lawn and garden, and Trevor walked home in the din of gas engines.

***

Steven agreed that he would take the fall if there was a fall coming.

Dylan would be just a co-author for the rest of the story. She wouldn't type anything, wouldn't press any buttons, wouldn't click on anything. All the technical elements of this lark would be Steven's. This was his suggestion. Dylan thought his "I'll take full responsibility" was overdramatic. Or maybe it wasn't. Was any of this technically against the law? She considered googling the answer but thought better of it.

Dylan sat in a bean bag chair beside Steven's bed. She held a spiral notebook and a Bic pen. Steven sat at the computer.

"Well, I guess the question is what kind of story do we want to tell?"

"Right," she agreed.

"What kind of story do *you* want to tell?"

"Like what genre?"

"I guess."

"Well, it's already a mystery of sorts. I think we should just introduce a character and see what happens."

"Just make it up as we go along?"

"Sure. Isn't that how you write a story?"

"Well, we could plan out all the parts." Steven wasn't arguing, just thinking aloud.

"We could. But I think it would be better if we see how people react. Wait to see how it goes over."

"I see your point," Steven said.

"Plus, it's an invitation, too. The way that Les set it up. It's like an announcement that comes in the mail."

"Right. But it can still introduce a scene."

Dylan liked this. This felt like an important, if silly, conversation. She missed this kind of conversation with Steven—when they had a project and dreamed it up together. She liked the idea that they would focus on someone else's story instead of their own for a change. It felt like there were so many minor decisions to make on a daily basis. Most of the time, she wanted someone to tell her what to do. She had little problem offering an opinion on what other people should do. It was the same way she felt about cleaning her bedroom. She would much rather clean a friend's bedroom than her own. In fact, she was straightening the books in Steven's bookcase when she came up with an idea.

"*Darling Energy gathered the throng.*"

"The *throng*? Oh, I like that. Just that sentence?"

"Yes."

"Why is she gathering a *throng*?"

"I don't know. Let's wait and see."

"I love it," Steven said. Dylan smiled. "I *love* it," he emphasized this time. Staring at Dylan now, he felt something stir—in the room, in his heart? I love *you*, he thought in Dylan's direction.

"I love it, too," she replied.

They stared at one another for a beat.

A toilet flushed somewhere down the hall. It relieved both of them.

"I'm going to go. But this is good, right?"

"It is. It is good. When should we send it out?"

"Sunday night, before we all go back?"

"I'll set it up for then."

"Do you know how to do it?"

"It worked the last time."

"Text me tomorrow."

Dylan didn't always go back down the ladder, but it was late, and they didn't want an interaction with Mrs. Lilly.

At the bottom of the ladder, Dylan looked back up at Steven and waved. Steven held his hand up and let it stay there until Dylan had passed the mailbox and disappeared into the night.

FIFTEEN

The following is a message from the Great Valley School District:

Darling Energy gathered the throng.

Message number four was spoken only once. Steven read it slowly and enunciated it clearly. He let the recording linger a beat or two past the sentence's end, letting the ambient room noise of his bedroom act like an ellipsis. Rather than just let it repeat, he figured he would "imbue the line with gravitas"—an explanation he practiced in case Dylan asked.

He tried on a different voice this time, too, something a little lower in pitch and, unintentionally, slightly British. Later, hearing it on his own phone, it sounded more affected and less authentic than he'd intended.

Mr. Drake wasn't in class, so they had a sub. The fact had made its way over texts and through the hallways like it was breaking news. The arrival of a sub—even with a well-liked teacher like Mr. Drake—was always met with a combination of excitement and relief. It meant nothing important was happening today. You might watch a video or silently read. Maybe half fill out a pathetic busywork handout that the teacher had no plan on collecting. There would be no real instruction. You could probably get homework for another class done during the period. You could take long walks to the bathroom, maybe play on your phone the whole time. The only better prospect would be substitute students, a concept Steven couldn't seem to get off the ground.

Substitute teachers provided for a forgivable—and often needed—sort of lawlessness. There weren't many institutions that operated like a high school. Steven was sure the adult world didn't work like this: three or four hours straight of direct instruction and constant observation. A half hour break for lunch, and then another two hours of the same thing. Even if you worked in a factory, on an assembly line, they left you alone for most of the day. He remembered some of the employees at his dad's engineering office, sitting alone in their cubicles, unbothered. He knew everyone complained about cube work, but it looked nice to Steven. He would have loved to have a personal, walled-in cubicle in every classroom, a place to be unbothered. In lieu of that, it was at least nice to let your guard down when you had a substitute. Subs had no real relevance and even less authority.

And what a cast of characters they were. There was Miss Betty who was sweet and brought in candy. There was Polly—he could never remember her last name—who must have been eighty and wore a wig she readjusted every few minutes, her lipstick smeared over her teeth. There was some little guy in his fifties with a big mustache, messy gray hair, and a chain wallet who looked like he might be a weekend biker. There were a few subs who looked a lot like students, recent college grads who wandered around the building looking for the right room. It was a ragtag group, for sure. The school had adopted a group of refugees and let them loose in the building.

Kids were quick to sniff out the subs' fear or hesitancy. Because subs had no currency in this relationship, the whole system of the classroom could disintegrate. Some students would try to act all tough around subs; others would act like the subs weren't even there. Steven preferred a third, more curious option: coercing them into detailed conversations about their lives. They seemed more rooted in the outside world than his teachers did. They had accepted an invitation to work and so seemed like visitors from another country, ones who might tell them what life was really like. His questions began modestly—"How's your day going so far?"—but if the sub didn't squash them quickly enough, Steven would wind up questioning them about their honeymoon.

Today's sub for Mr. Drake was his favorite interview subject—the bow-tied and mothballed, Jim Ryerson. Mr. Ryerson, who was no taller than five foot five, looked like he was in a barbershop quartet. There was no straw hat or red pin-striped suit, no suspenders, but Steven could imagine them hanging in the teacher's closet. When he would walk into the room, he'd let out a long sigh, like he'd been holding his breath down the hallway. His favorite activity—his *specialty*, Dylan called it—was taking roll. It was a formal event under his direction. Reading from the class lists, he would slowly enunciate each student name—including the middle names—pausing dramatically to look around the room for the matching body. His default disposition was suspicion. It was like a schoolhouse scene from *Tom Sawyer,* like he was checking to see if any of the boys were hiding a frog. It made no difference to the students that he butchered every one of their names—it certainly made no difference to Mr. Ryerson.

He would dryly read the plans the teacher had left, sit down, confident that his part was then over, and read a hardcover book. Over the last three years Steven had asked him many questions. Steven found that Mr. Ryerson enjoyed talking about himself.

Questions like:

"Were you ever married?"
"Were you in the army?"
"What's your favorite song?"
"What was your first career?"
"What was your favorite subject in school?"
"What do you do for fun?"

Each elicited a story and explanation, but Steven kept the short answers in his notebook:

"No."
"Yes."
"Swanee River."
"Banking."
"Latin."
"Singing with my barbershop quartet." (Steven called that one!)
He wasn't sure what he would do with this information. He just wanted to remember.

Steven was ready to try out some new questions, but before he could,

Mr. Ryerson surprised the class with a question before they all had settled down.

"What is the meaning of all these phone messages?" He seemed annoyed. "Could someone explain to me what I'm supposed to make of them? The last one woke me up from a very deep sleep." Dylan turned to look at Steven. It hadn't occurred to them that even Mr. Ryerson would receive them.

Steven realized Mr. Ryerson likely only had a landline. Whereas these calls and messages reached most people in the district on their cell phones, Mr. Ryerson received word probably through a corded phone perched next to his bed. Steven made a bell ring inside Mr. Ryerson's house, waking him from a dream. What a strange new power Steven had developed. He wondered what he dreamed about. He'd ask that next time.

"You get them, too?" Marta Wainwright asked.

"Of course I get them. I'm a district employee," Mr. Ryerson said.

Marta didn't mean anything by it. "I'm sorry, Mr. Ryerson. I just thought that because you're a substitute—"

"A guest teacher," he corrected. The district recently had tried to switch to that terminology, but it stuck with no one. No one except Mr. Ryerson.

"This one was stupid." It was Ted Lavender again. "It didn't make any sense."

"None of them make any sense," Molly added. "That's why I like them." Steven and Dylan turned and smiled at Molly. Molly was okay, they thought at the same time. "I think someone's trying to tell us something."

"This is a very inefficient way to tell someone something," Mr. Ryerson said. "I was having a very pleasant dream."

"What were you dreaming about, Mr. Ryerson?" Steven asked. He wanted to hear more reactions from the class, but he didn't want to be too obvious about it. Plus, he wondered what he dreamt about.

Molly interrupted before he answered. "First I thought it was directions. Like coordinates, or details, to go look for something. On that day, at that time and place."

"That is what it is, isn't it?" asked Wyatt.

"Well, it still could be, yes. But 'Darling Energy'. . ." Molly took her phone out to check the rest of her note on the message. "'Gathered the throng.' Now it sounds like the beginning of a story."

"I thought it was 'gathered-up *thong*.'" Everyone ignored Ted's joke, except for Marta Wainwright, who screwed up her face.

"My friends and I have been keeping a log. The first message was October 8th at 12:03 am. *The March 15th* one. Message number two—*3:33*—was October 13th at 5:30 p.m. Message three about the Memorial Arch—the one that sounded a little different—was right before Thanksgiving break, November 22nd. This last one—the first that is a whole sentence—came in at 11:15 p.m. last night. The voice was different on this one, too. Although, it sounded like the same person, just using a different voice."

"Did anyone else think it sounded like a fake British accent?" Wyatt asked.

Steven and Dylan found it hard not to look at each other.

"So, I'm keeping a spreadsheet about them now. See if there's any patterns or anything."

She's keeping a spreadsheet?! Steven marveled at how into it everyone was. *CSI: HS*! Why wasn't there a high school CSI show yet?

"It's the Darling Energy thing that's got me confused," Molly went on.

"Is it a band?" Wyatt asked.

"It sounds like a band," Molly agreed. "It would make sense that a band 'gathered a throng.'"

"Or it's a person," Dylan suggested. Steven looked at her. What was she doing? Let it play out.

"True. It could be a person," Molly thought out loud. She made a note on her phone.

The suppositions went on for another ten minutes. Mr. Ryerson eventually lost interest and went back to his book—a biography of Ronald Reagan.

The bell rang. Before Steven left he repeated his question to Mr. Ryerson: "What was your dream about, Mr. Ryerson?" Mr. Ryerson marked his place on the page with his finger and looked up at Steven.

"It was about my father." He went back to his book. Steven nodded to himself. It seemed impossible to imagine Mr. Ryerson having a father, Steven thought. The thought necessitated imagining Mr. Ryerson as a boy, and that picture couldn't be conjured. Not that it was easy to conjure his own father these days.

By the door, Dylan motioned for him to walk with her to her next class. "Have a great day, Mr. Ryerson," Steven said.

***

Trevor bought two tracksuits at The Sports Authority. He'd never owned one before. He had always jogged in some mismatched combination of sweatpants and T-shirts. These new suits—one in blue, one in black—had white piping down the sleeves and legs. They were made of a lightweight material that swished together in a calming pattern with each stride. It sounded like a gentle shushing, and Trevor's breath fell into synchrony with it.

He had called out sick. It was understandable, given how yesterday had turned out. He wasn't sure it was his place to visit the hospital to see how Royce was. It had been less than twenty-four hours and his parents would need time to process everything, to find a way to help their son. The following morning, it took Elizabeth to state an obvious point: Trevor was a hero. He had saved that boy's life. Trevor did not think of that way.

"It wasn't a house fire," he said.

"What does that matter?"

"The boy was trying to kill himself."

"And you saved him." Trevor nodded. "Isn't that heroic? Not everybody would have done what you did. You might have hurt yourself."

Trevor's rescue didn't seem heroic. Maybe he would have felt more if there hadn't been a small part of his brain that thought it understood what Royce was feeling. Your sense of heroism diminished by your empathy with the particular distress. Obviously, there would be no newspaper headline.

It took great effort for Elizabeth to get the whole story from him when he walked back home yesterday. She might not have noticed anything if he hadn't walked so slowly into the house, the smell of smoke on his clothes.

"The neighbor boy helped, too."

"He's a hero, too. Who are they? The Caulders' neighbors?"

"I have *no* idea." Trevor threw up his hands. He didn't know anybody in this neighborhood.

"Okay." It was too soon to hash this out with him, so Elizabeth let it drop.

Trevor had no plan, but it was the realization that he didn't really know anyone in his own neighborhood that inspired the tracksuits. He'd run around the neighborhood today—and maybe some of the surrounding ones—and see what he could see.

When he came downstairs that morning, Elizabeth raised her eyebrows at the sight of this blue tracksuit. An attached hood swung from his jacket as he came down the steps. They kissed as she opened the front door to go to work.

She grabbed the jacket hood. "You even have a cape." She smiled at him. He managed a smiled back. They kissed again.

***

Dylan promised Steven the first ride in her car. She didn't mention the honor had actually gone to Daphne when Dylan drove her sister to the train station the afternoon before. She waited by the lobby exit and stared at the small fleet of yellow school buses. She wasn't beholden to their schedules any more. Dylan could come and go as she liked. Driving still made her nervous, but she couldn't understand why she had waited so long to get her license.

Nicole hobbled by on her crutches. "Hi, Dylan," she said cheerily. The image was a far cry from the last time she saw Nicole. Dylan had given up her prejudice against freshman—for Nicole, at least. Once you spend

Halloween night at the ER together, once you witness someone in agonizing pain, you're linked for life, she reasoned.

"Hey, Nicole. How's the leg?"

"It's fine. It's the crutches that hurt."

"See you later."

Two senior boys held the door for Nicole as she hopped out. She watched as Nicole tried to negotiate around a circle of kids who were standing by the flagpole. She saw Nicole turn around and look back at the commotion. The senior boys motioned her over to the circle. Everyone was looking at the ground. Dylan texted Steven again.

Dylan: Let's go!

Steven: Be right there.

Now that she had her own car, should she pick up Norman the next time they went out? If they went out. They texted only a few times over Thanksgiving break. Norman was visiting family upstate and said he was out of cell range for most of it. She couldn't come up with a good reason, but she doubted that was completely true. It was only the past weekend that they had last gone out: he picked her up and took her back to his house where they watched *Casablanca* with his dad. (Lester stayed up in his room the whole night.) The night ended with some familiar fumbling in his car. She'd give him one more chance. It's not that she wanted to put out or anything, but if he wasn't going to tell her what he wanted out of their relationship—physically or verbally—she'd needed to rethink things.

When she looked at photos of Norman online—Snapchat, Instagram, whatever—she found herself very attracted to him. He was definitely handsome. In some of the photos, he was hot. There was one where Norman was toweling off his hair by a pool and laughing—just a candid shot. There were a few girls in bathing suits in the background. One photobombed the shot, as she held onto Norman's shoulder. The photo was taken July 3rd, 2014, more than three years ago now. She didn't know who the girls were, but she envied how close they seemed to him, how natural they all looked. Sometimes she would even hate them. When she looked at *that* Norman, she wanted to climb in his car in the summer and go find a swimming hole. She imagined the ride back, wet, sitting on a towel in the passenger's seat, blasting the radio, her hand porpoising the air outside the window.

In person, he was so nice and kind that it confused her why that wasn't enough. They never argued over anything, and for some reason, this annoyed her. He was just so *agreeable*. Maybe that would be fine if he just reached for her a little more. He never came up behind her and grabbed her shoulders and made her guess who it was. She knew that was a stupid teen movie cliché, but the idea that he would be seeking her, looking for her, didn't seem like too much to ask.

While she didn't have to be on the bus's schedule anymore, she was still waiting for Steven. The circle had grown around the flagpole. Kids had their phones out, taking photos of the ground. Dylan decided she had to have a look for herself.

She went out and looked over Nicole's shoulder. "What is it?" Nicole hopped to her left to let Dylan in.

In pink sidewalk chalk, someone had written "Darling Energy" in big bubble letters. In a neon blue underneath, it read "gathered the throng."

Ha, she thought. Ha!

The circle was hardly a *throng*, but you have to start somewhere.

Steven came up behind her, grabbed her shoulders and looked on the scene. She widened her eyes at him. "You?" she whispered and gestured at the writing. No, his expression told her.

They walked into the parking lot. "That is hysterical," Steven said.

"That was pretty quick."

"It's become graffiti, already."

The fact that Dylan was about to drive Steven around in her car should have been the big story, but the story they were writing together stole the rest of the car conversation.

"It's on Snapchat." Steven fiddled with his phone. "And Instagram, too." He laughed. "Someone made 'Darling Energy' a hashtag. It has three posts."

Dylan turned out of the parking lot.

"Where we going, Darling Energy?"

"Let's go for a drive."

***

Trevor managed a few waves to passing cars, neighbors whose faces he recognized. He kept jogging but turned to see which driveways they turned into. Gray Explorer, 487 Orchard. Black Jeep Patriot, 402. White Tahoe—the squirrel killer?—356. He repeated the details to himself.

Outside of 304, he watched a girl ride her bike in a circle in her driveway. It was a slow, mindless loop. She leaned into her orbit, going just fast enough to keep from stopping. She stared at a fixed point where a small mound of melting snow remained.

The circle took her as far as the mailbox on one side. Trevor slowed to a stop and caught his breath.

"Hi, there," he said. The girl, who was maybe twelve, looked over at Trevor before the loop took her back toward the house. She had black hair that spilled out onto a gray hoodie. Trevor looked over the house. It looked like his own, like the Caulder house. The garage door was open.

The girl, on the next loop, noticing Trevor still standing there, stopped pedaling and removed a pair of white earbuds. "I'm sorry," she said. "I didn't hear you."

"Oh, nothing. I just said hello." Her hoodie read Agnes Irwin—the girls' private school down the road. The girl resumed pedaling and maneuvered into the garage. A horn blew from behind Trevor. Another white Tahoe. It was trying to pull into the driveway, but Trevor was standing in the way. He recognized the face inside. It was the woman who had struck the squirrel yesterday. She rolled down her window.

"Can I help you?" It only then occurred to Trevor how sketchy the scene must have looked to her: middle-aged, mustached man in shiny tracksuit talking to a twelve-year-old girl on a bike.

"I'm sorry, no. I just stopped for a second to catch my breath. How are you?"

"I'm fine." But her face did not look fine.

"I live down the street. 503." The mother didn't reply.

"Your daughter goes to Agnes Irwin?"

She gave him the queerest look. "What are you doing?"

"Just out for a jog. Catching my breath. We saw each other yesterday. The squirrel?"

The woman reached for her purse and took out her phone, holding it in the frame of her car window. "I'm taking your picture," she said and pulled the rest of the way into her driveway.

Trevor called out to the car. He could see the girl look out from behind a door in the garage. The mother got out and slammed her door. She gave one quick, disgusted look back at Trevor.

"I'm a teacher." He thought this explanation might help. "I live down the road. I didn't mean to—" But mother and daughter were already inside. He stared back at the house and listened to its silence. Then he an away.

He crossed over Warren Avenue and into another neighborhood. This one had a name: The Cobblestones at Thornbury. Who came up with these names? What does that even mean? Was the name likely to increase property values? Was it how you gave directions to friends who wanted to visit?

"Just look for the cobblestones."

"What cobblestones?"

"The Cobblestones at Thornbury, of course."

Where even were the cobblestones? It was all just black pavement and blond sidewalks. In all the years he'd lived in the area, he may have only turned down this road twice. Trevor was pretty sure one time was for a birthday party—a classmate of Benjamin's. The Goodwins was the name that popped into his head.

He remembered picking Benjamin up and how excited he was about a gift bag they'd given each kid. Benjamin sat in the back seat and inventoried the haul for his dad. He held each item up so Trevor could see them in the rearview mirror. Was one of them a joy buzzer? The memory seemed right in his head, but it might have been his own childhood he was remembering. He used to love gag gifts. Maybe it was a whoopee cushion? It bothered him for a second to think that he couldn't remember. He didn't remember finding anything like that among Benjamin's things.

He remembered parts of the conversation on the ride home, though. It was something like:

"Why did they give us gifts if it wasn't our birthday?"

"I don't know. I guess, it's just a nice thing to do." He remembered smiling back at Benjamin in the mirror. And he remembered Benjamin smiling back.

"It *is* nice," Benjamin agreed.

Trevor was glad his memory wasn't completely failing him. He was right about the name, too. It read "Goodwin" on one of the mailboxes halfway up the street. There were two guys struggling to lift a heavy box into the back of a truck. It looked like a dad and his son. Trevor watched their progress as he jogged by, but turned to face the street when he noticed they had spotted him. He would not get into another failure of a conversation.

He'd almost made it past the driveway. "Trevor??" The call was from the father, presumably Mr. Goodwin.

Trevor slowed and tried to smile. He pretended he was more out of breath than he was. He squinted at the man as he and his son lowered the box to the driveway and walked out to the road.

"Trevor, right?" Mr. Goodwin said. "It's Bob Goodwin."

Bob, right. "Bob! How are you?"

"You remember Andy, right?"

He didn't. Not really. "Andy, sure! How are you?"

They both answered: "Good." Andy went to Great Valley. He recognized the face a little.

"Getting a little jogging in?"

"Yeah. Just trying to run off Thanksgiving?"

"Yeah." They all just stared at each other for a beat.

"So how are things?" Bob Goodwin asked. He had that apologetic look on his face that people get when they haven't seen him or Elizabeth since Benjamin died. He assumed that now, ten years later, there wouldn't be these interactions, but he was routinely wrong.

"They're good." Trevor would help him out. "How's your school year, Andy?"

"Good."

"Great." He was always upgrading responses during small talk. "Who do you have for English?"

"Mr. Whitermore."

"Oh, good. He's a good teacher," Trevor said to Andy. "He's a good kid," he said to Bob.

"Yeah, he looks like a kid. Met him at back-to-school night. Did we have teachers that looked that young?"

"I'm sure we did."

Bob looked back at the box by the truck. "Any chance we could use you to lift this box into the truck?"

"Sure," Trevor said. This was more like it. Some friendly neighborhood interactions—that was what he was looking for. People just helping out people. It wasn't a community barn raising, but it would do.

"What's in the box?"

"It's leftover tile for a bathroom project. I made the mistake of thinking it would be easier to transport if I put all the smaller boxes into one large one, but clearly that was a stupid decision, and I've already sealed it shut. I'll let the store deal with it. I just want to take it back and get a refund for what we didn't use."

Trevor bent at his knees and grabbed one end of the box. Mr. Goodwin and Andy grabbed the other side.

"It's heavy, so let's do it together," Bob said. He counted: "1, 2, 3—"

Trevor lifted his end on the 3. Bob and Andy didn't.

"Wait!" Bob yelled. But it was too late. In their panic Bob and Andy tried to balance their end, but the box had already slipped from their fingers. They both jumped out of the way of all that weight, and the box thudded on the ground and popped open, tearing the packing tape. Some loose tiles spilled out and broke against the pavement.

"Shit!" Bob yelled. "You okay?" he asked his son. Andy grabbed his hand. He'd jammed it.

"It's fine." Andy practiced opening and closing his fingers.

Trevor grew red. "I'm so sorry. I lifted on 3. I thought—"

Bob surveyed the damage. "It's okay. That was my fault. I should have specified. I was going to do "3" and *then* lift. But I forgot to tell you that. Damn. That's my fault."

"I'm really sorry."

"Don't worry about it. It's not a big deal. My fault." The tile was a geometric dark green. It broke off like little emeralds. Trevor started to pick up the pieces.

"Oh, don't bother. I'll just sweep that up. Andy, why don't you go grab the broom out of the garage." Trevor got down on the ground and reached under the truck for some of the larger shattered pieces.

"Don't do that. I'll move the truck. Not a big deal. I mean, the bathroom's done already. It's just the leftovers."

"I'm really sorry," Trevor tried one more time.

"Where is it?" Andy couldn't find the broom.

"I'll help." He turned to the garage. "Well, let's get together soon or something," Bob said. "I don't want to keep you from your jog. Next time I won't put you to work." Bob meant it as a joke, but Trevor felt like a failure. For the first time since he left his house, he saw himself in the tracksuit. What a ridiculous outfit, he thought.

"It was good to see you. Tell your wife we say hello," Bob offered as Trevor walked back to the road.

"You too," Trevor said. He ran up the street and didn't look back.

***

Dylan and Steven decided on a bookstore. There was still a small, privately owned bookstore in their town run by a young English couple, the Cartwrights. It was called Bookend, and the sign hanging outside had been designed by Dylan's mother. It was a simple serifed font, but the vertical line of the capital *B* jutted out into an ornate-looking bookend, paired with another off the side of the lowercase *d*.

Lionel Cartwright greeted them as they walked in. He had a small moustache, and Dylan and Steven had fun with the idea that he was Mr. Drake's younger brother. Dylan thought there must be some correlation between books and mustaches.

"Was that you parking that car?" he asked.

"I just got my license."

"Was this your first stop?"

"It was. Besides school."

Mrs. Cartwright—Helen—was older than her husband. Her long pony-tailed hair was already graying. She wore an off-white cardigan sweater and had several chunky bracelets that rattled around her wrists.

"I've got something for you," she said to Steven as she walked up to the counter. "Come with me." Dylan used to joke that Mrs. Cartwright had a thing for Steven. Steven loved the attention.

"I'd follow you anywhere," he said. Helen Cartwright laughed and walked Steven back into the nonfiction section. Mr. Cartwright rolled his eyes.

"They're a cute couple," he said. "How's your mother?"

"She's good."

"What's she working on?"

Mr. Cartwright meant what new art piece was she working on. Besides the sign out front, Bookend had hung and sold two of her mother's smaller dog portraits. Dylan was never sure what her mother was working on because she worked so quickly. She never talked about it, but two weeks would go by and three paintings would be finished. They would be wrapped in brown paper and twine, delivered to the customer as soon as they dried.

"I don't really know."

"Well, tell her I still want to hire her to paint Deacon." Deacon was the Cartwright's springer spaniel who liked to sleep in the self-help section. He raised his head when he heard his name.

"I will." Deacon would make a fine subject for a portrait. His face was so sad, so serious. His eyes and his ears drooped as if they'd slide off his face.

"Can I help you find anything today?"

"No. Just looking."

"Well, let me know if I can help."

On the way over in the car, Dylan and Steven had decided they would let the rows of books inspire their next message. They'd look for something for Darling Energy to do, or an occasion for her gathering. They'd let the book spines and first pages give them direction. She passed by the nonfiction, the history, and travel sections, and made sure to avoid, at all costs, the education section, filled with big dumb study guides for the SAT and AP subject area tests, along with Barron's guide to colleges and universities. Every cover featured horrible bold fonts and ridiculous stock photography of smiling students gathered around a desk. She wanted to punch them—the books, the models, the College Board itself.

Dylan tried to put off thinking about her future—colleges, majors, careers. She liked a lot of things a little bit, and the idea she'd be making a decision that would affect the rest of her life, and would need to make that decision in the next year, made her want to take a nap. Many things made Dylan want to nap. She'd always thought that if they wanted to make an authentic, realistic teen movie, it would need to have entire scenes where the characters did nothing but nap. Or at least a montage of napping.

Dylan was a terrific napper, and there was no decision too great that she couldn't fall asleep to. The only future planning she let herself do dealt with the apartment she would get in college and how she would decorate it. She'd fallen in love with Daphne's apartment in Providence. She and her roommate Emily's place was filled with interesting artwork and colorful, modern lamps. The walls were painted a "Tibetan Red," as Daphne described it. It was warm and cozy. It was sexy, somehow. It was hard to imagine how her life now could lead to a scene like that.

At school she was surrounded by many ambitious young students, peers whose sole purpose, it seemed, was to create a college résumé so profound it would embarrass an admission counselor to reject them. They grubbed for the best grades—arguing over quiz points, negotiating extensions, monitoring their grade book like a stock portfolio. They joined every club regardless of interest. Dylan's friend Melanie joined the Young Republicans, the Young Democrats, and the Libertarian club because she thought it would show range. They played as many sports as they could fit into their schedules. If they couldn't manage a sport that required actual coordination, they would join track and cross-country—they took quickly to the dull ache of running. If they couldn't sing, they'd mouth the words in the back row of Concert Choir. If they couldn't play an instrument, they would learn to twirl a flag. Dylan's friend Mike who played viola since he was six had learned to fake-play his way through high school, hovering his bow over the strings, replacing his sheet music with Physics notes.

"Why don't you just quit?" she used to ask him.

"The music helps me concentrate."

They all knew, however, that their résumés weren't complete without a healthy dose of service. So they joined those organizations, too. Key Club, Lion's Club, American Red Cross, Interact, Youth Service America, Kiwanis, Leader Corps, Peer Mediators, Habitat for Humanity, the Food Bank, Project Linus, UNICEF, Best Buddies, Meals on Wheels. If the sign-up tally for these organizations were any indication, the high school contingent would cure cleft palates, prostate cancer, and homelessness by prom.

Dylan supposed it wasn't so bad to have selfish reasons for good deeds, but all of this manic résumé-padding would often shut her down completely. It seemed impossible to keep up with the Joneses—or anyone from Abbott to Zhang. Dylan was aware enough to understand that whatever skepticism lay behind fellow students' enthusiasm for these interests and good works, she was no better.

She ran track, sang in the choir, did the makeup and costumes for the play and musical, and volunteered for SADD and Key Club—and she only enjoyed two of those things. Her parents had made her take two SAT prep classes, and she had been known, from time to time, to interrogate a set of multiple choice answers on a vocabulary quiz. Why would they ask for the *best* answer? Shouldn't there just be one *correct* answer?

Some kids took it way too far and adopted a cutthroat attitude. They would openly challenge teachers; they would enlist the help of their parents to question administrative decisions; they would study the system, looking for the right combination of courses and teachers to ensure their success. They brought all the science and math of advanced metrics to the classroom.

Dylan didn't have that competitive gene—or was it learned behavior? She didn't need to have the last word. She didn't need to be first in line. When a plane deboarded, she would wait in her seat until everyone else had grabbed their carry-ons and walked off. She was patient, and she hoped that patience would pay off someday. She wasn't quite sure how to make patience a marketable virtue, or if it qualified as a Darling Energy superpower.

That's why she loved the bookstore so much. All those stories, all of those voices and ideas cohabiting in the same room, the same shelves—but quietly, modestly. Some books were bigger or glossier than others and some were best sellers, but there was no jostling in the room. There was equality. There was order and community. Maybe the authors and publishers had different motivations, but for the consumer it was a haven.

And so, of all the futures and occupations that awaited Dylan, the only one she could imagine enjoying at this point in her life was to own and run her own bookstore.

"You don't want to do that," Mr. Cartwright told her last year.

"Why not?"

"The best you can hope for is to break even."

"What's wrong with breaking even?"

Mr. Cartwright considered that. "Well, there's not many independent booksellers left. People buy their books online. They don't want to leave their house."

"*I* want to leave my house."

"That's different."

"Why?"

"Because you're still young."

"Old people don't want to leave their house?"

"Not really."

"That's sad."

"Yes, I guess it is," he agreed.

Dylan found Steven and Mrs. Cartwright huddled in a tiny reference section. "I love it," he told her.

"I thought you would," she said. "This one's good."

Mrs. Cartwright was holding open a book titled *Lost in Translation: An Illustrated Compendium of Untranslatable Words from around the World.*

Steven sounded out the word: "Tsundoku: *leaving a book unread after buying it, typically piled up together with other unread books.* Yes. That's my life."

Dylan reached over his shoulder and turned a page. "This one is mine," she said. "Iktsuarpok: *the feeling of anticipation that leads you to keep looking outside to see if anyone is coming.*"

"No, you're this one. Luftmensch: *refers to someone who is a bit of a dreamer and literally means 'air person.'*"

"That's not nice," Mrs. Cartwright chided Steven.

"I meant it as a compliment."

"Let me see that." Dylan took the book, and Steven and Mrs. Cartwright moved back to the front of the store.

Dylan thought it was a lovely book. The illustrations were pretty and simple. Another Drake vocabulary word sprung into her head: *winsome.* There were words for all sorts of things she recognized: the time you spend after lunch or dinner talking to the people you shared the meal with (*sobremesa*); the road-like reflection of the moon in the water (*mangata*); even a word for the time needed to eat a banana (*pisan zapra*).

It was a relief to know that there was a book for ideas that couldn't be translated neatly, that even the unknowable and indescribable could be known and described if you were willing to try, that even those observations and sentiments you were sure were yours alone were actually shared by other people across the world.

She lingered on the page for *mamihlapinatapai*. It came from the Yaghan language of Chile, and it referred to "a silent acknowledgment and understanding between two people, who are both wishing or thinking the same thing (and are both unwilling to initiate)." Isn't that what love is, she wondered—a silent and wished for feeling between two people? She wasn't sure she had ever experienced *mamihlapinatapai*. What if you thought you were experiencing *mamihlapinatapai*, but you were mistaken? The silence in that case wasn't understanding; it only moved in one direction. Was there a word for the desire to experience *mamihlapinatapai*? If so, she lived it all the time. Maybe everyone did, she thought—until she realized that was something Steven would say: "Everyone feels that."

She took a photo of the page to remember. She didn't have any money. She'd come back for the book some other time. Looking out the window, she noticed a low and dark cloud pass over the sun.

***

Maybe the problem, Trevor thought, was he kept running through residential areas. Maybe if he ran into town—just another mile down the road—he'd have better luck. He could pick up some groceries or buy some cut flowers. Trevor liked having errands to do. He liked making checklists and crossing things off. It was getting darker earlier though, and he had no plan for how to get those things back home, but those were details. Maybe he'd call Elizabeth and she could pick him up and they could go out to dinner, even though it was only Monday.

She'd say, "What about the groceries? We can't leave them in the car."

And he'd say, "They'll be fine."

The way he imagined it, he would grab her hand, look in her the eyes, and she'd smile. In reality, he knew her practicality would win out, and she'd grab the groceries from him and suggest they go out to eat later in the week. It seemed sad to Trevor that his idea of throwing fate to the wind, of giving into a romantic gesture, was letting groceries sit inside the car for a while.

The borough of Malvern where Trevor's run had taken him ran along the railroad tracks. The town couldn't make up its mind what it wanted to be. Twenty years ago, it was just a small collection of shops: an Italian restaurant, a hardware store, a funeral home, an electronics repair shop, a tailor and a cobbler, a beverage store, and a bank. After the collapse in 2008, it was briefly a ghost town, with more closed businesses than open ones. The restaurant managed, the beer store stayed, and business for the funeral home was never better. Somehow the tailor and cobbler survived, too. Those two shops, on the opposite side of the tracks from where Trevor was running, seemed impervious to any outside influences. He guessed the tradesmen owned their buildings, and whether or not anyone was getting their shoes cobbled was beside the point. The point was you show up to work.

Which is exactly what Trevor wasn't doing. He wondered what the tailor, mid-stitch, would think if he saw Trevor running past his window at 3:30 p.m. on a weekday. It occasionally occurred to him how odd it was to have a job where you could call in for a substitute when you didn't feel well or had planned a trip. What other jobs could possibly allow that? He was relieved there were no substitute cops, no substitute doctors, and no substitute pilots. He could imagine what the tailor would say about the tracksuit.

"I remember when men used to dress well. When they didn't run around the town in glorified, polyester pajamas."

"You're right," he'd tell him.

"Of course, I'm right. Men used to have class. They wore hats and tipped them at the ladies on the street."

"I'm just trying to get in shape. You've got to admit our health is better. We live longer these days." Trevor thought this might trip him up.

"Live longer??" he imagined the tailor saying. "How about just living?? What about working? What's wrong with that?"

"I do work. I'm a teacher."

"That's not working. Women teach." The tailor in his head was a chauvinist. "Done by three o'clock. And your summers off!"

A Walk signal blinked, and the tailor's voice quieted in Trevor's head.

God, that's what they always say: "Must be nice to have your summers off." Trevor had been in the game too long to let that one bother him. He was used to people thinking they knew what a teacher's job was. Most people feel their experience as a student gave them a good insight into what it's like to be a teacher. Trevor did not pretend to know what it was like to be a doctor despite visiting several of them over the past year. He'd been so often to the mechanic recently he knew the names of his kids and where they were going to college, but the inside of a car was still a mystery to him. He could understand how it had gotten this way. It makes sense: you spend fifteen to twenty-plus years of your life in a classroom watching some old man or lady prattle on about something or other. You think to yourself: how hard could it be?

The disregard for teachers in the United States had a long history. Sure, everyone will tell you a story about a favorite teacher who inspired or helped them, but then they'll complain about the summers and the "Cadillac"-pension plans and the favorable insurance rates and the tenure and the union bargaining. Teachers become an odd target for conservative anger and frustration when things are going badly. A life of public service didn't always beget a life of public appreciation. It brought public scrutiny instead of public interest. Trevor worked in a district that had a great number of retired households, folks who had already sent their kids to school and resented having to still pay school taxes. He couldn't understand how they missed the point—that the schools were shaping kids who would one day build their decks, install their hot tubs, service their cars, extinguish their fires, pilot their jets, teach their grandchildren, represent their state, defend their rights, rehab their limbs, discover their cures, manage their portfolios, write their novels, serve their country, prepare their food, wipe their ass, and treat their impotence.

Trevor knew education couldn't take sole credit for society's accomplishments, but a successful education could—at the very least, and perhaps most importantly—help increase the chances that folks weren't bigoted, selfish, small-minded bores, but tolerant, empathetic, curious citizens. That wasn't an argument for the Humanities; it was an argument for humanity.

"What do you think of that, Mr. Tailor?"

Unmoved, the tailor continued his alterations under a bright light. Trevor ran past the train station and observed the different ways people waited. The train could take him right into the city. It was less than an hour, but Trevor didn't make the trip often enough.

He passed the Painted Plate, a store that invited its customers to paint their own plates. He knew it was unreasonable, but he hated this shop. He had never been inside but could see the poorly painted plates displayed on the shelves.

At first glance, it seemed like the kind of place that Trevor would want to support. Elizabeth would bring this up any time he complained about it still being open.

"They're getting people painting. That's a good thing. You should like that."

"Yeah, but they're not. . ."

"They're not what?"

"They're not painting *well*."

"Who cares?"

The argument would always end there. It was a stupid one to have anyway, but passing the shop today, it emerged again.

It's like this, he thought:

The modern commercial world didn't seem to notice the death of arts and crafts, or the devaluing of the education and practice it took to master them.

You ever look down at your dinner plate and think, man, I wish I could paint some half-assed abstract blob on it? Stop wondering and paint your own plate! A store invites you to build your own frozen yogurt. You can pick your own toppings! You can concoct your own mix of flavors! In fact, serve yourself! We'll just stand here on our phones and ring you up. Hey, want to check out more quickly at the grocery store? Well, you'll enjoy our self-check-out lanes! You can use the bar-code scanner yourself! Even learn the UPC code for bananas! While you're at it, bag your own groceries! Did you ever wish you could build your own bear? Now you can! Pick the stuffing! Pick the accessories! Do you like music? Of course you do. Tell you what: tell me a song you like, I'll feed it into a computer, find its algorithm, and then recommend other songs that have its particular pleasure indices!

Businesses sold "experiences" because the world had forgotten how to have them on their own. If they could get you in their doors, they could let you personalize your experience, customize it to your preferences. It's not that Trevor hadn't benefited from this—he and Elizabeth enjoyed taking vacations that offered planned excursions. But the expertise of artisans and craftsman wasn't as valued anymore. Four art studios opened and closed in the Painted Plate's vicinity since it had opened. Rather than support the original artist, people valued the artificial, knowable commodity. Beyond that, Trevor worried about how much of his brain and taste he was outsourcing: his Spotify-suggested playlists, his GPS-reliant brain, his social media news suggestions. Trevor wanted to explore. He wanted to search for something, and he was embarrassed to find that he couldn't figure out what he was searching for.

He wondered if Royce felt that way. Were the drugs an attempt to control an empty or turbulent inside, to allow him to have a genuine "experience," or avoid one? Was it Vicodin from his parents' medicine cabinet, left over from some dental surgery? Was it an action that could have been prevented or avoided? If not, what influences would make a young person no older than seventeen try to kill himself? He had his parents. He had a nice home in a nice neighborhood. He went through a good school district, had access to a supportive community with sports and piano lessons and day camps. Could your biology betray you so hopelessly, so helplessly? Trevor wondered if this was happening to him. Were his insides changing on him—and was it beyond his control? Did Benjamin's death activate some slow fuse that would snake its way to his brain? Was everyone born with this fuse?

Some clouds rolled in, covering the sun, changing the unusually warm November day to a brisk one. The wind picked up and lifted Trevor's jacket hood up into the air.

In less than a minute, it was a downpour. Heavy raindrops pounded the streets and sidewalks. In the next minute, it erased what snow was left alongside the curbs. There would be no running home now. Trevor would have to wait out the storm and call Elizabeth. Standing under the awning outside the Bookend bookstore, Trevor reached into his tracksuit pants pocket for his phone. The screen was dark and unresponsive. He pushed the home and power keys a few times, but nothing.

"Shit."

He'd have to call Elizabeth from the bookstore. He was friendly with the proprietors, the Cartwrights. They'd let him use their phone.

He caught another glimpse of himself in the door window. His shiny tracksuit had grown shinier, and through the reflection, he saw Dylan Geringer and Steven Lilly standing and talking by the counter.

"Oh, come on," he whispered to himself.

His thinning dark brown hair was plastered against his forehead. He hadn't been able to figure out the fastener on the hood in time. If what the cat dragged in looked beaten, wet, and pathetic, then he looked like that.

He tried to open the door slowly, but there was no silencing its bell. In fact, it sounded twice when he tried to close it again. Dylan and Steven and the Cartwrights turned to face the door. He had to come in now.

The scene unfolded like two cross-generational American Gothics: Steven and Helen Cartwright side by side, and next to them Dylan and Lionel, two perplexed-looking odd couples. Deacon wagged his tail and greeted Trevor by the door.

"Oh, man," Mr. Cartwright started. "The rain got the best of you. You okay?"

Briefly—Trevor hoped so at least—he considered answering truthfully. Seeing two of his students out of the classroom, on a day he called out of school, made him feel like the tables and desks were turned.

He could just blurt out everything right now. "No, I am not okay. I feel like I'm trapped in my body and my brain wants to push out through my ears. I feel like I am entirely alone, even when I'm surrounded by my wife and family and friends. I feel like I've been phoning it in at work and that my students can tell. I miss my son and I want to rip out my heart and stomp on it to keep it from hurting. I want to run home in the rain because I deserve to. I have no idea how to get out this place I'm in. I'm old and I'm getting older. And I'm wearing a ridiculous tracksuit that makes me look like an overweight Russian gymnastics coach."

But all he managed was, "It's really raining out there." He was grateful Deacon allowed him to lean down and pet him.

"Hi, Mr. Drake!" Dylan and Steven spoke at the same time.

"Trevor, do you want a cup of tea?"

That sounded like a great idea and distraction. "No, that's okay. Really."

"I'll get you a cup of tea," Helen said anyway.

"I didn't know you were a runner, Mr. Drake," Steven said. Here he goes, thought Dylan.

"Oh, not much of one really." He had knelt down to give Deacon his full attention. He was leaving a small pool of water on the floor. "Not now at least." He turned his attention to Mr. Cartwright. "Say, Lionel, can I use your phone? Mine's died."

"Of course." Lionel grabbed the phone by the register and turned it around on the counter so it faced Trevor.

"We missed you today," Dylan said. It seemed like the right thing to say.

"That's nice. Yeah. I wasn't feeling well." He looked down at himself in the tracksuit. "I thought maybe I could run it off." He gave a short laugh.

"Mr. Ryerson was in," Dylan explained.

"Was he?" Trevor allowed himself to smile. "Did he sing for you?" Sometimes Jim would sing a French song if the students badgered him enough. The performance often ended up on Facebook and YouTube.

"Not this time. He was telling us about his dreams." He didn't really, but Steven thought it was a good line.

"Really?? Well. . ."

He grabbed the phone receiver and froze.

He didn't know the number. He didn't know his own wife's cell phone number. Mrs. Cartwright came back with the tea and placed it on the counter next to Trevor.

"It's Earl Grey," she explained. She noticed the puzzled look on Trevor's face. "What's wrong? Do you want something else? I might have chai."

"No, thank you. This is great. It's just. . ."

Mr. Cartwright guessed. "You don't know the phone number??"

"I don't." Dylan and Steven were still just standing there. Didn't they want to go browse for a while? Trevor tried to laugh. "I have it set on my phone. I think it starts 4-8-4, and then it's 3-6-something-something. I don't think I've ever known it."

Dylan tried to commiserate. "I don't know my mom's number either. No idea."

"No one knows anybody's numbers anymore," Steven philosophized. "Well, I know Dylan's. That's about it."

"I guess I'll call a cab, then."

"Dylan just got her license!" Dylan gave a quick panicked look at Steven.

Mr. Cartwright chimed in. "It's true. This was her first stop."

"We could drop you off," Steven suggested. The prospect of Mr. Drake as a passenger in her car was too much for Dylan, but she didn't want to appear rude. Maybe this is what drivers do. They give people rides when they need them. This wasn't in the driver's test.

"It's just down on Orchard, right?"

"Well, I think that's nice," Mrs. Cartwright said, as she smiled at Steven.

"I don't know. I don't want to put you out. I'll just call a cab."

"That's silly. Take your students up on the offer. You don't get a chance to help out your teacher every day." Trevor thought Mr. Cartwright was enjoying this a little too much.

"It's a mile down the road. No biggie," Steven said.

Dylan was going to beg off, but then she stopped herself. Why not? It would make a good story. He would do the same for them. She wasn't going to let this become Steven's success.

"It's not a big deal. I'd be happy to," she said.

Trevor considered Dylan's face. It was such a sweet face. She was doing that nodding thing like she did in class.

"You sure it's not a big deal?"

"It's not." Dylan looked at Steven. "Let's go."

They had to step over Deacon, who was blocking the door.

"Take your tea," Mrs. Cartwright had already put it in a to-go cup.

"That's very nice. Thank you."

As she pulled out of the parking lot, Dylan would have been more surprised when she made eye contact with Norman, who was looking out the window of Anthony's Pizza, but the afternoon had already turned into a recast Jane Austen novel, as she had just rescued Mr. Drake from the pouring rain. Dylan was Elizabeth, of course, but who exactly was Mr. Darcy, she wondered. Or was it *Sense and Sensibility* she was remembering? Norman's face looked green under the neon light. She looked into the rearview mirror where she found Steven grinning back at her. She shook her head in disbelief. She drove slowly, concentrating on the road. Dylan hadn't driven in the rain before, and Mr. Drake had to help her find the wipers.

It was a short trip. Along the way, Trevor was overcome with this simple act of generosity from his students. He made himself look out the window because if he'd looked over at Dylan driving the car, he would have cried.

They pulled into the Drakes' driveway and parked.

"Hope you feel better," Dylan said.

Trevor still felt like he was catching his breath. He smiled at Dylan and then turned to Steven. "I'm glad I ran into you two. Thanks." Something buzzed inside him. He couldn't tell if it was the slow fuse, or where it was headed. Water welled in his eyes. He hoped it looked like rainwater.

Steven noticed something off. Mr. Drake held the door handle but wasn't pulling it. "Are you okay?" he asked.

"I'm fine," he said, but he still wasn't opening the door.

"You have your keys?"

Trevor fumbled in his pockets with the other hand and retrieved them.

Dylan was struck with a thought. She reached into her wallet and pulled out a long thin white label, the one Mr. Drake had given her.

She tried to think of something appropriate to say, some reason she presented his gift back to him now, but nothing came out. Instead, all she did was hold the label out to him.

I'll be fine, it read.

Trevor looked at the label. He could manage only a brief glance at Dylan or he would completely lose it here, and he'd had enough embarrassment for the day.

He grabbed the label and opened the door in one motion. Steven and Dylan watched Mr. Drake open his front door and disappear behind it.

SIXTEEN

S teven's dad had only recently become a texter. Foster Lilly, who
could take apart and build computers with ease, had resisted the
smartphone for years.

It was the least interesting of his recent transformations, but it
opened a line of communication between them where there was usually
silence. He wasn't particularly good at it, Steven thought, but the trans-
missions were frequent, and he would take what he could get. Mr. Lilly
would sometimes text Steven by mistake. Steven would read through the
messages looking for any insight into his dad's new life.

"No—I okayed it with Ron."

"Skim milk?"

"I'm leaving now. Italian?"

"You can't be serious!!!!"

Four exclamation points?? Steven's father had never used an exclamation point in his life—verbally or otherwise. He assumed he was

receiving texts meant for Vernon, his dad's boyfriend. It felt wrong to say "boyfriend"—not for the question of sexuality, but because his father was forty-three, and forty-three-year-olds shouldn't have boyfriends and girl-friends. Steven should.

Vernon worked with his father. Steven had a picture of Vernon in his head from a holiday party years ago. He was a tall, black man in a light blue polo shirt. He wore glasses. He let Steven photocopy his hand on the Xerox machine. Steven was surprised he wasn't more interested in him. He wasn't obsessed with finding out what was so special about Vernon that made his father leave his mother. Maybe if he'd left his mother for another woman, it would have invited comparison, but as it was, Steven's questions were for his father alone.

He'd always admired his dad for his stoicism. As a child, it was a comfort to know how his dad would react to something. Even when his father's logic annoyed Steven's child brain—in explaining why they couldn't have something or go somewhere—its predictability was a safe place to grow up in.

Foster Lilly was always patient with his son. He weathered homework meltdowns and temper tantrums. He drove to any museum or attraction that Steven expressed an interest in, including multiple trips to Philadelphia's Mütter Museum of medical abnormalities, where Steven marveled at the world's largest colon and the woman with an eight-inch horn in her head. He would take Steven and his mother to Valley Forge Park to go hiking, despite having little interest in the outdoors. He would sit for hours with Steven at the dining room table putting together jigsaw puzzles. Mr. Lilly would work on the difficult sections—wide swaths of blue sky or sandy, patternless dunes—while Steven worked on the borders.

Being an only child, Steven had everything he needed. His father's patience and control, his mother's kindness and love. Sometimes he wished his father were more outwardly affectionate, but by middle school, he assumed that his father's affection *was* his silence. It occurred to him now that he'd been copying his father's personality for years. A family of three didn't allow for complicated politics, but he enjoyed those days when the two of them were out on the porch—his dad with the newspaper, he with a book—while his mother talked on the phone in the kitchen. They were bonding, weren't they?

Aloofness was coolness, Steven thought. The quiet observer became the novelist, the musician, the photographer—the philosopher. Or at least an engineer, like his dad. That was the narrative in all the biographical documentaries Steven had consumed. If Steven had any chance of becoming any of those things, he'd have to remove himself from the scene, like his dad did. He'd have to develop a healthy skepticism. He'd have to be patient like his dad and sit on the outskirts. Or that had been the plan. His dad's leaving forced Steven to observe himself, and that wasn't nearly as fun. It was too late by the time Steven had realized the outsider status would doom his reputation in school. By then, it was more likely that he would become the Unabomber than a philosopher.

Steven hadn't realized you could be an outsider to yourself. That his dad's long silences might be the result of emptiness and longing, instead of thoughtfulness, unbuoyed Steven. That seemed like another betrayal, Steven thought. Had they been sharing different silences all along? To consider that there were quieter and more unspoken thoughts in Foster Lilly's head, ones Steven would have never guessed at, unnerved him. If it were true of his father, it could be true of anyone. What else was he missing? Silence no longer seemed a comfort. It was loud, like the ring after an explosion. These new phone texts from his father were like intermittent chirps from a smoke detector's low battery. Just when he'd be settling into some comfortable routine or drifting into a nap, his phone would light up with the word "Dad."

It had been the spring of eighth grade when his father had driven out of the driveway for the last time. He'd forgotten a lot of it—not because it was a traumatic moment, but because he didn't realize it was a final exit. He understood it was serious, but his parents had communicated the news with a confusing sense of diplomacy, devoid of emotion. Every sentence began with "We just. . ."

"We just want you to know how much we love you."

"We just want you to know that everything will be fine."

"We just want you to know that we're still a family."

His parents took turns with these lines, the other one nodding his or her head. It was hard for Steven to comprehend the content and sentiment of these lines because he was too put off by their practiced and robotic recitations. His parents never had spoken as a unit before, and it was disconcerting to see them working together like this.

"We want you to know this has nothing to do with you," his mother said. The thought had never occurred to him until she mentioned it.

"Why would it have to do with me?"

Neither of them had a response to that.

"Well. . .it doesn't," his father said.

There was some conversation about where his father was going to be living—Phoenixville—and how he'd be close by if Steven ever needed him, and that they'd see each other often. They didn't use the word *visitations*, but Steven had watched enough bad television to know that was a thing. The scene unfolded only two years ago, but it was already a faint memory.

When he called it up now, only three slides remained in his head. The first one was of his father at the kitchen table writing a list of passwords onto the back of an envelope. It lingered with Steven because he had saved the scrap after his father left. It read like a piece of found poetry:

Wifi: Lilliputi@n65
Netflix: RearWindow1954
Bank: Moneyba!!
Apple ID: Pythagora$

The second slide was Foster Lilly holding onto the banister with one hand and holding a pair of New Balance sneakers with the other. His father was talking to him in the image but staring at the sneakers. Steven couldn't remember what he was saying. Strangely, despite Steven's actual position in the foyer, the view of the scene was from the top of the stairs.

The third slide was of the blinking hazard lights on his father's silver Camry as it pulled out of the driveway. Because their driveway met the street by an overgrown hedge, Mr. Lilly often put on his blinkers when he exited to signal any cars that might not see him. Steven watched the red flashing lights disappear behind the greenery.

So to recap: his father left behind his passwords, took his sneakers, and drove out of their lives like he was in a funeral procession.

In truth, his parents' promises and assurances did not come to pass. They had definitely stopped being a family. Everything was decidedly not fine. And Steven had only seen his father five times in two years. Foster Lilly bought a house in Phoenixville, just twenty minutes away, but was living with Vernon in North Carolina after Vernon had been transferred to Asheville. Foster came up for two Christmases, two June birthdays, and once when his PA home had been broken into.

So Steven was surprised to learn from his father's most recent text that he was in town and wanted to meet up after school. It was still a few weeks before his usual Christmas visit, and months before Steven's birthday.

"How about Anthony's?" Mr. Lilly texted.

"When?"

"Thursday?"

"Okay."

"Check if your mother can drop you off."

"I can get there."

"??"

"Dylan has her license."

"How's Dylan?"

"Good." Steven would stick with stoicness until he knew what the meeting was about.

Foster Lilly kept to a restricted and healthy diet. When he still lived with Lillian and Steven, one of his few "rules" was that there had to be at least one vegetable side dish on their dinner plates. He rarely snacked, except for the occasional apple or small bowl of raw almonds. He allowed himself a glass of wine or two on the weekend, but beyond that it was coffee, tea, or water. Knowing what he knew now, Steven realized his father must have been in a constant state of self-restraint.

Or had he been? It only recently occurred to Steven that his dad hadn't just had a sudden epiphany. Right? He hadn't woken up one day and thought: I don't love my wife anymore, I love a man, and his name is Vernon. Change like that didn't come by way of a flash bulb; it must have developed in a dark room for forty years. It wasn't out of the blue. It had been *in* the blue, the whole time maybe. Had his dad been having affairs with men the whole time? The prospect seemed more logical than a lifetime of abstinence.

Maybe it would have been easier to weather a deliberate hurt. If something specific had happened, like his mother had caught his father having an affair and then threw all of his clothes and golf clubs—not that Foster Lilly had any golf clubs—out onto the front yard and yelled, "And stay out!" Or if his mother had died suddenly, but painlessly, in her sleep. Steven didn't wish for either of these scenarios, of course, but he thought they would be easier to understand. They would have visuals. Biologically, he could imagine the emergency response to trauma, the adrenaline, the increase in heart rate and breathing. He'd watched with fascination how characters on TV shows would breathe into paper bags when they were experiencing tremendous anxiety. He tried it in a leftover lunch bag once a few weeks after his father had left for good, but it smelled like turkey and left him light-headed. If there had been a death, there would have been a funeral and a wake. There would have been formalities. He could have put on a suit and stood in a receiving line in the back of the church and accepted condolences. But there were no traditions for divorce, no planned moments for reflections, explanations, no eulogies.

If Steven's parents' divorce wasn't a deliberate, sudden act, then he wondered if it was inevitable. He preferred this thought to thinking the marriage had been a mistake, because then he would be a mistake. A more positive outlook on the events might interpret Foster's acceptance of his sexual identity as a victory. He was sure his father must have felt this way. It didn't make Steven feel any better, but maybe that was his source of solace, that his father's true love was inevitable, not his divorce. *That* was just collateral damage.

The only sign growing up that he didn't completely know his father was his frightening appetite for pizza. It was the one exception to his strict diet. Foster Lilly would order an extra pizza because he could routinely eat five or six slices on his own. Steven used to marvel at this feat.

"Where does it even go?" Steven's mother would ask. It was just something else he was good at hiding.

About once a month, they would order a Friday takeout pizza from Anthony's or the Pepper Mill. They'd eat it in the living room as they watched *Jeopardy*, the only show they watched as a family. The living room filled with questions: *What is the Suez Canal? Who is Buster Keaton? What is trickle-down economics? What is the Pythagorean theorem?* Alex Trebek's moustache was more condescending than Mr. Drake's, but Steven still enjoyed the premise of getting the answers first and supplying the questions. He wished everything else worked like that.

Steven couldn't remember ever eating inside Anthony's. When Dylan dropped him off, he waited for a moment on the sidewalk to watch his father, sitting at a booth, looking at his phone. She had asked if he wanted her to go in with him, but he declined. His father would drive him home. "I'll text you if I need you," he told Dylan. He glimpsed concern on Dylan's face—was it love?—when he closed the car door. He turned around hoping to see Dylan still idling at the curb, but she had already left.

His father turned and put his phone away when he heard the door open. He made a move to get up out of the booth, probably to hug Steven, but Steven slid in across from his dad before he got the chance.

"Hi."

"Hi."

"That was Dylan driving? When did she get her license?"

"Last week."

"When will you get yours?"

He wanted to say something hurtful like: *As soon as my dad who's left us teaches me how.* But he was angry at himself for being unable to be angry. He could only manage resentment.

"Maybe next month."

One complication of how he felt about his dad had to do with Steven's support of the LGBTQ community. It was the times, thought Steven. The *zeitgeist*, Mr. Drake would have instructed. He'd grown up at a moment in time—as gays won the right to marry, when sexuality and gender were more on the news than war and poverty. He was happy about these liberties. He argued for them, reposted his profile pics with a rainbow gradient after the Supreme Court ruling. He was a member of the Gay-Straight Alliance at school. His own past was marked by bullying about his suspected sexuality. He wasn't gay, but having been bullied as someone who was made him feel like he was, and here was his dad, finally liberated, able to be the person he really was inside. It was a narrative Steven was used to celebrating for people who weren't his dad.

"How's Vernon?"

"Vernon's good. How's your mother?"

"Good."

"Good." His father looked over at the pizza ovens. "You want to get a pizza?"

It would have been easy to say yes. That's why they were here and there's never any reason to turn down a pizza, but Steven didn't want to give his father this.

"I already ate." He hadn't already eaten. "Maybe a salad."

It wasn't the response Foster Lilly wanted, but he got up from the booth and placed their order. When he returned, he looked like he'd figured out how to proceed.

"So. . ."

"So."

"I'm selling the house in Phoenixville." His father said it like a pronouncement.

"Okay." He didn't live there much anyway.

"I'm moving to North Carolina."

"Aren't you there most of the year anyway?"

"Yeah." Steven wasn't sure where this was going.

"Is that it?"

"I'm getting married, too."

"Okay," Steven said. "Makes sense." Steven tried to be magnanimous. "That's good, I guess."

Steven's dad searched his son's eyes to check if he meant it. "It is good. Yes." He reached for the grated Parmesan shaker and shook it. "I want you to be there, of course. Just a small ceremony at Vernon's house."

Mr. Lilly paused again. Steven wasn't sure what he wanted to hear, so he settled on just nodding his head.

"Listen, Steven: I just want to tell you how much I love you. How sorry I am. How—"

"Foster!" A man behind the counter yelled his dad's name. Their order was up. Steven watched as his dad tried to think of a way to carry both the pizza, the salad, and the drinks back to the booth. He saved him from that negotiation and helped carry the order back to their seats.

Steven watched as his dad sprinkled healthy doses of Parmesan and hot pepper flakes onto the pie. "You sure you don't want any?" Steven looked down at his sad chef's salad—just a bunch of leaves with chopped ham and egg on top. Whose idea was this? What kind of chef had okayed chef salad?

"I'll take a slice." He and his dad devoured a slice before Mr. Lilly tried to regain the thread.

"I just want you to—" he began again.

"Can I ask you a question?" Steven interrupted.

"Sure." Foster Lilly grabbed his second slice.

"When did you know?"

"When did I know what?" He was talking with his mouth full.

"Anything. All of it. When did you know you were gay? Or when did you know you didn't love mom anymore? Or when did you realize you loved Vernon?"

He finished the second piece. "I love your mom."

"You know what I mean."

Mr. Lilly worked on a piece of crust. "Well, that's a lot of questions." He took a moment to finish the crust and pick up another slice. He held it in his hands for a while. "I grew up in a different time." He put the slice down but stared at it as he went on. "I don't know. I really did fall in love with your mother. When I tell you that I love her, I mean it. She was beautiful. She's still beautiful. And we've told you already about meeting, how we met in Astronomy—"

"And she was Lillian, and you were a Lilly."

"Right. And I know that seems like a silly point. Just a coincidence." He picked up slice three and took a few bites. "But it seemed more like fate at the time. It still seems like fate."

Steven enjoyed this story, though he'd never really heard it from his father before. It was always his mother who told it. His father would merely add color commentary—how it was December, what it was like inside the observatory, their professor's lisp.

"We hit it off immediately. We just sat in the dark, staring at the ceiling with its projected constellations, and talked. We were both painfully shy, but inside there, it was comfortable to just be yourself."

"But you weren't yourself."

"Well. . ." Steven's dad considered this point. "Maybe not completely. But as completely as I had ever felt before. I was myself for the first time, nearly. I don't think I knew what parts of me were still missing. But it didn't matter." He eyed a fourth slice. "We held hands and joked about getting married. 'You'd be Lillian Lilly!'"

His mother usually said that line. Out of his father's mouth, it sounded more like a piece of magic, like the two of them had cast a spell over one another. They looked for a sign, said an incantation, and then became husband and wife. Mix the petals of two lilies and the reflection of the stars. And now, here was Steven. He had more questions, but he realized that he was just listening to the answers for parts of himself. Was it chance, fate, magic, a mistake, the stars? Did it matter?

"What about Vernon?" Steven took another slice and continued to ignore his salad.

"How did you meet Vernon? I mean, just at work?"

"Yeah. You know. We met at work."

"No stars?"

"No stars."

"What then?"

"What then *what*?

"Well. . ." Steven wasn't sure what his question was. "How did you know?"

Foster Lilly was just about to down slice four. "I don't know. I just knew."

"There's not a story?"

"Yeah. There's a story. Not like—it's not like. . . I don't know, it's different."

Steven had trouble understanding anything without a story attached to make it whole. Were stories out of our control, unfolding of their own accord? Or were they man-made, simply forged out of a desire for truth? Or was it desire? Was that all you needed? Steven wasn't sure why this question was so important to him.

"I'm sorry you haven't met him."

"I've met him. He let me Xerox my hand."

"What?"

"He let me Xerox my hand. When you took me to work one day."

"Oh. I didn't realize." This threw Steven's dad. "Well, I want you to meet him again. Before the wedding. I was thinking you could come and visit over spring break. Take a look at some colleges. Lots of great schools in North Carolina. We can do a whole tour of the South, if you like. Have you thought a lot about it? About schools?"

"Yeah, I guess." Steven hadn't been thinking too much about all of that. Whenever anyone asked about college and the future, it made him want to run away or take a nap. He changed the topic.

"When are you getting married?"

"June. June 25th. You'll be out of school by then."

The chime above the door rang and in walked Mr. Lewis and Norman. Shit. Steven had no interest in any small talk right now.

"I wonder if I could ask you a favor," Foster said. Steven watched Norman and Mr. Lewis place an order at the counter. "Steven?"

"Yes?"

"I was going to ask your mother to do it, but maybe you could help me out instead. Especially if Dylan's got her license." Steven turned his attention back to his father. What was this?

Mr. Lilly took a key chain out of his pants pocket and held it out for Steven. "This is a set of keys for the house in Phoenixville. I've had the place staged by the realtor, but I still have a few of my own things there. Some art and some furniture. It's a terrible time to try to sell anything, in the winter. But I was hoping that maybe you could just check in on it from time to time. I've stopped the mail, but every once in a while, they still drop off catalogs and junk mail for some reason. And something has been knocking over the trash cans."

Norman and his dad sat at nearby table and waited for their order. Steven looked away when Norman looked over, but not before Mr. Lewis made eye contact.

"And then there's the snow. If we have any more snow, I'm going to need someone to shovel the sidewalk out front and the front steps and porch. I'd pay you, of course. I'm sure you could use some money, right?"

Steven could use some money. He liked the idea of taking care of a house and having it all to himself. "I can do that." He grabbed the keys.

"I'm not coming back for Christmas this year." Steven's dad delivered the line, thinking it might hurt Steven.

"I understand." Steven put the keys inside his coat pocket. He wasn't facing them, but he was sure the Lewises were coming over. He could sense Norman's dumb shadow.

"How about two hundred bucks a month? I'll give you a hundred today, and then I'll send you a check for the rest in January." Mr. Lilly took out a hundred-dollar bill and handed it to Steven.

"Sure, that's great." Steven took the bill. "Thanks." He tried to think of something to say that could make them up get up and leave, but it was too late.

"Hey, Steven." Norman's greeting wasn't very enthusiastic. Mr. Lewis must have dragged him over.

"Hey, Groucho!" Mr. Lewis slapped Steven on the shoulder. "Is this your dad?"

"Yes." Steven's dad stood. He reached out to shake their hands, but realized his hands were still greasy from the pizza. He grabbed a napkin instead.

"I'm Evan Lewis. Norman's dad."

"Foster. Foster Lilly. Nice to meet you."

"I'm Norman, sir." Listen to Norman with his 'sir,' thought Steven.

"How's the pizza?" Mr. Lewis asked.

"It's great. Love their pizza."

"Yeah. We live only a block away, so we're here a lot."

"Oh, yeah?"

"On Theronside. Next to the tailor's."

"Oh, sure."

Steven didn't have a clue how to get out of this conversation. Norman was staring around the room, pained. What was his problem? Steven found this more painful than Norman, surely. They hadn't talked much since Halloween. Steven had been trying to keep his distance when he saw Dylan with him.

"You guys close by?" Mr. Lewis asked.

Steven shot a look at his dad. Steven lived "close by," but his father lived five hundred miles away.

"Here and there."

The strangeness of that response struck Mr. Lewis, but it didn't slow him down. Was this his private investigator persona? "Okay," he said. "Steven helped us hand out Halloween candy this year." It was an odd detail to share with his dad, but perhaps Mr. Lewis could tell somehow that Mr. Lilly knew few details about Steven's life these days.

"Oh yeah?" Foster looked over at Steven. He furrowed his eyebrows. It didn't seem like something his son would do. But maybe he didn't know his son.

Steven caught the look and its intention. "What?"

"I thought you hated Halloween?"

"I don't *hate* it." Steven did hate Halloween, but Steven hated more when someone summed up his feelings and presented them in front of other people. Steven disappeared into another slice of pizza.

Mr. Lewis continued: "Well, I can't say I get it much. Everybody pretending to be someone else, wandering around the streets at night." Norman stared at Steven. Steven kept chewing, starting at his plate. He looked up long enough to see Lester Lewis standing right outside the door. Mr. Lewis noticed.

"Well, we better get going. The oldest out there is getting a little impatient."

They all turned to look at Lester. Steven had never seen him in the daylight before. Lester's hair was already thinning and his face was bright red from the cold. He was holding a plastic bag from the pharmacy. His stare back was somehow empty and focused at the same time. Steven thought Lester was looking directly at him.

"Evan!" someone yelled from the counter.

"That's us," Mr. Lewis said. "It was nice to see you, Steven. Good to meet you, Foster."

"Likewise."

"Nice to meet you, Mr. Lilly," Norman said. He walked to the counter, grabbed the pizza, and didn't look back at Steven. He and Mr. Lewis opened the door and followed Lester as he took off ahead of them. They crossed the street and made for the railroad overpass bridge.

"They seemed nice."

"You ready?" Steven answered. He was piling up the used napkins and paper plates onto the tray.

"Sure." Mr. Lilly had been holding onto a piece of crust for a while now. "So maybe you'll come down for spring break then?"

"Sure. Maybe. Yeah." He stood and slid the tray off the table. "I need to check."

"Of course. I mentioned it briefly to your mother, but you should check to make sure. It could be fun. And you could see Vernon's place. See our place." Steven was already walking across the restaurant to the trash can, but his dad kept talking as he followed him. "We can drive down to New Orleans even. You'd like it there." Now his dad was telling him things he'd like. He didn't like that either.

On the car ride home, Mr. Lilly rattled off a dozen colleges in North Carolina and the nearby states. He could tell that his father had googled some of the information or maybe had bought a book. He knew the relative sizes of the schools and programs they were known for. Dylan had told him that this was something parents do. They gather all this college info, save brochures, print articles off the computer, and leave them in piles on the kitchen counter. Their children, after all, are their biggest investment. All that time and money better pay off. His mother, thankfully, had other things on her mind and left no passive-aggressive piles on the kitchen counter for Steven. In fact, she had rarely, if ever, brought up the topic of college. Maybe that was more worrisome. But apparently, in Vernon's house in North Carolina, there was a pile his father was amassing.

"I'll text you later in the week," his father said as his dropped him off. Steven wanted to ask him to come in, but it felt wrong to invite his own father into a home he had bought but later abandoned. He wasn't sure his mother would want to see him anyway. They spoke on the phone, but Steven may have only seen them together three times since Foster Lilly left Lillian Lilly.

The shape of the Lilly driveway necessitated a three-point turn to turn around. It was already dark when Steven walked toward the front door. His breath made tiny clouds in the December air, illuminated by the warm window light from his mother's miniature Christmas village inside. Steven was already looking out his bedroom window to watch his father complete the turn, turn on his hazards, and disappear into déjà vu.

SEVENTEEN

Mr. Drake thought it would be good for the students to attempt a few different college essays junior year. "Then when you come back as a senior, you already have a few different ideas down on paper." Dylan looked over the prompts on the handout. It seemed to her that the Common App essay prompts were different versions of one another.

1. *Some students have a background, identity, interest, or talent that is so meaningful they believe their application would be incomplete without it. If this sounds like you, then please share you story.*

So *meaningful*? Well, no, as a matter of fact, she was 0 for 4 there. What was so interesting about her background? Not a lot. She knew better than to feel bad about this. An uninteresting background probably meant a safe one, one without a lot of struggle or adjustment.

Did she have an interest so meaningful she needed to share it? She enjoyed the costumes and makeup she did for the play and musical, but she couldn't imagine writing about it. It didn't move her. Maybe if she picked up her guitar once in a while she'd have something to say about that. She liked books and bookstores, English class, but is that something she could turn into a college essay?

A meaningful identity? Dylan wished. Darling Energy maybe did, but she wasn't her yet.

Talent? Nope.

2. *The lessons we take from failure can be fundamental to later success. Recount an incident or time when you experienced failure. How did it affect you, and what did you learn from the experience?*

Well, here was a rich prompt. The challenge with this one would be the 650-word limit. Dylan had failed plenty of times but wasn't sure what lessons she learned besides not enjoying it and trying to make sure it didn't happen again.

3. *Reflect on a time when you challenged a belief or idea. What prompted you to act? Would you make the same decision again?*

Interesting, Dylan thought. Her mind was always challenging beliefs. It was a constant argument in there. She was less certain about the "acting" part. The boldest thing she had done lately—and it wasn't really her—was partner with Steven on sending these phone messages. If she had to pick an idea she and Steven were challenging, it was boredom. Was that a righteous enough case? And anyway, it wasn't her idea. It was Steven's, wasn't it?

4. *Describe a problem you've solved or a problem you'd like to solve. It can be an intellectual challenge, a research query, an ethical dilemma—anything that is of personal importance, no matter the scale. Explain its significance to you and what steps you took or could be taken to identify a solution.*

The problem with this prompt, Dylan thought, was avoiding writing a rant. Dylan could think of dozens of queries and ethical dilemmas she'd like to answer. "No matter the scale"? Maybe she could write an essay that was entirely made up of questions. That was something Steven might say or do. She'd entertain the idea with him but would warn him not to really do it. She was always so cautious, and Steven knew that. Steven could talk her into things she wouldn't normally do, but they never took on a shape until she fought it some. If Steven didn't have her, he'd be talking to himself and that never led anywhere. So was she a catalyst? It sounded so passive, like she was just a spark—maybe not even a spark, a source of friction, the nailed down carpet to Steven's socks. God, that was a horrible metaphor, Dylan thought. She should spare her reader from any figurative language.

5. *Discuss an accomplishment or event, formal or informal, that marked your transition from childhood to adulthood within your culture, community, or family.*

That's awfully personal. What did they want here? Did they want her friend Michelle to write about her bat mitzvah at thirteen? Dylan was impressed that she memorized all that Hebrew, but she was far from an adult now. She still collected Pez dispensers and Pokémon cards. And what was an *informal* event? A birthday party? A swimming meet? Blasting through seven seasons of *Gilmore Girls* in one week was impressive, but Dylan didn't remember suddenly becoming an adult because of it. And what high school junior or senior was an adult already? She didn't think of Daphne as an adult either, and she was twenty-one. What was an adult? Thirty?

She underwent no cultural transition. She had little sense of her community, and didn't have any expectations of it providing a transition—not until she graduated and left it, at least. Her community was high school, and to this point, while it had filled her with knowledge, she felt no more an adult than when she started it. She was more jaded. Was that what it meant to be adult? If so, maybe she was becoming an adult. But there definitely hadn't been a single event. School had chipped away her youthful enthusiasm in small, imperceptible ways. Oh god, Dylan thought. I sound like a cliché: a spoiled, whiny kid. Essay writing always brought out this side of her. She wanted to write something she would be proud of, that was authentic, but she didn't know how to start. Hackneyed phrases and ideas weaseled their way into her sentences. She tried working with a thesaurus. Mr. Drake hated the word *amazing*. He thought it was overused, that it was too easy of a choice. She knew better than to use *awesome*, but Roget didn't offer a satisfactory fix. *Incredible* and *unbelievable* sounded just as dumb. She remembered one day last month when Mr. Drake said, "People who say it was 'beyond words' just don't have the words yet. If you have the right words, nothing's indescribable."

She wanted to impress Mr. Drake. He was kind and encouraging with his comments on her papers, but she never felt like she was giving him what he wanted. He always talked about *voice*, but Dylan had had trouble finding one. One she liked, at least.

She sat staring at the blinking cursor on her computer screen until Steven's text interrupted her. She hadn't heard from him since she dropped him off to see his dad.

Steven: Vernon Williams = Vermillion Swan

Dylan: Who's that? Your dad's boyfriend?

Steven: That's my dad's soon to be husband.

Dylan: What???

Steven: Yep.

Dylan: Wow.

Steven: Yep.

Dylan: Vermillion is a red, right?

Steven: Yes. My father left my mother for a red swan.

Dylan: How did it go?

Steven: We saw Norman and his dad.

Dylan: I know. He told me.

Already, Steven thought. He just got back ten minutes ago. That's annoying. The minute-long break in their texting indicated Steven's annoyance. She broke the visual silence of the thread.

Dylan: Just that he saw you with your dad. What else? Or was it just to make that announcement?

Steven waited one more minute just to punish Dylan a little.

Steven: And that he's moving permanently.

Dylan: To NC?

Steven: Yes. And to invite me to the wedding.

Dylan: When?

Steven: Spring break.

Dylan: This was fast. Wasn't it?

Steven: Want to be my date?

This seemed like a harmless promise. Dylan liked weddings. Maybe this formal event would mark her transition from childhood to adulthood, she joked to herself.

Dylan: I'll need a dress.

Steven: You've got four months.

Dylan: I'm in. What does your mom think?

Steven: Haven't talked to her yet. She was putting some final touches on the village and I didn't want to ruin the moment for her.

Dylan: What's new there?

Steven: I told you it was Western themed?

Dylan: Yeah.

Steven: She staged a train robbery. Santa is holding up a train full of stolen presents.

Dylan: Who stole them?

Steven: That's a little unclear. I think they're elves.

Dylan: Renegade Elves!

Steven: Exactly!

Dylan: Is there a saloon?

Steven: Of course!

Dylan: Are there little mugs of eggnog?

Steven: Whoa! You're good.

Dylan: Are there really??

Steven: Would my mother kid you?

Dylan: No.

Steven: What are you doing?

Dylan: Ugh. Trying to write a college essay.

Steven: Ew.

Dylan: What do you write about when nothing has ever happened to you?

Steven: Nothing?

Dylan: Exactly.

Steven: Make something up.

Dylan: That sounds like a lot of work.

Steven: Write about a monsoon that hit your service trip to Guatemala.

Dylan: That's good.

Steven: Or about how your amputation just made you realize all the things you could do with one arm.

Dylan: Keep going.

Steven: How you once saved a fireman from a tree.

Steven: How you started a library for local prisoners.

Steven: How you stole all the bullets from all the guns in your town, smelt them, and built a hospital for children.

Dylan would have liked reading any of those essays.

Dylan: Those are great. But I think I need something real.

Steven: Boring.

Dylan: Yes. That's the problem.

Steven: Well, why couldn't you just make something up? How would they know?

Dylan: They'd notice that I still had both of my arms when I showed up for orientation.

Steven: True.

Dylan: You should be allowed to make one up. That would show more creativity.

Steven: Speaking of which. . .

Dylan: Next message?

Steven: So "Darling Energy gathered the throng." Now she needs to tell them something.

Dylan: Yes, but what?

Steven: You tell me, Darling Energy.

Dylan: I need help, obviously. I can't write my own story, even.

Steven: Come up with three or four ideas and text me back later.

It was a better assignment than drafting this college essay.

Dylan: Okay.

Steven: What do you want to tell everybody?

Dylan: I'll think on it.

Steven: Oh, and my dad gave me the keys to the Phoenixville house.

Steven: I'll be its caretaker.

Dylan: Rager!

Steven: HA!

Steven wouldn't have a rager, but maybe he could plan something there. He and Dylan had plenty of work ahead of them.

Dylan: Talk tomorrow.
Steven: Goodnight.

A familiar sound rattled the water glass by her bed: another helicopter. She turned her phone over on her desk, closed her laptop cover, and perched on the window sill to watch. In December it was easier to see the scene unfold through the bare tree branches.

When it was over, she closed her eyes and listened for the rest of the story.

EIGHTEEN

Lester Lewis had been told from the age of six that he was gifted, special. His placement in an academically talented program began when a woman in a blue pin-striped pantsuit asked him to rearrange four red-and-white blocks into assigned geometric patterns. Lester completed them in record time. The evaluator's excitement over the accomplishment made him feel uncomfortable.

"My word. That was so fast, Lester. How did you do that??"

Lester didn't like the look on her face. Surprises bothered him, and surprised expressions were worse because he never understood where they came from.

"Honestly, that was remarkable." She clasped her hands in front of her body like she was going to say grace. Lester didn't like grace either. When he was ten, he refused to hold his younger brother Norman's hands at the table. The idea of prayer upset Lester, too.

"Who are you talking to?" he would ask his dad.

"God," his father answered.

"Where?"

"In heaven." His father pointed up in the air. Lester followed his finger and stared at the water stain on the ceiling.

It helped for a while when Mr. Lewis stopped beginning grace with the word *Lord*. It was easier for Lester if a character wasn't evoked. By the end of the year, it was easier still to just stop saying prayers altogether. Mr. Lewis didn't believe in them anyway. It was just something he did out of respect for his wife.

Esther Lewis died when Lester was six and Norman was three. Mr. Lewis was forty-four, but no one ever asked for that detail. The pancreatic cancer that took her was so swift that her husband and sons barely had time to prepare or say goodbye. It was exactly three months from diagnosis to death.

Norman kept close to his father, always holding onto his hand. It broke his father's heart when he looked in Norman's eyes. They were so wide and unblinking, so like his mother's. But the expression annoyed Lester.

"Stop staring!" Lester yelled at his brother.

"He's not staring," his father answered. "That's just how he looks."

"Look different."

Mr. Lewis found hope and solace with Norman. Wide-eyed Norman liked to stare out the window at the bird feeder. The image comforted Evan Lewis. The outside world fascinated his youngest son. He bought him a field guide on Northeastern birds. Norman couldn't read most of the words, but he enjoyed looking at the pictures and tracing their shape with his fingers. When he was old enough to venture outside by himself, that's where Norman spent his entire day. Next it was insects and spiders. Then trees and leaves.

Lester did not care for the outside world. He found no joy in the birds on the bird feeder or with the insects his brother trapped inside old mayonnaise jars. In fact, he hated those things. The only distraction that kept Lester engaged involved a screen. When he could barely hold objects, it was handheld travel games like Yahtzee and Hangman. It was his father's deactivated phones. It was the Gameboy, the Nintendo 64, even an old Atari his father had saved and hooked up for him. It was remote controls—to the TV, the air conditioner, and the stereo. It was the "family" computer that moved almost immediately from the kitchen to his bedroom after it arrived at the house. It was iPods and iTouches and briefly iPhones, before he realized he needed an Android so he could make it do what he wanted it to do. Whatever that was.

Mr. Lewis, like other parents, worried about "screen time," but it was the least of his worries. Despite his gifted status and easy way with shapes and numbers, Lester was, as his fourth grade teacher had referred to him, a "menace" at school. Mr. Lewis was offended by the term and told Ms. Hudson that, but after listening to her list of Steven's offenses, he knew he had a problem—and that he would need help. Lester had: poked, punched, kicked, and bit; he pushed kids out of their seats; he sneezed *at* people; he called his teacher "fat"; he smushed sandwiches; he carried matches and, on one occasion, flicked a lit one at a student. When he wasn't acting out, he would just fall asleep at his desk or in circle time. His teachers were sympathetic to this boy who had lost his mother so quickly and early on, but their patience was tested. It was becoming impossible to have him around other students.

At home, Lester was surly but never quite that disruptive. From time to time, he would push Norman down on the ground or yell at him to get away. But once Norman found the outdoors, and once Lester found computers, peace was restored to the house. It was an uneasy peace, thought Mr. Lewis, but it was livable. It was calm enough to exist.

Medication helped Lester, too. His fourth grade behavioral report was just the first of many Mr. Lewis would be offered about his son. The school counselors and psychologist chimed in. They recommended testing. Lester might be autistic, they suggested. While he exhibited behaviors that fell along the spectrum, they never diagnosed autism definitively. When they sought outside help, a psychologist diagnosed Lester with manic depression. He was only thirteen, younger than when most people are diagnosed. Mr. Lewis worried that his son would fight the diagnosis, but he was relieved when Lester accepted it, and even seemed interested in it. It took them a while to find the right drugs and the right dosage.

The science behind the medication interested Lester. He'd have detailed, medical conversations with his doctor as they added and subtracted milligrams. Realizing that there were numbers behind his emotions brought some relief to Lester. Once they found the right combination and dosage, Lester was able to sit at his desk at school and not want to scream and kick. By the time he got to high school, he had found other introverts like himself, other computer whizzes, who made school easier. Lester never referred to them as his friends, but they tolerated Lester's eccentricities and were impressed with his skills as a coder. He'd found a haven in front and behind the computer screen. Norman had the outdoors; Lester had the indoors. Mr. Lewis could finally relax a little. Until he couldn't.

By the tenth grade, Lester had filled his schedule with as many math classes and electives as were allowed. The school couldn't offer him much more in the field of mathematics, so three times a week, he took an Advanced Trigonometry class at nearby West Chester University. That summer he took a combination of courses (Health and Chinese, among them) to assure that his junior and senior years could be filled with as many independent studies as possible. Having completed the credits required for Foreign Language, Health, Math, and most electives, Lester was free to spend the majority of his school day studying with Mr. Dawson in his computer lab. Lester already knew as much math as his teacher, so the instruction that Mr. Dawson offered provided challenging questions or tasks.

Use the Linden Meyer system to draw the Heighway dragon curve.

Create a webpage that allows users to interact with fractal images.

Map an Xbox controller to open and close the hand of the school's underwater robot.

Lester liked this kind of instruction. It required no group work, no discussion, no handouts, no social intelligence at all—just crunching numbers, designing a plan, trial and error. Lester worked swiftly. About halfway through his junior year, Mr. Dawson was running out of new prompts and challenges, and instead invited Lester to design his own research query. Lester didn't like the idea at first. He preferred being told what to think about, but he also knew Mr. Dawson was likely at his limit, that Lester had advanced to a level of knowledge and competence that limited his teacher's ability to devise new problems. Given this freedom, Lester's mind wandered around the room. Mr. Dawson often left Lester alone in the room to go make copies and grab coffee.

It was during one of these moments when Lester found himself staring at his teacher's computer screen. Outlook was open, revealing a long queue of district emails. Maybe his query was in this program. He'd noticed that teachers spent a lot of time on email. It was a technology he and his peers rarely used. It seemed remarkably outdated to Lester. Mr. Dawson often complained about the amount of email he got every day. A high-pitched ping sounded in the classroom every time a new one arrived.

It did not occur to Lester that his sitting down and using his teacher's computer while he was out of the room was completely inappropriate. Lester could make sense of so much information, but common sense still eluded him. There was nothing particularly interesting to Lester in Mr. Dawson's email. That didn't stop him from reading some of the messages anyway. Emails about fire drills, upcoming in-service days and faculty meetings, and field trip attendance announcements. One had an Excel attachment that listed every student allergy. Lester wasn't sure why, but he forwarded that one to his own home email address.

He was about to give up out of boredom when he noticed one email subject heading with his initials. It read: "Re: LL?" It could have stood for any number of things, but, with the message coming from his guidance counselor, Mr. Overton, Lester immediately knew it was about him. His head ached. It made him uncomfortable when people talked about him. Most of his childhood had been marked by adults discussing Lester in front of Lester. To know people were still doing it behind his back made Lester crazy. He wanted to read the email and also to never read it, all at the same time.

Mr. Dawson would be coming back soon. Maybe that was him in the hallway now, Lester thought, suddenly aware he was doing something wrong. He swiped the mouse's arrow back and forth over the email. His index finger hovered over the left-click button. He wouldn't read it now, he decided. He'd forward it to himself and decide later if he would read it. He clicked it. Outlook remembered his address from the allergy email. He was about to get up and go back to his seat when he noticed that the forwarding icon popped up next to the email. He wondered if Mr. Dawson would notice that. Lester convinced himself he would, so at the last minute he deleted the email. He hit the "x" for delete, and then went into the deleted emails and deleted it from there, too. He was sweating. He got up quickly, accidentally knocking over a coffee cup filled with pencils. He was picking them up when Mr. Dawson returned.

"You all right?"

"Fine." Lester put the cup and pencils back and sat down at his computer. He considered waiting until he got home to read the email, but he couldn't help himself. He opened his Gmail and read the thread. Even four years later, Lester could still recite most of the correspondence word for word.

Lester read it from top to bottom in its reverse email chronology.

To: overtonj@gvsd.net
From: dawsonb@gvsd.net
Subject: Re: LL?

HA!

—

To: dawsonb@gvsd.net
From: overtonj@gvsd.net
Subject: Re: LL?

This whole job would be easier if we could just get rid of the kids!

—

To: overtonj@gvsd.net
From: dawsonb@gvsd.net
Subject: Re: LL?

Nothing. Met with the dad. He's unconvinced. Tried to bring up how an online charter might benefit Lester.

It would make my job a lot easier! :)

—

To: dawsonb@gvsd.net
From: overtonj@gvsd.net
Subject: Re: LL?

Any news? He's been especially quiet this week.

—

To: overtonj@gvsd.net
From: dawsonb@gvsd.net
Subject: Re: LL?

Sure.

—

To: dawsonb@gvsd.net
From: overtonj@gvsd.net
Subject: Re: LL?

Don't think I can get into it over email. Can you swing by my office after school?

—

To: overtonj@gvsd.net
From: dawsonb@gvsd.net
Subject: Re: LL?

Really? That's a shame. I like having him here. He's definitely weird, but he's clever and interesting, too. He fixes the computers!

Is it for emotional stuff?

—

To: dawsonb@gvsd.net
From: overtonj@gvsd.net
Subject: Re: LL?

We're looking into some alternative placement for next year. Some better kind of fit for his needs.

—

To: overtonj@gvsd.net
From: dawsonb@gvsd.net
Subject: Re: LL?

Sure, no problem. Everything okay?

—

To: dawsonb@gvsd.net
From: overtonj@gvsd.net
Subject: LL?

Bill—I'm going to need Lester on Thursday and Friday if that works for you?

Joe

—

Lester was so upset he didn't hear the bell ring.

"Les. . .that was the bell," Mr. Dawson said.

Lester looked up but couldn't make eye contact with his teacher. He closed the browser, grabbed his book bag and left the room without a word. His guidance counselor and his emotional support teacher advised him to come down to Student Services if he was feeling overwhelmed, but he couldn't trust them anymore, and maybe never did. Instead he found a dark corner in the auditorium, sat on the floor, and seethed.

He read the thread over and over again on his phone. More people talking about him behind his back. His counselor was no surprise, but Mr. Dawson, who was kind to him and let him do whatever he wanted, and his own father holding meetings Lester knew nothing about? Just the casual nature of the exchange. The jokey nature of it all. The "HA!" The phrase "alternative placement," like he was some product that wouldn't sell, to be placed on a different shelf. "A better kind of fit"?? Like something could fit the horrible feeling of being young and angry and confused all the time. Like everyone didn't feel that way, Lester answered to himself. "Emotional stuff"? What the hell is that supposed to mean? Is that what he's been feeling all this time? Just *stuff*? And *I'm weird, but I fix the computers!*—was that the takeaway? Was that Mr. Dawson's assessment? People "swinging by" other people's offices, having quiet conversations about him?

The following morning Lester pretended to be sick and stayed home. He was a little surprised how easy it was to figure out Mr. Overton's email password. After a few variations, he tried simply *gvsd1234*—Great Valley School District 1234. It was the same temporary password students received when they forgot their own. Because it came so easily, Lester considered not even going through with his idea. Something seemed off about it. But he had the whole day to himself, and he'd already decided. Maybe it would even be fun, he thought.

Most of the emails were as dry and boring as Mr. Dawson's had been. Lester would never want a job where there was so much communication, so many meetings. At least Mr. Dawson could talk about math and computers all day. But to be a guidance counselor? All those feelings to talk about. All the talk of the future. The few times he had to visit the office to talk over his schedule, he'd seen kids crying in front of these men and women. Sometimes they would put an arm around a kid. It was gross.

If they wanted to talk about Lester behind his back, he would do the same to them. Mr. Overton didn't trash any of his emails. There were over two hundred messages, dating back to the summer. He sorted by sender and looked for any sort of personal correspondence. Halfway down, he saw emails from overtonk@gvsd.net. He hadn't put it together until this moment, but Mr. Overton's wife must be Kathy Overton, a librarian at Green Tree Elementary. She was a cruel woman, Lester thought he remembered. She was a shusher and stared meanly at the children when they came in for a book. What a weird pair—Mr. Overton's treacly friendliness and his wife's stern disgust.

There was nothing of interest in any of Kathy Overton's emails. Lester wasn't sure what he expected to find, but he was disappointed by the short sentence fragments they sent one another. Shopping lists, an Amazon link, a receipt for some deck furniture. Is this what his own parents talked about before his mother died? This was marriage, he guessed.

This irrational disappointment compounded the personal affront and violation Lester already felt. He'd see if they liked being talked about.

But no idea came to him. He opened an email in Mr. Overton's account. He found the option to send an ALL STAFF email and selected it. He stared at the blinking cursor for a while. When he couldn't think of anything to write, he settled.

Dear Staff—

Fuck you. Fuck you all.

Best, Joe
—

It was juvenile and stupid, but it made Lester feel good. It had been a while since he pushed or kicked anyone. The drugs he took made him feel empty. Safe, but empty. He missed this feeling. Missed feeling reckless. He laughed. He read it over to himself, laughed at including the "Joe" as the sign-off, at its formality. He said it aloud and liked it. Then, he sent it out.

"Fuck you all," he said to himself in his bedroom.

It didn't seem enough, though. They would know it wasn't Mr. Overton that sent it. It seemed the exact opposite of something Mr. Overton would say. It wouldn't hurt him enough. Maybe they'd all laugh at it in the guidance office. They were always laughing about something down there.

So, he opened another window, registered for a new Gmail account, and sent an email to Kathy Overton.

Dear Kathy—

You don't know me. I'm sorry I have bad news for you. Your husband has been cheating on you with another guidance counselor for the last three weeks. I just thought you should know.

He thought twice before he hit send. After thinking it through a third time, he clicked and sent it on its way.

That was better. That was mean. It still wasn't enough, but at this point, a headache descended on Lester, and he didn't feel well. He felt winded for no reason and laid down on his bed. "Fuck you all," he whispered to himself and fell asleep.

Everyone would talk about Mr. Overton now. Let's see how he feels about that, Lester thought.

He was right. People talked about Mr. Overton, and they were doing it with him absent from the building. Lester's counselor was not in school for the rest of the week. Five days later, when Mr. Overton returned to school, Lester was called to his office. He had been in the computer lab with Mr. Dawson when it happened. The class phone rang. Mr. Dawson answered it, listened for a moment, and then looked right at Lester.

Lester knew what was happening.

"Guidance wants to see you, Les," he said.

Mr. Dawson wouldn't look at him as he left the room. Lester thought he'd been weirdly quiet the past few days. They'd be in his office, waiting for him. He could just say he didn't do it. He could play dumb, but he didn't know how to do that. How would they know anyway? Maybe this was the meeting that his father had been planning behind his back, about going to a different school. They'd all be lying in wait. His head pounded again. His palms started to sweat. Maybe he could just walk out of the building. He could just go home. He could be sick for the rest of the week. He was sick. He was always sick, right? All that "emotional stuff," right?

He made it to the guidance office, and could see inside Overton's office from the hallway. His dad wasn't there, but Dr. King, the principal, was there with Mr. Overton, and his emotional support teacher, too. He paused for too long and Dr. King noticed him. He felt dizzy and twisted his fingers inside his fists. He wasn't going in there. He ran. Right out of building. Someone called his name, but he wasn't sure who. He ran through the parking lot, the woods behind the fence, and across a few lawns. He didn't stop to turn around until he had walked the two miles to his house. His dad was on the front porch waiting for him. He walked right past him and went up to his room.

"Les," his father said outside his door. "Can I come in?"

Lester didn't answer.

"Les, let's just talk this over."

"It's not locked."

The door wasn't locked and Mr. Lewis walked in. Lester was on his bed, playing with the abacus.

There was no use pretending to his dad. He told him the whole thing. Lester had stopped listening when his dad explained how hurtful those emails were, about how it might be a prank to send the all-staff email—a stupid one—but to send a stranger a hurtful—he kept using the word "hurtful"—message about a loved one was crossing a line, that it had caused the Overtons a good deal of pain and confusion, and that maybe it was time to find Lester a place where he could find more success. He would finish at the online charter school.

He never went back inside the high school building. He never talked to his fellow computer lab kids, or to Mr. Dawson. They asked him to write an apology to Mr. and Mrs. Overton, but he wouldn't do it, and by that point, Mr. Lewis was just happy the whole thing was over. But he was still worried—worried that he'd failed his son somehow, that bringing Lester back home to finish school online, removing him even farther from the outside world, would result in him never leaving; he'd never find a job, a loved one, a future.

When Norman returned home from school that day, Lester watched his brother bounce a tennis ball off the garage door until it got dark.

NINETEEN

Dylan's first shift at Terry's Christmas Trees and Sundries was on the first Sunday in December.

"Terry Christmas!" the sign read. She had to ask someone what sundries were. Turns out she was in charge of those. She sat with the cash register in a cold shed with an electric heater. She sold ornaments, wreaths, and garlands, and rang up the tree purchases.

It was better than Halloween Adventure, but only because Christmas was better. Her playful idea of a life of seasonal employment didn't seem so playful anymore. It didn't help that she and Norman had agreed to take this job together back when they worked together in October. They hadn't spoken much since Thanksgiving, and it was clear to Dylan now that Norman wasn't that interested in her.

She convinced herself she felt more relief than disappointment. And anyway, she had better things to do now. A gathered throng was waiting to hear what Darling Energy had to say next. It took a lot of willpower to resist telling her friends that Dylan Geringer was indeed Darling Energy, the trending hashtag, the mysterious specter inspiring Facebook groups and bathroom graffiti over the last two weeks. *For a good time call DARLING ENERGY!* She smiled when she saw a club fair poster that read, "Gather the throng!"

Mr. Kim, in a lesson about relativity, wrote on the board: *Darling E = mc²*. She snapped a picture of it and sent it to Steven. She thought about potential versus kinetic energy after class, and how she was tired of being potential energy. The messages could be kinetic, she thought.

A father and his daughter walked into the shed of sundries. The little girl was stuffed into a pink coat with a faux-fur-lined hood. She stared at the blinking lights up around the ceiling and pointed at them with her mittens.

"Hi, there. Douglas fir. Six feet," the man said.

"That'll be $45." She pressed a few buttons on the register.

"Oh, shoot." The man patted his pockets. "I left my money in the car. I'll be right back." He left the shed and his daughter behind.

Dylan was no parental expert, but she was pretty sure the father didn't mean to leave his daughter there among the glass ornaments and the electric heater. The girl, who was no older than four, Dylan guessed, didn't notice right away. She was still looking at the lights and waving her hands around. She noticed Dylan and smiled. Dylan smiled back.

"Do you like the lights?" Dylan tried her best kid voice.

The question froze the girl for a second. She looked away from the lights and stared back at Dylan.

"I like your jacket. It's pretty. Do you like pink?"

The girl looked down at her jacket. She nodded her head, and looked to where her dad had been. Seeing he was not there, the girl's eyes opened while the rest of her face closed in toward her nose. She was about to cry. Dylan was angry with this stupid, oblivious father who left his child alone in a cold shed. She did not want to deal with a crying kid.

"It's okay. Your daddy will be right back. He's just going to grab some money for the tree. Are you excited about Christmas??"

The word *Christmas* rescued the situation for the time being. The girl smiled and pointed at the Nativity set on the shelf above her.

"You are? What do you want Santa to get you?" Surely this line of questioning would keep the girl from crying. Where was this stupid dad? The girl kept pointing at the Nativity scene. It was an expensive Italian-made Nativity scene that Dylan had enjoyed setting up earlier that day. She flanked the baby Jesus with two camels and kept the wise men outside the manger.

Wordlessly, the girl kept pointing at the scene. Did she really want this for Christmas?

"Do you want a stuffed animal?" Dylan racked her brain for what a four-year-old might want. "Do you like horses?" Dylan was terrible at this. The girl's insistence with the Nativity scene was making her a little uncomfortable.

"No. You don't want to do that. You should wait for your dad." The girl was getting a little too close to the shelf. Stuffed into this pink winter coat, she looked more like a cannonball than a powder puff. It happened in one movement, and when Dylan thought about it later that night, she remembered it with faint yellow laser lines connecting the girl's movements, like the outline of a constellation.

It started with "Don't touch that!" a millisecond after the girl's arm reached up to touch the Christmas scene. Her mitten curled just enough onto the shelf to make contact with little baby Jesus's foot, hanging just over the side of the manger. Her oversized Gortex elbow scraped against a box of stacked ornaments on the row below. Hearing Dylan scream, the girl jerked her arm away and smacked a metal Christmas tree stand on display on the shelf. In one swift motion, the box, the stand, and the baby Jesus fell—and in the direction of the little girl. Dylan took two strides from behind the counter to the scene. With her right arm she pushed the girl enough out of the way and grabbed one of the metal legs to the Christmas tree stand. To balance herself, she extended her left arm behind her, and was surprised when she turned to see baby Jesus in the palm of her hand. Had she another hand, maybe the box of ornaments would have made it. Instead, they crashed to the ground. One ornament rolled from the box and was promptly stepped on by the returning dad.

"Mary!" he yelled and yanked his daughter by the arm. Mary was already out of the way, so the yank seemed unnecessary to Dylan.

"Are you okay?" The man was asking Dylan, not his daughter.

"I'm fine. Are you okay?" Dylan asked the little girl. This was too much for Mary and so she cried. Her dad picked her up.

"I'm very sorry about that. We'll pay for those ornaments." He'd been holding the cash in his hand since he walked back in. He picked up the box and read the sticker. "Here's eighty dollars. For the tree and these. I'm sorry for the inconvenience." He threw the bills on the counter and turned to leave.

"Let me give you your change." But she was just saying it to Mary, whose face looked out over her dad's shoulder on the way out the door.

Dylan's heart was racing still. She went to grab the broom and noticed she was still holding the baby Jesus. She placed the child back in the manger and had to reposition a camel that had fallen on Joseph. Maybe Mary had just been pointing at her virgin namesake.

Norman walked in. He was wearing an old army coat of his dad's. His gloves were dark from the tree sap and his black winter cap stretched over his ears and eyebrows. The added padding made the already enormous boy even bigger. He ducked his head enough to come through the door, but for the second time that day ran into the hanging mistletoe. This time it didn't fall but instead swung in a wide parabola until Norman settled it with one of his paws.

"What'd you do to her?"

"To who?"

"That girl. She was balling her eyes out."

"I saved Christmas." Dylan looked over at the Nativity scene. The camels laughed. "How're things out there?" She would treat him nicely, despite knowing it was just that.

"Slow. Charlie's here, too. I don't think they need the both of us." Norman had spent that Saturday afternoon trimming and netting Christmas trees and tying them to the roofs of cars. He had a ball of twine in one of his coat pockets. One end hung near the floor. Dylan could tell he wanted to say something else, but she was nervous to hear what it was. They both ended up staring at the shelves. When it became too awkward, she took out her phone and pretended to check something.

Norman broke the silence. "My dad never really took us to church." He was still staring at the Nativity.

Dylan swiped through the apps on her phone. "No?" Dylan tried. He needed help getting where he needed to go.

"No. Before my mom died, we'd go on Christmas and Easter." To this point, Norman had never talked about his mother. Dylan had been afraid to ask. "But I was only four. Which one is supposed to be Joseph?"

Dylan came out from behind the counter again. "Really?"

"Yes, really. I don't know the story. I mean, not the whole thing."

"Well, I'm hardly an expert." Dylan walked over to the scene with Norman. The Christmas playlist switched to "Silent Night."

"This one," she said pointing to a very solemn-looking Joseph.

"And these are the wise men?"

"Those two are. That other one is just a shepherd. I put the last wise man over here by the donkey."

Norman picked up the donkey and inspected it. He looked at its face as though it might speak.

"I wouldn't mind having a donkey."

Terry walked in. He was a short and stout man in his fifties.

"Dylan, how many so far today?"

Dylan grabbed the donkey from Norman and put it back next to a wise man. She walked back behind the counter and checked a ledger where Terry had instructed her to keep a tally of trees sold.

"Twelve overall. Mostly Douglas firs."

"Can you two help me with something?" Dylan looked at the register. She wasn't supposed to leave it. "It's okay. It will just take a minute."

Norman and Dylan shared a quick look and then we're following Terry out into the cold, past the rows of trees, and into the parking lot.

Terry led them to his black Audi A3. He had a vanity license plate that read "T O2 Y." Norman saw her trying to figure it out.

"It's T- 'AIR' -EE," he sounded out to her. "O2" as "air"? It was just another thing Terry didn't quite get right.

Terry smiled, opened the trunk, and stood to the side, inviting Dylan and Norman to look.

"Well? What do you think?" Norman and Dylan peered inside. "Do you think she'll like it?"

Dylan tried to describe to Steven later that night what she and Norman bore witness to in the back of Terry's car, but it was difficult to do it justice. Lying side by side was a half-sized Santa and a Mrs. Claus, each standing about four feet tall. It may have been an unsurprising idea for a gift from a purveyor of all things Christmas if it hadn't been for the eerily lifelike faces of Terry as Santa and Terry's wife, Charlotte, as Mrs. Claus. They were not painted faces, but rubbery, sculpted likenesses that looked more like sex dolls than giant Christmas statues.

"Well?" Terry asked again. "Do you recognize those faces?" He was giddy.

Maybe Dylan was wrong about the faces, she hoped, but she could tell, looking at Norman, that they were exactly who she thought they were.

"It's you and Charlotte?" she said through a tight smile. It occurred to her she didn't know if this was supposed to be a funny gag gift or a serious one.

"It's. . ." Norman tried.

"It's pretty *amazing* is what it is, right?" Oh, it's serious, thought Dylan. "There's a guy online who crafts these. All you have to do is send him a few photos, and he does the rest." Terry marveled at the bodies in the trunk. The image of them standing there, looking into the trunk at lifeless bodies, made Dylan feel like she was in some awful mobster movie.

"Wow, Terry," was all Norman managed.

"Right??"

"Yeah, those are one of kind," Dylan said and hoped.

"I know. I can't wait till she sees them. She'll be decorating the house tomorrow and I want to surprise her with them before she gets home tonight."

"Cool," Dylan said.

"That's great, Terry." Norman kept saying Terry's name, but he was saying it to Santa-Terry in the trunk.

"So I need your help." Dylan didn't like the sound of this. "Could you two drop this off at my house? On the front porch? I'd go myself, but I need to stay here until closing. I'd pay you, of course. I just want them to be there when she gets home. I can give you each fifty dollars." There were only two hours left on her shift. She'd only make sixteen dollars at the register.

Norman spoke first, out of his spell. "Sure!"

It was a strange request, but it was money. "Sure," Dylan agreed.

"They'll fit in your car, Norman."

And they did, but not in the trunk. Terry worried they'd get damaged, so he helped Norman and Dylan position Terry and Charlotte as Santa and Mrs. Claus in his backseat.

She and Norman just laughed as they buckled in.

"Should we put their seatbelts on?" Dylan asked.

"They're like crash test dummies."

"What is he thinking?"

"I don't know."

"They're too lifelike. It's creepy."

"They are creepy. Maybe if they were a little more cartoonish?"

"Maybe," Dylan said. "Either way, they're disturbing."

Norman pulled the car out onto route 30. "Maybe she'll like them. Some people just love Christmas."

"Look, I love Christmas. But I don't want my face on a Mrs. Claus doll sitting outside my house."

"Right, but the Thompsons *love* Christmas. It's their life."

"Then maybe they could just dress up like the Clauses. Like regular Christmas weirdo fanatics."

"Christmas cosplay."

It was the kind of conversation Dylan might have with Steven. It was easy and effortless. It was good to have a prop for conversation. Maybe that's what she and Norman needed. Something to bounce off of. Something to take away the focus on them. Why was she still thinking they were something?

It was going well. Dylan thought she would fish for the story of Norman's mother since he'd brought her up earlier in the evening. Before she could, Norman told her to put Terry's address into her phone.

"106 Grubb Road."

"Grubb?"

"Yeah. With two *b's*."

And like that, Steven floated into the car. 106 Grubb Road was only two houses down from the Lillys' house.

It seemed impossible sometimes, Dylan thought. Impossible to do anything out of the ordinary and not be witnessed and accounted for by perfectly placed onlookers. There were always faces watching her every move. Some were just in her head: Daphne—especially when the context was guys—and Steven pulling her along in different directions. In this case, she pictured him sitting between Mr. and Mrs. Claus in the backseat.

These witnesses were real people, too. When they'd made their way into the Grubb neighborhood and passed the Lilly house, there was Mrs. Lilly, pushing the trash cans out to the street. It was dark, but the street-light illuminated Norman's car. Dylan watched as Lillian Lilly squinted into the glare and at the last moment recognized Dylan in the driver's side seat. Her wave and smile withdrew as Dylan waved back, and her eyes widened—either at the strange cargo sitting in the backseat or at Norman; it was hard to say.

Whatever, she thought.

However weird Terry Thompson's Christmas obsession, it had provided him with a lovely modern house tucked back a hundred feet from the street. He must sell a load of sundries. It didn't seem the sort of house that would get the Christmas treatment, but according to Terry, folks came from around the county to drive by their house during the season.

Norman parked the car in the driveway turnaround against the garage. They got out.

"So where does he want them? Just in front of the door??"

Norman opened the passenger door on his side. "The front porch."

Dylan looked again. There wasn't a front porch. There was a cement slab leading up the door.

Norman grabbed Santa by the head. His foot got stuck on the seat belt, and his hat popped off. It revealed a bald head.

"Terry's not bald," Dylan said.

"Santa is."

"Is he?" She opened the door on her side and had better luck getting out Mrs. Claus, though her dress rode up a little, revealing bloomers.

"Sexy," Norman said.

Dylan followed Norman to the front door, but not before she turned and looked out to the street. With her luck, someone would be watching now, as she and Norman unloaded the bodies.

"Right here, I guess." Norman put Santa down in front of the door. In the soft glow from the door light, the doll looked even worse, like some oversized holiday voodoo doll of Terry. The smile was unsettling.

"Don't put it right in front of the door," Dylan said. It would be the second time today she staged a Christmas character tableau.

"Why not?"

"It's too close. She'll have to move it when she gets home."

"But it's in the light."

"Just move it back a little." She put Mrs. Claus down on the walkway. She grabbed Santa by the shoulders and shimmied him forward a foot. "There." She was trying to imagine how Mrs. Thompson would come up on it. Dylan grabbed Mrs. Claus now and moved to put her into place.

"Wait, you can't see the sack from that angle." Norman grabbed Santa to reposition, but didn't notice Dylan moving into place. He barreled into

Dylan, her lowered head thudded against his chest.

This time her powers couldn't save her from falling back, and neither could Norman, who reached out to catch Dylan's arm but only managed to grab Mrs. Claus's leg before it hit the ground. Dylan fell flat onto the hard ground, right on her ass. A split second later, Mrs. Claus, with a face like Charlotte Thompson, and minus one leg still in Norman's hand, toppled over her.

It was a strange scene made even stranger by the headlights that spotlit the four of them. Like a deer in the headlights, Norman and Dylan were just as frozen as their Christmas counterparts.

The side of the sedan read "Smith Security Systems."

Dylan got up to her knees, but doing so knocked Mrs. Claus onto the ground onto her new stump, her dress up over her shoulders. Norman still couldn't decide what to do. Wearing the old army coat and the black winter cap around his eyes, in his work boots pushing him over six and half feet, he knew what he must look like. He was still holding Mrs. Claus's leg.

A voice came from a speaker under the hood of the car.

"Stay right where you are! Do not move!"

Dylan recognized the name and the car. The Smiths lived across the street from Steven. Norman noticed he was holding the leg and made a move to put it down on the ground.

"What did I just say? Stay right there. Do not drop that leg!"

She noticed Mrs. Claus's dress and grabbed the hem to pull it back down.

"You too!" There was a floodlight mounted to the side of the car that turned on and shined at Dylan. "The police have been notified. They'll be here any minute."

Dylan looked at Norman. It looked like he was holding his breath. She wasn't going to just stay there until the police came.

"Mr. Smith?" Dylan called out. It got nothing from Mr. Smith. "Mr. Smith?"

"That's what it says on the car. Stay right where you are."

Something inside her switched on. They'd done nothing wrong. This was just a misunderstanding, and this guy was just Mr. Smith, from across the street. She stood up despite his orders.

"Do not come any closer!" Mr. Smith yelled through the speaker.

Dylan walked a little closer to the car.

"Dylan, stop it!!" Norman yelled. The leg he was holding was shaking.

"Mr. Smith," she tried again. "It's me, Dylan Geringer." Dylan held her hands out. She'd met him many times over at Steven's house. He always warned them about keeping the ladder up to Steven's window. "You might as well invite a thief," he told them. After a year or more, he stopped. Steven and Dylan used to joke he didn't even have a security business, that he was just a rogue Neighborhood Watch guy.

"I'm Steven's friend. Steven Lilly." While Norman still hadn't broken his curious pose, Dylan had reached the hood of the car. She waved to Mr. Smith inside. There was a pregnant pause, and then the floodlight turned off. A few seconds later the door opened and, tentatively, Mr. Smith emerged from behind it.

Dylan couldn't figure out what to say next, so she settled on: "Hi."

Mr. Smith wouldn't leave from behind the safety of the open door. He looked at frozen Norman again.

"Who's leg is that?"

"It's hers," Norman said and pointed to Mrs. Claus on the ground. Mr. Smith grabbed a Maglite from his belt and shone it on the body. He traced the beam up from her legs and settled onto her face. His eyes bugled out, his shoulders rose up, his mouth opened. It was Charlotte Thompson's face pressed against the ground.

"What. . .what have you done??" Mr. Smith looked back at Dylan.

Now aware of the absurdity of this crime scene, Dylan tried to explain.

"Mr. Smith, that's just a doll. Mr. Thompson had it made for Mrs. Thompson." None of this news cured Mr. Smith's face. "See." She walked back and picked it up with both hands. She held it out in front of her for Mr. Smith to examine. She knocked on the head. "See? And that one back there," Dylan motioned back to Terry's Santa by the front door. Mr. Smith trained the Maglite beam onto Santa's face.

"That's Terry!" Mr. Smith let out. This misunderstanding wasn't becoming understood. Under the light from the walkway and the flashlight, it really looked like Terry.

Norman sensed an opportunity to lower the leg to the ground and break his stance. He tried on a smile. "We were just waiting for Mrs. Thompson to get home."

The response and the sight didn't sit well with Mr. Smith. He looked like he'd seen a ghost. He grabbed the handle of his car door and muttered something to himself. He got in and slammed the door shut. Dylan wasn't sure what this meant for them. "Mr. Smith," she said again.

He came on though the speaker. "Do not move. The police have been called." The speaker clicked off, and Mr. Smith put the car in reverse.

This was ridiculous, thought Dylan. She looked back at Norman, the leg on the ground, Mrs. Claus and her bloomers resting on her stump, and erupted in laughter. Norman smiled and got one good laugh out, but they both stopped when they heard a loud crunch of metal. At the end of the driveway, Mr. Smith had backed up into a patrol car. He really had called the police. He must have hit his microphone button by accident because Dylan heard an amplified "Shit! Shit!" coming from the street.

The police car put on his swirling lights. The door opened, and a policeman popped out.

"Goddamn it, Jim! What are doing?" Mr. Smith got out of his car. "You didn't even have your lights on. Look at this!" The officer was pointing to his dented front fender. "Goddamn it!"

Norman, out of his spell, ran down the driveway to see if everything was all right. Dylan couldn't get a hold of herself. She burst into laughter again. Tears streamed down her face. She was gasping for breath. She looked up long enough to see Mr. Smith pointing back down to her and the scene, but it had no effect. Nothing would stop her laughing now. She had to steady herself against the light post.

After the police and Mr. Smith had left, after Dylan stopped her laughter long enough to help Norman explain what they were doing there, they fixed up the dolls enough to pose them in front of the door. Dylan was able to balance Mrs. Claus by wedging the leg against its stump and a large planter.

Dylan still couldn't stifle the occasional burst of laughter while they brushed grass off the doll's clothing.

"What is wrong with you?"

"Nothing."

"I don't see how this is funny."

"You don't?" Dylan couldn't believe how that was possible. Norman didn't answer. "You don't?" she repeated.

Norman scrubbed the lapel of Santa's suit. "Why aren't you talking to me?" she asked him.

"I'm not!"

"You're not what?"

"I'm not *not* talking to you."

"Yeah. Okay." She stopped fussing with the doll and just looked at Norman. "What are you upset about?"

"I'm not upset." He stood and stared back. "It was just embarrassing. And there was a car accident. And the doll broke. I mean, the cops were here." To hear the description like that, from giant Norman Lewis, was too much for Dylan. A quick laugh escaped her mouth. She put her hand up to stop herself.

"I'm leaving. Let's go." Norman made for the car. "Come on," he said. "I'll drive you home."

"What's wrong??" she asked again.

He was opening his door. "Fucking shit! Let's just fucking leave already!!" The curse was so loud, a neighborhood dog barked. "Let's just get this over with!"

Dylan wasn't sure what the "this" was, but she didn't like the sound of it, and she didn't like how Norman was talking to her. It was rage. "Okay?!?" Norman yelled.

Dylan just looked at him. Who was this? She didn't like it. She felt uncomfortable. "Forget it," she said as she turned and walked down the driveway.

"Where are you going?" Norman had gotten a hold of himself. Dylan kept walking. "Where are you going?? I'm not going to let you walk home." He closed his car door and walked after her. "Dylan. I'm sorry. Let me just take you home."

"It's okay." Dylan had almost made it to the end of the driveway. Norman, right behind her, grabbed for her elbow. She turned around, and Norman let go.

"I'm not going home. I'm walking over to Steven's." She looked for traffic and stepped over some plastic left over from Mr. Smith's taillight. She didn't turn around, but she knew Norman was still watching her. When she'd made it past some tall evergreens, she looked back through the branches. Norman was walking back down the driveway to his car.

Steven's bedroom light was on. The ladder sparkled in the moonlight. Before she made it to the top, Steven was already at the window waiting for her. He opened the window for her, and Dylan crawled through the opening.

"What's going on?" Steven said.

Dylan put her arms around his neck and brought his face next to hers.

"Nothing," she said. She leaned in and kissed him on the mouth. Her lips were freezing, but Steven's were warm and soft. She kept kissing them until they felt the same. Out of the cold now, her red hands burned against Steven's neck and face. She felt Steven's hands around her waist. His fingers found her ribs, and he tried to bring her in closer. But they were already as close as they could get.

Dylan broke away and said, "You'll never guess what happened."

TWENTY

Dr. Cruz's waiting room hadn't been updated since the '80s. The Lucite coffee table had a mirror top, and there were pastel prints of creamy sunsets over the ocean. The walls were an eggshell white and featured two chrome dolphins, jumping towards the corner of the room. Royce saw his face reflected in the lead dolphin, pinched and stretched out as if in a carnival mirror. He moved his head around until his eye reflected back to him through the dolphin's eye.

He wanted to tell Dr. Cruz how much it infuriated him, all these mocking reflective surfaces in his waiting room. It was bad enough with all the self-reflection that went on inside the doctor's office. He had to get it out here, too?

This was the arrangement, though. He knew his future would be filled with more doctor's visits, with more rehab, with serious conversations with his parents. It had been impossible to explain to his parents how this whole plan had just been a lark, that he'd never meant to kill himself. He didn't think so. Not really. Not all the way. He knew it was serious, or whatever the word was—*severe*? He knew it would lead to this, and part of him was relieved—relieved that there was a routine now, a routine that would involve his parents' attention, and not involve school in any form. Royce wouldn't be able to convince his parents of his real motive. Royce wasn't interested in dying. Not yet, at least. He was death-curious, sure. But mostly he just wanted to see the look on their faces. He wanted to hear the concern in their voices. He thought maybe the drugs would do it, but to his parents there was a neat and tidy answer to that problem. He could be fixed with other drugs and month-long stays at resort-like rehab centers. They'd have to take a suicide attempt more seriously, he thought.

It was poorly planned. He'd set his timer for three minutes after he started the car. He thought that would be enough time for the garage to billow up with smoke, from what he'd read. Royce thought he had his mom's trips to the drug store timed perfectly. She wasn't someone to go browsing in the supermarket. She hated shopping, and Royce knew her trip would take her to the pharmacy, and the pharmacy only. Usually, he would accompany her. For the last six months, he went along for the ride. They were fetching drugs for him, anyway. He might as well go along, he thought. Then, as now, staring at the chrome dolphin, Royce often found himself lost in an unbroken gaze when he traveled with his mother in the car. They didn't speak to one another, and it was easy to zone out with his headphones in and just pick a spot to stare at.

On that first trip to the pharmacy the digital car clock was his target. The colon separating the hours and minutes blinked by the second. If he stared at it long enough, he could almost fall into a trance. But that wasn't the idea. The idea occurred to him on the second trip. He would time their trips to the pharmacy. If he knew how long his mother was gone, he could plan something for her, something for her to walk in on—on the days he stayed home.

It took, on average, eighteen and a half minutes—from driveway to driveway—to complete the pharmacy trip. If he stayed home the next time, and waited fifteen minutes, give or take, he could be ready by the time she came home.

He'd spent a good month or two googling—*researching*, Royce told himself. Even as a child of the internet, he was surprised there was so much information about suicide there. He expected all the preventative sites, all the sites with advice and support and offers of help, all the testimonials. What he wasn't expecting were the sites that offered step-by-step instructions on how to commit suicide successfully. Some of them had FAQs and tips. From what he could gather, the goal of the authors was to prevent a botched attempt. Despite all the anger and rage Royce felt inside, despite how much he enjoyed hating himself sometimes, he was a little appalled at the frankness of this guidance. But the information provided him with what he was looking for: a way to stage a realistic suicide, so it looked earnest, so they would know he was serious, that he wasn't fucking around anymore, and, importantly, enough information to make sure he didn't *really* kill himself. Not *really*, he thought.

"Lester? You can come back now."

Dr. Cruz's office assistant was motioning for some guy to come back with her. Royce thought he recognized Lester. He remembered kids talking about a Lester, some kid who got expelled a few years back. Royce was sure this must be the kid. What—was he twenty or something now?

Now *there* was a kid who looked suicidal. He looked like a ghost as he raised out of his seat, in front of the jumping dolphins, and followed her back into the office area. He must be seeing the other doctor. It was some woman. Royce would not be talking to a woman. He made sure his parents knew that.

The way he'd planned it, Royce thought he could fill the garage with enough smoke at just the right moment when his mom would return from the store. She'd pull into the driveway, hit the garage door opener, and witness the smoky cloud billowing. She'd see the hose, too, he thought. At worst, he would get a little light-headed. Just in case, he would set his phone's alarm for three minutes. From what he read, he figured that would both be enough time to get a good cloud of smoke, just enough time to look convincing. If she wasn't home by the time the alarm went off, he'd turn the car off, open the garage, and put the hose away.

Royce assumed he'd planned it right. His alarm hadn't gone off and he could hear something behind him, outside the garage. But there wasn't the slow rise of the door as he had imagined. He wondered if it had been two and a half minutes already. His mother, if nothing else, was punctual. But something was off. The door didn't raise. Someone was hitting it from the outside. He noticed in the side-view mirror a bar of light appear and disappear, getting wider and wider with each loud bang. Maybe the door was stuck.

A man walked into the smoky haze. Royce tried to get up, but his body was heavy and his eyes burned. He went to lift the handle, but his hand wouldn't work. He couldn't tell if he was awake or not. Royce worried for a second that he was caught in a dream. When the man opened the door, he decided to just close his eyes. It wasn't his mom, and it wasn't his dad, but it felt good to be grabbed. He could feel that, at least. There was a burning in his lungs, too. Royce wanted to cough, but nothing came out. Nothing at all. Not even a breath.

The man wrapped him in his arms and dragged him out. He could feel his feet and his sneakers as they dragged against the cement. It was like he was watching someone else. For a moment, he felt like he might be the man who was doing the dragging. It seemed like minutes until he found his breath again. When he found it, it came out in fitful coughs, in spit and smoke. His face was in grass. He tried to look up at the man, but it hurt to open his eyes. It was easier to just keep them closed. He thought about closing them. Maybe if he held his breath, all the pain would stop.

His mother told Royce later it was Mr. Drake. *Fucking Mr. Drake?* he had been saying to himself the past month. He wasn't the right audience at all. He didn't even know that guy. He had never been his teacher. He knew his face. That mustache, yeah. And always giving him shit about his hat. What's such a big fucking deal about wearing a hat? Fuck that guy. And he's the one? The one that drags me out of there? "He saved you. . ." Royce's mother said later in the hospital. Fuck that. Fuck him. And *outside* of school? Royce thought he was safe from teachers on the outside. But that was just another thing he was wrong about. His mother, who got caught behind a school bus, didn't even get to see all his effort, all he planned for her.

It was always the wrong people, all the time.

***

Maybe Trevor was feeling better. When he passed the signs for the emergency room, he no longer wanted to go inside and fill out a form. It was the second week in a row he was going to meet his wife at work for lunch. The first week he surprised her, surprised himself, too. He had to ask the lady at the front desk where the claims department was. Trevor had picked up Elizabeth from work before, but it was only ever outside in the circle. Until last week, he'd never been to her office. He'd met many of her coworkers over the years, as she made her way up the ranks. He and Elizabeth had attended charity dinners and holiday parties together, but he only had a mental image of her office and its desk, and he was touched to see a framed picture of the two of them from last year's holiday party next to her computer. He liked Doug, the hospital CFO, and his wife, Janice, but Doug was more handsome and successful than Trevor, and he would get jealous at the shorthand communication Elizabeth had with him, and their inside jokes.

But that was a different Trevor, he told himself. Walking through the lobby to the elevators, Trevor felt a bounce in his step he didn't remember having when he made the same trip last week. It helped that the holiday break arrived early this year. The last few days at work had helped. It started that rainy day when Dylan Geringer and her friend Steven Lilly had driven him home. It was a small gesture when she offered Trevor his own label back—*I'll be fine*, it read—but a knowing gesture, and its simple kindness, had filled Trevor's heart with something like love.

There was a crack, and through it, Trevor let in a little light. It helped that his neighborhood and town had strung tiny white Christmas lights around town. Here in the hospital lobby it was no different. They outlined the circular visitor's desk and the stones around the water feature. They shone especially bright around the hospital gift shop. There was a piano outside the store, available to passersby. A little boy ran his hand over a few keys before his mother whisked him away.

It was completely out of character, but Trevor dared himself to sit down at the piano. He used to play a little, but piano was not like riding a bike. It was years ago—maybe his early twenties, Trevor thought—when he'd last tried to play anything. The one melody he could recall, he could only plunk out with his right hand. His mother had taught him, though she had no memory of it, he found out later. It was, fittingly enough, "God Rest Ye Merry Gentleman." He remembered how to find middle C and from there counted up to E. He remembered the first fifth jump up to B, but scaling back down, forgot about the F#. He caught it quickly enough and corrected it the next time through the opening line. That was all he had, just the first two repeating lines. He played them again now that he had it down. He wouldn't push it any further. As he pushed the bench back in, the boy and his mother smiled at Trevor. Smiling: it wasn't hard, really. "I'll be fine," he told himself. Thank you, Dylan Geringer.

God rest ye, merry gentleman
Let nothing you dismay

Trevor sang it quietly to himself as he passed by the gift shop.

"Mr. Drake?"

The voice came from a woman standing inside the gift shop doorway. He recognized her face. He would smile, so he did. This was getting easy, he thought.

She helped him out. "I'm Mrs. Lilly. Steven's mother."

"Is that right? Mrs. Lilly? It's nice to meet you."

"We met at back-to-school night."

"Oh, sure. Good to see you again."

"That was nice of you." Lillian pointed to the piano.

"I'm afraid that's all I remember. Does it get played often?"

"Here and there. One of the cardiologists studied at Juilliard."

"Really? That's great."

"There's a piano teacher who brings her students here." Trevor nodded. He noticed the stuffed monkey Lillian Lilly was holding. "That's a good idea."

"Well, we thought so at first. Then she started giving lessons here and tried to hold a recital."

"What? Really?" Trevor and Lillian laughed.

"How's Steven?"

"You tell me."

"He's great. He's really a great kid." Mrs. Lilly raised her eyebrows. She needed convincing.

"Honestly. He's a great thinker. Really intuitive about literature. About stories and characters." Lillian let the monkey she was holding hang by her side.

"I'm really sorry about what he said. What he said in class. There's really—"

"It's fine—"

"Well, it's not fine."

"It was really out of character. He was just having a bad day." Mrs. Lilly considered that. "It's high school." Lillian thought *that* over. "He's just a kid."

His last few weeks of teaching, Trevor had found himself thinking this simple notion more often: "They're just kids." Sometimes it would come to him in sadness when he thought of Royce. "He's just a kid," he'd say as he shook his head. *Why did terrible things happen to kids?* Trevor's own life sparked that guiding question over the last ten years. In the past few days, however, the same words took on a different meaning. Dylan and Steven were *just kids*, and look at all they had to offer the world.

"Are you visiting someone?" Mrs. Lilly asked.

"Yes."

"I hope it's not serious."

This confused Trevor. "Oh! No. I'm visiting my wife."

This confused Lillian. "How's she doing?"

Trevor caught on. "Sorry. She's not a patient. She works here."

Lillian lit up. She squeezed the monkey, and it made a high-pitch wheeze. "Oh, yeah? I probably know her."

"Her name is Elizabeth. She works in—"

"Oh sure. I don't know why I didn't think of it. Elizabeth Drake, sure. She's in claims."

"That's her."

"Okay, then." They both stared at the monkey for help finding the next line in the conversation.

"The shop looks great. Festive."

That's all Mrs. Lilly needed to turn on her Christmas cheer. "Come in. Check it out."

Lillian had continued stringing the lights throughout the store. They dangled, somewhat dangerously Trevor thought, over displays of stuffed animals, flowers, scarves, and coffee mugs. Trevor spun a card carousel.

Lillian had placed herself back behind the counter. She pressed a mechanical Santa that Ho-ho-ho-ed. Trevor smiled at it and then at Lillian.

"Wait till you see this," she said. Lillian pushed two buttons. The first one dimmed the store lights. The second caused the Christmas lights to twinkle intermittently. Out of the ceiling speakers, Nat King Cole sang about chestnuts.

"It's wonderful," Trevor said. He meant it, too. Christmas spirit was difficult for him, but somehow here, with this mother of one of his students, in a hospital gift shop, he let it float into his head and heart. He felt a little dizzy.

Lillian turned the lights back on. Trevor was still staring at the ceiling.

"This is nothing," she said. "You should see my Christmas village."

Trevor bit. "Oh, yeah?"

"It's a Langley Village. You know it?"

"Langley? No. I don't."

"Really? Oh, it's something else. They're an old American company that fashions decorative and seasonal miniatures for the home."

"Is that right?" Trevor didn't mean it sarcastically. The Christmas spirit filled him with earnest curiosity. "Like with the tiny homes and shops. The ones that light up?"

"Yes. But these are the best brand. The level of detail is stunning. All American made."

"It sounds lovely."

"It is. This year I'm going Western."

"I'm sorry?"

"Western themed. It's taken the better part of the last two years, but I've put together a pretty authentic-looking Western Christmas village. In the living room. It's set up year-round, but I don't turn the lights on until the second Sunday of advent."

Mrs. Lilly was beaming. Trevor wondered if he loved any hobby the way Lillian Lilly loved her Christmas village. Look how easy it is to love, he marveled. "That sounds like a lot of fun. I'd love to see it."

Lillian put down the stuffed monkey down on the counter.

"You should come see it."

"Oh, I couldn't," was the right response to this prompt. She was just being friendly. She wasn't really inviting him over to her house to look at a light-up Christmas village.

"You and your wife should come to the lighting." Lillian saw the hesitation on Trevor's face. She tried to preempt his refusal. "I'm serious. Why not?"

Nat King Cole gave way to Bing Crosby's "White Christmas."

Wasn't this what Trevor had been looking for? Some sense of neighborhood and community? Why shouldn't he and Elizabeth visit this tiny Cowboy Christmas town?

Trevor nodded his head before he answered. He smiled. "I'd like that. That's nice of you." He smiled again. "Thank you. We'd love to come."

"Oh, wonderful!" Lillian made tiny claps with her hands.

"You don't think Steven will mind?"

"What?? No."

"Having his teacher over at the house?"

"No. He loves you. He's always been more comfortable around adults, anyway. I won't even mention it to him. It would be a fun surprise."

"What night again?"

"The second Sunday. This weekend. It's the fourth. Sunday the fourth."

Trevor and Elizabeth never had plans on Sundays. It was a day of chores. She was always saying she'd like to get out more.

"Six o'clock. Here," Lillian grabbed a piece of paper. "Let me take your email address, and I'll send you an invitation. Directions to our house, etcetera."

Before he left to find his wife and tell her he'd accepted this odd invitation, he stopped in the doorway. "Merry Christmas, Mrs. Lilly!"

"Merry Christmas! And it's Lillian."

"Lillian Lilly!?"

"That's me."

"How about that?" He waved from the door. "See you Sunday."

Trevor had just about made it to the elevator when he saw Royce Caulder's parents, pressing the up button. How was it they managed to look as cheery and as affable as ever? He wasn't sure what to do. For a moment, he thought they might want to talk to him if they saw him. He would have wanted to talk to them if the tables were turned. But what was he supposed to say? The second and stronger thought, the one that pushed him to the stairs instead, was that they wouldn't want to see him at all. Do you feel shame when something like that happens? When your son tries to commit suicide, and a neighbor saves him? Trevor didn't want to find out.

Trevor was on the first step up the stairs when he couldn't help himself. He wanted to look back at the Caulders one more time. Maybe there was something he missed in their expressions. It was a mistake, and it almost ruined his Christmas cheer. Right before the elevator doors closed with the Caulders behind them, they saw Trevor from his perch on the step. Trevor tried to smile, but he knew it must have looked off. The Caulders' eyes widened. In that long second, they recognized Trevor. It looked like Mr. Caulder may have been trying to wave, but the door closed before his hand had made it past his waist. Maybe he was shaking a fist. Trevor had become just another staring townsperson, like the ones that gawked at Elizabeth and him.

Trevor ran up the rest of the stairs. He could still hear "White Christmas" from the gift shop. Or maybe it was in his head. He wanted to keep it there until he made it to Elizabeth's office.

Where the treetops glisten
and children listen
to hear sleigh bells in the snow

***

Steven couldn't figure out why there was a bench by the hospital helipad.

"What possible reason could there be?" he asked Dylan.

"I don't know. Why not?"

"Why not?? Because helicopters land here. It's not safe."

"It's safe now." Dylan stared at her feet but squeezed Steven's hand. Steven had come over to Dylan's house that afternoon. They took a walk, but had gotten no further than the helipad bench.

Besides those Thanksgiving appearances, Steven was rarely at Dylan's house. It was always Dylan climbing into Steven's room. Since their kiss, though, life had become more unpredictable. He felt selfish about it now: how she was always the one who trekked over to hang out, how he got to sit in his room and wait for her to come over. He had grown so used to having to win her over, convince her to come by, like it was an argument to be won. He thought his room was an escape for her. She'd complain about her parents and say she just needed to get out. Steven was never sure he believed her. The Geringers were sweet people. Steven envied their predictable kindness and support. Dylan wouldn't mention any specific slight. She would sit on Steven's floor and breathe a sigh a general annoyance.

It didn't occur to Steven that Dylan escaped to his room solely to see him. I mean, yes, they were friends, but until she kissed him last week, he never once had entertained the thought she liked him that way. *But of course, she did, right?* She could have gone anywhere else, could have gone to another friend's house. But she kept coming over to his house. For the last three years. Maybe he'd won her over, he thought. It's not how he imagined falling in love—through persistent and dogged familiarity. Steven's love for Dylan happened over night, in a flash of kindness—if not at first sight, certainly by the second. So what if it took Dylan longer to figure it out?

It annoyed Steven that he was even trying to figure this out, so instead he leaned into to Dylan and kissed her again. Since the night Dylan left Norman to deal with a creepy Mr. and Mrs. Claus and walked across the street into Steven's room, they had become more inseparable than usual. Long silences replaced their long and often silly conversations, punctuated by the occasional kiss and the squeezing of held hands. Steven was content just to stare into Dylan's eyes, looking for some sign that this wasn't all a fabrication of his imagination.

"What are you looking at?"

"I'm looking at you."

"I can see that." Dylan would make a funny face and look away. So instead, Steven would stare into the palm of Dylan's hand and trace its lines with his finger. He wasn't sure which one was the love line, but they all appeared long. He'd never noticed Dylan's hands before this week.

It was neither hot, nor heavy, but it felt like a new world had opened up. Dylan broke the silence. "So I've been thinking. About our story."

Steven was startled. He didn't like how this sounded. "What story?"

"What story?!" Had Steven missed something? "Darling Energy's story."

"Oh, yeah. Of course."

"We've got to plan it out, I think. I don't think we can leave it up to improv anymore. What do we want to happen? What do we want to tell people?" Dylan got up from the bench and walked around the perimeter of the helipad.

Dylan suggested a few ideas, but Steven wasn't paying attention. A smile crept up onto his face. Look at her, he thought—her long, brown hair and how it fell in front of her eyes. And her eyes, the ones she always complained about—*they're too buggy*, she'd say—a green indistinguishable from the pine needles surrounding them; and the shadow that disappeared into the nape of her neck, the only bit of skin visible on this December day.

"Well? What do you think?"

Steven stood up to stall. He hadn't been listening, and he didn't have any ideas for the Darling Energy story. "Well. . ." He took his own path around the helipad. Dylan circled clockwise and Steven counterclockwise. When they passed each other, they reached for each other's hands and held on until their momentum swung them back around for another cycle.

"Maybe we just leave it as is."

"What? No. What are you talking about?" Dylan asked.

"Well, it's pretty mysterious now. Just unfinished like it is."

"That's stupid."

"I don't know then."

"Well, you can't start a story and not finish it."

"Sure, you can. There's lots of unfinished stories. Most stories are unfinished."

"No, they're not. What does that even mean? A story needs a beginning, middle, and end. We're hardly in the middle." Dylan was more annoyed than Steven had anticipated.

"Most endings are a disappointment, though. If we wait a little, we put off the eventual disappointment."

"That's easy for you to say." This time when they passed, Dylan kept her hand to herself. "It's not your story."

"What do you mean it's not my story?"

"You're not Darling Energy."

"Neither are you." They were at opposite sides of the helipad now. They both stopped and faced each other.

Dylan did not want this to become a thing. She felt like yelling at Steven, but she wasn't sure what she was angry about. So, instead, they stared at each other and said nothing.

"I'm sorry," Steven said. Although, he was not sure what he was sorry about it. But he knew he'd said something wrong. "If you were Darling Energy, what would you want to tell the throng? What would you want to do?" Dylan didn't have an answer. "What superpower would you want to have?"

Dylan thought about it. "I'd want. . .omniscience. I'd want to be all-knowing."

"I think that one is going to difficult."

"Okay," Dylan tried to come up with another one. "How about mutation?"

"That's a solid choice. What would you mutate into?"

"*Who* would I mutate into?"

"Okay, *who* would you mutate into?"

"Anyone I wanted."

"Okay." Steven moved into the center of the helipad. "Like a kind of shape-shifting?" Dylan followed Steven's lead and soon they were both standing on the giant painted *H*.

"Yes. So I could look and feel and be like anyone." Steven grabbed her hands.

"What would you use this superpower for?" He brought her closer to him.

"I don't know yet."

"But how would I recognize you? If you shape-shifted?"

"You'd just know."

"I like your shape now." It was a horrible line and Steven knew it as soon as it escaped. Luckily, Dylan laughed. Steven grabbed her again, but stopped when they heard a low rumble in the sky. The lights circling the pad lit up blue and red. They both looked up.

They spotted the helicopter off to the south, through the trees.

"I never see one during the day."

"Well, we can't wait here."

"Hold on." Dylan wanted to look at its approach a little longer. The rumble grew, and the helicopter hovered out over the trees now. Steven looked back at the hospital. The outside door lit up, and he saw a few workers run past a window.

"Come on!"

"One second," Dylan repeated. What was her problem? He finally just grabbed her and they ran off into the woods.

A member of the hospital team waved angrily at them as they disappeared behind a tree. The man mouthed something, but the sound was too loud now. The force of the air pushed the branches around over their heads. The force was stronger than Steven would have imagined.

Dylan tried to say something, too. Steven thought she said, "I've never been this close," but he couldn't make out the last part. He stood behind her and held onto her shoulders. He needed to plant his feet against the tree, the noise and wind was so strong. Steven tried to tell Dylan that they should walk back to her house, but she wouldn't budge. "Hold on," he thought she mouthed.

They had a good view of the staff members as they lowered the body from the copter onto a stretcher on the tarmac. A doctor leaned over the stretcher. Dylan pointed.

"Look!" she shouted.

"What!? Look at what?"

"The face!"

They were too far away to really see it, but Dylan was insistent on something.

"And the jacket!" She was yelling now into Steven's ear.

"What about it?" he yelled back. He looked closer, but by that point his view was obstructed again.

"It's—" Dylan said a name, but Steven couldn't hear it.

"It's who?!?" he yelled again.

"It's Mr. Ryerson!"

"It isn't!"

"It is! That was his face. Look at the jacket! I'm sure of it."

Was the jacket striped? It looked red and white, but maybe that was from the lights blinking. "Really?" Substitute teacher, Jim Ryerson? It *did* sort of look like him. "No. . ." He didn't believe it. But it could be his barbershop quartet outfit. How did Dylan even recognize him from there? Super-sight?

He noticed a look come over Dylan's face—not like she'd seen a ghost, but like a ghost had seen her. She was weirdly calm.

Dylan grabbed him now, and they walked back through the woods, into her yard, and sat down on the patio steps.

"Are you sure?"

"Positive." She picked a pine needle off her sleeve. "I'm sure it was him."

"Shit."

"Is he married?" If anyone knew this information, it was Steven. He'd been keeping notes on subs since freshman year.

"No," Steven recalled. "He said he never found the right girl."

"Does he have friends?"

"I think so." Steven didn't know. "Well, he's got his barbershop quartet. So three friends."

Dylan leaned into Steven. She rested her head on his shoulder. "It's sad."

"Yeah," was all Steven could manage. He stroked her hair because he thought he should. It was soft. He could smell her shampoo—like oranges.

They didn't speak for a while. Mrs. Geringer passed by the window and made a face—and then she made another face, something like a smile. Steven had trouble deciphering either one, but whatever they meant, he stopped stroking Dylan's hair.

The whirring of the helicopter in the distance slowed to a stop. Steven was about to say something when both their phones vibrated at the same time. Steven reached for his first.

"What?" He let go of Dylan altogether and stood up. "What??" He shook his head back and forth.

"What?" Dylan asked.

"Did you do this?" Steven asked, indicating his phone.

"Did I do what?"

"I'm serious. Did you do this?"

"Did I do *what*?" But of course, she hadn't done this. They'd been to-gether the whole time.

"Hold on. Look at your phone. Did you just get this same text?"

"What text?"

"Look at your phone!"

"Okay, okay. . ." Dylan stood up, pulled out her phone from her back pocket.

"Where is this?"

"It's the trestle bridge. Before you get to Downingtown." Steven was still looking at his phone.

"It's massive."

"It must be a hundred feet long."

"How did they even do this?"

"How high up is this?"

"Oh, it's gotta be ten stories. Easy." Dylan looked back at Steven. "We don't need to write the story." Her face opened in wonder. It was the same expression she held looking up at the helicopter. "They're writing it for us. Or actually," she looked back at the picture. "It's just an invitation. The real story is taking place on March 15th. That's what we need to be planning. This event, not the story."

Steven looked back at the photo. In graffitied letters about six feet tall, the message read, "Darling Energy Gathers The Throng: 3/15 @ 3:33 / VF ARCH / RSVP."

"RSVP?" Steven finally noticed that part. "How do you rsvp a giant graffitied invitation a hundred feet in the air?"

"Very carefully." The lights on the helipad turned off. They hadn't noticed, but it had grown dark outside. "Wait. Who sent this picture?"

Steven hadn't considered this point. "Oh." He looked back at the phone. Unknown name and number. "Lester, right? He's the only other one who knows about the messages."

"Lester." Dylan said his name to herself. "He didn't. . ."

"What, paint that? God no."

"So why is he sending this?"

"Well. It's his invitation, too."

Dylan had forgotten that point. None of this would be happening without Lester.

A few minutes passed without comment as Steven and Dylan fiddled with their phones. Steven stopped and stared back through the woods to the helipad.

"Poor Mr. Ryerson. I hope he's okay."

"Yeah."

"It didn't look good."

"No, it didn't."

TWENTY-ONE

Steven couldn't understand why his mother was waiting for the second Sunday of Advent. Why would a woman who devoted a large part of her entire year to planning, arranging, and maintaining a miniature Christmas village inside her house refuse to "power it up" until only two weeks before the holiday? It wasn't as if his mother was working on it until the last minute, tweaking the lights and moving the buildings around. Lillian, even with this new Western theme, had stopped "production," as she called it, back in October. Moreover, it was a year-round feature. The display did not disappear into the basement for a year. It sat on a table by the bay window at the front of the house, day after day. True, you couldn't see it from the driveway, as the curtains were always drawn, but that was true for the rest of the house, too. Since Foster Lilly had left, there were few visitors to the Lilly household. While Mrs. Lilly fretted over the display and the snacks, Steven fretted over the prospect of a household of witnesses, invading his house, upsetting his delicate snow globe existence.

When it became clear that he would not be able to avoid "the show," he insisted that Dylan come over and keep him company. Steven expected he'd have to convince her to come over, but Dylan didn't even let him finish his pitch.

"Look on Sunday, I'm really hoping—"

"Oh, of course. I'm not going to miss this."

"You can't make fun of it."

"What? I wouldn't. Plus, I think it's cool."

"You do not."

"I do, too. Think of all the work your mom has put into this."

Steven didn't need to think that over. He was center stage. He was his mother's second set of eyes at each new feature placement. Lillian had Steven hold certain characters and buildings in temporary poses so she could judge the effect from across the room. For the past week, he'd been dreaming about the village, about being one of its inhabitants, about cowboys and cowpokes, and cacti with tinsel. Steven had never done any LSD, but now he didn't have to.

Dylan arrived early. They hoped to start a list of what they would need to put together a show of their own—on March 15th in Valley Forge. Despite all her trips to Steven's house, she was rarely downstairs, and more rarely, in the front formal living room. This was her first close look at Mrs. Lilly's masterpiece.

"Are you ready for this?"

"I am. But I wanted to tell you, I talked to Mr. Ryerson's friends. The barbershop quartet."

"What? How? How is he?"

"He broke his back. And a leg. And has a concussion."

"Car accident?"

"Yes."

"How did you find them?"

"Would you believe they are the only local barbershop quartet?"

"Yes. Yes, I would believe that."

"Well, they said yes."

"Yes, what?"

"They can come on the 15th."

"Really??"

"Yes."

"To Valley Forge?"

"At 3:33. Well, I told them 3:30."

"So this is happening."

"Oh, it's happening."

"It *will* be your birthday. What did you say it was for?"

"A party."

"Just a party?"

"I'm not sure they've ever been asked to perform anywhere before. They just said, yes, right away."

"So what are—"

"Oh, stop it, and let me see this thing!" Dylan walked past Steven into the living room.

"Oh my." Dylan stared. "It really is amazing." Dylan circled around the table from a safe and respectable distance.

Steven reluctantly agreed: "It is."

"It doesn't seem so. . .weird, really." Steven let Dylan try to finish. He stared at the miniature Western jail. One of many Santas was slipping a tiny present to a man behind bars. The sheriff on duty was asleep in his chair.

"When you think of all the time it must have took." Dylan was right, but it was hard for Steven to appreciate that point. Despite his mother's enthusiasm and single-mindedness for this Western Christmas village, it was also a reminder of how far she had removed herself from the life-sized real world.

"What are these?"

"What do you think?"

"Oh!" It came to Dylan. "It's the song! Is it the whole song??"

Steven nodded. It *was* the whole song. Out on the ranch, Lillian Lilly had placed characters for each day of the "Twelve Days of Christmas." By the stable at the edge of the town, eight maids went about with their a-milking. The four calling-bird crows perched in a tree; a tribe of twelve Native American drummers were caught in mid-strike up in the hills; five cowboys made five golden-ring lassos; and two "Lonesome Doves" stared at each other from a safe distance. The pear tree was a cactus, of course.

"Was she always into cowboy stuff?"

"Beats me. I didn't think so."

"Well???" Mrs. Lilly had floated into the room. Her face was already alight with excitement. It needed no special effects tonight.

"Mrs. Lilly, it is amazing. It's just. . ." Dylan circled around the table again—leaning in to see the details. "It's unbelievable." She smiled and turned to share her enthusiasm with Steven, hoping he'd join in. "It's like a dream."

"You are so sweet." Lillian hugged Dylan. Steven stared, wide-eyed. His mother liked Dylan a lot, but he was sure they had never even touched before. However, it looked completely natural, like they were old college friends. He marveled at how easily women can emote. He wondered if it was genetic. The sight made him a little dizzy.

"I'm excited for the lights," Dylan said.

"You're going to love it!" Mrs. Lilly looked over at Steven. He tried out a smile. He didn't want to be the embarrassed son. He had the presence of mind to know that was a cliché. Still, the premise of the night was hard to get behind.

"It does look great." This, from Steven, pleased her immensely. She grabbed them both by the shoulders.

"Could you help me with some things in the kitchen?" That seemed more like it, thought Steven. That's a normal thing to do.

Dylan was certain she'd never been inside the Lilly kitchen. To hear Steven tell it, Mrs. Lilly rarely cooked—even before Foster left. They were a takeout, microwave, prepared-food family. The kitchen seemed to confirm this. It was spotless, like something out of a kitchen makeover TV show. On the counter, there was a bowl of fake fruit next to three purposeless, decorative orange bottles. There were no pictures on the refrigerator or on the walls. Surfaces were polished to a high sheen, and the brightness, combined with the recessed lighting on the ceiling, made Dylan feel like she was walking into a desert mirage. It was brief, but it was the first of two light shows that night. She shaded her eyes. Mrs. Lilly noticed.

"Sorry about that." She dimmed the lights over the kitchen island. "Could you two help me arrange these cookies and candies on these plates over here?" Lillian motioned to a stack of store-bought treats. "And maybe when you're done that, you could fold these cloth napkins?"

"You're using the cloth napkins," Steven said.

"Yes. Why?" It wasn't a question, so Steven let it drop.

Steven and Dylan got to work on the arranging as Mrs. Lilly retrieved plates from a tall cupboard. It was quiet. Christmas music played in the living room, but it was hard to hear in the kitchen.

"I love your dress, Mrs. Lilly," Dylan said. Lillian was wearing a royal blue A-line dress, and a chunky red glass necklace that matched her shoes.

"Thank you!" She put the plates down on the counter.

"I bought one that looks just like it for the wedding."

"Really?"

Steven squeezed Dylan's hand and glared at her. She shot a look back, unsure of what she'd done wrong. Dylan assumed Steven was telling her to avoid small talk.

"What wedding are you going to?" Mrs. Lilly turned to face them as she put down the last of the plates.

"To—" She'd realized it too late. Steven was still staring at her. Dylan couldn't imagine Mrs. Lilly didn't already know about Mr. Lilly's impending marriage. Dylan turned to look out the window, hoping the right answer was floating around somewhere in the December air.

"Well, that's not a good sign. If you can't remember—" Mrs. Lilly stopped short. Her attention swung over to her son. Steven, who could often rescue a situation with a quick line, stared at the Christmas cookies. "What? What did I say?"

"Nothing." Steven noticed a plastic cookie container, half-open. Its opening looked like a mouth. His mother was its ventriloquist.

"Steven. What is going on?"

Dylan waited for Steven to say something, but nothing was coming. *Was he just going to stand there?* Mrs. Lilly shifted her attention back to Dylan. Something had changed in her eyes. If Steven hadn't been standing between Dylan and the hallway back to the front door, Dylan might have considered leaving and walking home. It surprised both Dylan and Steven when Mrs. Lilly grabbed a cookie and ate it over the sink.

"You weren't going to tell me?" she began.

"No," Steven replied.

"You weren't?"

"It's not really my job, is it?"

The logic stopped Mrs. Lilly. "No, you're right. But that doesn't mean you couldn't have told me."

"Is it that much of a surprise?"

Lillian thought about this. Dylan noticed a band of headlights sweep through the windows. Lillian grabbed a wine glass from the cabinet next to the stove. She opened the refrigerator and grabbed a black box of wine.

"It's been three years." This simple fact floated in the air.

"I know," Mrs. Lilly said finally. She grabbed two cookies, put them in the empty wine glass, and made for the back door, back through the laundry room.

"Where are you going?" Steven asked. "We have people coming over." A door slammed in the driveway. Mrs. Lilly said nothing as she closed the door behind her and disappeared into the back yard.

Steven shifted his eyes back to Dylan. He just stared.

"What??" Why was he angry with her? How was she supposed to know his mother didn't know about the wedding? "You didn't tell me your mom didn't know."

"So you thought my mom might want to talk about the dress you're wearing to his wedding?"

"I was just saying I liked her dress." The doorbell rang.

"Then just say that." Steven turned and left. Dylan watched him go upstairs.

Whoever was at the door had resorted to knocking. She heard Steven's door close upstairs. She heard the click of the lock. Mrs. Lilly had vanished with a box of wine and Christmas cookies. Dylan Geringer would answer the door, then—if that's how these two wanted to play it. Darling Energy would have to save this night from further disaster.

"You?"

At least Mr. Smith—of Smith Security Systems—recognized her this time. He couldn't hide his grimace. Dylan understood. When she saw him last, he had backed into a patrol car.

"Dylan?" Mrs. Smith was carrying a bottle of something. "How nice." She let herself in and gave Dylan a hug. Dylan and Steven could never understand how someone so cheery could be married to someone so unpleasant. Trailing behind both Smiths were their twin daughters. Was it June and Julie? she tried to remember. They were eight and wore matching Christmas sweaters—little snowflakes and stars.

"Are you the help tonight?" Mr. Smith.

Dylan tried a laugh. "No. Just a guest."

"Do you remember Dylan?" Mrs. Smith asked either June or Julie.

"No," one of them said. Mr. Smith laughed.

"I do," the other said. "Steven's girlfriend."

"Oh, I don't know about that, June," Mrs. Smith said. She looked at Dylan to see if the answer was written there. Something dropped upstairs. "Is Lillian still getting ready? We're not early, are we?"

"She said seven o'clock. It's seven o'clock. We're right on time." Mr. Smith tapped his watch. The girls whisked past Dylan and into the living room.

"Mommy!" June said.

"Look at it," said Julie.

The village was unlit, but even in its darkness, it was a sight.

"Don't run in there—be careful!" Mrs. Smith warned. "Oh my!" Mrs. Smith followed her daughters into the living room. Mr. Smith followed, but kept one eye on Dylan.

"Look at this! It's—it's amazing." Mrs. Smith looked back at her husband for confirmation. "Is Lillian in the kitchen? Does she need help?" Mrs. Smith said.

"Where's Steven?" asked Julie.

These were all good questions, thought Dylan, but another doorbell ring was the only answer.

"Excuse me," Dylan said as she made her way to the door. Out the front window, Dylan saw another car pull into the driveway. Dylan had no idea how many people had been invited—or if she would be the only host for the night. She looked back into the kitchen and out the back door, hoping to see Mrs. Lilly walking back in—but no luck.

In the next ten minutes, she welcomed five more guests. First it was Rabbi Elysse from Kesher Israel Congregation. Steven had mentioned her once, back when he was considering converting to Judaism. While it was another one of his short-lived obsessions, his mother and he got to know Rabbi Elysse well. She and Lillian became friends. Ironically, Rabbi Elysse was easily the most enthusiastic about the Christmas display.

"Doesn't this just get you in the spirit?" she asked the Smith girls.

The next were the Joneses from across the street, who, in some weird bit of reciprocal neighborhood DNA had twin boys about the age of the twin Smith girls. Mrs. Smith acted as a surrogate host when she saw Janet Jones. "We're just trying to keep up with the Joneses," she told her. This must have been an old joke as it simultaneously pleased Mrs. Jones and Mrs. Smith and forced eye rolls from Mr. Smith and Mr. Jones. Men could be such bores, Dylan thought.

Mrs. Smith took Dylan aside. "Is she okay?" she whispered to Dylan. "What happened? Where's Steven?"

"They had a little fight. Steven's upstairs. Mrs. Lilly is out back."

"Oh, dear. I'll see if I can talk to her." The doorbell rang again.

"Do you need help?" Rabbi Elysse asked.

"That's okay. I know where she went. Could you just get the door?"

Before Dylan walked back into the kitchen toward the back door, she turned up the Christmas music on the stereo. Maybe that would fill the awkward spaces.

She found Mrs. Lilly in the dark, sitting on the cement slab at the end of the patio. It was too cold to be sitting outside in her pretty blue dress. Without turning around, Mrs. Lilly spoke first. She knew it was Dylan.

"Do you know any of the constellations?"

It sounded like an invitation, so Dylan sat down next to her. "I know Orion. That's him, right?" Dylan pointed up into the sky. "That's the belt?"

"Yes, that's right. That's probably the most recognizable one." Lillian pointed to his left shoulder. "That star is Betelgeuse."

"My dad taught me a little. Orion's the hunter?"

"Right." Mrs. Lilly handed Dylan her wine glass. "Could you hold this for a second?" Lillian held the box of wine at an angle and poured herself another glass. "Thank you, honey."

"That's about all I remember, though."

"The one I like," Lillian took a sip of her wine, "the one I always look for is the Pleiades. You know that one?"

"I don't think so."

"The Pleiades are the seven sisters."

"Oh, right. We read about them in English."

"In English?"

"It's in *Streetcar Named Desire*. Something Blanche says."

"Is that right?"

"It's when Blanche is all alone."

"Hmm." Lillian looked over at Dylan. "I must seem like a character in a book. Do I seem like a character in a book?" she asked. Dylan wasn't sure how to answer that one. She used a Steven strategy.

"Don't we all seem like characters in a book?" Mrs. Lilly thought that one over. She raised her eyebrows and grinned. She said nothing, but Dylan was sure she heard her son's voice in that line. Dylan wasn't convinced that she herself seemed like much of a book character, but why not? Dylan changed the topic. "Where are they?"

Lillian pointed up to the sky. "If you draw a line through the three stars of Orion's belt to the right, you'll see this v-shaped pattern of stars. You see? With a real bright star in the middle."

Dylan followed the belt and found the misty sisters.

"It's visible from virtually every place on the Earth. As far north as the North Pole, as far south as the southernmost tip of South America."

"I didn't know you know so much about the stars."

"I don't. I mean, I did. Briefly." Lillian took another gulp of wine. "In college. It's where I met Foster—Mr. Lilly. In Astronomy class."

"Oh, right." Dylan had heard the story from Steven before—how their love was in the stars.

"Steven's a lot like his father." Dylan nodded and took her word for it. "Their focus. Their odd. . ." she looked for the right word, ". . .ambitions." Dylan knew better than to interrupt. Mrs. Lilly was trying to figure something out. She sighed and changed gears with another gulp of wine.

"You like Steven." Dylan couldn't tell if it was a question or not.

"I do." She searched for the right thing to say. It finally occurred to her: "He's my best friend."

It was a simple statement, but Dylan had never said it before. She wasn't sure, however obvious it may have been to everyone else, if she had ever thought it before. Dylan always expected she would have had one close *girl* friend at this point in her life, someone besides her sister who would have rivaled her friendship with Steven—but it never seemed to happen. Sitting under the stars and out in the cold, with a progressively drunker Mrs. Lilly, the statement took Dylan by surprise. She wasn't sure why, but her eyes welled up. Lillian noticed and started bawling.

Their sweet moment under the stars had turned on a dime. Mrs. Lilly's cries were heaving yawps, and Dylan didn't know what she was supposed to do. She settled for rubbing Mrs. Lilly's back. At one point, her sobs were so melodramatic, Dylan thought they might be laughter. However, they were not.

"I can't go in there," Lillian spit out.

"Okay."

"Are they all here?"

"Some people are."

"I can't."

"Okay." It was the only word that made any sense right now.

"I think I'm drunk."

"It's okay."

Mrs. Lilly pulled her dress further down over her knees.

"Is there anything I can do for you?" Dylan asked.

"Will you turn the lights on for me?"

"The patio lights?"

"No. The Village lights. That's why they're here."

"Okay. What do I have to do?"

"There's a power strip behind the couch."

"Sure. Okay. But you can't stay out here."

"I can't go in there either."

"Just hang out in the kitchen."

"No."

"Okay. How about just come into the laundry room?"

"I don't want them to see me like this."

"It's too cold out here, though."

Mrs. Lilly eyed up the garden shed. "I'll wait in the shed."

"In the shed?" Mrs. Lilly got up, but almost tripped over the black box of wine.

"Here, let me take that," Dylan said.

"I got it." Mrs. Lilly grabbed the box and glass and made her woozy way to the shed.

"Be careful, Mrs. Lilly."

"I'm fine. The power strip is behind the couch," she repeated. Then she disappeared into the shed.

When Dylan returned to the living room, she found Mr. Drake and his wife among the honored guests. On a normal day, this may have surprised her. Tonight it elicited only a smile of recognition. There was a show to put on, and Dylan would not disappoint. Rabbi Elysse helped Dylan move back the couch.

"Mrs. Lilly isn't feeling well. She asked me to the flip the switch on this beautiful village," Dylan announced. Dylan had never *announced* anything before.

"We should turn these overhead lights off," Mr. Smith said, suddenly interested in the evening.

It was a good decision because when Dylan flipped the power strip on, the room positively glowed. From her kneeling position behind the couch, Dylan's first view was of the audience. Everyone stood silently, catching their breath at the sight. Both sets of twins, standing in the front row, stood slack-jawed. Mrs. Smith and Mrs. Jones covered their mouths. Behind them Mr. Smith, Mr. Jones, and Rabbi Elysse each drew a long, slow breath. In the back row, Mr. and Mrs. Drake, though equally struck, seemed frozen in indecision. When Dylan thought about it later, she wasn't sure what she was witnessing. Was it fear or pain or exhaustion or relief—or some combination—that washed across the Drakes' faces? When she stood up, the music switched to "Hark! The Herald Angels Sing," and she joined the tableau.

Inside each house, saloon, and general store; on every ranch, farm, and crossroads—a light glowed. A tiny choir outside the tiny church held miniature candles that flickered on and off. A circle of cowboys gathered around a tiny fire out on the prairie. On the far edge of the farm, a small barn was alight with the glow of an angel perched above it, casting its light onto the manger. Inside, a cowboy version of the Nativity played out. Had Dylan never flipped the switch bringing this whole world to life, this scene, with its cowboys substituting for shepherds, may have only sparked a chuckle, but illuminated as it was now, it made Dylan wish her parents took her to church.

A Jones boy—Jack—sang along to the chorus:

Hark! The herald angels sing / 'Glory to the newborn king.'

The second verse came along and when the words failed him, he hummed along.

The other kids joined in—June, Julie, and Jack's twin brother, Max.

And then Mrs. Smith.

And then Mrs. Jones. They sang the words to the first verse over the second verse, but no one seemed to notice or care.

Mr. Smith looked suspiciously at the power strip and followed the cord as it disappeared under that table.

Mr. Drake and his wife forced a smile. Trevor put his arm around Elizabeth. Listening to little Jack and Max sing wasn't easy for them.

Somehow the group entertained themselves for an hour, staring at this tiny village. Dylan brought in two plates of cookies. She distributed the cloth napkins. Small talk was made. June Smith played the piano.

Dylan would have liked to talk to Mr. Drake, and meet his wife, but she found it hard work to meet the group's requests for drinks and treats, to fend off questions about Mrs. Lilly and Steven, to small talk with the Smiths and Joneses about her college interests and plans, to show the twins where the bathroom was. She was not a natural host. In between songs, she would hear Steven moving around upstairs. She watched a light go on and off. When she stopped moving for a minute, she'd get angry at Steven for leaving her down here by herself. Or, she wondered, why wouldn't he go check on his mother, alone in the garden shed? Finally, Rabbi Elysse could no longer shirk her duties as counselor and made her way out the back door to find Lillian.

Dylan thought she'd be the adult, too, and was about to make her way up the stairs to find Steven, when Mr. Smith let out a scream.

"It's on fire!"

"What?!"

"The power strip! Get an extinguisher!" A chorus of voices joined in. "Call 911."

"I've got it. Just get an extinguisher!"

"I don't know where there is one," Dylan said.

"Well, look for one," Mr. Smith yelled. Dylan disappeared into the kitchen.

"We should call 911."

"Call 911! Call 911!" Mrs. Smith kept yelling.

"I've got it! Just help me move this back." Mr. Smith ordered Mr. Drake to his side. They both grabbed an end of the display table. It was hard to budge.

"Just yank it." The table screeched out from under the window. Horses and cowboys fell to the ground. The jail fell into the saloon.

"Shouldn't we unplug it?"

"Take the kids outside," Mr. Jones yelled at his wife.

"Did anyone call 911?"

"Where is Lillian??"

"Get Steven!"

"I'm still waiting on that extinguisher!"

Steven came barreling down the stairs.

"What's going on?"

"It's on fire!"

"Get the kids out already!" The Smith and Jones moms grabbed the twins, who were more interested than scared, and ran out the front door.

Steven ran into the kitchen as Mr. Drake and Mr. Smith and Mr. Jones tried to create more space around the fire. The flames popped out of the empty sockets and up the cord toward the curtains.

"Grab it before—shit!" The flames leapt up onto the curtains. Mr. Smith stomped at the fire in the power strip. Mr. Jones grabbed at the curtain and yanked it down with the rod into the center of the room. The curtain rod slammed into Mr. Smith.

"Ow! Watch it!" But now they had a fire in the center of the living room. The curtain lit up like a fuse.

"What are you doing?"

"Containing it?"

Mr. Drake found the outlet where the power strip was plugged in and tore it out of the wall. When he backed up, his back hit a loose end of the village table. More buildings fell. The town lights flickered off. The angel and two horses fell on top of the baby Jesus.

Steven ran into the room with the fire extinguisher. He let loose on this Christmas inferno. He squeezed the white foam on the curtains, on the power strip, on the center of the Christmas village where two cowboys lined up for a showdown. He got some on the shoes and pants of Misters Smith, Jones, and Drake. When he finished, a gooey, snowy mess covered most of the living room floor, rug, and all of the Christmas village.

The fire extinguisher was still oozing when Rabbi Elysse and Lillian Lilly ran into the room. Dylan followed right behind.

There was a pregnant pause—a nine-month pregnant pause—punctuated only by the heavy breaths of men—and Steven. The relief of extinguishing was short-lived. It was replaced by the shamed reverence for the *Christmas village that was,* for the tiny, Western world of Mrs. Lilly's imagination, somehow both smoldering and drenched. Only the eight maids a-milking found a dry spot out on the range.

Steven thought about saying something, but as he drew a breath to begin, sirens filled the air. Dylan and Steven joined Rabbi Elysse, Lillian, Mr. Smith, and Mr. Jones by the side of the front window that was saved from the propellant. They formed an odd, and unintentional lineup, unable to move. When a firefighter jumped off the truck and ran toward the door, Dylan, aware now that no one else would take point on this moment, met their late rescuers at the door. They were followed in by Mrs. Smith and Mrs. Jones, checking on their husbands. Dylan saw Mrs. Drake huddled with the children by the garage door.

Lillian was in no condition to handle questions, so the witnesses there handled the narrative for the firefighters and EMTs. Steven tried to speak, but nothing came out. Instead, he heard Mr. Drake's voice from behind him. Steven hadn't realized Mr. Drake had been there the whole time. Steven also hadn't noticed that he was still holding the fire extinguisher.

It dawned on him that he'd been holding his breath the whole time, too. While Mr. Smith took the firefighters over to the offending power strip, Mr. Drake grabbed Steven by the shoulder.

"Here. Let me take that." Mr. Drake grabbed the extinguisher and put it down on the ground. Steven still could not move. Trevor noticed Steven's head, bobbing up and down in small almost imperceptible movements, still in shock.

"What are you doing here?" Steven managed to get out.

"You saved the day, Steven." It was clear Steven still wasn't following. "Come here." Trevor, still holding onto Steven's shoulders, turned him around so they were facing each other. "You okay?" Trevor hugged Steven. Steven rested his head on Trevor's shoulder. The foam on the floor gathered around their feet like they were standing in snow. Neither of them said a word.

Lillian watched her ruined world from a bench by the staircase. The rabbi had found a blanket. She used it to cover Mrs. Lilly, who, though she showed no signs of it, was frozen from being outside for so long.

Dylan fought the urge to join the Steven-Mr. Drake hug. It wasn't easy. If she could, she'd hold onto the both of them, and maybe, somehow, the three of them could just disappear, disintegrate into tiny parts, and then reassemble in Mr. Drake's classroom on the first day of school, and just start the year over—or reassemble in Mrs. Lilly's Christmas village before the great fire, out on the plain by the campfire, far from the jail and the schoolhouse. Maybe if she squeezed her eyes shut, it would be March 15th, her birthday—and the anniversary of Benjamin Drake's death—and the town would be assembled around Valley Forge's Memorial Arch, and Mr. Ryerson and his barbershop quartet would be singing "You Must

Have Been a Beautiful Baby"; and Mr. Drake would speak about his son; and Daphne, home for spring break, would bring her boyfriend, Jay; and her parents would stand alongside Mrs. Lilly; and Norman and Lester and Mr. Lewis would come; and Mr. Lilly with Vernon; and maybe even Royce Caulder and Chris Strawbridge would be there, and Nicole, hopping around on her crutches; the entire school, the borough businesses; a plane with a banner, a marching band, a hot air balloon; and Steven and Dylan would stand under the arch and just breathe it all in.

Dylan hadn't realized that her eyes had been shut. When she opened them, Steven had left Mr. Drake in the living room. He was trying to talk to his mom.

"Mom. Mom." He tried again. "Mom?"

"Let's get you upstairs, Lillian," Rabbi Elysse said.

Dylan came over to help, but there was already a circle of help surrounding Lillian. The rabbi and Steven grabbed Mrs. Lilly by her elbows and steadied her for the trip up the stairs. They moved so solemnly up the stairs that Dylan couldn't help thinking it resembled some nineteenth-century period drama, that Mrs. Lilly was Miss Havisham wandering around a mid-celebration shamble of a house. By the time she turned around to look for Mr. Drake, he had already stepped outside to join his wife. Dylan was the lone guest left in the house. She watched out the window as Mr. and Mrs. Drake put their arms around each other, as they watched the Smith and Jones children walk with the parents down the driveway and out into the darkness.

"It's not really safe for you to stand here." A fireman was talking to her. "Do you live here?"

Dylan looked up the staircase. "No."

"Do you have a ride home?"

"My car's here."

"You should call your parents."

"They live in the next neighborhood over. I'll just—" Dylan took one last look around the ruined living room, the Christmas village shrapnel, scattered over the floor. "I'll just drive home. Thank you."

On her way out the door, she noticed the angel figurine, the one that had been perched over the manger, stuck against the baseboard, nearly hidden under the foam. She took it and put it in her pants pocket. She grabbed her coat from the hall closet and walked down the driveway to her car.

"What's that ladder doing there?" a fireman asked another fireman.

"It was there when we came."

"Well, take it down. It's dangerous to just leave it up there like that."

And so, the fireman took down the ladder to Steven's room, walked it back inside the garage, and just like that, the gate to her three-year friendship with Steven was gone.

Looking into her rearview mirror up at a ladder-less Steven's bedroom window, Dylan knew something had changed. But she wasn't sure what. All she knew was that she had a lot of work ahead of her. March 15th was only three months away.

TWENTY-TWO

Dylan was glad Daphne was back for Christmas, even if she had to share her with Jay, her boyfriend since July. They seemed like a good match.

"What do you think?" Mrs. Geringer asked her husband after the two left for a movie.

"He's tall."

"Okay. And?"

"Friendly." He noticed that Dylan was paying attention. "I think he's tall and friendly."

"That's it?"

"What do you think?" he asked Dylan.

"I agree."

"On which part?" her mother asked.

"Both parts. I think he is both tall and friendly."

"Well, I guess it's settled then."

When they arrived, Daphne had adopted a strange affectation. It wasn't accompanied by a British accent, but there were echoes of a judgmental tone that was a good bit posher than Dylan expected of her sister.

"Oh, please, we're not drinking that stuff," she said to the Heineken in her father's hands when he offered it to Jay. Jay took it anyway, and from what Dylan could make out, enjoyed it. In this tall and friendly man's hands the bottle looked airline-flight-sized.

When politics came up, suddenly Dylan and her parents weren't progressive enough. When traveling came up, they weren't cosmopolitan enough. When education came up, Daphne came dangerously close to questioning if it had any real value, but retreated when she saw the look on her benefactors' faces.

Daphne had planned on studying theater until the end of her freshman year, but then realized that Brown's theater program was flighty even by Brown standards, after which she drifted for a bit into modern culture and media, until somebody pointed out she'd never get a job with that major, until finally, when she had no more time to conceive of the right trajectory, she somewhat reluctantly landed as a poli-sci major.

Dylan could understand her interest in politics. Daphne had always been an activist of some sort. Dylan used to marvel at all the PowerPoints her sister would make for her parents: why they should get a dog, better distribution of chores, why they should pay for her car insurance. But still: she wouldn't tell Daphne this, but Dylan was disappointed that the political Daphne beat out the theatrical Daphne who used to put on plays with her sister. That was the side Dylan liked talking to. She'd met Jay in a poli-sci class, and she and her parents suspected this played a large part in the decision process, but they knew better than to suggest such a sexist conclusion to Daphne.

Steven had been avoiding school lately, staying home with his mother. He and Dylan still texted, but Steven thought it was best if she not come over for a while.

"It's just not a good time," he told her. Dylan knew it was true, but, vainly she thought, still took it personally.

Dylan enjoyed her own mystery-fame so much, she wanted to present Daphne with her own Steven-conceived anagram name. He provided one, but the combination of letters wouldn't play nicely for Steven. He found *endanger, angered, enraged, gangrened,* and *grenade,* but the rest eluded him. He settled on *Hip Gender Anger* or *Hip Green Garden*—Dylan could take her pick. *Hip Gender Anger* was too on point, and the other too hippie-dippie. Dylan would wait to see how the rest of Daphne's visit would go first.

Later that night, Daphne invited Dylan to go out to dinner with Jay and her.

"Without mom and dad," went the invitation. "Bring Steven."

"I don't think he can make it."

"Check."

"Trust me," Dylan said. He hadn't left his house for anything since the Christmas party. "I don't want to leave her here," was the excuse. Dylan knew his concern about his mother was authentic, but also knew him well enough to know it was a convenient excuse for shutting down and disappearing into his own depression.

"Just check," Daphne insisted.

Dylan took out her phone and held it in front of Daphne, as she texted Steven.

Come out to dinner with Daphne and me? she wrote.

"Don't phrase it like a question. Tell him he's coming."

In less than five seconds, the typing bubbles appeared on her phone.

I can't. Need to stay in. Steven wrote.

"Ask him what for?" Daphne said.

"See?" Dylan scrolled up on her text thread with Steven to show her sister. It was a series of recent curt responses from the past two weeks:

Staying in.

Can't make it.

She's not doing well.

Not a good time.

Daphne was convinced. "Fine. Okay, then get dressed and let's get going."

Dylan looked down at her red and black plaid shirt and jeans. "I am dressed."

"We're going out to *dinner.*" Daphne walked back into the kitchen where she'd left Jay with her parents.

Dylan couldn't think of a restaurant in town that wouldn't welcome jeans, but she needed to get out of the house and didn't feel like defending herself. When she came down the stairs five minutes later, Daphne made a face at the shift dress and sweater combo Dylan had chosen.

"What?"

"Nothing."

Jay was already in the car as Dylan followed her sister through the front door.

"What is that?" Jay asked.

"What is what?" Daphne was making a left turn and didn't see it right away.

"What does it say?"

Daphne looked up at the trestle bridge. Dylan had hoped they might come this way. They were passing the *DARLING ENERGY* graffiti painted high up on the side of the bridge.

"What is this *Darling Energy*?" Dylan wanted to tell her sister about the messages, about March 15th, about everything—but she hadn't had the chance, and besides, she wasn't sure how to start.

"I keep seeing that," Daphne said.

"You've seen it before?" Dylan asked.

"Yeah. Why? What does it mean?"

"Where have you seen it before??" Dylan couldn't imagine anyone outside of town would have heard the phrase before.

"All over."

"Yeah," Jay agreed.

He knew, too??

"It was painted on that cell-phone lot wall. At the airport. Wasn't it?" Jay asked Daphne.

"Yeah. And then there was the church sign. The push letter one. It was like "Come and dore Him" because someone took the *a* from *adore* and used it to spell *Darling Energy*."

"Are you serious??"

"Who or what is Darling Energy??"

Dylan was a little delirious. She hadn't realized that her anagram alter ego had escaped her sleepy suburb beyond a few school signs and one very impressive bridge lettering. What was it doing at an airport parking lot? Or on churches? She wanted to text Steven about these developments, but it "wasn't a good time." Even for *this*, she wondered? There was some thrill to having this information, and that she would be able to fill in her sister at dinner, that for once, she'd have the answer to something her sister wondered about. She thought she might tease them with a little tidbit, but before she could, Jay held up his phone for Daphne as they sat idling at a traffic light.

He read a headline. "'Police Investigate *Darling Energy*.' He continued reading. "'Weeks after police first noticed a Malvern bridge defaced with graffiti, area residents have complained to police that the mysterious phrase has been found at local businesses, churches, and schools—both in the form of graffiti and social media posts.'"

"Where are you reading that?"

Jay passed his phone back to Dylan. Dylan scrolled through the story. It mentioned the school's automated phone messaging system, with each message transcribed. The effect of reading those words, conceived haphazardly on a whim with Steven—and before by Lester—here, inside an actual article in an actual newspaper, or at least in an actual online one, rattled Dylan. They were sandwiched between quotes from Dr. King at school and a police chief. Toward the end of the article, the irony of reading a quote from a Mr. Jim Smith, "a security professional," of all people, who seemed to follow Dylan around like a shadow this last month, prompted no chuckle out of Dylan. She could only scan the quote after the word *terrorist* jumped off the phone screen. Her face flushed, and she shut off the phone and handed back to Jay.

"Maybe it's an environmental activist," Daphne started. They were pulling into the restaurant parking lot. "Some sort of alternative energy company. A viral, grassroots PR thing. That happens all the time up at school."

"It doesn't sound like a company," Jay said. "Maybe it's an allusion."

"Well, yeah."

"I mean, maybe it's a literary allusion."

"From what?"

"I don't know. I'm just saying maybe it is. I'll google it."

Daphne pulled into the parking spot. "Wait till we're inside." Daphne and Jay opened their doors and closed them, still mulling it over. Dylan didn't move.

It was all getting away from her, this story. She should tell Daphne. But not if the police are involved. But it's not like she did anything wrong. I mean, not *much* of anything. They sent a few phone calls out. It was all for fun. She didn't do any of the graffiti stuff. Nothing illegal, really. Had she? "Area residents" are complaining? *Terrorism?!* It's not terrorism, and it's not an alternative energy viral campaign nor a Shakespearean allusion. It's just her name, scrambled up. A discovery of Steven's. It's just a bunch of letters, signifying nothing.

"Dylan!" Daphne knocked on the window. "What's wrong?"

It must have been written on her face. Daphne opened the car door. Dylan was still strapped into her seat belt.

"What's going on?" Jay stood behind Daphne, looking in.

"You feeling okay?" Jay asked.

"It's Darling Energy, isn't it?" Dylan said nothing. Her sister saw right through her. "What do you know?"

"I—" she started, but she stopped.

"Get out of the car. Tell me everything. But over dinner. I'm starved."

"Look!" Jay was pointing at the pole holding the restaurant sign.

Darling Energy gathered the throng! March 15th! it read.

"Look, they've even got stickers," Jay said. He smiled and opened the restaurant door for Daphne and Dylan.

"The ides of March! Caesar! See, I told you it was a literary allusion."

"Well, let's hope no one gets assassinated then," Daphne said.

Dylan's phone buzzed. *Norman?* What does he want?

It read: "You need to tell someone." A link to the same article followed.

Shit. *Norman* knows Darling Energy, too. She shut that fact—and Norman—out of her head somehow. Who else had they told about her anagram name? *She should "tell someone"? Who is Norman to tell her to do anything?*

***

Mr. Drake poured another bourbon. He took a sip and put the tumbler down next to the labeler. He'd taken to labeling again. He needed to think this over. Elizabeth had been offered a job. "Not exactly offered," she explained. "They would be creating the position for me." The proposal would require them to move out west, to just outside San Diego. Her sister lived in the city. She didn't push the idea, but it was floated out there, and it hadn't landed yet.

"You could find a teaching job out there."

"I could."

"Or not. Do something else. You don't have to be a teacher forever."

She was right. Although, that's what most teachers did. They taught forever. It was a secure job. What would he do if he didn't teach?

"You could write a book."

Trevor exhaled. "Just think about it," she said before she headed off to bed.

So that's what he was doing. Thinking and drinking. If she had asked last week, before that party at the Lillys' house, he would have thought of better arguments for staying. Something about that night, those twin boys singing carols, a drunk Mrs. Lilly, that dark cul-de-sac so much like his own. When the fire broke out over that Christmas town, he imagined himself as one of its figures—even as he pulled the curtains off the wall. It was an out-of-body experience, and he hadn't found his way back in since.

It would be a new start. There was no denying that. And Elizabeth would be happy. Shouldn't one of them be happy? And couldn't he, for once, do something unexpected, something unpredictable?

The last bourbon offered no answers, but he wouldn't give up asking it. He'd leave the ice out this time. He knew that's how you're supposed to drink it. Trevor remembered the shame he felt at that small pub in Doolin—on a trip to Ireland with Elizabeth—when the bartender shook his head when he asked for his Jameson's "on the rocks." On the same trip, he reached for a Guinness before it had properly settled. It was an unpardonable sin, and he was glad they were leaving the next day.

It was the summer after Benjamin died. While he and Elizabeth agreed they needed a trip to get away from things, they both knew—though neither spoke it aloud—that the trip would be a disaster. He put a giant scratch on the side of the rental car, trying to squeeze past a roadside rock wall. As they sped past beautiful green pastures and ocean vistas, Trevor was only aware of how narrow the roads were. He gripped the steering wheel so tightly he gave himself a headache. Elizabeth tried to point out a castle here and there, but she felt Trevor's tension in the car. When they finally would get out to walk around thirteenth-century ruins, the history didn't comfort them. Everywhere they walked, the rocks—when they weren't tombstones—reminded them of tombstones, older versions of the one Benjamin hit his head against, of the one he lay beneath.

The only pleasant part of the trip was all the rain. The rain was commiseration. At another pub in Donegal, Trevor was happy to learn about all words the Irish had for rain. His teacher was an old woman who sat at the bar next to them. "We say, *it's a grand soft day*," she explained, "when the mist only gathers around the mountains. Then, there's *spitting* when it looks like things might clear up any second. A bit more than that is a *wetting rain*. It's a pretty tricky mist that might just soak through your clothing if you didn't have a good umbrella."

Trevor marveled—he'd had few beers and shots by then—at all the verbs that followed: *pissing, bucketing, hooring, pelting, lashing.* "*Hammering*'s the worst," she said as she finished. "It will ruin you."

"There's only seven types of rain in Ireland," a man at the end of the bar piped in. The bartender smiled at the joke that was coming. "Sunday, Monday, Tuesday, Wednesday. . ."

***

The rain kept following Trevor. January didn't even have the good sense to snow. There was no blanket, just puddles. Trevor walked over to look out the window. It was coming down hard—somewhere between a *pissing* and a *pelting*, he thought. He still hadn't put the hose away. Not since Dylan Geringer tripped over it. For a moment, he let himself imagine the two of them back in his yard. The bourbon made his head swim.

He pictured Steven by the lamppost.

"You can't move out west," Steven told him.

"Why not?"

"You're not a West Coast guy."

He pictured Dylan walking past the tree, stopping a few feet from the window. She didn't speak. Just stared at Trevor.

"It's three hours behind there. All the time. They never catch up."

"I don't want to catch up."

"So you'll just retire?"

"Maybe."

Dylan took another step closer to the window.

"What about your students?" Steven continued.

"What about them?" he said. Dylan took another step. She was only two feet from the window where Trevor stood.

"You can't leave them."

"Why not? They leave me every year."

Trevor scored a point with imaginary-Steven. Steven walked toward the window to join Dylan.

"Every year I get to know them, and every year they leave."

"But you get new ones," Steven said. He was standing next to Dylan now.

"It's not the same. I don't want new ones."

Trevor didn't know what lines to give Dylan. She just kept staring at him. Finally, he decided she would reach out to the window, and lay her palm against one of the panes.

Trevor tried to elicit some magic realism, tried to make a light emanate from Dylan's palm—to do what, he wasn't sure. But it was harder than he thought. The harder he tried, the more she and Steven faded from the scene. They were gone when he heard the whoosh of the toilet from upstairs.

***

"*Hip Gender Anger??*"

Jay thought that was hilarious. "It's perfect."

Daphne slapped his hand that rested on the table.

"See. There's the anger. Perfect."

"That's the best one?" Daphne asked her sister.

"Well, there's *Hip Green Garden.*"

"I don't like that one either."

"It wouldn't make for great graffiti," Jay added.

"No. It wouldn't." Daphne took a sip of wine. "Well, what are you going to do?"

"I don't know." Dylan had told her sister mostly everything. "I mean, unless someone figures out it's my name. But it's not my name. Not really. And anyway, just because it is, it doesn't mean I was responsible."

"But you *were* responsible."

"Not for what it's become."

"Here's another one." Jay was reading off his phone. "Oh, it's your school newspaper. This is a pretty good-looking site."

"What is it?" asked Dylan. She wanted the summary. She wasn't sure she could read through it right now.

"Different theories." He scrolled a little farther. "It says there's a club??"

"For what?"

Daphne interrupted. "Okay. But what should we do about this?"

"We?" Dylan said. "I told you, I don't know if I should say anything—"

"No. I mean about March 15th? About your birthday party?" The waitress came over to clear their plates. Dylan waited for her to walk away. "You cannot give up this plan now. You've invited everyone to come to your party. You can't cancel."

"I don't want it to be a birthday party. I want it to be a party for the town. An event."

"Well, it doesn't look like you have any choice." Jay was looking at his phone again. He'd found a subreddit forum that someone had started already: /darling energy. "It's going to happen whether you show up or not."

"People are going to take over your story."

"They already have."

"Well, then. What are you going to do about it?"

"I've got a barbershop quartet coming." It was the only thing Dylan had to offer.

"A what?? Listen: you need to think big here. No matter what anyone else is planning, you are Darling Energy. It's your alias they're using. Imagine the reveal." Daphne was getting a little too excited.

"My reveal??"

"Yes. Let's say a bunch of people show up. Then what? You've got to have some plan."

"We need Steven for this." Dylan felt lost having this conversation without Steven. She wasn't sure what Steven would think if he knew Daphne knew.

"Yes, you do. We're leaving tomorrow. And it's only two months away.

You two need to get on this." Daphne finished her wine. She looked at Jay and back at her sister. "This is exciting! Don't you think?"

Jay looked at Dylan for her answer.

"We'll come, of course."

Dylan nodded her head. She tried to convince herself with each nod, but she was staring at her lap.

***

At school, February was the longest month of the year. Despite its twenty-eight days, it was a slog for students and teachers alike. The winter vacation was a distant memory, and spring break was nowhere in sight. You might be more than halfway through the school year, but it never felt like it. It was a purgatory of punishing tedium. Every assignment was a struggle. You were treading water, sick of the winter, sick of the dark, sick of your assigned seat, sick of your teacher, sick of your students—and just plain sick: with the flu, with whooping cough (When did that come back? Trevor wondered), with mono, with stomach bugs, with bronchitis. Trevor couldn't keep his room stocked with enough tissues. Students would parade back and forth to the tissue box by the classroom door. Each blow was thick with rattling snot, nostril by nostril, never completely emptying. And the coughing! Dry, sharp coughs from one side of the room would be answered by wet ones that sounded like clogged garbage disposals.

In February, it was easy to imagine quitting.

The students had no choice, but Trevor did. He could make plans to sell his house, to pack all of his belongings, and move out to San Diego, where it was comfortable and perfect every day. An earthquake would be his only worry, he figured. But even that seemed like a fun alternative than February right here, right now. Swallowed up by the earth didn't sound that bad. Not right now.

After twenty-six years, Trevor knew things would get better. He knew March, once he got past the 15th, would shake things out, and that April was *almost May*, as his students would remind him. May, of course, was almost June, and June was the end. Things seemed a little different this year, though. This Darling Energy thing wouldn't go away, and while there hadn't been one of those messages in weeks, it was still a *thing*. Someone had made magnets and put them on the lockers around the school. Some clever Sharpie-work had changed the GVHS sign outside the gym to DEHS—*Darling Energy High School?* There could be worse honorees, he supposed. Trevor's wife reported that she overheard the hospital chaplain talking to an orderly about Darling Energy outside the chapel. And Trevor's students wouldn't stop talking about it. He'd learned to tolerate their curiosity, but it was a constant reminder of March 15th, and the ten years that had passed since Benjamin passed away. It was a countdown he couldn't get behind, and not to mention, it confused him. I guess that was the point, but still: why did everybody care so much? So he asked.

He was supposed to be leading a conversation about Tim O'Brien's *The Things They Carried*, but it could wait a few minutes.

"What is it about this Darling Energy thing that interests you so much?" he began. The class quieted down. They remembered how Mr. Drake flipped out last time the subject was broached in class. An old teaching rule said he should wait at least seven seconds to see if someone would venture a response. He gave them fourteen seconds, but no one spoke up. Dylan stole a look over at Steven.

"Seriously. I get it's mysterious, I suppose. But what is it exactly? What are you hoping for?"

Dylan wanted to help Mr. Drake out here, but she had been growing more and more anxious as the date approached. She knew she would go to the Memorial Arch at 3:33 that day, but she was still unsure if she had any real role in the event. Ted Lavender spoke up first.

"It's interesting." He thought it over more. Dylan noticed that he'd grown less annoying as the year went on. Someone told her his mother was sick. "And. . .nothing else is as interesting. Not in this way, at least. I mean, it's—"

Molly took over. "It's unpredictable, right?" Molly would often end sentences with *right?* It was hard to disagree with her this way. "Just objectively, it makes for a great story. Strange phone calls come in the night. They tell us about a day and a time and a place. They mention a strange name of someone who will gather us all together, right? Don't you think that's interesting?" The question was for Mr. Drake.

He tried nodding. "Yeah, but what if it's a hoax? What if it doesn't mean anything at all?"

"Don't we always take that chance?"

It was Dylan who uttered the rhetorical, but she didn't recognize the voice resonating in her throat. She wasn't even sure what she meant. She was trying to convince herself of something. She hadn't meant to say anything at all. Steven looked over at her. Dylan stared back and could feel the eyes of the class on her.

Dylan shrugged her shoulders. It was a carefree shrug. A zen-shrug.

"Don't we always take that chance?" she repeated.

"Don't we always take *what chance*?" Trevor took a step closer to her desk. Maybe he needed to listen more to his students. Wasn't it Dylan who came to his house and listened to him talk about Benjamin? Didn't Dylan drive him home after he got stuck in the rain? Hadn't she offered that *I'll be fine* label back to him—the one he keeps in his wallet now? Come to think of it, wasn't it Dylan Geringer who helped him put out a house fire? Trevor tried to think of the right analogy. She wasn't a guardian angel or his shadow or his ghost—nothing like that. But she was about the right age—Steven, too. This whole class, maybe—alternate Benjamins, phantom limbs, younger versions of Trevor himself. And everything is new to them, all the time. Each question and discovery. Every happiness and disappointment. They never get older. They just graduate, and then there are new ones. It wasn't ignorance or naiveté, or even innocence. That's not what he saw when he looked and listened to Dylan. *Is it hope?*

"Is what hope?" Dylan asked. Trevor must have said that out loud. How much had he just said?

"I'm sorry." Trevor's thoughts were written all over his face. He hadn't realized that he'd walked right up to Dylan's desk. He was too close to elicit a follow-up response from her.

Molly broke the tension. "March 15th is Dylan's birthday, anyway. I think this whole thing has been an elaborate plan for a birthday party." The class laughed. Dylan, too.

Trevor had forgotten that. Steven had told him, at his house. Despite spending a career looking for symbols in literature, Trevor resisted looking for signs in his own life. He didn't believe in fate. He knew his ebbs of depression made him a more susceptible target for *signs*. The voice in his head was good at keeping those vain interpretations silent, but here was Dylan again, not just showing up in person, but showing up in the past, as well. "What if it doesn't mean anything at all?" he had asked. "Don't we always take that chance?" she had said. What chance was he supposed to take?

Steven kept staring at Dylan. Dylan couldn't tell if Steven was as invested in the question. He was a little better, but things still weren't back to normal. It was the first day this week he was back in school.

"You like a good story, Mr. Drake," Ted added. "And this is a good story."

"I guess you're right." Trevor sat down. "Speaking of which: let's talk about this book."

Trevor looked at the blue and black cover, the shadowed outline of soldiers marching in a line, looking for a sign.

TWENTY-THREE

Steven liked being the caretaker of his dad's house. Save for a few days of school here and there, it was the only time he'd leave his own house, leave his mother there by herself. She didn't like it, but he'd promised his dad he would check in every week, and besides, he was getting paid. His dad made weekly deposits into his PayPal account, and after a month and half, he had enough money to scour eBay and Etsy for his new collecting obsession: Russian nesting dolls. His favorite set was a vintage set of Ukrainian Matryoshka dolls. The seven dolls made for an odd family—the men wore long, dark handlebar mustaches and the women sported headscarves knotted across their foreheads. The smallest male doll looked just like its patriarch: a receding hairline, a red and raw nose, and heavy lidded eyes framed by dark eyebrows. Big or small, everyone was a suffering adult.

The Phoenixville row home afforded Steven the opportunity to play house. In his version, he had no kids and no spouse. He was just a bachelor with an entire house to himself. He liked that there was no TV and the internet was spotty. When he would go over to check for the mail and make sure trash cans hadn't blown over and that all the windows and doors were shut tight—and to "keep up appearances," as his dad explained—he'd bring a book and just read by the front window. He'd been by more times than was required over the last two weeks and had gotten to know some of the neighbors. "Hey, Steven," they'd say, as he came up the walk, swinging his keys. Sometimes he'd fix something for Mr. Walters, who lived in the other half of the twin. Maybe he could convince his dad to not sell the house. Steven could live right here. Skip college. Get a job down the street at their bookstore, or maybe at the old movie theater.

He missed Dylan. He knew his exile was self-imposed, and that he could just decide to be a part of things again. He could show up to school every day if he wanted to. He could see Dylan every day after school, like always. He could try to be a better friend to her. He could try to get his mother the help she needed. He could start looking at colleges. He could *apply* himself. But there were so many *coulds*, and as they piled up on top of one another, they stuck together and formed a heavy weight on Steven's chest. Feeling the weight, sitting there reading his book, he imagined having a heart attack. That seemed like the adult thing to do. He imagined how he'd fall to the floor, gripping his chest. In the vision, he was wearing suspenders and one side came loose as he knocked a rotary phone off the table. He could picture the view from the floor, his right eye blinded by the carpet, the coarse bristles against his face. He felt like a dropped camera.

Steven would read at least two chapters of *The Things They Carried* before he headed back home. He'd be letting Mr. Drake down if he didn't at least try to keep up with the rest of the class. In his frequent absences, he'd started a thread of emails with Mr. Drake to keep tabs on the class. Despite his anxiety over possible mistakes in grammar and mechanics, he liked composing them. Mr. Drake always told them that writing could present the best version of themselves. Steven appreciated that interpretation. So he tried to be the best version of himself in emails, rewriting and revising his inquiries and apologies. He was humble and magnanimous, but confident and self-assured. He was who he wanted to be.

He owed Mr. Drake an email actually, so Steven put the book down and walked out to the front porch where his cell phone reception was better. It was below freezing, and Steven could see his breath escape into tiny clouds.

"These people are crazy!" Steven could easily hear Mr. Walter's voice in the adjoining twin house. He often talked to his television.

"Come look at this," he yelled for Mrs. Walters. Steven leaned over the railing separating the two porches.

"Steve? Is that you?"

Steven put his phone away. "Yes, it is."

"Come in here, boy." From someone else, being called *boy*—or "Steve," for that matter—might have rankled Steven, but not from Mr. Walters.

"Leave him alone." Mrs. Walters must have been upstairs. Her voice was muffled.

"Come here and look at this, Steve."

Steven opened the front door and let himself in.

"You're young. What is the deal with this thing anyway?" He pointed at the television. Steven was Mr. Walter's source for all topics that caused confusion, which was, at this point in Mr. Walter's life, basically all topics. Youth was the only requirement.

"Do you believe these people??"

Steven sat down on the love seat, to the right of Mr. Walters. The television volume rattled a row of framed photographs on the radiator—or maybe it was the heat.

"What are they talking ab—" Steven stared at the screen. *What was he seeing?* Dylan mentioned that Darling Energy signs and graffiti had been spreading beyond just the trestle bridge. She mentioned something about the airport, he thought. He knew the school newspaper wrote something about it. Once or twice this last month, he'd read through the comments on Reddit, amusing himself with the wild theories. He was aware of the memes. He found it amusing, but he was under the impression that it was dying out, that its purposeless mystery would be replaced by some new viral interest. He let himself imagine he and Dylan gathering at the arch on her birthday. Maybe he'd feel better by then. Maybe his mom would feel better. If they were lucky, they could sit in a car and watch to see if anyone showed up for their invitation. At best, maybe they'd see a recovered Mr. Ryerson and his barbershop quartet drive through the parking lot, looking for an audience. Maybe he could convince them to sing "Happy Birthday" to Dylan.

But reading the ticker at the bottom of the TV screen, Steven realized he'd underestimated the town's interest: *"Cult" Welcomes Darling Energy.* Above it, dressed in yellow robes, the Bobbies, Bob Robertson and Bob Bannon, addressed a news reporter.

Steven remembered his dad telling him about the Bobbies. He pointed their meeting house out one day on the way home from a piano lesson. The building was part of an abandoned quarry. A few outbuildings circled it, forming a pathetic-looking village. "They're not a bad cult," his father explained. "They're not a bunch of murderers or misanthropes. One of the guys used to work at our office. They're more like hippies. Living off the grid." Indeed, Steven did have some memory of the taller Bob selling books and soaps at the farmer's market.

The shorter Bob answered a question: "Again, we're not a cult. We're a *society of thinkers*."

The reporter corrected herself. "So what plans does your *society* have planned for the 15th?"

"We will be on-site, at the arch at 3:33 p.m. To welcome Darling Energy."

"Who exactly is Darling Energy?"

"Or what," the bigger Bob interjected.

"*What* do you think Darling Energy is? What do you think will happen?"

"It's not up to us to think about it."

"I thought they were a society of *thinkers*!" Mr. Walters was back to yelling at the screen.

"We'd like to welcome anyone interested in hearing the message to join our group on the 15th," the shorter Bob said.

"Did you send the phones messages?"

"We don't send messages. We are receivers."

"Darling Energy sent the messages," said the taller Bob as he looked into the camera. The line would have had a more unsettling effect had tall Bob not had such a pronounced lisp.

"What is it with these guys?" Mr. Walters asked. "You're young, Steve."

Steven's jaw was open. He felt his phone buzz in his pocket. "I'm not sure."

The reporter threw it back to the in-studio team.

"The park service at Valley Forge is also extending an invitation for

March 15th. An array of historians, actors, and performers will be on hand to answer questions and provide a taste of colonial America."

"Sure, sounds like the place to be, Leslie," the anchor replied. "Now over to Hurricane Schwartz for the weather. . ."

"I've to go. Sorry, Mr. Walters." Steven opened the door to the porch.

"Good to see you, boy."

Steven opened his phone. He read Dylan's text.

Dylan: Did you hear?

Steven: I just saw it.

Dylan: Saw what?

Steven: The Bobbies.

Dylan: What about the Bobbies??

Steven: Wait, what are you talking about?

Dylan: The Scrabble Club.

Steven: What?!

Dylan: They unscrambled it.

Steven: There's a Scrabble Club??

Dylan: They know it's an anagram.

Steven: They unscrambled DE??

Dylan: Yes. But not into my name.

Steven: Into what?

Steven watched the flashing ellipses as Dylan typed.

Dylan: LEGENDARY RING.

Steven did a quick check in his head. It was all the letters.

Steven: Whoa. That's good.

Dylan: No it's not.

Steven: I'm upset I didn't think of that one. Your name keeps on giving.

Dylan: They could keep unscrambling it.

Steven: How did you hear?

Dylan: It got around school.

Maybe Steven would join the Scrabble Club. They sounded like his kind of people.

Dylan: The Medieval Culture club is making plans.

Steven: There's a Medieval Culture club??

Dylan: There's a club for everything. You should come to school once in a while.

Steven: Plans for what?

Dylan: The 15th. I don't know. Cosplay or something.

Steven: They're going to dress up??

Steven's head was spinning.

Dylan: What did you think I meant? What are you talking about? The Bobbies? The cult people? What happened?

Steven: They're not a cult. They're a society of thinkers.

Dylan: ???

It occurred to Steven, as he described to Dylan what he had just witnessed on TV, that maybe Steven didn't need to snap out of anything. Maybe, like an anagram, the world was snapping into place and rearranging itself. Maybe, if you waited for the right moment, order would push out chaos. Was it just about finding a different perspective? Maybe Steven A. Lilly didn't need to be *Silent Valley* anymore. Maybe he could transform again. Could he embrace Mr. Walter's *Steve*, even? Were all these people really going to show up on the 15th? Maybe Dylan's birthday party wouldn't be a private affair after all. Maybe it would be more than a birthday party. Maybe there would be room for Dylan and Steven among the barbershop quartets and robed cultists—between the medieval warriors and the Revolutionary War soldiers.

Steven: Come over?

Dylan: I'll be right there.

TWENTY-FOUR

The tailor set down a bucket frothing with suds. Lathering up a soft-bristled brush, he worked it in tight circles over the letters. Norman had offered to help, but Mr. Rutigliano didn't even respond to Norman's voice. From the living room window, Norman watched the tailor work, scrubbing the defaced window until only a slight, black smear remained. Norman knew he was angry, but the tailor didn't show it in his body language. He was a man used to manual labor, used to working at a thing until it was done. He grabbed a rag and removed the last traces of the *Y* in *Energy*. Even this he did gracefully.

Norman was angry, about a lot of things. But he couldn't decide what angered him most. There was the fact that the tailor had to deal with this defiling of his personal property. Norman had always admired Mr. Rutigliano and Mr. Myers, the cobbler whose shop was right next door. Neither was warm to Norman or Lester or Mr. Lewis. Most of the conversations they had, in fact, were about trash cans blocking the alley or questions of snow removal. Last winter, Norman, hoping to impress the tradesmen, shoveled the snow from their sidewalks before either had arrived at work. The act rewarded Norman with a quiet thank-you from Mr. Rutigliano. It wasn't much, but it felt like ample payment from the quiet man next door to the Lewises.

Norman knew Dylan hadn't written her anagram name on the store window, but he knew she and Steven inspired it. He also knew his brother Lester had been involved somehow, that they were using his *system*, whatever that was, to send out these messages. Watching Mr. Rutigliano finish washing the window, Norman didn't care about their motive. If it was conceived out of playfulness or boredom, it didn't matter. It was affecting people. It was just so. . .stupid, he thought.

He tried to talk to Lester about it, but that was impossible. Even more than usual, Lester had exiled himself to his bedroom, coming down only for meals. Their dad had grown more concerned. There was an argument when Mr. Lewis suggested Lester increase the frequency of his therapy visits. It prompted a single, yelled, "No!"—the loudest sound Norman could remember his brother making in years—followed by a slammed door. Norman had been standing in the hallway outside his room. He thought he might try reasoning with his brother. He was about to knock when he heard his brother grumble to himself: "That's not what I need."

What *did* he need? Norman wondered. Wasn't that always the question?

The police's interest in Lester had died down. They were satisfied he wasn't involved in the phone messages, but that was before this thing with the Bobbies and the park service. He'd just watched their interview on television, and while he laughed at his dad's assessment of them, part of Norman felt bad for them, too. If they were expecting to meet Darling

Energy, they would be disappointed to learn the messages were coming from two high school juniors. He didn't like the idea of a hoax, of putting people on, and that went for Darling Energy *and* Dylan Geringer. And Steven. Maybe Steven most of all. It was to Steven that Lester had given his hard drive. It was just the kind of plan Steven would come up with.

He had wanted to give Steven the benefit of the doubt because of how close Dylan was with him, but Steven was a disrupter. He was one of those kids who was too smart for his own good, for whom things came so easily. Those kinds of boys drove Norman crazy. Norman had to work hard for every success that came his way. Steven's kind, however, sighed and muttered sarcastic remarks in the back of the classroom. They were smug. They'd say a thing—something only *they* would get, or worse—a quote from some film no one had ever seen—and then just walk away, laughing to themselves. Norman saw through these kinds of kids. Why Dylan couldn't see it, too, aggravated him. The more he thought about it now, the more infuriated he grew. None of this would be going on if it weren't for Steven. And now, with all this new attention, maybe Lester would be dragged through all of this again. What if whatever he had given Steven on Halloween could be traced back to him? He didn't like that Steven had possession of his brother's stuff, had control of it. What if there were something else on that hard drive that was even worse? Norman had no reason to expect anything else, but he also had no reason not to. He'd watched too many police procedural TV shows and listened to too many stories from his private investigator dad to not worry.

Norman couldn't text Dylan, and he didn't want to text or talk to Steven, but of the two options, he settled on Steven. He would try to reason with him—if he could even get him on the phone—and if that didn't work maybe he would get to punch him in the face. This aggression wasn't a feeling Norman often felt, but as he looked back out the window and watched Mr. Rutigliano put away his soapy bucket, come back to the window, lick his thumb and work on a persistent remaining smudge, he thought of grabbing Steven by his shirt collar and holding him off the ground to take a good, long look at what he had started. If he could arrange it so Dylan was watching, even better. Norman allowed himself a cartoon fantasy. He imagined placing one hand on Steven's head and another on the soles of his feet, squeezing them together like he was playing the accordion. He'd reduce Steven to the size of a Rubik's Cube and throw him in the trash can behind Mr. Rutigliano's shop. The image came easily to him, but conjuring up an expression of appreciation on Dylan's face at the sight was impossible. He'd start with a text to Steven and play the accordion stuff by ear.

Norman: Hey man

Norman didn't think "man" sounded right, so he started again.

Norman: Hey

Keep it simple, he thought. He'd feel him out first. Norman figured a simple *hey* out of nowhere might get Steven to bite. Norman watched his phone for a response. When none came, he realized he didn't have a plan for what to say next. He toyed with a couple lines until Steven responded.

Steven: Hey.

Norman had his attention. Maybe he'd agree to meet. He'd mention his brother.

Norman: Can we talk?
Steven: Shoot.
Norman: In person.

Steven didn't respond for a minute. Maybe that was too strong. Norman worried he'd made it sound too dramatic. The flashing ellipses blinked to indicate Steven was typing, but Norman interrupted the composition.

Norman: It's about Lester.

That was vague enough. He figured that would interest Steven.

Norman: Is he okay?

He had him hooked.

Norman: Not really.

Not a lie at all.

Norman: I'm worried about him.

Also true. Norman would save his anger for the in-person meeting.

Steven: How can I help?

Was Steven actually considerate? Or maybe he was just worried for himself.

Norman: He's upset. He says he needs his hard drive back.

It took Steven a while to respond.

Steven: Okay.

Norman: Can I come pick it up for him?

Steven: I'm in Phoenixville. At my dad's house.

Norman: I can drive out there. He's worried about something on the drive. It will calm him down to have it, I think.

Norman had added the "I think" after a brief pause. It seemed generous.
A quiet minute followed. Norman imagined Steven texting Dylan. That thought annoyed him until Steven responded.

Steven: Here you go. I'll be here for another hour.

Steven sent his address. Norman grabbed his keys and walked to the door.
"Where are you going?" his father asked.

"I'll be right back," he said as the door slammed behind him.

Before he pulled out from the curb, he could feel his brother's eyes staring down at him from his bedroom window. He looked up and saw what he imagined. Lester closed the blinds, and Norman unfroze and drove away.

***

On the drive over to see Steven, Dylan entertained the idea of not showing up on the 15th. If she didn't show up, her role in these messages might be more easily hidden. Maybe the park had a webcam she could watch from the privacy of her bedroom. What if Norman said something to someone about her name? She didn't like crowds anyway. Meeting with Steven now meant each of these anxieties would be replaced by bigger questions and more plans. He had sounded excited on the phone, something like his old self, which was a relief. She'd been missing him. The past few weeks were another reminder of how much time they spend together, and of how her other friends, at least mentally, had moved Dylan to the periphery of their phone contacts and social media tagging—let alone any face-to-face meetings. It wouldn't be that big of a deal if she and Steven had spent the last month driving around together, maybe going to a show or the movies, studying after school, making out in Steven's room. But she'd spent the month on Netflix, avoiding schoolwork by watching space documentaries and rewatching episodes of the *Gilmore Girls*. She was becoming a cliché.

By the time she had parked outside Steven's dad's house, she'd swung back on the pendulum. No, she thought. She was Darling Energy. She was a feminist, or something. She would not approach her future worrying about what other people thought about her. She would be the best version of herself and take what she wanted.

That was the thought when she ignored Steven's "Hi" from the porch, marched up to him and kissed him on the mouth, just as she'd done back in December. She didn't let Steven react, she just got down to business.

"Okay then. How are we going to handle this?"

"Dylan," Steven motioned to the open front door.

"We've got a lot of competition now, from lots of different groups trying to make March 15th their own thing, but let's remember where this began." Steven tried to interrupt again.

"Just let me finish."

"Norman's here." Steven pointed to Norman's hulking presence as it filled up the doorway.

"I'll tell you where it began," Norman said as he walked out onto the porch.

On seeing him, her eyes widened, but she was proud of herself that she didn't miss a beat.

"You don't know what you're talking about." That seemed like a good place to start. She wasn't here to talk to Norman. Her brain hadn't questioned his presence at this place yet.

"Dylan," Steven said again.

"Norman, I don't know what you're doing here, but I can assure you this isn't your business." She was still annoyed at what he'd said to her that last time they spoke.

"Oh, it's my business."

"Guys, let's take this inside." Their raised voices had brought Mr.

Walters to his window.

"How is this your business?"

"Because you're using my brother."

"We're not using your brother." Finally Steven said something, Dylan thought.

"Yes, you are." Norman took a step toward Steven. "You're using his computer, his stuff, to send out these stupid messages."

"What's going on out here?" Mr. Walter's voice showed more curiosity than anger.

"He gave that stuff to me. He wanted me to have it."

"What right have you to take my brother's stuff?"

"It's not about rights," Dylan said. "He *gave* it to Steven."

"Well, you can't have it." Dylan wasn't sure why she had turned so quickly to rage, but something about it felt great. She clenched her fist. She took a step toward them both. It must have looked ridiculous, this triangle of close-talkers.

"I told you. Just text your brother first. I want to make sure it's okay with him," Steven said.

"I'm his brother."

"I'm aware of that, but he told me to take the drive and that he didn't want it back. Shouldn't have it back."

"Well, he changed his mind."

"Fine. But I need *him* to tell me that."

"What's going on out there?" Mrs. Walters was watching from the bedroom window.

"Nothing, Mrs. Walters. Sorry. Let's go inside," Steven tried again.

"I'm not leaving without that hard drive."

"Well, I guess you're not leaving then," Steven responded.

Later that night, Dylan couldn't recall the punch in any detail. It happened as quickly in the moment as it did in her memory. It may have been the snapping sound of Norman's nose, like a magician snapping his fingers after finishing a trick.

"Yes, you are leaving." Dylan's arm shot straight up from her side. There was no arc, no step forward, just a spring unleashed at just the right distance. Norman's nose was right at the limit of her reach. The strike was so sudden and surprising, the crack of his cartilage so immediate, that the three of them just stood there, looking at Norman's nose, in shock. Maybe Dylan most of all. She felt an apology form in her throat but before it fell out, Mr. Walter let out a whoop.

"Oh my! She just up and hit you. Did you hear that sound??"

Norman, Steven, and Dylan still hadn't moved.

"Boy," started Mr. Walters, "your nose is bleeding."

Norman stopped staring at Dylan and felt for his nose. "Ow," he finally managed.

"We'd like you to leave," Dylan said. She broke her stance and stood by Steven's side. Norman wiped away some of the blood and looked back and forth at Dylan and Steven. For a brief second, Dylan imagined Norman punching her back, the crushing thud of his meaty paws. She saw the same look on Steven's face. Instead, he exhaled and walked down to his car at the curb.

Steven stared at Dylan.

"That was a good punch, little lady," Mr. Walters said.

Dylan looked back at him. *"Little lady?"* she said.

Mr. Walters didn't like what he saw. "It was a very good punch," he said and closed his window.

"What was that?" Steven asked, smiling.

"I think I broke my hand." Dylan's hand was already purple. "Can you take me?"

Steven knew she meant the hospital, but all the other possibilities lit up his mind. "Of course," he said. "Let's go."

Dylan was in tremendous pain, but she still hadn't let out a gasp or a yell. She thought the impulse might be behind her now. As Steven fastened her seatbelt for her and they drove off, Dylan wondered if you didn't react right away, maybe you could control your pain.

TWENTY-FIVE

"I'm going for a walk," Trevor said.

"Where?"

"Just want to stretch my legs."

Elizabeth knew what was going on. "Are you going to investigate every siren and alarm?"

"I'll be right back."

"Take your coat, at least."

Trevor grabbed his coat and walked out the door. He knew what he'd see before he made it to the street. For the minute it took to walk around the curve in the road to confirm his fears, he tried to imagine other possibilities. It could be the Wilson lady—was that her name? The one who fell on the ice last year. It felt terrible to think, but she was in her eighties—how much longer could she last? Last year, an ambulance came for the boy who broke his leg on the trampoline. That one had almost sent Trevor over the edge. It was too close to home, he thought—and too close to home in the other sense. What was the point of these trampolines he saw in so many backyards? Where were the kids trying to jump to, if they were just going to come back down? A few years back there had been an electrical fire in someone's pool house.

"A pool house?!" he remembered saying to Elizabeth. "Only in this neighborhood would someone have a pool house!"

"We have a pool house."

"It's a shed!" It was only a shed, but sometimes Elizabeth liked to needle her husband's liberal guilt.

Trevor picked up the pace a little. He would know for certain in another minute. He didn't want to appear too interested or too nosey. But why shouldn't he? Wasn't that the same complaint—that the way they lived now, privacy was more important than community? Was it even more important than casual interest? Was it nosey to wonder if someone in your neighborhood was okay?

He heard the thud of a door as he rounded the curve. The ambulance was where he feared it might be, right in front of Royce Caulder's home. It was like he was walking back into a scene from a movie he had already appeared in. The same boys from next door watched as the ambulance pulled away. This time the scene ended as Mr. and Mrs. Caulder loaded into their Tahoe and followed their son to the hospital. Did they see Trevor walking up the street, a repeat conspicuous witness, a stalker of their personal, private tragedies? They had been home this time, Trevor thought. And they still couldn't stop it??

Trevor was too hot for his coat. He took it off and turned back home. He felt a burning in his head.

***

Dylan and Steven were twenty minutes into their ER wait when an ambulance came to an abrupt halt in front of the hospital. It was a different view than the one of the helipad from her bedroom, but it played out the same way. EMT techs and hospital staff unloaded the injured and whisked the gurney through the sliding doors. Dylan and Steven's view of the emergency through the window was separated by a row of hedges and another set of sliding doors. Dylan used her unpurpled hand to squeeze Steven's tighter.

It was a diverse group that sat around Dylan and Steven. There was a boy with an ice pack on his head. An old man attached to a portable oxygen concentrator sat next to his wife, who was reading a magazine. A man in army fatigues held a tiny baby. He paced in front of the windows looking for someone.

"It's weird to think this plays out every day here," Dylan said.

"What does?" Steven asked.

"All of this. All these *emergencies*. Every day, new people, new injuries, new accidents." Steven nodded.

"You should call your parents."

"I know. I will."

"They're like two minutes away."

"I know." Dylan didn't want to call them yet.

Steven stared at Dylan's hand. It had been wrapped quickly—and not altogether gently, Steven thought—by the attending nurse. The ice pack left tiny droplets on her wrist.

"There's just so much we don't see." Dylan wasn't sure what she was trying to say.

"I know."

"The view from my bedroom, the helipad. All the blinking lights and the sound overhead. As close as it is to my bedroom, it still seems so far away." Dylan grimaced a little at her pain. She told the nurse it was a 2 on the pain scale, but she wondered if she had underestimated it. Compared with all the pain she'd ever had in her life? Compared with the perceived pain of the other waiting patients? On a cosmic scale?

The man in fatigues walked outside to meet a woman. He passed the baby to her. "They took him back an hour ago. Still waiting," he said.

"Do you want me to call your parents?" Steven tried again.

"What are you worried about?"

"They should know you're here."

Dylan knew Steven was wright. "Okay, but I don't want to talk to them. Can you text for me?" Dylan handed over her phone.

"What should I write?"

"Write that I punched a giant and broke my hand."

"I'll figure it out."

***

Trevor circled the garage maze two times, looking for a parking spot. How could all these spots be filled? Has there been an epidemic? He was about to circle a third time when he decided he'd just park in the hospital chaplain's spot. Elizabeth told him he was rarely there anyway. He'd leave his hazards on.

His wife's question was still ringing in his ears: "What are you going to do when you get there?" "I don't know" was his answer then, and his answer now. It wasn't his business, except that it was, he told himself. He needed to be there. That was the best he could come up with.

He walked up to the admitting counter and inquired about Royce.

"If he just got here, I don't have his information yet," the nurse said.

"What does that mean?" Trevor was surprised to hear his raised voice.

"Sir, are you a relative?"

"No."

The nurse stared at him, trying to assess the situation. "He's in good hands. You can take a seat over there."

Trevor followed the nurse's finger and found a seat underneath the TV. He had to pass right by Dylan and Steven, and while they both noticed him immediately, Mr. Drake was oblivious. They watched him run a hand through his hair, unzip his jacket, and roll his neck back and forth. CNN's Wolf Blitzer, muted on the screen above, welcomed viewers to the Situation Room.

"Should we say something?" Dylan wondered.

"Leave him be. We don't know what's happened."

They sat for a minute. Mr. Drake rubbed his eyes.

"What if it's his wife?" Dylan's mind raced. Steven squeezed her good hand harder. Dylan relaxed. They tried to stare at the screen instead.

It took Dylan's parents two minutes to walk through the sliding glass doors of the emergency room. They scanned the room, and Dylan watched them recognize Mr. Drake under the TV. Mr. Drake looked up and took out his phone. Following the Geringers was another set of parents, the ones Mr. Drake was looking for. Mr. Drake got up out of his seat and took a step before he realized he didn't know what to say. Mr. Caulder noticed him on the way to the counter. He stopped briefly, or so it seemed to Trevor, a curious look on his face. Mrs. Caulder stopped in her tracks, a few steps behind, like a force field kept her from approaching.

Trevor took a step back. He was too close. He wanted to overhear what Mr. Caulder was being told, but he knew it wasn't for him. Mr. Caulder whispered something to Mrs. Caulder. Were they arguing? A nurse came back and whisked Mr. Caulder away. His wife just stood there.

It seemed clearer now—what he was there for.

"Mrs. Caulder?" he said. He wished he knew her first name.

She turned and took in Trevor, her hands down by her side.

A curious thing happened, a wordless and sudden intimation pushed them together. Trevor held Royce's mother. She rested her head on his shoulder. He rubbed her back and said, "I know." He said it like there was something to know. He guessed there was.

Trevor wasn't surprised when he noticed Dylan and Steven. They'd been appearing all over the place—in his classroom, at his house, in his imagination. His eyes softened at them, like he was looking at an old photo. Dylan raised her bandaged hand. Steven smiled. Dylan's mom and dad eclipsed the view.

"What happened?"

"I punched Norman."

"Norman Lewis??"

"Why?" Mrs. Geringer asked.

"That tall kid??" Mr. Geringer always referred to people by their physical traits. It made sense in Norman's case.

"Where'd you punch him?" her dad wanted to know.

"At Steven's dad's house."

"No. Where on his body?"

"What kind of question is that??" Mrs. Geringer wanted to know.

"On the nose, Mr. Geringer." Steven didn't bother suppressing his smile.

"Let me see it," her mom asked. "Good lord. It's terrible."

"What did he do?" Mr. Geringer asked.

"Nothing."

"Then why did you punch him??" her mom asked.

"It's complicated," Steven said.

"No, it's not. He tried to take something that wasn't his." Dylan looked at Steven. "And he wouldn't leave Steven's house."

"I thought you said it was your dad's house."

"I'm looking after it." Mrs. Geringer raised an eyebrow.

"Why would you punch him, though?" Her mother was unconvinced of this story. "Just call the police. Did he try to hurt you? Norman??"

"No. We didn't need the police."

"Why didn't *you* punch him?" Dylan's dad asked Steven.

"She beat me to it."

"Is Norman okay?"

"Where's he now? Where's Norman?" Mr. Geringer noticed Mr. Drake. "And isn't that your English teacher?"

Trevor pulled away from Mrs. Caulder, but held onto her shoulders. He was repeating something to her. She nodded. They watched as his shoulders shook. His chin dropped onto his chest. Now it was Mrs. Caulder who was doing the hugging.

When they called Dylan back for an x-ray, Mr. Drake and Mrs. Caulder were still consoling one another. Dylan missed it play out, but Steven and the Geringers watched the scene unfold as Mr. Caulder joined the huddle, spoke a few words, shook Trevor's hand, and walked with his wife into the ER. Steven watched Mr. Drake's indecision as he looked after them. Where he was standing kept triggering the automatic doors. By the fourth invitation, he was out the door, making his way to the garage.

Before he turned the ignition, he pounded the steering wheel with his fists, accidentally turning on the wipers. They fell into an odd syncopation with his hazard lights, but every now and then, they fell into synchrony.

The hospital chaplain knocked on the driver's side window.

"Can I help you?"

It took Trevor a second to notice, and longer to find the switch.

"Can I help you?" the father tried again.

Trevor looked up at the man. His eyebrows were unruly and white. They reached up to his hairline. Maybe it was a sign, Trevor thought.

"I don't know. Maybe."

"You're in my parking spot."

"What?" Trevor noticed the sign again. "I'm sorry. I was just—I'm sorry. . ." he said as he motored the window back up. He put the car in reverse and waved at the chaplain. In his rearview mirror, he watched the old man hold up his hand. Was he waving, giving a blessing? He turned the corner before he had a chance to figure it out.

***

Steven accepted the invite to dinner. He wasn't ready to face his mother, not after the day he'd had, and besides, he hadn't been to Dylan's house since, when? Two Thanksgivings ago? He really liked the Geringers—Tom and Sarah. He liked Daphne, too, and was disappointed he missed her over the holidays. At first, it had been a marvel to see this perfect little family, sitting around the table, having conversations together that lasted until after dessert. How many families still eat together, or hell, stick around to eat dessert together? Have dessert, even? For a while, it had been a fun shtick with Dylan. Steven would make fun of her Norman Rockwell family. He'd compliment Mrs. Geringer's drinking glasses and centerpiece—drinking glasses, they had! It's not that their neighborhoods were so different. If anything, Steven's had a greater number of McMansions than the Geringer's. Steven's house had some nice furniture, too, but there was nothing on it. There were no people sitting on the loveseat, no coffee-table books on the coffee table, no photos on the refrigerator. The Geringers', however, was positively *lived* in: Mrs. Geringer's framed paintings, a place for bills and correspondence, a built-in bookshelf where books and family photos fought for space, a piano with a vase filled with flowers—fake, sure, but still, thought Steven. And of course, a mother and a father living together, starting conversations, even once or twice kissing in the kitchen. The prospect of visiting this bit of theater last year offered too much painful comparison. It was sadder but safer at home. Halfway through dinner, they noticed the snow falling.

"Was it supposed to snow??"

"I don't think so," Mrs. Geringer answered her husband. Sarah was a weather fanatic. She would have known.

"That's strange."

Steven gathered dishes and glasses.

"Oh, leave them there," Mrs. Geringer said as he joined her husband and daughter by the patio doors.

"That's okay," Steven told her. He went back for the cloth napkins—cloth napkins?—when he stopped to watch the Geringers—minus Daphne—stare out at the mounting snow. Tom Geringer had his arm around Sarah. Dylan pulled at the sleeves on her sweatshirt. She bit on one of the hood strings.

Dylan felt Steven's stare and turned to face him. She let the string fall from her mouth and smiled at him. For a moment, seeing Dylan framed by her snow-watching parents, Steven imagined this was their house, that maybe they'd have a place this nice, or any place really, maybe the Phoenixville house, or some place by a body of water, and they would link arms and stare out at the world as it snowed, or rained, or fell apart.

Dylan felt it, too. She looked at Steven holding a pile of napkins, wearing a few of her mother's wooden animal napkin rings around his fingers, and wanted to take him upstairs to her room. She thought about kissing him again, but instead she walked up to him and felt his cheek down to his chin with the cold metal splint that held two of her fingers. It seemed another daring act from Dylan, from Darling Energy in the flesh, steps away from her parents. Steven grabbed her free hand and something fell into place. He would tell her later that it was his heart, but in reality, it was a whole body rush. His legs wanted to buckle, but Dylan squeezed his hand harder and brought it up to her chest. Where had her parents gone? Weren't they still standing there?

"There's already four inches," her mother finally said. Steven moved his hand away.

"I'm not sure you're going to want to drive in this, Steven," Mr. Geringer said, turning around.

"No. You're right," Steven said.

"Can you call your mom? Tell her you'll stay here?"

"Oh. Sure." Steven looked at Dylan. He could still feel the cold metal against his face.

"Yes. You're not driving in this. Here, give me these." Mrs. Geringer grabbed the napkins and napkin rings from Steven. "Dylan, can you go up and get some blankets and a pillow for Steven? We'll set him up on the couch."

"It's only eight," Mr. Geringer said.

"Well, get them now. Do you want me to call your mom?"

"No. That's fine."

***

They watched an hour of TV with the Geringers. Some sort of *Law & Order* program. Dylan and Steven said little. They nodded and muttered agreement with Mr. Geringer's guesses about who the real killer was. They sat close together and shared a blanket under which they held hands. Sometimes Dylan's good hand brushed against Steven's thigh.

After the Geringers headed off to bed, and Dylan and Steven promised to turn everything off, they pulled an ottoman over and watched the snow pile up outside on a bird feeder.

Dylan's phone buzzed. It was her friend Michelle—part of a group chat, one she was surprised she was still a part of. It reported Royce

Caulder's death by suicide. How that information arrived so quickly, the cause so confidently verified, unsettled Dylan. She thought she recognized Mrs. Caulder as the woman Mr. Drake had been hugging, but she couldn't understand why Mr. Drake would be holding her. She knew about Royce's other attempt, had heard something. Whatever she had heard lacked any details to make the story stick. He'd spent most of the last two years in and out of treatment centers. She wasn't sure exactly, but she felt something like sympathy for her former tormentor.

It annoyed her, actually angered her now, as the replies came buzzing in, to witness all the exclamation points and OMGs and emojis over this boy's death. This fake sympathy. It was fake, right? True, she didn't like Royce. She never had. He'd been a bully and a *freak*—as the kids called him in high school, once his bully powers had vanished in a skinny teenager frame. More recently, he was the face they imagined when they pictured school shooters—not so much a villain, more an ignored supporting actor. He was mean still, really mean, but he was so sad, too, or that's how his face appeared in her brain now. He was just so sad, wasn't he? Why was he sad? And now he was dead and the news of this was already being spit out over wireless plans, with insincere exclamations and horrified gasps by the dumb-stupid thumbs of her classmates. How did Mr. Drake know? Why was he there?

"What's wrong?" Steven asked.

Dylan handed him her phone. He stared at it. For a while, they both said nothing, just stared at the mounting snow.

"Royce was an asshole," Steven said finally, but not unkindly. It was true, and he was just stating a fact, working something out. "He was an asshole, but he shouldn't have died. He was just a kid."

"Yeah," Dylan agreed.

"It's just so stupid. We're just—I don't know." Snow covered the bird feeder now. It looked like a man, a white head and shoulders, a black pole for a body. "What are you feeling?" Steven asked.

Dylan tried to come up with an assessment. "I don't know." Their legs were tangled under the blanket. Dylan dropped her head on Steven's chest.

"Everyone's just a kid," she said finally. It was the kind of line Steven would say. Out of Dylan's mouth, it was more truth than deflection. "Right? We're all just kids and things happen and—" The ice machine in the fridge rumbled. "We went to elementary school with Royce. He was just a kid like us."

"He liked popsicles." Steven wasn't sure where that factoid came from, but the memory found him on its own.

"Our parents are just grown-up kids," Dylan continued.

"Some more than others."

"I'm serious. Your mom and dad. They were just college kids when they met. Not much older than us." Dylan fixed the tape around her splint. "Mine too. They're just—"

"You're right. It's easy to picture my mom as a kid. And I don't mean that like an insult. Her attention span. Her. . .I don't know. I wish she were more like an adult." Steven moved closer to Dylan. "I can never picture my dad as a kid. Even in his childhood pictures. It doesn't look like him. Like maybe the photos are fakes and he's hiding some different past from us."

"And Mr. Drake was a kid," Dylan added. September seemed a lifetime ago, back when they wondered who he was and joked about his secret life. They'd seen little moments of his secret life now, and while she was happy to see him as an actual person, she knew that maybe she'd seen too much. If adults, if teachers and parents, were just as sad as their kids, what did that say about her future? It was unreasonable and silly maybe, but Dylan felt guilty that her life had been so free of the pain and anguish she witnessed in her friend and his parents, in her teacher and his wife.

"Mr. Drake was a kid, sure. But he also. . .*lost* a kid."

"Yes. Yes he did, didn't he?" She bit her hoodie string again. "I can't imagine."

They couldn't imagine. It was like imagining their own demise, their own disappearance—to be here one minute and gone the next. It would be the Caulders' story now.

Steven thought about it more. "I don't know. I used to want to hurry up to adulthood. I would have done everything to just get out of here and be an adult somewhere. I guess I'd still like to. But I'm less sure. What's the rush?"

The conversation ended there. If they were headed to an epiphany, the snow hypnotized them out of one. The answer wasn't out in the snow, and it certainly wasn't in the text messages that were still buzzing in. It was right in front of them. They'd spent so much time *musing*, so many hours pondering and second-guessing, staring out at the world as if it would give them answers—and for what? When all they needed was right here under the blanket.

Dylan kept her injured hand up in the air and out of the way the whole time, like a permanent swoon. They were slow and careful with one another. Dylan remembered later how quiet it had been, how the voice in her head had shut off. She didn't even remember the sound of their breathing. She just remembered feeling like one person, like Darling Energy manifest, once and for all.

When it was over, they held each other for a long time without moving—except for their lungs, contracting and expanding against each other's skin.

TWENTY-SIX

Dylan was surprised how quickly the first two weeks of March went. She and Steven enjoyed the buildup to the 15th. They didn't fret about the details and the what-ifs anymore. They were excited now, excited to see who would show up for their party.

"Lester's party, too," Steven reminded her.

"He still hasn't gotten back to you? None of this would have happened if he hadn't sent those first messages. Really, he did most of it."

"And everybody else did the party planning. We didn't even need to invite anyone."

"Oh, I meant to tell you! Mr. Ryerson will be there. The barbershop trio will be a proper quartet."

"That's great."

It helped that the snow had kept them out of school for four days so far in March. They spent days and nights together at each other's homes. Steven's newfound happiness lifted his mother's spirits. He was eager to get Dylan back over to his house, to hang out like they used to, and Mrs.

Lilly liked the company and distractions. She liked to see Steven happy again. She was able to talk about Mr. Lilly's wedding without losing it, and even bought airline tickets to North Carolina for Steven and Dylan. After what had seemed like a lifetime of inactivity, Steven and Dylan now had two big events in as many months.

The only sour note in this new song had been Mr. Drake's absence from school. They hadn't seen him since that night at the hospital. Earlier in the week, Steven and Dylan drove by his house and parked outside. After a little deliberation, they knocked on the door, but no one answered. There weren't any cars in the driveway either.

The student directory informed them the Caulders' house was in the same development as Trevor's, so before they went back to Steven's house, they slowed down to take a look. It, too, was dark and empty.

There was little news about Royce's funeral. Steven and Dylan had planned on going but could find no details of the Caulders' plans. They must have decided against any services, they figured. The school responded with a brief student assembly, a letter home, and an automated phone message informing families of the support the school was offering for any students who were struggling in the wake of Royce's death. With this announcement and the four snow cancelations, the district's automated phone message system was finally being used for its intended purpose.

Lester's choice of date and time may have been random, but the fact that March 15th fell on a Saturday seemed like another stroke of luck. Kids were out of school; many were off from work. The only worry was whether it would snow again or not. The five-day forecast said 60 percent chance.

***

Trevor was never one who drank to get drunk. He was, however, over this past week, someone who drank to stay drunk. Taking days off work was Elizabeth's idea. If he was serious, she told him, if he was ready for this new chapter—leaving everything behind here and following her job offer out to California—maybe he should take the rest of his personal days. Maybe, too, he should take some of his paid sick leave. She couldn't ignore his depression anymore. It had morphed and changed from the shared version they had carried together since Benjamin's death. The counseling they went to back then prepared them for the different ways they would grieve, but at some point, Trevor's grief had turned inside out. It was a new virus that found no reflection in her own controlled one. She managed one day at a time, but Trevor's days were months, and it was harder to see how he was doing. Looking back at the last few years and seeing now how hard he had taken this death of a neighbor's boy, Elizabeth was a little ashamed she didn't recognize his descent sooner. She thought she had been looking at their regular misery, not this expanding fractal. His grief had developed grief.

"Are you hungry?" she asked him.

"Not particularly," Trevor responded as he poured another finger of bourbon. It was the 14th of March and it was snowing again. "I'm just going to watch this." Trevor pointed at John Wayne on the television. It was a few days early, but some cable channel was already showing The Quiet Man, three days before its usual St. Patrick's Day presentation.

"You should have something to eat," she tried again.

"I'm fine." Trevor plopped down in his chair and picked up the remote to turn up the volume. It had been three days in a row he'd stayed home from school. He wasn't feigning sickness. He was tired of feeling guilty about feeling sick, anyway—tired of self-diagnosing it, rejecting it. He couldn't be in front of kids right now. He couldn't look at their stupid, sweet faces. He couldn't answer all their questions. He couldn't stand the idea of watching them laughing in the hallways like everything was all right. He didn't want to talk about books, all of those quiet interiors, and all the characters, and how, year after year, they did the same things, every time, on the exact same page. Said the same things. He didn't want to talk about Gatsby's American Dream or Blanche's neediness. He didn't want to talk about Winston Smith's pointless fight against Big Brother. He didn't want to try to convince a bunch of seventeen-year-olds that they'd understand all of this a lot more when they got older. He didn't want to help them connect with these pathetic adult failures, these horrible people—or see themselves in them. He didn't want to talk about walking in someone else's shoes, for god's sake. What was the point of imagining Boo Radley's abused childhood? There would be so much time—so many days—for his students to discover this pain on their own.

The Quiet Man was already at the end, the long fight sequence where John Wayne's Sean Thornton battles his wife's brother Red, a fistfight that takes them all over the village, even for a drink at the pub along the way. Sean gets all the physical justice he needs, the love of Maureen O'Hara's Mary Kate, and the grudging, bloodied respect of Red. It was so satisfying. It was Trevor's dad's favorite movie. Trevor remembered watching the movie with his dad a few years before he passed away. His father tensed and smiled with each landed punch. It was so satisfying to watch how neatly everything tied itself up. As the credits rolled, Trevor got up to fix himself another drink. He could hear Elizabeth shut the bedroom door upstairs. Tomorrow it would be ten years since Benjamin died. He would at least stay up until midnight. It seemed disrespectful to go to sleep now.

Midnight came and went, and with it more old movies. He fixed himself a snack, but only because he wanted to keep on drinking. He only felt drunk when he stood up—or when he tried to lay down on the couch—but sitting just perfectly, just so, slowing sipping his bourbon, he felt almost alive.

"Have you slept??" Elizabeth asked when she came downstairs in the morning.

"A little bit," he lied.

"You need to sleep this off." She grabbed her coat and the snow shovel by the door. She had to head back to the hospital to help train the woman who was taking over her job at the end of the month. It had snowed overnight, and the walkway was covered with about three inches.

"I can do that," Trevor said without moving from his seat.

"No, you can't. Sober up and let's go out to dinner tonight." Today would be hard for Elizabeth, too. She needed Trevor later.

Trevor knew she was right. "I will. I'm sorry."

"You don't have to be sorry. Just go to sleep, take a shower. I'll need to get out of this house tonight."

Elizabeth walked back to Trevor. She leaned the shovel against his chair and laid her hand on his shoulder. He didn't turn around, but he grabbed her hand. They held on for a minute, only letting go when the Paramount mountain logo faded onto the screen, announcing the next feature. Elizabeth grabbed the shovel and walked back to the door.

"I love you," Trevor called back to her. His hand hadn't moved from his shoulder.

"I love you, too." She opened the door, and Trevor could hear the shovel scrape against the walkway outside.

Sleep and a dream found Trevor. Someone who looked an awful lot like John Wayne—at least from the backseat view—was driving Trevor around in a white and wide SUV. They made a slow circle around a familiar-looking cul-de-sac. Despite their slow speed, Trevor kept sliding along the vinyl backseat, from window to window. He tried to yell at John Wayne but couldn't summon any words from his mouth. They kept circling and circling until Trevor opened the car door and jumped out. His escape opened up a new setting: his classroom. Instead of student desks, the room was filled with park benches and couches. A few low-lit floor lamps cast their light into dim Venn diagrams on the floor. Trevor thought about sitting on the floor, but before he could, he heard a knocking. It was from the closet behind his desk. He didn't want to open it. He wasn't sure what he'd find, but even in his cloudy dream logic he feared he'd find Benjamin, or maybe Royce, or John Wayne mid-punch, behind the door. A lucid dream-thought found Trevor inside his subconscious, and he was suddenly scared he wouldn't find anything. The knocking grew more persistent, and it froze Trevor by his desk. He watched helplessly as the door opened—with a haunted-house creak, even—but there wasn't anyone there. Instead, a twin-sized Murphy bed lowered to the floor. It was already made up—white sheets and a scratchy-looking army green blanket. No longer afraid, Trevor sat down at the end of the bed and was surprised to find its parts labeled. A white tape label read "Pillow" on the pillow. "Blanket," it read, on the center of the blanket.

The drinks were finally catching up to him. The opening credits of *Vertigo* weren't helping either. Bernard Herrmann's score, with its flutes and vibraphones, floated over spinning kaleidoscopes. It was all too much for Trevor. It too closely narrated his mental state, so he switched the channel over to the local news station—but the spinning didn't stop. What was he looking at, exactly?

"What!?" he said to no one. It was a shot from the traffic helicopter. He couldn't concentrate on what the newscaster was saying, but he recognized the arch at Valley Forge Park and the snowy hill that sloped down below it. As the shot widened, he saw the refurbished cabins where General Washington's troops huddled together almost 250 years ago. But it couldn't be Valley Forge, because it was crawling with people and cars, and it looked like there was a marching band there—or maybe two marching bands—and who was this clown with the balloon animals they were interviewing now and why were there two drag queens behind him? He thought he recognized a few of his students in a panning crowd shot, but it was hard to say as most people were bundled in winter coats and scarves. Many held signs: *Darling Energy!*, *Your Throng Awaits You!*, *Et Tu, Darling Energy?*

Was this really happening, Trevor wondered. How drunk was he? It was infuriating, all of these people gathered—and for what? On the tenth anniversary of Benjamin's death there was a giant costume party, apparently. Hundreds of people "yucking it up," he said out loud. How asinine! Valley Forge was a battleground, for god's sake. How long had it been since *those* kids died? Almost 250 years?! Where was the solemnity?

Where was the quiet respect?

"This is. . ." He had trouble finding the word. "It's just. . .stupid."

His phone rang. It read *Ben Whitermore*. Ben Whitermore? What was he calling for? On a Saturday? Ben was earnest and diligent, but he was also twenty-five. He wouldn't want to talk shop on a Saturday afternoon. The last day Trevor was at work, he'd counseled Ben about a difficult parent meeting he was still reeling from. He was not in the right frame of mind to talk on the phone, but somehow the fourth ring sounded sort of desperate, and his name was Ben, and yes, it was stupid to look for a sign, but watching the madness out at Valley Forge Park, it felt like the world was splitting—so he picked up.

"Hello?"

"Trevor?"

"Hi, Bern." The word *Ben* didn't form right coming out of his mouth.

"Hey, I'm sorry to call you at home."

"That's food—good, I mean." Trevor sat up. He would need to power through these slurs.

"I wasn't sure if you'd be home. Wasn't sure if you were headed out to the park, too."

"The park?"

"I just figured I'd see you there."

"For what?"

"Well, I don't know, I guess." A dog barked on Ben's line.

"What was that?"

"That's Holden."

"Your dog?"

"Yeah, I'm headed out there now. To the park."

"For what??" he asked again. Holden barked one more time.

"Well. I'm not sure. Everyone's going. I just want to—"

"Can you hold on a sec—" Trevor threw the phone on the coffee table and ran to the bathroom. The puke hurt coming out. Most of it made it into the toilet. He was surprised when he came back to the phone to see that Ben hadn't hung up.

"You still there??"

"I wanted to get your help on something. I meant to ask you at work but I know you've been taking some time off."

"Shoot."

"I don't mean to bother you if it's a bad time."

"If it's a bad time? As opposed to what?"

"I'm sorry, if this isn't a good time—"

"Which is it then? Are you sorry if it's a good time or a bad time?"

"Trevor?

"Yes!"

"Are you okay?"

"I'm fine," Trevor said through a belch. "Look, it's fine. Go ahead. What do you need?" Trevor thought he heard Holden's collar jangle in the background, but it might have been the ringing in his head.

"I need a letter of recommendation. I'm applying for this summer program in England and they only take twelve students—"

"Oh, sure. I can do that. No problem. I can definitely—" Trevor looked back at the TV screen. He recognized one of his students, Marta Wainwright, dressed like a medieval wizard. She was holding a two-sided sign. On one side it read *Darling Energy*, but when she flipped it over it read *Legendary Ring.* She kept flipping it back and forth and waving a wand over the letters. Was it an anagram??

"What the living shit?!"

"What's wrong?"

"Are you watching this?"

"What?"

"The park. On TV."

"No. Like I said, I'm headed over there now." The line went quiet.

"Trevor?"

"Yes?"

"You still there?"

"Yes." But he sounded unsure. "Where are you?"

"Where am I? I'm in my car. Holden and I are headed out to the park."

"Can you swing by my house?"

"I don't need the letter now or anything."

"No. I want you to pick me up. Can you pick me up?"

"Uh, yeah. Sure." Holden barked again. "You want to come with us?"

"Yes. Could you pick me—pick me up?" Trevor tried to stand again. He held onto the armrest.

"You bet!" *You bet,* thought Trevor. Who says, *You bet!*

"Do you remember—"

"Yes, I remember where you are. I'm just a few minutes away."

"Ben?"

"Yes?"

Trevor reached the hall closet to get his coat.

"Thank you. I just want to say thanks." Trevor eyed up the bottle of bourbon.

"Sure. I'll be right there." Holden barked again.

Trevor discovered the bourbon bottle fit well enough into the inside pocket of his winter coat. The label maker fit into the other.

Throwing up made Trevor's head feel a little better, but now he was just angry. It felt kind of good. A car horn honked outside.

"This is Holden," Ben said, motioning to the black lab in the back seat. The dog sniffed Trevor's shoulder as Trevor took a seat in Ben's old Camry.

As Ben pulled out the driveway, he turned to Trevor. "It's none of my business, but. . .are you drunk?"

Trevor took the bottle out of his pocket. He tapped it with his wedding ring. "I am drunk." He slapped Ben on the shoulder. "I'm very drunk. Now, let's go to the park."

***

Norman Lewis couldn't remember the last time he and Lester did anything together. Even the sound of Lester's voice came as a surprise when he asked Norman for a ride out to Valley Forge.

"Don't question it. Just take him," his dad told him.

"Okay. It's just. . ." Norman decided not to tell his father what he knew about the phone messages that prompted the gathering at the park. He didn't want to implicate Lester any further, and he wasn't sure he'd be able to explain it anyway. Besides, the tape crossed over his broken nose made him look cartoonish. He didn't particularly want to be seen in public and, judging from the news coverage, there could be no more public setting than the one he was about to drive his brother into.

"Pick some dinner up on the way back. Anthony's maybe?" his father asked.

***

"Can you just tell me what you're expecting to see there?" Norman asked his brother as they pulled away from the curb. Norman thought he was owed an explanation. Lester thumbed through his phone's Twitter feed. "What was the point?" Lester ignored his brother. "Lester. Lester!" Norman pulled off into a parking spot along King Street. Lester turned and looked at him.

"I'm not driving you there. Not until you tell me what this is all about."

Lester looked back down at his phone. "I'm not sure," he said as he pointed at a picture on his phone. Someone at the park was holding a countdown clock. It read 58 minutes. "I guess we'll find out at 3:33."

"You sent out the date?"

Lester nodded and added, "And the time."

"But not the place?"

"I didn't send the place. Or the other parts. I didn't have any plan. I just wanted to see what would happen. I just did it because. . ." Lester turned off his phone. "I just did it because I could do it." Norman stared ahead, unsatisfied. "Isn't that a good enough reason?"

Norman thought it over. "No," he decided.

"Can we go? We'll be late."

Norman pulled back onto the road. It was 2:37 p.m.

***

Steven couldn't believe it. He and Dylan had arrived around 11, figuring they'd make a day of it. The picnic basket and blanket he brought was out of place, seeing as how the park was still covered in an inch or two of snow. By noon, the sun had come out and the weather report called for highs in the low 50s. It wouldn't melt in time for lunch on a picnic table, so they ate in the car and stretched the blanket over their laps. By the time they had finished, the rest of the parking lot was full. A pair of school buses sat outside the Memorial Arch circle with their lights blinking. Dylan and Steven counted at least two news vans. Up the hill, they watched two park officials confer with a policeman in front of the arch. A man put a speaker on a stand.

"This is amazing. Shall we?" Dylan asked as she reached to open the car door.

"Hold on." Steven reached behind his driver's seat and pulled out a small, wrapped box. "Happy birthday."

"You didn't need to get me anything."

"Of course, I did. I wanted to." Dylan kissed Steven. "Now if you don't like it—"

"I'll like it." Dylan tore the paper off.

"If you don't like it—"

"Can you stop? Let me open it. You don't have to say anything." Dylan smiled at Steven and he quieted. She opened the box. Inside was a silver chain with a small, rectangular pendant attached. "It's lovely." Dylan held the pendant in the palm of her hand. Six short strands of silver joined two long strands. "I love it." Dylan leaned in to hug Steven, but he stopped her.

"Do you see what it is?" Dylan looked at the design again.

"It looks like a railroad track?"

"Hold it the other way." Dylan followed Steven's direction and held the pendant vertically. The railroad track became a ladder.

"It's a ladder."

"It is."

"Steven," she said. "I love it."

They held each other without a word until someone knocked on the car window. And there he was: Mr. Ryerson in a straw hat. His pin-striped suit peeked out from behind his black winter coat. Dylan noticed a stress fracture boot on his left leg.

Dylan rolled the window down. "Mr. Ryerson. It's great to see you!"

"Do you know where we're supposed to perform?" Dylan noticed the rest of his quartet standing over the trunk of a black sedan.

"I'll be right with you," she told him. She rolled the window up. "I love it," she repeated to Steven as she put on the necklace.

"Are you ready for your birthday party?"

A group of revolutionary soldiers walked by the car.

"I may be underdressed. But let's see what happens. How much time is left?"

"There's a little less than an hour."

**

Lester did not want to get out of the car. "There's too many people," he told his brother.

"You're the one that wanted to come. You can stay in the car. I don't care." Norman got out of the car but had to wait for the Great Valley marching band to move past him before he could make his way to the crowd that gathered in front of the arch.

When the last bass drummer crossed in front of him, Norman looked back for his brother. Lester Lewis stood outside the car and took a deep breath. If he hated crowds, he hated noise even more. He almost turned back to the car when five kids in medieval costumes ran in front of him, laughing and screaming.

"To the arch! To the arch!"

He took another deep breath and crossed the street to meet his brother.

***

By 2:30, it was clear that no one was in charge. A park official, using a makeshift PA system and wireless mic, tried to welcome everyone to the park, but it brought mostly feedback. One of the reenactors, the one with the fanciest hat—was it supposed to be George Washington? Dylan wondered—tried to help by twiddling knobs on the mixer. His troops looked annoyed. A few of them kept pointing at the Bobbies and their followers. Dylan and Steven were trying to be a good audience for Mr. Ryerson's barbershop quartet, but it was impossible not to stare at the white-robed Bobbies. There weren't many of them—maybe fifteen—but standing against the snowy backdrop, they looked like snowmen come to life. The effect would have been greater if half of them weren't wearing ski hats and scarves. They stood in a semi-circle facing Bobbie One and Bobbie Two.

"Are they humming?" Steven asked, motioning over to the robed ones.

"I can't tell." It was hard to hear anything over the drum cadences of the marching bands.

"This next one is called 'You Oughta Be in Pictures,'" Mr. Ryerson announced into the chaos. The tenor blew into a pitch pipe. If being ignored bothered Mr. Ryerson, Dylan couldn't tell. It must be all that substitute teacher training, she thought.

You oughta be in pictures
You're wonderful to see

Washington must have figured something out because a man in a suit stepped in front of the microphone and made the following announcement.

"The Valley Forge National Historical Park is nationally significant as the site of the 1777–78 winter encampment of the Continental Army under General George Washington. Few places evoke the spirit of patriotism and independence, represent individual and collective sacrifice, or demonstrate the resolve, tenacity, and determination of the people of the United States to be free as does VALLEY FORGE!"

"USA! USA! USA!"

The chant was led by a group of boys who were standing between the fire-breather and a woman who held a sign that had a crossed-out "John 3:16" and a scrawled-in "Darling Energy 3:33." Mr. Ryerson and his quartet broke into a bouncy "My Country, 'Tis of Thee." The park official could not get everyone's attention back.

Steven enjoyed watching the Scrabble Club who, despite numbering only thirteen, had staked out a prominent spot by the west side of the arch. Each member held a Scrabble tile above their head. In one formation, they spelled D-A-R-L-I-N-G E-N-E-R-G-Y. Every few minutes, one of them yelled "Bingo!" and they ran into new positions. The redhead holding the Y left the end of one word to form the ending to another: L-E-G-E-N-D-A-R-Y R-I-N-G, they spelled. The Medieval Culture club kids yawped. The ones that held plastic swords and shields banged them together. To the great laughter of the crowd, the tiles re-formed one time into N-E-R-D-I-E-R G-A-N-G-L-Y.

Dylan pointed at two drag queens who were spinning their boas. "I get that she's supposed to be Marilyn Monroe, but who's the other one?"

"I think it's Judy Garland. But she would never have a boa."

"I don't know what to look at. It's all so overwhelming."

"It's amazing. Your throng has been gathered."

"I guess it has." Dylan allowed herself to enjoy this moment. Whatever worry she felt in its anticipation vanished. No one would ever know that she and Steven—and Lester—had brokered this madness. What a sight!

"Is that Lester?" Dylan spotted him standing next to a tree. "Should we go talk to him?"

"That's definitely Lester because that giant boy next to him with the tape all over his nose is definitely Norman." Norman must have seen them looking his way because he walked back behind the crowd.

Before Steven and Dylan could make their way to Lester, a frantic, red-headed lanky man and his dog interrupted them.

"Hey, Steven."

"Mr. Whitermore! Is this your dog?" Dylan bent down to pet Holden.

"Have you seen Mr. Drake??" Ben scanned the crowd.

"Mr. Drake is here?" Dylan asked.

"Yes, I drove him here, but I can't find him."

"Is everything okay?" Steven asked.

"I don't know. I don't think so. He's. . .he's not feeling well."

Dylan saw the label on Mr. Whitermore's jacket. It read "Ben."

"Did he give you that?" Dylan pointed at the makeshift name tag.

"Yes. He's been labeling everyone." Dylan noticed three kids across the crowd with their own labels.

"Ten minutes left," someone yelled into the PA system microphone.

"Just let me know if you find him," Ben said as he and Holden ran into another clump of people.

"Where will you be?" Dylan asked, but Mr. Whitermore was already out of sight.

"That didn't sound good." Steven and Dylan looked into the crowd, hoping to see Mr. Drake.

"I'm worried," Dylan said.

"Do you think there's going to be a countdown? My god, there's going to be a countdown, isn't there?"

"Yes. There's a guy holding a timer," Dylan answered, but she was still looking off into the crowd.

"What's going to happen when nothing happens? What happens when it's 3:34 and nothing has changed? Is everyone just going to go home?"

"I don't know," Dylan said. "Should we look for him?"

"Let's wait till after." He took Dylan's hand and squeezed it. The sun was peeking through now. The snow around the arch was mostly gone. Dylan took off her scarf.

The two marching bands—Great Valley's was joined by neighboring

Conestoga High School's—had formed a flank off to the east side of the arch. Both joined forces for a rousing rendition of the National Anthem. The colonial reenactors filled in their formation and stood at attention. The timer hit two minutes and somehow one of the drag queens—Marilyn—had commandeered the mic.

"Two minutes, Mr. President!" she cooed at General Washington. The crowd erupted.

Dylan watched the Bobbies. They were backlit by the sun and curiously unmoving. They seemed to be the only stakeholders here with anything at stake. They were waiting for Darling Energy to show up—or something. Everyone else had just shown up for the party, it seemed. At the moment Dylan realized the two main Bobbies—Bob Robertson and Bob Bannon—were missing, she noticed some scuffle erupt off to her left. She didn't know why, but she was filled with a sudden fear that it must be Mr. Drake, that there must be something wrong. The premonition was right, but the location was wrong.

"Look," Steven said, pointing in the opposite direction at a man who was fighting with Marilyn Monroe for the wireless microphone. "What's he doing?"

The skirmish off to her left revealed the two head Bobbies carrying a ladder. Two more of their clan were unraveling a banner. A policeman and park official ran over to intervene. The scene hardly registered with Dylan, as she was already making her way over to Mr. Drake, who was yelling something unintelligible into the microphone. At least, it *looked* like Mr. Drake. His hair stuck out at odd angles. His face was beet red, and he was missing his glasses. But the feature that stuck out most to Dylan was the bottle of booze he held in his left hand. Maybe this was *Dr. Overtaker.*

By this time, the crowd was singing along:

And the rocket's red glare
the bombs bursting in air

No one heard Mr. Drake except for Dylan, who was close enough now.

"Ten years ago today we lost our son, Benjamin Drake." Trevor didn't notice Dylan moving toward him when he began again. "It's been ten years since we lost Benjamin," he said into the bottle before he realized it wasn't the microphone. Dylan looked around the crowd and was relieved to see that their attention had moved to the Bobbies and their ladder and banner on the other side. The rest of the crowd was mid-anthem. Trevor took another swig from the bottle but it was already empty.

"Mr. Drake? Are you okay?"

"He was a beautiful boy. Are you listening?" He turned to yell at the people around him. Some finally noticed. Among them were Norman and Lester Lewis. The sound of Lester's voice surprised Dylan.

"You're Darling Energy, aren't you? Dylan Geringer."

"What?" Dylan put her hand on Mr. Drake's shoulder, but he didn't notice.

"It's your name. An anagram, right?"

"What? Yes." Dylan tried to turn Mr. Drake toward her.

"I knew it," Lester said.

"What's going on?" Norman grabbed the bottle away from Mr. Drake, and for a moment, Trevor gave them his attention.

Dylan didn't want Norman's help, but she clearly needed it.

"Ten years!" Trevor yelled into the microphone. Dylan noticed some students had pointed their phone cameras in their direction.

"Hey, why don't I take that?" Dylan reached for the microphone, but Trevor spun away.

"Why are you here??" Trevor said, turning to face Dylan. "Why are you always here?" His eyes bulged. "You're always lurking around."

The line stopped Dylan in her tracks. Trevor looked more angry than drunk now. She was just trying to help. She didn't know what to do, so she turned to the kids who were filming. "Put those away!"

"Here, Mr. Drake, why don't you just walk over—" Norman made a move to take Mr. Drake away from the arch and the crowd, but he spun away again, this time almost tripping over his feet. The label maker fell from his coat pocket. He ran into the guy who had been making balloon animals earlier, knocking him and his bag of balloons to the ground. Trevor didn't stop. He ran through the crowd to the opposite side of the arch.

He was about to run into a scene that Steven had been monitoring for the last minute. Bobbie Bannon was leaning his ladder up against the arch. He'd gotten himself up to a narrow ledge about ten feet high. Bobbie Robertson and a few of his robed friends were trying to keep the officials away long enough to allow the Bobbies to duct-tape up their Darling Energy welcome banner.

"Did you see him?" Dylan asked when she'd made it back to Steven. She was holding Mr. Drake's label maker.

"He ran back here," Norman added.

Steven noticed Norman's voice sounded different. The broken nose made this big boy sound pretty silly.

"Who? Trevor? I don't know. I've been watching—" Steven pointed over to the ladder and banner, but the park officials had already torn the banner in half and were ordering Bobbie Bannon down. One end still hung down by a persistent piece of duct-tape.

Another crowd had formed around the man with the digital timer. Someone yelled, "Twenty seconds!"

A few Revolutionary War reenactors mistook their role and formed a circle around the Bobbies like a real-life militia.

"Guys, could you back it up?" a cop said as he motioned the group to make room. The other policeman and a park official had cornered the two Bobbies. Dylan, Steven, and the Lewis brothers were the only ones paying attention when Trevor found the ladder and climbed it. It wasn't that high—maybe twelve feet—but Mr. Drake was drunk, and who knew what he would do? He'd made his way onto the narrow ledge, no longer balancing on the ladder. This wouldn't end well.

The countdown grew louder. The snare drums in attendance went into a roll.

"10. . .9. . .8. . .7. . ."

"Trevor. Just climb down." Ben Whitermore had found his department head finally. He stood at the bottom of the ladder, looking up. His dog Holden was barking up at Trevor.

"6. . .5. . .4. . ."

"Mr. Drake. Come back down for a minute," Dylan tried.

The "3. . .2. . .1" of the countdown grew louder and louder with each number, until it gave way to a rapturous hooting and hollering. Steven noticed some of the Bobbies look up into the sky for Darling Energy's arrival.

3:33 p.m. also prompted a very choreographed pantomime from the

Medieval Culture club with assistance from the Scrabble Club kids. The kids holding the letter tiles over their heads once again re-formed *Darling Energy* into *Legendary Ring*. Someone dressed as Arthur pulled a sword out of another kid who pretended to be a rock. Steven and Dylan witnessed none of that firsthand. It wasn't until a week later that they saw the footage on YouTube.

Trevor, despite his drunkenness, stayed balanced on the narrow ledge. He still had the wireless microphone.

"My son was eight years old!" he yelled. "Benjamin Drake!"

The marching bands were still trading songs back and forth, but the crowd around the arch had finally noticed Trevor standing up there.

"And what about Royce Caulder? How did we help that boy? We didn't do enough," he shouted.

"Sir, you're going to need to come down that ladder right now." The policeman joined the others at the ladder base.

"Why don't *you* come down the ladder?!" Trevor yelled back.

"You are going to fall."

"I'm not coming down!"

Steven ran over to the Scrabble Club kids. He'd been thinking of requesting a rearrangement earlier, but now seemed as good a time as any. He gathered them in a huddle and motioned them into new places. If people really wanted Darling Energy, they were going to get her.

Dylan tired of watching these men yell at Trevor up on the arch, so she climbed up to the top step of the ladder and tried a more private word with her teacher.

"Mr. Drake—"

"See! I was right. You're always lingering around me."

"Can you pass me the mic? You need an extra hand up there. Do you think you can get back down?"

Trevor looked at his hand. He realized suddenly that he was balancing on a very narrow ledge with only one hand to brace himself.

"Why don't you just drop the mic?"

Trevor looked at the mic in his hand again. "I want to." Trevor stole a quick glance out at the crowd that had formed around him. He dropped the microphone, which let out an ear-piercing feedback. It barely missed hitting Norman Lewis on his broken nose.

"I want to come down," Trevor said.

"Jump!" one of the USA-chanting boys yelled.

"You *should* come down. Do you need help?" she asked him.

She was concentrating on Mr. Drake, but she couldn't help but notice Steven and the Scrabble Club kids. What was he doing?

A police car chirped and a few more policeman descended on the scene. Steven had the tiles in their new positions. It was hard for the group to read their new formation, so they leaned out of line, trying to figure it out.

"D-Y-L-A-N G-E-R-I-N-G-E-R," it spelled.

"Who's Dylan Geringer?" one of them asked.

Marta Wainwright in her wizard robe spoke: "She's in my English class."

"Isn't that her?" the letter *D* asked.

"On the ladder. It's her birthday, according to Facebook," said the red-headed *Y*.

"Is she. . .?" the boy holding *A* started, but he was uncertain about what he wanted to ask.

Up until this moment, the TV reporters had a tough time knowing exactly what their lede was. It was a town event with an uncertain origin. However, Drunk Local Man Climbs Historic Arch was a headline they knew how to cover. As the news cameras and citizen cell phone coverage converged around Trevor, the rest of the crowd followed. What was once a wide swath of competing groups had now transformed into a horseshoe of alarm and fascination.

At the angle Mr. Drake was standing, it was difficult to figure out a way to turn and find footing on the ladder. The only sure footing he found was by pressing his back against the arch itself, like some modern gargoyle. Dylan realized she wouldn't be much help standing at the top of this ladder, but she didn't want to leave him there either. It wasn't lost on her that she resembled a crisis coordinator or hostage negotiator, albeit without the bullhorn.

There was a drone photograph in the morning paper the next day that looked like some sort of Hieronymus Bosch painting: a lone man teetering on the ledge of a monument, watched by soldiers and citizens, dogs and drag queens, policeman and druids—and a barbershop quartet. The sun had broken through at this point, and the remaining snow glittered like diamonds. The moment didn't freeze for any of its participants, however.

Trevor tried closing his eyes, but it only made it worse.

"Isn't that your name?" he asked Dylan. The letter-holders were still formed in Dylan's name.

"What are you doing?" she asked Steven, who was back at the bottom of the ladder.

"It's your birthday," he answered. "Everyone should know." He thought the fact would inspire Mr. Drake to come down. "It's Dylan's birthday!" he called up to him.

It took a moment to register with Trevor. "Her birthday," he repeated.

The Medieval Culture club broke character. *Legendary Ring* suddenly became a less interesting solution to their scramble. Bobbie Bannon asked a kid standing next to him, "Which one is Dylan? The one on the ladder?" The rest of his crew watched Dylan with greater interest.

Trevor looked at Dylan curiously. "What are you doing?" Dylan wasn't sure how to answer the question. It was a better question for Mr. Drake anyway. The man on the arch seemed less and less like the teacher she knew.

"Miss, please come down off the ladder," the policeman said.

"One second!" Mr. Drake answered for her.

"It's just your name scrambled up? It's just an anagram?" he asked her.

"Yes. It's just a thing—it's just a thing we did."

"What else can you spell with it?"

"What?"

"What other words can you spell with it?"

"I don't know." She looked down at Steven. "A bunch of things, I guess."

"It can also spell *Daringly Green*," Steven shouted up. It was an appropriate description for the grass that revealed itself under the melting snow. The hill beyond the arch was filled with growing circles of daringly green.

"Make it spell his name."

"Who?" Dylan asked. "Steven?"

"Can you make it spell Benjamin's name?"

Dylan looked down at Steven. Steven looked at the tiles. He turned back and shook his head.

"I don't have enough letters."

It wasn't the response Trevor was hoping for. He looked down at the ladder. His left leg buckled a little, but he caught his balance. The crowd gasped.

Steven saw a firetruck and EMT van pull into the parking lot, followed by two food trucks. The policeman tired of asking Dylan to come down the ladder, so he climbed onto one of the lower rungs and grabbed her leg. "Let's go!" Dylan obliged.

"Wait a second, Mr. Drake. Hold on!" Steven yelled. He grabbed Dylan and pulled her over to the letter tiles.

The fire truck seemed an unnecessary choice. It would take a little planning, but Trevor was only twelve feet up in the air. He could have just slid down into a few strong, outstretched arms maybe. More park officials and policemen had shown up by then and forced the crowd to back up off the circle and onto the grass surrounding the arch.

Steven was busy with a marker and a few of the letter tiles. With Dylan's help, they had changed an *R* into a *B*. Two diagonal lines made the *I* into a *K*. A few of the Bobbies had taken to following Dylan around. Steven directed the letters into the right order. He brought them as close as the emergency responders would allow, right in line with Mr. Drake's line of sight.

"Hold them higher," he told them.

"B-E-N D-R-A-K-E," it spelled.

They were too far now to read his face, but Dylan and Steven saw Trevor's posture change. A reporter from the news crew asked Dylan who Ben Drake was.

"Benjamin Drake was a boy who died ten years ago today."

"And you're Dylan Geringer, is that right? Are you Darling Energy? Can we get a word with you on camera? Is it true today's your birthday?"

"Not right now." Steven grabbed her hand and brought her over to the other side of the fire truck where they could get a better view. The truck extended its long ladder out toward Trevor on the arch. A fireman waited at its end and helped an exhausted looking Trevor out on the rungs. The crowd cheered again, desperate for reasons to celebrate.

The motorized ladder brought Trevor and the fireman closer to the truck where Steven and Dylan could see Mr. Drake. They watched him stare at the signs spelling out his son's name. He turned back to them.

They couldn't hear what he said over the beeping of the fire truck but, watching his lips, they thought they made out "Happy birthday."

It felt silly to wave, but it was the only motion that occurred to them.

Lester Lewis appeared out of nowhere. He smiled at Steven and Dylan.

"This was a great party. Thank you," he said. He laughed and clapped his hands.

"We couldn't have done it without you, Les," Steven said.

"No, you couldn't have. Anyway, thanks." Lester Lewis away walked toward a taco truck.

"I'm not sure the last time I heard my brother laugh," Norman said, watching his brother order a taco.

"I'm sorry about your nose," Dylan offered. She couldn't remember why she punched him.

Norman straightened the tape around his nose. "It's okay."

"Dylan!" Daphne and her boyfriend emerged from behind the crowd. "This might be just be the craziest day I've ever witnessed." She spotted Steven. "Steven!" She gave him a hug. Norman Lewis took his cue and walked away to join his brother. "It's great to see you! Was that your idea with the letters?"

***

March 15th. 3:33. Memorial Arch. Darling Energy gathered her throng.

All it took was an invitation. By 4:30, after Mr. Drake was released into the custody of his wife and taken home and most of the news vans were gone, Dylan and Steven retreated to one of the reconstructed soldier cabins. Dylan had spent the last hour accepting Happy Birthdays from classmates and strangers and inquisitive glances from the remaining Bobbies.

She and Steven stared out at the crowd who had made no moves to pack up and go home. The temperature was nearing 60 degrees, and the last of the snow evaporated into the March air. It didn't take long for everyone to forget what brought them there in the first place. The lines for the food trucks were long. A bunch of kids were playing Ultimate Frisbee. Balloon animals were still being made.

***

"I guess some people just need a formal invitation," Steven said.

"What's the Shakespeare quote?"

"You'll need to be more specific."

"The one about greatness. How some people are born with greatness."

"From *Twelfth Night*, right?"

"I think."

"What about it?"

"Maybe it applies to invitations, too." Steven wasn't following. Dylan turned it over in her head. "Maybe some people are born with an invitation. Like, they just know how to enter a conversation, they're naturally social. They know what to say and how to say it. People that are just comfortable anywhere."

"And the others?"

"What's the rest of the quote?"

"Some *achieve* greatness?"

"Right. Some people figure it out over time. They work hard to show up. It's not easy for them to say what they have to say, but they make it work."

"So the rest of us need the invitation *thrust upon us*, if I'm following your thinking here?"

"Right. Some people need the invitation hand-delivered, with an embossed envelope—"

"Or a phone message."

"Right, or a phone message, a text—or better, a friend—or even someone they never really knew that well, who can grab their arm and yank them into life."

"Which one am I?"

"I don't know. Which one am I?"

They stared back out at the crowd. Mr. Whitermore's dog Holden was meeting a beagle.

"It's just good to show up."

Dylan was happy to help this day happen, happy to be Darling Energy, happy she and Steven, and Lester, helped thrust so many outside in the middle of March. Dylan didn't always know exactly what to say or when to say it, but she knew how to show up, how to be there. At least today she did.

"So that's your superpower then? You get people to come together?" Steven asked her.

Dylan thought it over. Was that her secret power? Could you even call that a power? She'd never displayed it before. Can you have a superpower that's a one-off, a onetime blast of influence? Or was this how her life as Darling Energy would start? Can a power be gentle and unassuming? Communal, even? Are there alternative version of superheroes, ones that are more reasonable? she wondered. Who work to force their enemies to see common ground—or at least, *arrive* at one? Is there a Superman somewhere who sits down with Lex Luthor and talks out his problems? Is there one who uses his heat vision to warm the rope tied to a hostage, fraying it just enough for the man to unravel it on his own?

Thinking about it later, Dylan and Steven agreed that the day played out a like a comic book, every moment a separate cell. Words—mostly exclamations—hung in the air like jagged speech balloons, the whole thing a swirl of colors and crosshatches. They knew it was vain to think so—and not really true—but standing there, looking out the cabin door, at how perfectly everything was playing out, they felt like they were finally in control of something, like it was a play they were directing.

"How do we get this feeling to stay?" Steven asked.

"I'm not sure we can."

"I think we can."

"Well. . ." Dylan thought it over. "Maybe we need to keep making wild, impossible plans."

Steven nodded in agreement. They watched as two sousaphonists walked by.

"What's next?"

TWENTY-SEVEN

Trevor and Elizabeth stayed at a resort and health spa on Mission Bay. Off to finalize the particulars of her new position, she left him on a chaise lounge, staring out at the water. He'd bought some books from the "Beach Reads" section at the Hudson Booksellers at the airport. He wasn't ready to jump into a story yet, so he read a pamphlet that listed "Things You Probably Didn't Know About San Diego." *1. San Diego produces more avocados than anywhere else in the country. 2. Two hundred cruise ships berth in San Diego harbor every year. 3. The San Diego Zoo was home to the first baby panda born in the Western Hemisphere. 4. San Diego County is home to the most missions in the country.* Maybe Trevor would find a seaside mission and go back to church. He'd only been in the city for one day, but he could see why it would be easy to believe in God out here. However, he was more excited to read about the Hotel Coronado, the filming location for *Some Like It Hot,* one of his favorite movies. Maybe he'd learn how to tango instead.

He had left his phone in the hotel room after an old college friend had sent him the link to one of the articles chronicling his scaling of the

Memorial Arch. He knew he shouldn't have click on it, but couldn't help himself. He only looked at the photo before he shut off his phone and made for the beach. He remembered the fire truck part, but the image of him holding himself up against the arch, as depicted in the photo, seemed like someone else entirely. Until that point, he had avoided all the news stories and accepted Elizabeth's assessment of the coverage: "It's not so bad," she said. "It could be worse."

She'd been quite supportive about it, really. She didn't question his actions or express any disappointment. It worried Trevor a little that she accepted it without judgment. Did that mean she thought he was capable of getting drunk in front of the town in a federal park? Anyway, it was her suggestion and arrangements that saw Trevor take a temporary leave from work that would result in his official retirement when the school year came to a close. He would not have planned it this way, of course, but on the plane ride out here, he warmed to the idea of his sudden disappearance. He'd watched other colleagues' retirements play out awkwardly over sad sheet cakes in the department room or with overwrought speeches in dim banquet halls. It wasn't a quiet exit, but at least it was sudden. He'd spent over twenty years watching his students disappear into the real world. Maybe it was his time.

It had only been five days, but some of the fog was lifting around Trevor. He enjoyed watching the beach birds—the cormorants, the pelicans, the gulls, and the tiny sandpipers as they ran along the water's edge. He watched the sails billow on the boats tied to the dock and a line of flags whose designs he didn't recognize. Striped beach umbrellas disappeared along the curve of the shoreline. Some people jogged; others walked dogs. A policeman pedaled by on his bike. Could it be like this every day?

Trevor relaxed at the prospect of not having to teach anymore. He made a list in his head of all the things he would never have to think of again: the fluorescent lights of his classroom; the Expo markers for the whiteboard; the dusty floors; all those off-whites and grays—of the walls and floors and the lockers; the piles of handouts and essays; the paper clips and staplers and Post-its; the Xerox machines and printer cartridges. The district initiatives and in-service days; the standardized tests and their scantrons; the grades and their silly percentage points. He wouldn't have to get up at 5:30 a.m. anymore, either. He wasn't sure if he was done with *teaching*, but he was definitely done with all of its debris.

It wasn't lost on Trevor that his list didn't include any people. Sure, some of his colleagues tried his patience, but they were good people. They were teachers, after all. And yes, he'd miss the students. He'd miss them generally and specifically. There was no escaping them anyway. Right here on the beach, he'd already seen two kids that reminded him of former students. He recognized the laughter and yelling from the volleyball game off to his left. He saw them in the waiters and bartenders at the resort, in the shuttle driver from the airport. They were everywhere. While he could still summon his own Benjamin when he closed his eyes, his specter was a little less resonant when they were open. If it was the students that Trevor would miss most, it was because they gave him something, other than himself, to worry about.

He thought of Royce a few times that first week in San Diego— whenever he saw a kid with a baseball hat—but more often, it was Dylan Geringer and Steven Lilly he found himself wondering about. He regretted abandoning his classes right at the end of the year. He knew they'd find someone who could ably fill in, but he didn't want them to feel rejected.

Dylan and Steven had been so kind to him. They were so earnest and authentic—in the way that only young people can manage. Steven reminded him of himself at that age. He wasn't as cool as Steven when he was in high school, but he recognized the manic enthusiasms and uncontrollable frustrations. Whatever problems Steven dealt with, he still seemed like a more evolved version of the student-Trevor. Were students evolving and developing faster, or were they the same as they've always been? With all of Trevor's experience, he still didn't have an answer for that one. He expected the latter.

It was Dylan Geringer he thought about most often. What was it about her? It had less to do with her anagram-spawned alter ego. While *Darling Energy* was a great name for a character—and captured both her strong and dear qualities—she didn't need another identity in Trevor's eyes. Was it her face—that open-eyed look she would give him? The way she would nod her head in class? The way she asked questions, and the look on her face as the possibilities piled up behind her eyes? Trevor had taught other students with these qualities before, but Dylan's generosities expanded out of the classroom and into Trevor's life. Dylan had taught him something, but he couldn't yet put it into words. March 15th was the day Benjamin died, but it was also Dylan Geringer's birthday, and that must mean something.

He owed them—Steven and Dylan—a thank-you.

***

Steven was a little nervous about leaving his mother behind when he and Dylan left for North Carolina. Thankfully, Rabbi Elysse had arranged a weekend retreat for Lillian and her up in the Poconos. It was spring break and Steven was leaving on a plane for a week's long vacation with his best friend. He would not have imagined the possibility back in September, but if the year had taught him anything, it was to stop measuring possibilities.

Still, he was surprised when his dad and Vernon drove them from the airport up to their new house on Nag's Head. It was conspicuous for its small size, as it was sandwiched between two large and looming newly constructed houses, but it was the aquamarine siding that cracked a smile across his face.

"What do you think?" his dad asked them.

"It's. . .blue."

"It's aquamarine," Vernon said.

"It's so cute," Dylan said.

"We love it," Mr. Lilly said.

Steven kept shaking his head and smiling. He still couldn't believe this was his dad, the one he'd grown up with. "It's amazing. I love it," he decided. These past few weeks it was so much easier to enjoy other people—and to love what they loved.

They arrived in the morning and were tasked with helping Foster and Vernon decorate the back deck and line up a few chairs they had rented. It was all so casual and thrown together, not an approach Steven thought his dad could permit. They stuffed mason jars with cut flowers and placed them along the deck railing. It was Steven and Dylan's job to create a playlist.

The guests, all seven of them, arrived by 1 p.m. for a few cocktails, and the ceremony, which started at 2, led by Vernon's uncle Will, a federal magistrate, was over by 2:15. Steven was a little put off by the nonchalance of the event. Shouldn't there be some pomp and circumstance? He thought the sight of his father kissing Vernon would make him feel weird, for lack of a better word, but it made no such impression. The whole night felt more like a movie he was watching than real life. If Steven was disappointed a little by the ceremony, the drinking and dancing that followed made up for it. Dylan had insisted on Motown for most of the playlist, and it was a great choice. There was a moment when their small party crowded around the firepit, dancing around in a circle to The Temptations' "Ain't Too Proud to Beg." Steven couldn't get over how beautiful Dylan looked in her blue dress. Vernon put a red carnation behind her ear before the ceremony, and it stayed put for what seemed like an endless number of twirls.

At the end of the night, after Vernon's parents and uncle and Foster's college roommate had all left, the four of them sat around the fire and watched the embers die out. Steven's father had heard the outline of the Valley Forge Park story, but Steven and Dylan hadn't yet found an effective way of telling the story yet.

"So you're Darling Energy?" Mr. Lilly asked.

"I am," Dylan answered.

"And is your teacher okay?" Vernon asked.

"I hope so. He took a leave of absence. They say he's retiring at the end of the year," she reported.

They grew quiet for a minute. Finally, Foster spoke.

"Can you imagine?"

"Which part?" Steven asked.

"Losing a child. . ." He looked up at Steven.

Vernon grabbed his hand.

"I just. . ."

Steven wasn't sure what the proper response was. He settled on "I know," but as he said it, his dad walked over to him, looking for something else.

Foster Lilly was crying. "I'm sorry," he said to his son as he brought him in for a hug. "I'm sorry."

***

Vernon and Dylan let father and son have their moment as they took a seat up on the deck.

"So does Steven just figure out these anagrams?"

"Yes." Dylan watched Steven and Mr. Lilly's shadows move across the next-door neighbor's house. "Actually," she remembered, "he figured out one for you."

"Oh, he did?"

"Ready for it?"

"I'm ready."

"*Vermillion Swan*."

"*Vermillion Swan*?" Vernon thought it over and smiled. "Oh, I like that." He laughed and then called back to Steven and Foster. "Okay, you two, we're not done dancing yet."

Vernon resumed the playlist on his phone and the bass drum and organ of "Devil with a Blue Dress" sprang to life. Vernon looked at Dylan in her blue dress.

"Oh, you're good," he told her.

When a few neighbors came over to congratulate the newlyweds, Dylan and Steven walked down to the beach. They watched a few sandpipers run toward the water. They took turns taking photos of one another in the moonlight.

"No filter needed," Steven said.

"I feel like this whole night has been on its own filter."

"Which one?"

"Maybe Rise. Or Mayfair."

"Hey," Steven's thumb was scrolling along his phone.

"What?"

They opened Mr. Drake's email and sat down on the sand. Dylan read it aloud.

Dear Steven and Dylan—

(Steven, I still have your email from our second marking period correspondence. I hope it's okay if I ask you to please share this email with Dylan when you see her.) I'm writing to you two from the sunny beaches of San Diego. My wife and I will be moving out here for good in the next few months. This week we'll be looking for housing.

I never imagined myself as a West Coast guy—always three hours behind and not much in the way of seasons. But I'll tell you: after three days, I don't think it will take a lot of convincing.

I'm writing to say thank you to both of you. You've both been very kind and generous with me. This last year has been very difficult, and it was a relief to know I could share the classroom with people like you.

Most folks can name their favorite teacher, someone who really made a difference, was a mentor or coach—someone who guided and encouraged them. It was Mrs. Eaton for me. She showed me how great books could say all the things you'd been thinking or feeling, but didn't have the words to say yet.

But we teachers don't do enough to honor and remember our students. It's easy for us to make an impression—good or bad. We stand in front of you every day, demanding your attention. We ask so much of you—to think and work, to focus and plan, to take risks and ask questions, and all of that, on top of whatever life throws at you outside the classroom.

So allow me to say thank you, Dylan and Steven. In just seven months, you improved my life immeasurably. There's a fearlessness in being young, and while some of it may come from inexperience, a lot of it comes from a natural hope and curiosity and ambition and empathy. It's lovely, really, and without your good natures, I'm not sure I would have made it even to March.

Please keep in touch, and feel free to use me for your college recommendations, if that's something you're even thinking about already. I look forward to heaping praise your way.

I don't know much about the schools out here yet, but if you make any college trips in this direction, please let me know.

Take care!
Your teacher,

Mr. Drake

—

***

They watched the moon reflect off the water.

"I'm trying to picture Mr. Drake on a beach," Steven said.

"I can picture it."

"In shorts?"

"Maybe in linen pants."

"And a big hat?"

"No. Not a big hat. Maybe a visor."

"There'd be a little suntan lotion stuck in his mustache."

The image made Dylan laugh. "I can see him with some cool aviators on."

Steven thought it over. "I could see that."

There wasn't as much to imagine anymore. You could get to know anyone if you were interested enough.

"So I've been thinking. . ." Steven formed the ellipses with his eyes.

"Yes?"

"What are we going to do next year?"

"For what?"

"For your birthday."

Dylan thought it over. "The movies?"

Steven A. Lilly, formerly *Silent Valley*, and Dylan Geringer, sometimes *Darling Energy*, stared out at the ocean.

"Do you know the anagram for *ocean*?" he asked her.

"No. What?"

"*Canoe.*"

ACKNOWLEDGEMENTS

There are many people I need to thank for helping me conceive, write, edit, design, and share this book. Without them, this story would still be just a few lines in my phone's Notes app—where it began one night back in 2016.

Special thanks go to my former colleague Trevor Drake and my former student Dylan Geringer. Had their names not spawned such compelling anagram alter egos, there would be no novel. Dylan and Trevor were generous to let me use their actual names, but, as the old disclaimer goes, the names, characters, places, and incidents in this work of fiction are the product of the author's imagination. I can't, however, say that it's only *coincidental* that there is any resemblance to persons living or dead. Trevor does indeed have a mustache, and Dylan and he are lovely, good people.

My students were not only great inspiration; they were great encouragement. After posting a monthly calendar in my classroom detailing my daily word count, I benefited from the cheery praise of Thomas Jenson in his assessment of a particularly fruitful week; and from the shaking head of Laura Liu after a week of zeros. I needed both of them. A lot of gratitude goes to Allison Hartman, who, more than a decade after she was our high school's literary magazine editor found the time to read the book twice, providing generous and thoughtful insight.

My teaching colleagues have provided a lot of support—and material—over the years. Teaching is a humbling profession, particularly when you're starting out, and I was lucky to find coworkers who not only knew their stuff, but generously shared it all with me. Many have become lifelong friends. I know how long to microwave their lunches. Ben Whitermore was kind enough to let me name a character after him in this story.

Of course, many thanks go to my own teachers, like Michelle Baird, Barbara Masters, Clarence Miller, Bill Byers, Kerry Beaumont, and Linda Child. I'm especially grateful to Lisa Eaton and Doug Wilfert. Backed by a public school district that valued the arts, they championed our creativity and gave us a stage to explore it on.

Many thanks to Kristen Solecki, who designed the wonderful cover to this book. Kristen and I have worked together on many designs for album covers. I'm glad her work is your first impression of this book. You can find more of her art at www.kristensolecki.com. Thanks also to my friend Scott Jefferson for so thoughtfully designing all the words and spaces inside this book.

I have newfound respect for the keen eye of a good editor. It helped that I already had respect for my friend Brian Baughan. He cleaned up my clunky phrases, plugged in every missing punctuation mark, and made sense where I made none. I didn't realize he would have to google whether *boy shorts* was one word or two. Sorry for the pop-up ads.

Final thanks go to my friends and family. Steve Hanna is the best kind of best friend. He was an early reader of the book and is a constant en-courager of my work—and one of the best writers I know. My first teach-ers were my parents, and they encouraged my every whim and invested in every one of my dreams. I have my mother to thank for suggesting I in-terview for some teaching jobs, and for getting me the first one at Sacred Heart, where I taught alongside her, just up the hill in the middle school. In elementary school, she bound my first storybook with red-checkered wrapping paper: *The Adventures of Wishy Washy*. My sisters, Suzanne and Leigh, must have listened to her, too. We're all teachers.

My wife Jessica is the love of my life, and I'm lucky I get to spend my days and nights with her and the dogs. Unlike my songwriting, which in-volves days of listening to the same chords and words over and over again, the quiet tapping of my typing has required less of her patience but has received no less of her love.

And thanks to you readers, too.